1

AVIELLE LEBEAU TRIED to focus on the last paragraph of her creative essay in the back seat of the packed black Nissan Rogue as she, her sisters, and their mother sped down the highway. They followed closely behind an SUV carrying her father and brothers. Avi wanted her words on the laptop in front of her to be all-consuming, but a new distraction popped up every two seconds.

If it wasn't her little sister's loud crunching of white cheddar popcorn beside her or the nonstop tapping of her big sister's acrylic nails on her phone screen in the passenger seat, then it was their mom belting off-key to another song on the radio, tearing away any semblance of Avi's focus.

Avi peeled her sweaty thighs from the leather seat, leaning forward to aim the air vent directly at her face, but the August sun beaming through the window, and her combined anxiety, rendered it useless.

With a huff, Avi sat back again, staring at the words, trying to stop her eyes from darting to the GPS screen on the dashboard. She had, maybe, two minutes before they reached the tail end of South Carolina and crossed the state line into

Georgia. Avi steadied her hands on the keyboard, instead pulling up the Briarcliff Prep website. Weirdly enough, the same thing that had her ready to pull her hair out doubled as a calming force.

Tomorrow morning, Avi would be joining the ranks as a young Black woman of prestige, honor, and distinction at Briarcliff Preparatory School for Girls. For years, she'd dreamed of starting her freshman year of high school in Georgia, being back with her older siblings and joining the *Cliff News* as a creative-writing columnist. Her dreams remained steady, but for the last week or so, a creeping fear of homesickness . . . failure . . . or maybe just general unease lay constant in her chest. She ran an anxious hand up and down her chestnut-brown arms before remembering to triple-check that her inhaler was in the pocket of the blue duffel bag lying at her feet.

The Briarcliff home page read "Number 1 HBBS" and featured a slideshow of smiling students playing instruments in class, dressed in costumes on Halloween, lounging in dorms, and playing volleyball. For a moment, Avi paused, seeing a picture of her big sister, Belle, and her dance team, the Cheetahnaires, posing in sequined lavender-and-gold unitards at a basketball game. Dancing wasn't Avi's thing like it was Belle's, but maybe she'd make friends just as quickly by joining the school's paper—if they'd have her.

"We made it," their mom, Toni, beamed as Avi pulled her AirPods out of her ears. Belle aimed her camera out the window, catching the peach on the giant blue "Welcome to Georgia" sign for her vlog.

Avi saw her mother's chin jut up and felt her piercing

upturned eyes (eyes they'd all inherited) staring at her in the rearview mirror. She fixed her face just a second too late.

"Is your writing not going well?"

Absentmindedly, Avi pulled at an escaped brown coil from her high puff. "It's fine; I just can't concentrate."

"Concentrate on what?" Belle squinted, and her left dimple deepened in her mahogany skin. "I thought you said you finished your sample for the *Cliff News* a week ago?"

"I mean, I did, but it still needs to be—"

"I thought it was really good, personally," Paisli interrupted, leaning forward in the back seat. As she moved, the Target bags full of new twin XL mattress pads, shower caddies, and velvet hangers crowding her crinkled.

Avi faced her in wide-eyed outrage. Her twelve-year-old sister had the face of an angel—the nosiest little angel walking on earth. "And who said you could read it in the first place?"

"It was printed and sitting on your bed like a nice present," she said, smirking. "Felt like an invitation."

Avi cut her eyes at Paisli but suppressed a retort, knowing her little sister's snippy attitude was a result of being "left behind." She remembered feeling like that when Belle left for her freshman year at Briarcliff Prep three years ago. And again, last year, when the twins, Moe and EJ, prepped to leave for Preston Academy, Briarcliff's brother school. Maryland had seemed dull in comparison, and Avi desperately wanted to be in Georgia with her older siblings then. She'd yearned to experience the sisterhood and embrace experiences her mother bragged about having at her alma mater. More than anything, Avi wanted to step foot on Briarcliff's campus and see what all the hype was about.

But her fairy tale was beginning to fade. The immediacy of it all, the idea of her parents leaving her there tomorrow . . . it had her feet freezing, while she simultaneously broke out in a sweat.

She pushed the edge of her clear-rimmed frames up the bridge of her nose with one hand and fanned her pits with the other. "I— Can we all just roll our windows down and be quiet for like ten minutes?"

"No, honey." Mom shook her head, and the pressed curls framing her face flowed. Though she did lower her window. "You get nervous. That's okay. Happens to the best of us, but this is exciting! You're about to start your freshman year of high school at a Historically Black Boarding School."

"The best one," Belle added.

"And there aren't too many people who can say that. You'll be surrounded by young intellectuals that not only look like you but have similar experiences, too!"

"Plus, you have nothing to worry about with your essay. I read it, too, and it was . . . compelling. You got a gift, doll."

Avi felt the corner of her lips twitch. But that was easy for Belle to say. She didn't have an insecure bone in her body.

"You even convinced Auntie Char to send Kai," Paisli said.

"I did not," Avi said, glaring back at the little brat this time. "Kai talked to Moe and EJ about Preston and convinced Godmommy Char himself. Preston was his choice."

"And Briarcliff was yours," her mom said pointedly.

Avi was sick of being the topic of discussion, so she did what she always did to evade unwanted attention—allow her sister to talk about herself.

"Belle, what was your top school other than Spelman and Southern U?"

Belle's soft brown eyes lit. "Either NCAT or Hampton. I haven't really narrowed it to three, but Spelman's my priority."

At the sound of her collegiate alma mater, their mom reached over to give Belle's full cheek a stroke. "And the double major is in Dance and what?" she asked, picking up Avi's slack.

"Dance Performance and Choreography and Comparative Women's Studies with a minor in Communications or . . ." Belle launched into the different major and minor combinations she'd been contemplating, her sister's first-day jitters forgotten.

Avi stuffed her AirPods back in her ear, thankful old reliable still worked. She already knew of Belle's plans to be in a position similar to Ashley Everett, Beyoncé's dance captain, and eventually start a business specializing in entertainment event planning.

She swiped her finger across the touchpad on her laptop and the screen lit. This time, she didn't hesitate to click the *Cliff News* link. For the past few months, her secret pastime had been to stalk old articles, poems, and short stories posted in the creative-writing section of Briarcliff's newspaper. Egypt Mack, the second-term president of the paper, stared back at Avi from the screen. Her smile felt like a welcome, and Avi was ready. It was fun to imagine her writing one day posted on this very website. To have someone looking at her story or poem and finding the inspiration to create. According to Belle, they only picked the best writers, and there was one opening available for the freshman/sophomore creative-writing column.

In no time, she found her favorite article, titled "The Transition." It was from last May's edition of the *Cliff News* by now-graduated senior Rochelle Harris. The journey it took Avi on in only 1,500 words was awe-inspiring. She closed Briarcliff's site and enlarged her own essay once again. Belle and Pai liked it, but Avi wasn't in love with her words yet. She would stick this ending if it was the last thing she did.

AVI AND HER FAMILY filled two tables in the outside sitting area of a rest stop about two hours out from Grandma Sugah's.

Kai, Avi's lanky godbrother, sat beside her on the bench. Their moms had been roommates back in college and ran Truehart Publishing together today. It was fate handing Avi her first friend when they were born a month apart. While it was true Avi didn't convince him to attend Preston, there was no denying she'd planted the idea in his head.

He brushed the sides of his hair, careful to avoid disturbing the short curls atop his head. Antonio, the youngest of the six LeBeau siblings and Paisli's twin, sat on the other side of him emulating the action.

"You didn't even reach out to Jasiri?" Avi asked about Kai's soon-to-be roommate.

"I know all I need to from his bio. He's from Atlanta, makes beats, and listed 'music producer' as his career aspiration. What else is there to know?"

"You wanna be a court justice," Avi said, smirking. "What if you have nothing in common?"

"And you'd want to know if he's a night or morning person. Also, if he's the showering type," Mom said, unwrapping a piece of chocolate from her purse.

"Or things like if he'll think he can just use your stuff 'cause it's in the same room. Like your toothbrush, for example," Belle said, camera out, snapping off-guards of everyone.

Kai looked sick at the thought but shook his head. "As long as dude doesn't watch me in my sleep or mess with my food, I'm good. We can figure out the details later."

"Aye, you're just lucky they didn't try to put you in a triple like they did us freshman year," EJ said from across the bench.

His twin Moe didn't bother to take his eyes off the screen. He was playing with the lighting on a frame he'd shot for his and EJ's newest short film. "Yeah," he said stroking the peach fuzz on his chin. "I was pissed when I found out they gave us a triple last year."

"Didn't you guys get a triple in Newton again?" Antonio asked.

"True. But Q's tough. We asked to keep it the same."

The twins' physical similarities were startling, from the strong jaws they'd inherited from their dad to the tone of their vibrant, dark skin. Getting their braces off earlier this summer only added an unneeded boost to their egos. The only real physical tell for those who didn't know them was the short fade Moe kept and EJ's ever-growing high-top fade.

"Newton's the livest dorm on campus," EJ said. "If you're cool with the RBs, you can pretty much do what you want.

Plus, the emergency exit door on the ground floor is faulty, so it's easy to . . ."

EJ's voice faded as their mom's head snapped away from Belle's camera with raised brows.

". . . to come back to the dorm before curfew." EJ's phone rang then, and a photo of his girlfriend, Noemie, crossed the screen. He gladly answered, leaving the table.

"Avi, you're lucky, too," Paisli said from Belle's lap. She was way too big to be sitting there, but Belle wrapped her arms around her baby sister's waist. "You get to be in Hollingsworth like Mommy and Belle were," she pouted. "Zazie seems really nice, too. And I *love* her TikTok."

"Two more years and we'll be there with them," Antonio said cheerfully.

"Wait. How did you find Zazie's TikTok?" Avi asked. Zazie was a Chicagoan with an affinity for photography and dreams of being an astronaut. But Avi only received her new roomie's IG handle yesterday. How would Paisli know that she seemed nice?

"I found it after I found her Instagram. If I look hard enough, I can find anything. Ooh," she said, grabbing her phone from the table, "somebody just delivered a package to the front door." She zoomed in further. "He has a blue mohawk and tattoos on his scalp. Look, Tony!" she said facing the phone toward her twin.

But their father, Ellis, snatched it out her hand, appearing out of nowhere. He'd been across the lot, chatting it up with some man he just met from Minnesota who saw the blue crabs on their Maryland license plates.

"I already told you, Pai. The new security system is just

that. A security system," he said sternly. "If you use it to people-watch, the app comes off your phone." He pretended to hand it back to her, only to snatch it away again with a broad smile plastered on his bearded face. The left dimple each of his kids inherited shone bright. He dropped the phone in her lap, and placed his large hands on Avi's shoulders, whispering, "Come talk to me," in her ear.

Avi sighed, annoyed, but she saw this coming. When they first parked, Dad had strode to their car to open Mom's door. As she stood on her toes to kiss him, Avi heard her name slip from her mother's lips.

"Do you wanna start?" he asked when they were feet away from their chattering family.

Avi's brow arched. "I would, but I'd hate to admit to something you have no idea about."

"Fine." He chuckled. "The first is good news. Your uncle Jovahn is coming to help us move you guys in tomorrow."

That was one of the positives about this move to Georgia. Living this close to Sugah, maybe visiting Auntie Naima's bridal boutique, and seeing Uncle Jovahn, too. He was her father's youngest brother and in his last year at Morehouse. Growing up, Jovahn spent holidays and most summers in Maryland with them. Over time, he'd come to be much more like a big brother than an uncle.

"Secondly," Dad said in a serious tone.

Avi fought the urge to roll her eyes. "Here we go."

"Yeah, here we go." He nodded. "I've been waiting for you to say something to me, but tomorrow's the day. Your mama, Belle, and even Moe—who literally pretends not to care about anything—have been tellin' me you're stressed about

Briarcliff? Not that I haven't noticed you hiding in your room." He leaned on the bench in front of her, and the cologne on his skin lingered. "Tell me what that's about? I thought I was the only one falling to pieces about you leaving me."

Avi took a moment to think, wanting to answer honestly. Her feelings were a jumbled, conflicting mess. The idea of starting her first year of high school tomorrow filled her to the brim with excitement. Avi knew it would be no *Glee* or *High School Musical* experience, though she couldn't deny the two weeks she'd spent binging *The Facts of Life*, hoping to somehow prepare herself. No matter how unprepared she felt, the urge to follow in her family's footsteps was . . . compelling.

Still, another part of her—the louder, aggressive part—wanted to road trip back to Maryland with her parents, Antonio, and Paisli tomorrow and leave all the worrying behind.

"I dunno." Avi shrugged. "You and Mommy let me decide if I wanted to go to Briarcliff or not. I've never made a big decision like this before. What if I picked wrong? There's nothing wrong with a regular high school in Maryland, and I didn't even consider them. What if I end up hating Zazie? She seems nice enough now, but that could be fake. What if I don't even get past the first-round picks for the *Cliff News*? What if I get homesick? What if—"

"Whoa, Avi." He chuckled, though his eyes filled with concern. "Have you ever considered a positive 'what if'? What if you love it? What if you find your best friends? What if you become an even better writer? That's what I've been thinking." He touched a finger to her chin. "Listen, Belle came back even smarter and more business savvy with her YouTube page, that a *professor* helped her start." Freshman year, Belle's music professor encouraged her to post her solo violin mashup performance at the Winter Orchestra Showcase. What started as a series of violin covers had branched into choreography videos and vlogs that gained a decent following.

"And your brothers have matured profoundly in one year at Preston. I'm still shocked," he said with a hand to his chest. "EJ studies under that vocal coach and earned his spot as the scarecrow in their production of *The Wiz* last year. And Moe's always talking about how much that film club professor is teaching them. Even encouraged him to send in his short film to that festival last year. And he got third place.

"As much as I'd like for your mama and me to take all the credit," her dad continued, "I can't. It takes a community, and you're entering a new one tomorrow. Look, I see your storyboards. I see you practicing and honing your craft. The regret and guilt you'll feel for not trusting yourself, your talent, and your instincts will overpower any comfort you'd get by us loading up the car and driving home right now. Tell me," he said, crossing his arms over his chest, "if we go to those schools tomorrow and drop off Belle, EJ, Moe, and Kai, and tell you it's okay for you to come home with us, would you hop in?"

She shook her head. "No."

He smiled again. "You didn't even hesitate, baby. This is going to be good for you. You're gonna find your place, and everything will fall in line." He leaned down to kiss her forehead. When he pulled back, Avi saw her cedar-brown eyes mirrored in his. “You can go back,” he said nodding toward their table, pulling his vibrating phone out of his pocket. When she was feet away, he called to her with the phone to his ear, “Avielle, your tuition is already paid. So, take what I said to heart.”

2

AVI LOOSENED HER death grip on the ceiling handle and bent to retrieve her buzzing phone from the floor of Belle's Nissan. She'd hit a hard-right turn, narrowly missing the curb.

"Whoopsie!" Belle smiled apologetically as Avi rolled her eyes. All summer, Belle had worked to improve her driving while Avi sat tense and terrified in the passenger seat. Missing the curb was an improvement.

> Don't sweat the small stuff.
>
> KAI

Avi repeated the mantra to herself but couldn't stop fidgeting in her seat, nervously twisting the rose-gold "A" charm on her bracelet between her fingers. She pulled the small car mirror down to check the state of her braid-out. The humidity was winning. As she tightened the belt to her blue tie-waist linen shorts, the sight of a new pimple on her chin drew her eyes back to the mirror.

Belle glanced over at her. "Will you sit still? You're makin' me itch."

"I'm trying to make sure everything's right. I don't wanna look silly meeting new people." Avi slapped the car mirror up.

"You look pretty," Belle said with a side-eye as she pressed her foot to the gas. "Cute shoes, by the way."

Avi looked apologetic, praying Belle wouldn't take back the powder blue lace-up ballet flats she'd stolen from her suitcase last night. They matched her outfit, and it really was important that she make a good first impression.

Belle didn't feel the need to try as hard in her ripped, fitted jeans and lavender dance-team shirt that read THE GOLDEN CHEETAHNAIRES on the front and CAPTAIN in all caps on the back. Her thick hair was half-up in a sleek bun.

Before Avi knew it, they were behind a long line of cars as the familiar sight of the two schools came into view. Briarcliff's and Preston's gated campuses literally faced each other. The U-Haul carrying their father and the boys turned left under a large sign in silver lettering reading PRESTON ACADEMY.

Belle made a right under a tall, wide stone archway. Written on the sidewall in gold lettering was BRIARCLIFF PREPARATORY.

Avi looked back to see Jovahn trailing them in a U-Haul with their mother in the passenger seat, cheesing.

"Pretty, isn't it?" Belle said in a soft voice.

Cherry blossom trees sprouted all around the washed river-stone buildings, giving the campus an ethereal glow. Avi watched as families avoided walking on the grass, so perfectly manicured and green that it could have been a desktop screensaver. Horns honked and traffic built until a campus security officer ran over to direct the flow of cars toward the roundabout encircling a tall bronze statue of the founders, Walton and Paulette Briarcliff, their arms held out in welcome. Once past the statues, Avi leaned out her window, embracing the breeze on her face as "Before I Let Go" played faintly from speakers in the distance. A silver-haired woman scuttled across the street, heels clacking on the asphalt, as she neared a tall stone building named the Morrison Center with lavender picket signs stuck in the grass outside reading, *Check-in Here, Welcome!* and *We're so glad you came!*

It was surreal being on campus as a soon-to-be student. Still terrifying? Absolutely. But this first glance at what home could be for the next four years wasn't half bad.

Avi opened the car door, feeling her insides rise in equal parts nervousness and excitement as her feet touched the pavement. She watched her sister's expression as she hugged a group of girls carrying boxes. The looks on their faces explained why Belle called Briarcliff her second home.

But Belle's delight at being back on campus was nothing compared to their mother's. Toni did a little jig after jumping out of the truck and skipped to her daughters on the sidewalk. She mimicked Belle, waving and hugging several older women who also wore small, round *BP* pins. But Toni had gone the extra mile, wearing her old lavender school blazer, rolled up at the sleeves. Tradition was that every student received their first official Briarcliff blazer upon completing their freshman year.

Jovahn opened the back of the U-Haul and examined the inside before jogging over and draping an arm over Avi's shoulder.

"Excited?" her uncle asked.

"I'm feelin' something," she said, seeing a copy of her father's reassurance plastered on his face. He could have been her father and Uncle Morris's triplet. The only differences were Jovahn's natural slim build and three-inch height advantage.

Mom poked Avi's stomach. "C'mon. We have to get you guys checked in."

"How long do you think everything's gonna take, sis?" Jovahn checked his watch.

"Not too long. We have to be at Avi's dorm by ten thirty to move her in, and Belle's at noon."

"No, it's okay," Belle said, looking up from her phone. "I could probably use your help decorating later, but Logan's gonna help me move."

Three weeks ago, Logan Walsh asked Belle to be his girlfriend—and she was obsessed. He was the headmaster's son, student body president, and precisely Belle's ambitious, pretty-boy type. As she said his name, a small smile played on her full lips.

Mom nodded. "That'll be the perfect time for Daddy and me to meet this kid and get a feel for him. Tell Logan to expect us."

And just like that, Belle's smile fell. "Seriously?"

"Yes," Mom said, peeking over her dark Chanel shades. "If we don't meet him, then whatever it is you two have going on stops today."

As they walked toward Morrison, Avi noticed that exiting students wore purple lanyards around their necks. Every couple of feet along the sidewalk were poles with signs displaying the Briarcliff crest and the school motto: TO BE THE CHANGE.

Inside the cool building, student leaders in lavender-collared shirts directed new students to the right and guardians to the left. Avi followed Belle across the white-tiled floor to a line of tables where faculty sat typing into laptops.

She wrapped her arms around herself, glancing nervously at two girls making introductions, as Belle approached the thin woman behind an open table.

"Hello! I'm free over here," said a full-figured woman two tables over. She had the whitest teeth, cat's-eye frames, an eye-catching wedding ring, and a Briarcliff pin on her bright yellow lapel.

"Hi," Avi said, giving the woman a tight-lipped smile.

"My name is Professor Lovette. Yours?"

"Uh, Avielle Emoni LeBeau."

"Is it? Any relation to Belle and the twins?"

"Yes, ma'am. They're my siblings." Avi pointed to where her sister had previously stood, but Belle was nowhere to be found.

"Honey? Avielle?" Professor Lovette said. "How do you spell that?"

Avi spelled her name and then typed furiously into her phone.

Why would you leave me??

AVI

Calm down. I'm getting a new ID pic.
You will too in a sec.

BELLEY

She looked around again, unable to place her mother or Jovahn in the crowded room either. Her foot tapped erratically, and she clutched the small purse at her side as she waited for the woman's nails to finish clacking on the keyboard. Where was everyone? And when had they collectively decided to leave her alone?

"Okay, Miss LeBeau," Professor Lovette said, cutting into Avi's panicked thoughts. "You're all set. Go through the glass door, up the steps, and then you'll see the Freshman ID line. And, honey. Relax." The smile spreading across her red lips was warm. "I promise you're not the only one nervous. This is a new experience for every freshman, but I'm sure you'll learn to love it here. I did."

THE BUZZ FROM the slow-moving picture ID line steadily increased to a loud murmur as students gathered in the small space. Every couple of seconds, Avi found herself peeking around a tall girl with perfectly spiraled curls, hoping to get a glimpse of her sister walking back toward the lobby. She scrolled mindlessly through her finsta, trying her best to ignore the two girls in front of her criticizing everyone who walked through the side door.

"Where do you even find embellished jeans anymore?" whispered the petite girl wearing a periwinkle spaghetti-strap sundress and a slick ponytail.

"I can't imagine, but look at this one, Fallon," said the second girl, who had brown waist-length crinkled locs. She nodded toward a plump girl walking toward them. "I'd love to take a pair of tweezers to her unibrow." She lowered her voice even more. "Do you think her back is hairy like that, too?"

"Her back is probably just as hairy as everything else we

can't see," Fallon said, raising her honeyed voice, ensuring everyone close enough heard her.

The girl paused for a moment, a hurt look crossing her face. She quickened her pace, this time with slumped shoulders.

Fallon and Waist-Length Locs exploded in giggles.

"That was nasty," Avi said in a rush, shocked to hear her thoughts vocalized.

Fallon faced her with a haughty look and one dainty hand on her hip. "Who are you?"

The tall girl standing behind Avi spoke up. "Probably a decent person if she's not harassing strangers like y'all have for the last half hour."

"Have you two tried minding your business today?" the girl with locs sneered.

"You know what, Kieley," Fallon said, taking a sinister step closer, "I don't think they have." All the honey in her voice was gone.

"Why don't you—" Avi started. But the photographer just feet in front of them cleared his throat.

"Excuse me, ladies," he said in a gruff voice.

They hadn't noticed the room go silent. Avi wanted to shrink.

"I have to keep this line moving," the photographer continued. "Who's next?"

"I am, sir," Fallon said sweetly, though her eyes were menacing. She turned sharply, forcing Avi to lean back to avoid the swing of her hair. The tall girl mugged Kieley until she turned, too.

Avi stared daggers at Fallon as she flounced over to the black stool and gave the photographer a winning smile.

Cattiness and mean-girl behavior were expected at any high school. It had definitely been prevalent in middle school. But Avi hadn't expected it on move-in day.

She peered back again, trying to catch Belle.

"Are you looking for someone?" the tall girl asked.

Avi really saw her for the first time, noticing the slight Spanish accent in her voice. All the attitude meant for Fallon and Kieley had vanished. She had a glowing almond skin tone, round inquisitive brown eyes, and wore a stunning diamond bow-and-arrow brooch on her floral blouse.

"Actually, yeah," Avi said. "My sister."

Kieley took her seat on the stool.

"I can't stand people like that," the girl rasped. She smiled, sticking her hand out. "I'm Rhy, by the way."

"Avi," she said, taking her hand.

"It must be nice having someone here to let you know the ins and outs."

"Maybe? I mean, I don't know how much time we'll get to spend with each other since we're all supposed to be super busy and involved. Plus, she's already focused on her own things."

The photographer grunted in annoyance as Kieley asked to retake her picture a third time.

"So, where are you staying?" Rhy asked.

"Hollingsworth."

"Same!" She smiled. "But I'm nervous about this roommate thing. I don't like sounding like a spoiled brat, but the idea of someone else in my room while I'm sleeping or getting dressed has me spooked."

"I've had nightmares about it," Avi said, laughing. She was about to ask Rhy what floor she'd be on when the photographer shouted, "Next!"

Avi gave her a small wave as she walked to the black stool, suddenly thinking that she'd seen that smile before. She shook her hair out, smiling softly for two quick pictures.

3

"OH, THIS IS BOMB," Belle exclaimed. She held the ID picture hanging from the purple lanyard around Avi's neck.

They were sitting in the car, waiting for their mom to finish chatting with an old friend and watching Jovahn sweet-talk a woman twice his age.

"My smile came out kinda lopsided, but I don't hate it," Avi said, looking down at the laminated ID with her full name, grade, and school year. This card would also hold her café dining dollars and serve as her key to get into Hollingsworth.

Belle rolled her window down, pointing a threatening finger at Jovahn as he walked to the U-Haul. "You can't talk to her if I know her daughter," she shouted.

"Watch me," he said with a laugh before slamming his door.

Avi took to trying to absorb every detail on campus as they pulled out of their parking spot. She knew from the website that every building was named after Black women who had contributed to the advancements of their people, whether it be in science, art, politics, or entertainment.

"The Hurston Bookstore," Avi said, reading the gold lettering on the front of one building. She squinted at the plaque of Zora Neale Hurston's face by the entrance. "Hmm. O'Day Dining Hall. Who's that again?"

Belle flicked her left indicator. "Claudia O'Day was the first Black headmistress in 1972."

"Right, right. I still can't believe it took sixty-four years for an all-girls Black boarding school to get a Black headmistress."

Belle shrugged. "Sounds ridiculous, but it's true. And not only for HBBSs, but HBCUs too. Dr. Willa Player didn't become the first Black woman president of Bennett College until 1955. Spelman didn't get Dr. Johnnetta B. Cole until '87, and that was a whole hundred-plus years after their start. Occasionally, Headmistress O'Day will pop up and stroll around campus. She's highly revered around here."

Avi stared wonderingly at each building. The stories these walls could tell would probably knock her off her feet. The girls who'd transformed into women sitting in these buildings created the path she was just beginning to walk. Following the U-Haul, they passed the (Shirley) Chisholm Learning Center, (Fannie Lou) Hamer Hall, the (Audre) Lorde Building, and a chapel.

Campus security looked stressed and overworked as they ushered cars in the right directions. People scurried in every which direction carrying bags, shading their eyes from the bright sun, and stopping to ask questions to student helpers in lavender-collared shirts. It became easy to differentiate the upperclassmen (who were having loud or energetic reunions) and the freshmen (who wore expressions of both amazement and confusion as their guardians cautiously shadowed their every move).

"Where are the dorms?" Avi asked after they passed the

small mail center and another campus emergency phone.

"Just around this corner," Belle said, nodding toward the right. She took out her lip gloss and clumsily tried to apply it as she steered. "Past our dorms are the academic buildings and the Angelou Auditorium. Toward the back of campus are the greenhouse and Zody—that's the student museum. And if we had taken a left at the golden cheetah statue back there, you would've seen the Cliff. It has more food options, and BP and Preston students hang out there."

At the right, Avi saw a cul-de-sac housing the four dorms. Hollingsworth and Union, the two identical freshman dorms, sat facing each other and looked to be the oldest of the four. Rashad, which was the tallest, housed sophomores and juniors. And the newly renovated Truth Hall existed exclusively for seniors.

According to their mother, back in the late eighties and early nineties, none of the dorms had air-conditioning. Avi couldn't imagine living in a stuffy, overcrowded building in the dead of a Georgia summer with her inhaler as the only line of defense.

The front, side, and back doors of Hollingsworth sat propped open as parents carried boxes and pushed dollies up ramps. Avi watched people moving in and out of window frames of rooms with drawn blinds up to the fifth floor.

The lobby of Hollingsworth was cramped with people trying to check in and get to the steps or elevators. Three girls with binders and name tags on their lavender shirts sat at tables handing out keys while two others walked around pointing residents in the right direction.

Avi and her mother approached one of the girls in purple sitting under a sign reading J–Q. She wore a TWA and spoke with a perky voice. "Hi, my name is Easlyn! I'm a senior RS—a Residential Sister, that is. Last name?"

After Avi gave her name, Easlyn flipped the pages in her heavy binder and detached a key. "Okay, Avielle, it looks like you're in room G-12B. Which means I'm your RS," she said, smiling broadly, before handing Avi the silver key, which she promptly attached to her lanyard. "Now, if you'll just sign here and here. Oh, and initial there. Great! Now, you can either use one of the elevators to your left," Easlyn said, motioning widely toward an impossibly long line of grumbling people. Another RS with a frizzy ponytail rushed over to stop an annoyed girl who was stabbing the up button repetitively with her thumb. "Or," Easlyn continued, "you all can use the stairs to the ground floor on your right. See you at the dorm meeting tonight at seven!"

"JOVAHN IS GONNA start bringing your stuff down in a minute," Avi's mom said as they headed down the steep steps of the sunlit staircase. Together, they passed a small kitchenette, laundry room, and a spacious study room. The walls were painted a glossy white, and each four-panel wooden door had the names of its future inhabitants on the frame. There were fourteen rooms on the ground floor, most of which were open as new residents and their families flowed in and out carrying fans, containers, printers, comforter sets, and chairs.

Avi and her mother bobbed and weaved to avoid a rolled-up carpet being carried by a tall girl with multicolored braces and her look-alike brother. Finally, near the end of the hall was Avi's name under G-12B. The door was cracked open, and they could hear the soft crooning of a soulful song neither of them was familiar with. Hints of lemon drifted in the air as Avi pressed the door open and peeked into the room.

A girl wearing sunflower-print overall shorts and white Chucks with her hair in light brown waist-length box braids waved what looked to be burning wood slowly throughout the room. Avi furrowed her brows at her mother, who nodded encouragingly and nudged her forward.

Her voice was barely above a whisper as she spoke to the girl's back. "Eh, hello?"

Startled, the girl shrieked and jumped before turning to face them. At once, Avi recognized her roommate from her Instagram, @ZinOrbit.

Zazie held a hand to her chest and bent over to catch her breath.

"I'm sorry." She chuckled. "I didn't hear you guys over the music." Her shocked expression resolved into a bright smile. She had a small gap in between her front two teeth, a deep bronze skin tone, and overwhelmingly kind hazel eyes. "I'm Zazie Lewis. Nice to meet you both," she said and extended her hand.

Avi's mom rushed forward to take it. "No, we're sorry for frightening you. I'm Toni, and this is my daughter, Avielle."

Avi hated how her mother sounded like she was trying to arrange her first kindergarten best friend.

She gave a weak smile and made herself walk forward to

shake Zazie's hand but was shocked to receive a hug pinning her arms to her side.

"You look exactly how you do in your pictures," Zazie said, pulling back and waving the smoking wood once more before placing it in a bowl atop the desk. "I was so happy when I got your first email, and now we're both *actually* here." She bounced on her toes.

"It's nice to meet you, too. I love your braids and your overall shorts, by the way. The print is pretty." She hoped she didn't come off as trying as hard as she was.

"Oh, this little thing," Zazie said, sticking her foot out and placing a hand on her hip. "I found it two days ago with the tag still on at Plato's Closet. You know the thrift store?"

Avi didn't, but she nodded anyway.

"And I did the braids on myself for the first time. It took almost three days, but I think it was worth it."

"Definitely," Avi said, impressed. "So, what is that?" She pointed toward the smoking wood.

"Oh, right. I was cleansing our room with Palo Santo. My grandma's friend harvests it! It's used to welcome positive energy and brings about peace and clarity."

"And that's where the lemon scent is coming from?" Avi's mom asked, intrigued.

Zazie nodded. "And pine, I think."

Avi looked around at the built-in wall divider. Each side held a twin-size bed, floor-length wall mirror, sink, desk, chair, and two mahogany dressers. The space was small, compared to her room back home. But Avi could at least appreciate that she would have her own window.

"How long have you been here?" she asked, peering around

at the bare room. She slid one of the closet doors open, revealing the tiny space in which she was expected to store her clothes.

"Mmm. Maybe ten minutes. My dad should be coming back with some of my stuff soon." She skipped to the door and peeked down the hall. "Here he is now . . . and it looks like he already made a friend," she said, amused.

A huge bearded man carrying three marked boxes ducked into the room seconds later. "My daughter's right in here," he said to someone behind him.

"So is mine," Avi's dad said, stepping in behind Zazie's father.

"I checked the boys in," he said to Toni before she could ask, "but they don't have nearly as much stuff as Belle and Avi do. So I sent Jovahn over there to supervise and came over here to help. We can meet the boy later."

"Logan."

"Yeah, him," he said dismissively. "Then I met Keith outside on the sidewalk," he said, clapping a hand on the man's broad back. Keith smiled, and Avi could see that Zazie got both her gap and hazel eyes from him. "Anyways," he continued, "we got to talking about his restaurant back in the Chi and his daughter being on the ground floor of Hollingsworth, too."

"This has been my baby's dream for a while," Mr. Lewis said in a deep, boastful voice. "I could've cried when she got that scholarship. And Briarcliff's only the first step. What is it you say, baby?" he asked, wrapping a log-like arm around Zazie. " 'When I'm done, the change will be apparent environmentally, socially, and radically.' Show 'em how you say it!"

Zazie moved out of his reach, and her brown cheeks warmed. "Daddy, they don't have to know everything right this moment." She smiled apologetically. "He's more excited than I am."

Avi's mom laughed. "You know what? Why don't we get some more of you all's things and get started unpacking? You two stay here and get to know each other a little." She pushed the men out of the room, bracelets clanging as she walked. "Now, tell me more about this restaurant you have, Mr. Lewis."

"Our dads hit it off," Zazie said, filling a long, uncomfortable silence.

"He's the friendliest person I know. Unless he's in a courtroom. But your dad seems nice too, so I'm not surprised." She searched the room, hoping for some inspiration to keep the conversation going, but there was nothing but the box on Zazie's desk labeled CHI→ATL. "So, Chicago, huh?" Avi asked.

"Yeah," said Zazie, perking up again. "I grew up on the south side, near the Hyde Park area with my big brother, dad, and grandma. My brother thinks the whole idea of boarding school is super bougie and elitist, and I know parts of it will be, but the history, the values . . . this opportunity"—she touched a finger to the pink crystal hanging from her neck—"it feels like a once-in-a-lifetime chance. Plus, my grandmother went here when she was a girl."

Avi sat down at a computer chair and watched Zazie pull a neatly folded Sierra Leonean flag out of a small box on the floor. She held it up, sizing it to the wall behind her bed.

"What about you?" Zazie asked.

"What about me?"

"Why Briarcliff?"

"Oh, that." Avi shrugged. An indifferent look settled on her face. "My mom went here when she was a kid and loved it. She was student body president, ran the newspaper, was voted 'Most Likely to Succeed,' and won the Harvest Queen title her senior year. Now, my older sister is a senior here, and my twin brothers and godbrother go to Preston, too. I guess you could say it's kind of a family thing."

Zazie faced Avi swiftly, her braids swinging behind her. The side of the flag she was about to pin into the wall slumped. "Wait. You don't want to be here?"

"No! Don't get me wrong," Avi said, shooting upright in the chair. "Briarcliff is my dream come true. The writing and fine arts programs alone were enough to get me here, but this will be my first time in school surrounded by people that look like me." She unconsciously stroked the small hairs on the back of her brown arms. "It'll also be nice to finally have more than one random Black teacher every couple of years." Avi's head tilted with a squint as she spoke, more so to herself than to Zazie. "Maybe it's just that I have a lot to live up to," she continued. "And a lot of expectations for myself that still feel super out of reach."

"I get it," Zazie said. Her lips pursed in a grin as she took a seat and rolled toward Avi. "You just have to remember that home is behind, the world ahead, and we have so many paths to tread."

Avi squinted at her. "Meaning?"

"If we ever wanna accomplish anything, we gotta leave our comfort zones."

Avi sat back in her chair, nodding slowly at the sentiment. "You know what? I like that a lot." She smiled back at Zazie, repeating her words in her head.

"Wait a minute," Avi said, remembering. "Did you just steal a *Lord of the Rings* quote?"

Zazie looked caught for a moment. In the next, the girls burst out laughing.

4

IT TOOK THREE HOURS for the group of five to get the girls' room set up. Ellis and Keith put together lamps and fans, hung curtains, and adjusted bed risers. Toni, Avielle, and Zazie transformed their new dorm into a home.

Zazie's side was full of bright yellows and mellow grays, completed with a sunflower comforter, yellow shag carpet, and a string of smoky quartz crystals hanging on her headboard. She hung a framed quote by Audre Lorde that read, "I am deliberate and afraid of nothing," and posters of Assata Shakur, Chloe x Halle, and Stephanie Wilson, the second African American woman to go into space. A printed collage of Zazie with family and friends lined the wall over her desk, holding an old laptop, a small succulent, and a tattered Black doll dressed in a blue, white, and green dress.

Avi's side was powder blue and white, with her monogrammed initials hanging over the decorative-pillow-covered bed. Wisely, she'd chosen only to bring her two favorite stuffed animals: the small Black rag doll she was gifted on her first birthday and a plush blue ladybug she'd won at a school giveaway four years ago. Two Vashti Harrison canvases were placed delicately over the desk that now held her writing journal, special pens, and laptop. Her glasses case, a shabby copy of *Legendborn*, and realistic-looking blue and white silk peonies sat on the baby-blue utility cart next to her bed.

"I might be able to get used to this," Avi said from her fuzzy white saucer chair.

"Yeah. It's finally looking homey," Zazie agreed, cooing at the plant on her dresser. "Thanks again for helping me set everything up, Mrs. LeBeau."

"No problem, honey. All your stuff was already adorable. It just needed to be placed correctly."

"Shouldn't you two be heading off?" Mr. Lewis said, dabbing at the sweat on his forehead with a white rag. He tugged on Avi's white curtains, ensuring they were secure.

Ellis stared through his glasses as he set up Zazie's laptop, muttering, "The Organization Fair began thirty minutes ago."

Avi scrambled to her feet. "What are you guys gonna do while we're gone?"

"Make sure Belle is settled, meet Logan, and check on the boys," her mother said.

"Wait," Avi whined, "I want to meet Logan, too."

"Later." She pushed the girls out of the room, despite Avi's protest, urging them to stay together.

IN HOLLINGSWORTH'S emptying lobby, the girls heard the voice of Alexandria Malone, headmistress of Briarcliff Prep, coming from the main lounge. The far wall of the lounge held an ornately painted school crest of a cheetah's head, praying hands, an open book, and the fern adinkra symbol for "endurance." A couple of their new dormmates sat in front of a grand fireplace on plush purple couches, watching a video of Headmistress Malone with her distinctive eye birthmark as she explained the genesis of Historically Black Boarding Schools on the plasma screen TV.

"HBBSs gave Black children in elementary and secondary schools the opportunity to prepare for higher learning and academic success, while simultaneously providing the chance to gain a profound sense of community and commitment to academic excellence," Malone said over the soft instrumentals of the Briarcliff song playing in the background. "The Briarcliffs envisioned a safe space in Georgia to educate and prepare young Black women for a world that did not want them and never intended to listen to them. We are proud to see their vision in action every day.

"But, after *Brown v. Board of Education* declared segregation in public schools unconstitutional in 1954, many HBBSs were no longer deemed 'necessary.' Enrollment decreased dramatically, and financial hardships hit. Prior to the 1970s, there were more than one hundred HBBSs. Today, there are only eleven remaining. Briarcliff Prep and Preston Academy are amongst two of the most prestigious boarding schools in the nation. The traditions, values, standards, alumni, faculty, staff, and students are what keep these institutions at the top. You all," she said, pointing at the viewers, "keep us where we are. Relevant and necessary."

Zazie tapped Avi's shoulder, waving her on to follow a group of students talking boisterously about the Cliff, out the glass doors and through a shortcut on a cobblestone path behind Williams Library. Past the gym was a courtyard holding four large academic buildings and a two-level rounded building called the Maya Angelou Auditorium. Representatives of the Student Government Association stood at tables handing out lavender bags and T-shirts with the school crest, their class year, and *To Be the Change* written along the back as Francesca Leong, SGA president, directed them toward the Organization Fair.

The Cliff was by far the most active place on campus. Some students were already trying out their new Cheetah Dining points at the surrounding chicken hut, sushi place, burger joint, and vegan spot, while others took the opportunity to interact with classmates. Outside, people sat at round picnic tables in the middle of the sunny oval, snacking as music played over a speaker. Current students held out flyers and handed out favors, trying to get those passing by to hear what they were about. The tables stood side by side, representing every Briarcliff student group and six joint Preston-Briarcliff organizations.

"They're going all out for this," Avi commented with a mouth full of chocolate éclair she bought from the campus convenience store. "Do you know what organizations you're signing up for?"

Zazie held up three fingers. "The Photography Club, the Environmental Protection League, and Motherland United—they're the African student club." She ate a handful of popcorn she'd picked up from a concession stand and took a pamphlet from a girl representing Cheetah Plans—an event-planning club Belle cofounded. They planned the school's SNAs (Saturday Night Activities), concerts, holidays, prom, etc.

"What about you?" Zazie asked. "Ready to introduce yourself?"

In the hours they had spent getting their room together, Avi's father couldn't help but spill her heart's desire to join the *Cliff News*. Zazie knew all about Avi stalking the paper's website and members for the last year. She even knew about the word-for-word intro her mom helped her prepare.

"I've been practicing what I'm going to say, but I wanna sign up for the French Club, too. And maybe I'll check out the BP Girl Scouts troop. My Grandma Rose would love that."

They walked together through the busy crowd as students gathered in front of tables to hear what various clubs had to offer. The modeling table held three students in four- and five-inch heels and striking makeup. Though she knew she'd never sign up herself, Avi meant it when she promised a particularly stunning girl named Lonnie to check out at least one of their runway shows this year.

In the very middle of the oval, a tear-stained girl stood on top of a table, performing a monologue from *Fences*, just as Viola Davis had, with snot bubbles and all. By the end, Zazie held a dramatic hand to her chest, swiping at a tear and blaming her sniffling on her allergies. They saw the back of the performer's shirt read "BP Drama Club" as she bowed in each direction to the applause of her small audience.

The Spanish Club and French Club representatives stood side by side with treats and dressed in traditional clothes. Avi listed her name and email on the French sign-up sheet, barely listening to the kid in a beret in front of her as her favorite song by Chika played over the speakers. Feet away, Zazie stood at Motherland United's table rapping along and waving her arms with a clipboard and pen in either hand.

Together, they passed the Young Democrats, Young Republicans, Debate Team, Cooking Club, Glee Club, and the Golden Cheetahnaires before Avi saw the *Cliff News* sign.

"There go your people," Zazie said, pulling Avi to her so they wouldn't split a pole. "I'm gonna go check out the Photography table. Good luck!"

Egypt Mack, the president of the student-run newspaper, spoke to the crowd of prospects. Seeing her in person felt surreal after months of studying the paper's site. Egypt's creative-writing piece two years ago, "The Melanin Chronicles," came off as corny to Avi. But the articles she wrote, "Domestic Violence in African American Teen Relationships" and "Neoliberalism in the Black Community," hinted at a serious future in journalism.

The sun glinted off Egypt's coconut-brown skin as she explained the acceptance process.

". . . so, we are always recruiting talented writers and editors who display a great sense of awareness and the drive necessary to maintain the standard of the *Cliff News*. Those interested in joining our team and filling openings can sign up for the email list. If it wasn't obvious, we do not accept everyone, as do many of our sister clubs," she said with a shady look toward the surrounding tables. "Putting in the time, hard work, and dedication, as I do," she said, holding a hand to her chest, "to improve your craft and the standard of the paper are necessary to earn and keep a position with us." Egypt plastered a tight smile on her face as she scanned students lining the table to sign up.

Avi watched as two parents spoke to Egypt about the

newspaper and the benefits of listing membership on college applications. She tried her best not to psych herself out and resisted the little irritating voice urging her to walk away. This was her first real chance to take herself seriously as a writer, even if it was just for a high-school newspaper.

Egypt rolled her eyes when the couple left and walked behind the table to stand next to another girl sporting shoulder-length twists.

"Hello," she said, almost shouting at Egypt, before sticking out a hand. "My name is LeBeau. Avielle LeBeau." She promised to slap herself later for that opening.

"LeBeau. I'm Egypt Mack," she said with a chuckle.

Avi smiled sheepishly. "Um, I wanted to introduce myself. I'm from Upper Marlboro, Maryland, and I write short stories, poems—uh, things like that. And I think I'd be great for the creative-writing column. I saw on the website that the *Cliff News* is looking for a freshman to fill the position. I've been reading the online paper for two years, and I've always admired the quality of the column and you all's overall work."

"Mhm," Egypt grunted as she looked down at a clipboard. "The position's open to freshmen *and* sophomores. Of course, I can't just take your word for it. Did you hear what I said about the application process earlier?"

Avi nodded.

"Great. So, I'll be up front and tell you now. There's only one creative-writing column position open at the moment, so the competition will be fierce. You can sign up, and when it's time to send your work in, do so, but make sure your sample is up to par. And I mean the best of the best," she said, raising her hand like a bar. "I'm not saying it's not possible, but we do have other candidates we're a bit more familiar with, so if you want to be noticed, you have to stand out and let your work speak." Egypt gave a nod before turning to her friend to resume their conversation.

Avi didn't let her shoulders slump, though it felt like her stomach was in her ballet flats. But the small smile she forced herself to hold faded as she took the dismissal. She'd been prepping for this moment for months and had been anxious to finally meet Egypt since she was announced as president on the *Cliff News* website. Never had Avi imagined she'd be so curt and dismissive. Even worse was hearing that there was already someone Egypt was leaning toward. Of course there was! Avi was just starting out here. There had to be someone who'd been prepping for this their entire freshman year—last year. Avi waited anxiously until the sign-up sheet landed in her hands and scanned the names of other students who'd marked the "creative writing" column under interest. There were only two others so far. A sophomore named Kyla Shephard—that must be who Egypt was speaking of. And the other was—

"Are you kidding me?" Avi whispered harshly under her breath as she read Fallon Walsh's name as the other contender.

"Almost done?" Zazie asked cheerfully, popping out of nowhere.

Avi quickly filled out her information on the sheet before passing the clipboard.

She pulled Zazie feet away from the table, as they weaved

out of the way of a cheerleader and two students wearing rainbow-colored BP LGBTQIA+ shirts.

"It wasn't that bad," she lied, folding her arms uncomfortably over her chest.

"Really? Because your face is giving . . . 'nauseated.' "

"I mean, I don't know. Egypt's more to-the-point than I expected her to be, but I did exactly what my mom said. Kind of. And there are other people going up for the same position I am."

Zazie chuckled. "You weren't expecting that?"

"Of course I was. But it may not even be worth the trouble." Avi sighed, annoyed at the situation, and dug in her small purse, pulling out a gold card. "Here it is."

"What?"

"My mom gave me her Starbucks card. Do you wanna—Agh!"

Avi bumped into someone in front of her, almost knocking them both over. She scrambled to pick up the purse and its belongings—brown print shades, lip gloss, a silver Tiffany bracelet, and Fendi headband.

"I'm so sorry!" she said, stuffing the items into the girl's hands.

"It's okay, really, Avi," said a familiar voice. She straightened at the sound of her name and smiled. It was Rhy from the ID line. They'd made their way completely around the oval back to the modeling table, where she'd been listening to Lonnie.

Avi handed her the bag. "I wasn't paying attention, but it's nice to see you again." People around them were slowing down to stare and whispering behind their hands. "Zazie, this is—"

"Rhyon Bloom," Zazie finished with wide eyes, mouth partly agape.

Avi took another look at the girl, and it all clicked.

"Bloom," Avi repeated slowly with raised eyebrows. That's why she looked so familiar in line. Avi had seen Rhyon and her family on the cover of magazines and endless blog posts practically her entire life. Weird that she hadn't been able to put two and two together earlier, even though her father just rewatched King Bloom's third stand-up special on Netflix this past weekend. Rhyon's father, who was deemed the hardest working man in entertainment, was a world-renowned comedian, producer, TV show host, and award-winning actor. His habit of putting work above all else and inability to be faithful led to his first divorce, from Melaine Flores. Rhyon's mother, Melaine, a proud Afro-Latina, made a name for herself way before marriage, taking the modeling world by storm in the early 2000s. Now remarried to ex-NFL star/current sports commentator Rodney Williams, Melaine owned several businesses, including a wildly successful fragrance line.

"Oh, great," Rhyon rasped with narrowed eyes and faux enthusiasm, "you already know everything about me from my last name, huh? Be sure to thank *The Shade Room* for me." She pivoted, turning her attention back to one of the tall girls in heavy makeup.

Avi looked guiltily at Zazie, who shrugged. Rhyon had been the first student to speak to her today. And she was really nice. Glancing around, she could see people sneaking extra-long peeks and distinctly heard King Bloom's name slip from the mouth of some kid feet away who looked no older than twelve. Avi could only imagine what it might feel like for people to have so much knowledge of your life and family, not to mention their own negative assumptions—and then starting at a new school on top of that. She was barely handling the first-day pressure herself.

"I'm sorry," Avi said with a soft tap on Rhyon's shoulder.

She turned back reluctantly with a haughty look on her face.

"I just didn't recognize you earlier, but I didn't mean anything by it, really. Um, this is my roommate, Zazie. Zazie, I met Rhyon in the picture line this morning. Oh, and we'll all be in Hollingsworth together."

They exchanged tight-lipped nods as Avi searched for words to make the situation better.

"We were about to stop by Starbucks before we head back to Hollingsworth," Zazie said, pointing toward Angelou, not being able to stand the awkward silence. "Wanna come?"

Avi nodded, holding the card up with waggling brows. "My treat."

Rhyon looked conflicted for a moment, then her shoulders dropped. "Okay," she sighed, shifting awkwardly on her feet. "I may have gone a little too hard just now. It's just that people have been whispering about my mom and me all day. And apparently, there's some PresCliff gossip page that posted a picture of us as soon as we stepped out of the car this morning. She told me to give people time to adjust, but I wanted things to be different here."

"No biggie," Avi said airily. "We'll get a frap and pretend like none of this ever happened."

"Cool?" Zazie asked.

Rhyon still seemed hesitant, but a soft smile found its way to her lips. "Let's do it."

5

BY EARLY EVENING the aroma of BBQ lingered in the humid air and the Georgia crickets chirped noisily. The long line of cars bordering the dorm cul-de-sac had dwindled tremendously as the girls headed back to Hollingsworth, their skin sticky with sweat and melting drinks in hand.

As they stepped onto the sidewalk, Avi decided the first thing she would do when she got back to G-12 was to give her legs a fighting chance against the vicious mosquitoes and change into pants. Unknowingly, they walked past their parents and Belle sitting on a bench under a tree in the courtyard.

"Over here," Avi's dad barked.

A tall, burly man called Rhyon's name from the door of Hollingsworth, and she ran toward him, promising to catch up with them later.

"We didn't know you guys were back from Preston," Avi called as they approached the maple tree. Avi's mom looked curiously at pictures on Keith's phone as he described the latest event at his chili bowl restaurant. Belle sat with a pinched face at the edge of the bench, her legs and arms crossed. The meeting with Logan must not have gone well.

"We didn't want to rush y'all after we got the boys settled and met Belle's little friend," Ellis said with a smirk.

"Boyfriend," Belle exhaled.

"Sure, baby," he said, draping an arm around Avi. "That's an arrogant boy. Keep an eye on them for me," he said under his breath.

Mr. Lewis nodded toward Hollingsworth. "Who was that you guys were walking with?"

"Her name's Rhyon. I met her at check-in."

"Wait. Melaine's daughter? Rhyon," Belle asked, suddenly intrigued. Her eyes widened in interest. "I didn't believe it when some girls said they tried to get a pic with her mom earlier, but I guess she would be about your age, huh? Mommy," she said, whipping around, "do you remember Melaine's 2017 spread in *Vogue Italia*? She's everything!"

"That's great," Avi said. "But when you meet her, don't mention it."

Belle looked over her shades. "You must think I'm grossier."

"Maybe, if I knew what it meant. Just promise you won't bug her."

She felt Zazie nudge her elbow and turned to see her meaningful nod toward Belle.

"Oh yeah, this is my roommate, Zazie."

Belle stood, smiling politely. "I know. I recognize you from your IG. Your page has an earthy, calm aesthetic and your eyes are stunning." She extended a hand, but Zazie quickly pinned Belle's arms to her side with a hug.

"I'm sorry," Zazie said as she released her. "It's nice to meet you. Avi's talked about you all day."

"I have not," Avi muttered indignantly to Belle's proud look.

Mr. Lewis stood, too, now holding his daughter at arm's length. "I asked Belle to watch out for you, Zaziena Amera," he said, suddenly somber. The teary look in his eyes made Avi think of the giant plush teddy bears you find at Costco.

"Daddy, I'll be fine," Zazie said in a comforting tone as he pulled her into a smothering hug. They walked to his truck to speak privately.

"It's about time for us to head back to Sugah's," Toni said with a proud gleam in her soft brown eyes.

Avi looked down at her glittering watch, surprised by her mother's words. "Already?"

Her dad nodded. "We hit the road tomorrow at five."

Avi shifted uncomfortably in the grass, glad that Zazie and Rhyon weren't here right now. She knew her parents had to head back home. Knew that they'd be leaving her here. But she'd been so caught up in the day and trying to make friends that she hadn't prepared herself for this exact moment. She dug her fingernails into her palm, trying to distract herself from the instinct to panic.

As if her mother knew her exact thoughts, she reached out, stroking her knuckles before embracing her. In Avi's ear, she said, "I left a little something in your room. A reminder." But before she could lean away, Avi tightened her grip, pulling her mother even closer.

Her father bear-hugged her then, raising her off her feet. But when he put her down, she took a few moments to lay her head on his chest, studying the familiar rhythm of his heart, like she had when she used to fall asleep on his chest as a small child. With a finger to her chin, he said, "The only way you'd come to regret this experience is if you're not putting your best foot forward. I promise."

Zazie's father had already driven away by the time their mom began shouting from the passenger seat of the car.

"Avi, you have your inhalers, right?

"You have to make sure you keep up with your EpiPens, Belle. I'm serious!

"Make sure one of you calls EJ, and tell him to give you a copy of his prescription, just in case!

"Look out for one another!"

Avi felt her chest tightening but refused to let a tear drop as her parents drove down the street. Funnily enough, she knew exactly why this moment felt so familiar. It was like the first day of kindergarten all over again. When she'd been so caught up with the touch-and-feel princess book in front of her that she hadn't realized her parents had slipped out the door. She couldn't believe they'd left her in that classroom full of strangers by herself. She cried and eventually hyperventilated, until she gave herself an asthma attack. Ten minutes later, they were back.

It wouldn't be like that today, of course. She was fourteen now and had been anticipating this day for so many years—even if it scared her. Briarcliff was supposed to become a second home, and that was exciting. But this very moment, watching the taillights of their parents' car disappear behind a corner made Avi feel . . .

"Bittersweet," Belle whispered.

Avi reached out, and without hesitation, Belle's hand enveloped hers. A second later, Avi warmed at the feel of her sister's arms wrapped around her shoulders. She wasn't alone this time.

AT 9:32 P.M., the girls were finally let out of the unnecessarily long dorm meeting. For two hours, they'd sat squished on the plush purple couches in the main lounge of Hollingsworth listening to Housemother Lisa, a stern woman with a bright smile and graying hair, and their RSs drone on about things Avi felt could have been sent in an email. They talked about keeping up the decency of the community kitchenettes and bathrooms and the Briarcliff app that they would use not only for school assignments and campus updates but for leave requests. Housemother Lisa emphasized that campus leave was a privilege that could and would be snatched away at any signs of rule-breaking. They spoke in detail about curfew and rules Preston students had to abide by in the dorms during visitation (checking in, no closed doors, out by 8:30 p.m.). Room checks, dry campus, appropriate makeup, and quiet hours were all covered in the detailed PowerPoint.

By the end of the meeting, the exhaustion from the activity-filled day showed on everyone's faces.

Everyone's except Rhyon's, that was. With a determined look, she made a beeline to Housemother Lisa. At dinner, Avi and Zazie had taken Rhyon's comment about never wanting to return to her room as a general dislike of the dorm. But the horror story she told of seeing Kieley, of all people, on the other side of her door was worse than Avi could have imagined. Avi explained to Zazie why this was so devastating as

Rhyon sulked back to them with defeat written all over her face. She'd been told, "A change like that is simply impossible so early in the school year" and "You two might turn out to be the best of friends."

Together, they walked down the steps, listening to their floormate Thalia Landon speak a mile a minute about her freshman class presidency campaign. She was a slim girl with vitiligo affecting the areas around her eyes, arms, and fingers. They took the custom "Vote Thalia 4 Prez" wristbands, while her roommate, Ashia, happily munched on a cookie she was supposed to be passing out.

"It's the first day," Zazie commented as she slid the gold band on her wrist. "How is she this prepared to run for freshman class council?"

"More importantly," Avi said, "how has Ashia kept her baby hairs laid like that all day in this heat when I look like every type of struggle?"

Many of the ground-floor girls were already in nightclothes and bonnets as they walked in and out of the bathrooms with towels and caddies. Other girls took this opportunity to explore Hollingsworth and meet their new neighbors. Rhyon jumped out of her funk long enough to introduce Dove in G-8, whose mother was a celebrity choreographer, and Raquel, from room 207, whose father was a retired Olympic track star. Zazie discovered that their neighbor in G-14, A'deja, had the same alumna scholarship sponsor as she.

Avi listened to them chatter distractedly until she saw a book tipping out of the class bag of a bored girl named Meme. The premise about a West African teen girl with white hair on a magic-filled journey to save her people was intriguing.

"I picked up that book last week, but ended up not buying it," Avi said, pointing to it. "Have you finished?"

Meme perked up. "I only have two chapters left, but it's *so* good. One of those books you know you'll reread a thousand times. You can borrow mine once I'm done!"

They were only three minutes into the conversation before realizing they lived about half an hour away from one another in Maryland. Meme's roommate Najah, from Tuskeegee, pointed out the *Beetlejuice* Broadway poster saved as Avi's wallpaper. The next thing Avi knew, the three of them were cheerfully singing all the parts to "Say My Name" on the floor outside of their rooms.

Around eleven thirty, Easlyn came down the hall in a puffy pink robe and fuzzy blue slippers, ushering girls into their rooms with reminders that they were well within quiet hours.

Rhyon gave a sorrowful goodnight before retreating into her room, which was directly across the hall.

Half an hour later, the new inhabitants of G-12 were in bed. Avi settled under her comforter to the echoes of noisy crickets over Zazie's soothing sounds-of-rain playlist. She sent a thank-you text to her mom for the wooden plaque with the Octavia Butler quote "All that you touch, you change. All that you change, changes you" before rolling onto her back.

"Zazie," Avi said barely above a whisper.

"Yeah," she answered, grogginess clouding her voice.

"Earlier before orientation, you asked about my siblings, but I didn't get to ask about yours."

"Like I said, I only have my brother, Tahj. He's seventeen and the smartest person I know. I don't know what I'd do without him."

Avi watched the ceiling fan whirl until she was dizzy. "Sometimes, I dream about it, but I can't even imagine only having one sibling."

"It's fine, I guess, but I always really wanted a sister. You're lucky to have two." She took a deep breath. "I figure Briarcliff is my first real chance to get some, even if they're not blood."

Avi flipped onto her stomach and exhaled with the weariness of the day, finally allowing her eyes to rest. "You can count me as your first."

6

AVI SAT AT A BOOTH in the café with Zazie and Rhyon the next morning, putting thoughts of her sample for the creative-writing column to the side for once. Belle and her best friend, Nevaeh Wilson, spouted knowledge only upperclassmen could know, and Avi needed to absorb as much information as possible. She nibbled on a bowl of fruit and oatmeal, trying to calm her nerves enough to focus.

"If you call Professor Simmons over during a test to ask a question, you can tell whether your answer is right or wrong depending on how deep the wrinkles in his forehead get," Nevaeh said. She shifted her loose brown curls before finishing the last of her blueberry muffin and downing her juice. Like all seniors did on their first day, she wore her official lavender school blazer.

Belle smoothed her tan pleated skirt out, saying, "And Madame Delcour wants everyone to do well, so if you ask a general question during a test, you can almost guarantee she'll let the answers slip."

Avi nodded nervously, running a hand over the crest on her lavender collared shirt. She wondered fleetingly if she should be taking notes, only to see Rhyon scribbling quickly in an emerald-green planner.

"What about Professor Akwi?" Zazie asked as she yanked her swinging braids up into a half ponytail. She had barely touched her pancakes or dry vegan sausage. "She's supposed to be our Women's Studies teacher, and I hear she's tough."

Nevaeh nodded. "A complete nightmare if you don't turn in homework on time or take detailed notes. She doesn't play, but she knows her stuff."

Rhyon yawned widely with a hand covering her mouth. That morning, before Avi's and Zazie's alarms went off, she had knocked on their door, fully dressed in a white button-down, bowknot necktie, and a purple plaid skirt, to complain about Kieley's bearlike snoring throughout the night.

"Sorry," she said, waving her second yawn away. An anxious look settled in her eye. "Tell us about Professor Blue? I have him on B Days."

Avi flipped her schedule over and sighed miserably. "Me too." She'd been placed in Algebra II because of her own stupidity. After wasting thirty-five minutes stressing over the first half of the timed online math placement exam, she decided to mark the multiple-choice options randomly and leave it to fate. She'd never expected so many of her random answers to be correct. Now she was being punished for her carelessness in the form of a class she was unprepared to take.

"He's *so* fine," Nevaeh said, flipping her hair. "Like a nerdy Chadwick Boseman, and his suits are always perfectly tailored. I swear, if he wasn't married to Professor Lovette, I'd—"

"No, thirsty." Belle chuckled. "Like, as a teacher."

"Oh—right. Blue's mad cool and hands out a lot of extra credit." Nevaeh shrugged. "Cute brooch!"

Avi looked down at the diamond and pearl–encrusted strawberry brooch Rhyon wore today.

"Thanks!" Rhyon adjusted her lucky pin. "They're kind of my thing, but this one was my abuela's favorite."

"Question," Avi said. "What does this small 'p' mean next to Professor Blue's name?" She pushed her glasses up, holding the schedule an inch from her face as she examined the sheet for a key code.

"Oh, you take that class at Preston," Belle said matter-of-factly.

The smell of the turkey bacon sitting in the middle of the table was suddenly nauseating.

Just as Avi prepared to launch into a string of complaints, Headmistress Malone's voice rang out over the intercom. She wished them a beautiful first day and gave a reminder that cell phones were prohibited on their persons during school hours. Belle inconspicuously slid her phone from the table into her blazer pocket. At the end of the announcement came a loud, annoying ring, signaling five minutes before first period.

Students all around the cafeteria cleared their tables of dirty dishes. Chairs scraped against the checkered floor as they headed for the exits.

"Good luck, Ellie," Belle said, before picking up her violin case and looping her arm through Nevaeh's.

BETWEEN RUNNING AROUND to find classes on time, numerous introductions, and explanations of class rules, the A Day flew by in a whirlwind. Students rushed past each other on sidewalks and in hallways on their way to classes, rehearsals, and meetings. Upperclassmen seeing each other for the first time since last semester hugged and squealed in the middle of busy walkways. And Headmistress Malone made herself visible during breaks to hurry students to class, check uniforms, and confiscate cell phones into her custom gold bucket.

The girls sat in the bare-walled room of their first shared class chatting until a woman wearing a tight bun and a polka-dot blouse entered. She set her bag down and wrote US HISTORY + in all caps on the whiteboard.

"My name is Professor Regine Shaw," she said, turning to face the class. "As you can see, I am your US History PLUS Professor. I say 'plus' because at this HBBS, I believe it is my job to give you all as much of the full history in the next two years as I possibly can." She paced back and forth, scanning the eager faces in front of her.

"That being said, because this country was born from the genocide of and cruelty to its Native peoples, the blood and backs of our enslaved African American ancestors, the exploitation of our immigrant siblings and the determination of the inhumane, it would be unfair and irresponsible to dedicate our three hours a week to feed you a nonsensical, revisionist history. So, I won't do that." Her eyebrows raised a fraction, with a shrug. "In exchange, all I ask is that you show up, work hard, and take advantage of this opportunity not everyone is afforded."

Zazie beamed. "Thank God!" she whispered when Professor Shaw turned to get a stack of papers out of her bag, "I was *so sick* of hearing about 'fair slave masters' at my old school."

During lunch by the Cliff, Avi and Rhyon pored over a school map on their table until they heard a passing senior snickering about "clueless freshmen." Avi stuffed the map in her backpack, mortified.

Exactly one minute before the bell, the girls skidded to a stop at the English 9 door, out of breath. Without their maps, they'd shown up at the wrong building and had to race across campus. It was Egypt Mack of all people who shouted, "Briarcliff women don't cut corners!" when the trio tried to take a shortcut across the perfect green grass. Avi tried to contain her wild thoughts about the encounter being the reason her sample would be discarded without consideration.

Just as the final bell rang, Professor Lovette peeked out of her room in her signature cat-eye frames and waved them in.

Unlike Shaw's bare walls, this room was full of color. One wall was a mural to honor Black novelists, poets, screenwriters, and playwrights. Quotes by well-known authors filled the adjacent wall, and the students' desks lined the room in a large circle.

Professor Lovette pulled her powder blue swivel chair up to fill the empty space. After giving a history of her educational past—a Briarcliff diploma, BA from Tuskegee, MA in education, and MFA from Columbia—she took a pile of papers out of the blue binder resting on her lap, restacked them, and with a southern tinge said, "Pass these out, darlin'," to the girl with braces in the desk to her left.

She gave them a moment to look over the syllabus on their own. It was straightforward—dates for upcoming quizzes and tests, lessons on grammar one month, detailed instructions on stylistic writing the next, learning to analyze poetry, and . . . highlighted in yellow, something about a biweekly student's book choice, presentation, and report.

When the timer went off, Lovette turned her attention back to the class, the chair squeaking under her full figure. "Questions?"

Avi's hand shot in the air, along with several others, but Professor Lovette's bright eyes landed on her. "Ah. Miss LeBeau," she said, remembering the nervous girl from check-in. "You first."

Avi returned her kind smile. "What exactly is the biweekly student's book choice?"

"I'm glad you asked," Lovette said, looking genuinely pleased. "Every other week, a student in this class will pick a book written by an author of color to read. They will do an individual presentation on said book and by the end of the next week, the entire class will need to turn in a book report. I know reading a whole book every two weeks may seem like a lot, but I won't be grading harshly, and it really is meant to be a grade booster.

"Look, I don't know about you guys, but reading the same books picked by teachers who had little in common with me through middle school, high school, and even grad school was . . ." She gave two thumbs down and blew a raspberry. "I just would've liked to have some say. So it doesn't matter to me the category or genre—and I mean short stories, full novels, poetry, comic books, fantasy and adventure, contemporary, romance—all of it is acceptable as long as it's written by a person of color, bonus points if they identify as a Black woman. Unfairly, I have decided that I'll have the first pick with . . ." She spun around in her chair before revealing the cover of *Clap When You Land* by Elizabeth Acevedo.

Avi beamed at her. Twice since fifth grade, she'd been forced to read *Lord of the Flies*. It wasn't that it was a bad book. That wasn't her problem. But to have a teacher prioritize books written by people who reflected *all* of their students was a dream. Avi felt like she could dance.

Then Professor Lovette's arms flew up, "But remember, let's keep books with outrageous graphic sexual references and gore to your personal reading time. Other questions?"

When the final bell rang, Avi waved her friends on and waited patiently for every other straggler to finish speaking to Professor Lovette before she approached the desk with her laptop in hand.

"I was just wondering, if you'd mind reading over my essay for the creative-writing column position of the *Cliff News*. It's due in a few hours, and so far only my siblings have read it. They think it's really good, but . . ."

"You don't know if it's Egypt good?" Lovette finished pointedly.

Avi nodded.

"I get it. The girl is tough! She has Gayle King journalistic dreams and something of a cutthroat-style work ethic when things aren't up to her standards." She chuckled. "Sure, honey, let me check it out!"

Half an hour passed before they were done. Lovette read

her three-page sample in five minutes, gave Avi her critical thoughts in another five, and sat down with her for the rest of the time answering Avi's questions about her time working as senior editor at Briarcliff in the early 2000s.

It was more help than she could've ever imagined receiving, and Avi worked in solitude as soon as she got back to her room. But ten minutes before the deadline, when her hand hovered frozen over the send button, Belle unexpectedly knocked on the door.

"Okay, you give three of your worst-fear cons to pressing send and I'll give three pros."

Avi inhaled deeply, giving in to her sister's games.

"You first." Belle shrugged out of her blazer and pulled Zazie's rolling chair up to the desk.

"Con: I submit it and realize everyone around me thinks it's good just because they don't wanna hurt my feelings and have to love me."

"Who? Me, Moe, and Paisli?

"Yeah."

"Eh. Doesn't really count. Lovette just told you it's good. Pro: You have 'my words written in print' on the goals list hanging in your room at home. Pressing send is a chance to see that happen."

"Con: Egypt will read it and personally blacklist me from the *Cliff News* even after she's graduated."

"I dare her to try it. Pro: Once you do it, it won't be a 'what if' situation anymore. And that alone will let you rest easy."

"Con: This is the first step toward me considering myself as a real writer and if I fail, I don't know what I'll do next."

"Pro: You're a writer with or without the *Cliff News*'s validation, and you've been prepping for this moment for a year now. You literally couldn't be more ready."

Avi looked into her sister's eyes, seeing their mom's comforting gleam reflected there. She turned back to the computer in defeat.

"Fine."

She stared at the email, checking once more that she'd selected the correct file before freezing over send again. But Belle bounced off her chair and was behind her in a second. Before Avi could pull away, Belle covered her hand and forced her finger to meet the touchpad.

It was done. Nothing she could do now but wait.

7

ON TUESDAY, Avi went to French I, her first course without Rhyon or Zazie by her side. That she could deal with. But Avi was less than pleased to discover Fallon fixing the collar of her button-down in the front row of the French room. Fallon's eyes brightened when she found Avi in the doorway, and she waved before pointing to the open seat beside her. Shocked, Avi looked to see if there was someone behind her. Nope. She took a deep breath and walked into the room. Either she was being set up, or they'd gotten off on the wrong foot. Avi suspected it was the former.

"Avielle, right?" Fallon asked, sliding a lock of hair behind her ear as Avi sat. "I heard through the grapevine that you'll be competing for the same writing spot I am. I never would've guessed that creative writing would be your thing."

Avi's brows furrowed. How would anyone guess that just from arguing with a stranger in public? "It's Avi. And who told you that?"

"Oh, I overheard it at the Cheetahnaire auditions yesterday afternoon. Belle brought it up in passing right before I earned my spot. She's like a *pretty* impressive dancer. Are you two blood sisters?"

Avi dug in her bag for her notebook to hide her face. What was that supposed to mean? "Mhm, same parents, and yeah I am shooting for the column."

"And you think you have a chance?" She asked it like a question, but there was doubt dripping in her voice.

"Uh—I . . ."

Fallon smirked at her fluster. Avi could be shy, but she'd never been a punk before. She sat up straighter in her chair, looking Fallon directly in the eyes.

"Yes, I think I do. My sample was strong, and I've gotten pretty decent feedback."

"Decent . . . that's cute."

The bell rang then, and the petite Madame Delcour flew in, giving two swift claps to silence the room. So Avi's instincts were right about Fallon: She was a young Regina George in training. No mistakes on that front. They'd talked for maybe a minute, and in that time, Fallon had managed to poke all of Avi's nerves. It was annoying. Avi had been looking forward to this class, and Belle always spoke so highly of Madame Delcour. She wondered for a moment if it would be ludicrous to try and switch into Spanish or ASL, but she already knew how awful it would be explaining to her parents that she let some girl run her out of one of her most anticipated classes. Avi headed her paper and began taking notes as Madame Delcour jumped right into the syllabus.

Things improved in Professor Akwi's Women's Studies class as she kicked off their first discussion, deciphering the difference between womanism and feminism with an

Alice Walker quote: "Womanist is to feminist as purple is to lavender." Quickly, they discovered that Akwi was just as intimidating as Nevaeh said and possessed the power to silence a room with the severity of her glance. But she was passionate about the subject, and Avi could appreciate that.

In the afternoon, Avi and Rhyon ran into Kai as they crossed the street heading toward Preston.

"I asked if you had an extra binder I could use for my computer science class earlier," Kai said. "Why didn't you text me back?"

Avi shrugged, not wanting to delve into how scared she was to get caught with her phone by a teacher or Headmistress Malone. "I must've forgotten to turn my phone back on."

"I thought you left it in the room this morning because of the rule," Rhyon said, oblivious. Avi glared at her.

They waved at the half-conscious Preston security officer, depending strongly on Kai's loose directions as they attempted to make it to their first Algebra II class in Valintino on time.

The stone brick buildings stood tall, bearing the names of men like W. E. B. Du Bois, Fred Hampton, Steve Biko, and Bayard Rustin. White-and-admiral-blue banners with the school motto—STRENGTH IN UNITY—flew high on flagpoles, blowing in the summer breeze. The sun shone brightly on a tall statue of the founding brothers, William and Carlton Preston.

Avi and Rhyon walked swiftly, arm in arm. It was apparent now why so many Briarcliff students were eager to visit PA. The campus was lovely, but after a while, Avi found her attention caught on the uniformed students going about their day.

"Maybe coming here twice a week won't be as bad as we thought," Avi said sagely after a guy in a Preston Lacrosse jersey flashed her a smile.

Right past the Robinson Library, the girls saw a towering stone statue of a roaring lion. Students periodically stopped to rub the statue's nose for luck and congregated in the grassy area surrounded by academic buildings.

As they passed the lion, a stocky guy with a Preston sweater draped over his shoulders left his friends on the brick walkway and jogged up to them.

"Hey, I'm Lamont. I don't know if you remember me from yesterday," he said, staring at Rhyon. As he blocked their path, Avi noticed he had perfect teeth and a look she could only describe as undeniably cocky.

"I remember," Rhyon said, quickly shaking his outstretched hand and yanking it back when he held on for a second too long.

"Can I help you out? It seemed like you were looking for something. Or maybe some*one*." He shrugged suggestively.

"Actually, yeah. We have a class in Valintino with Professor Blue, but this is our first time at Preston."

Avi tried to back up to give them the moment Lamont wanted, but Rhyon tightened her grip.

He pointed to the third building in the line-up, saying, "Right there. I have enough time to walk you over if—"

"Nope, that's okay," Rhyon flung over her shoulder as she pulled Avi past him and his sniggering friends.

"Catch up with you later, Rhy," Lamont called. She ignored him.

"You didn't think he was cute?" Avi asked when they entered Valintino.

"Doesn't matter," she said with an edge. "He stopped my mom for a picture yesterday, and last minute, he literally pulled me into the photo. Then the fool tagged me and a bunch of blogs in a caption *thirstin'* over my mom. He's a clout chaser, and desperation doesn't interest me."

They sat in Professor Blue's Algebra II class minutes later, listening to his welcome speech. He looked no older than thirty, with broad shoulders and an undeniable passion for teaching.

"The resources available to you all are plenteous," Blue said in his husky voice. "So, if your grade is struggling at the end of the school year, it most certainly will have been your fault." He smirked at the class's chuckles. "I'm joking, but at the same time, I'm not."

He leaned on the large rosewood desk behind him in his clean blue suit. One leg sat perched as he crossed his arms. "I mean, not to brag, but I'm an *incredible* teacher. In addition to doing everything I can during class, I'll be posting relevant practice quizzes on LionWeb. There will be extra credit opportunities; I'm always in my office outside of my classes; and my TA, who is of course late—"

Professor Blue's head swung toward the door as it flew open and a tall boy with a clean high-top fade, deep umber skin, a pair of small diamond earrings, and a face God clearly took extra care with jogged into the room.

Avi sat straighter in her desk with a silent gasp and pursed lips, suppressing the embarrassing urge to scream *Hi, I'm*

Avi and you're beautiful! out into the room filled with her new classmates.

"Ah, Mr. McClain, I'm so glad you could join us," Professor Blue said when he reached the desk with a mumbled apology. He clapped a large hand on the boy's shoulder with a proud smile. "Like I was saying, Mr. McClain is my Algebra II and Pre-Calc TA. He's a certified math whiz and more than capable of helping in any way needed, right?"

The TA looked bashful in response to Professor Blue's praise and said, "Call me Quincy," in a throaty voice to the class.

"Please pass these out, Mr. McClain. And when you're done, "I want you to put your tie on. School is still in session."

Avi watched entranced as the boy went from desk to desk, handing out papers from two stacks. Before today, she had been unaware that she had an exact type. But now that Quincy was right here in front of her, she could see that he was it.

Quincy stopped before Avi, and she took in his slim build, broad nose, midnight eyes, and a stunning smile worthy of all her attention.

She gathered herself, grabbing the papers still hanging in the air. Too late, she returned his smile.

Rhyon leaned over, giggling. "Stare if you have to, but you should probably close your mouth before you drool."

Avi snapped her mouth shut as Quincy sat at the desk next to Blue's and slipped the striped blue tie from his backpack over his head.

Throughout the hour, Avi alternated between playing with

the charm dangling from her bracelet and stealing glances at a dozing Quincy. Professor Blue received very little of her attention as he talked about five future tests and the math club he was starting. Avi tried to focus as Blue droned on about some major project that would be worth 15 percent of her grade, but she found her attention kept slipping back to the sleeping boy in the desk. Hopefully, Rhyon was taking enough notes for them both.

A pop practice test (which Avi was sure she would've failed regardless of this new distraction) took place during the last fifteen minutes of class.

"I'll be grading your practice assessments just to see where everyone is and then determine if early intervention is necessary," Professor Blue said, lining up the papers on his desk. "All right, guys, I'm here for questions. Everyone else is dismissed."

Avi gathered her belongings and followed Rhyon to a small line forming in front of Professor Blue's desk. He would soon be hearing the speech Rhyon had given each professor over the last two days.

"You'll be receiving 'A' worthy work because I'm an 'A' student and I will not allow my grades or your expectations to fall below my own 'A' standards."

Hopefully, she would receive a better response from Professor Blue than she'd gotten from their Health professor, who said dismissively, "Honey, this is a Pass/Fail elective."

Quincy sat slouched in his seat, arms crossed and head nodding by the time they were next in line. But there was something nagging Avi. She knew it would be a mistake to leave without at least bringing to his attention the fact that she existed. But how exactly was she supposed to get him to notice her if he was napping?

She quickly introduced herself to Professor Blue and got the familiar "Any relation to Belle and the twins?" before inching herself toward Quincy's desk. While Rhyon launched into her rehearsed speech, Avi scanned his desk for something to use. But there was nothing there except extra handouts and his phone.

She thought of purposely tripping over his legs. That wasn't a bad idea unless he had unpredictable reflexes when suddenly awoken. Her family learned the hard way—if Antonio was startled awake, anyone within reach could expect a slap in the face or a swift kick in the crotch.

Again, her eyes ran over the desktop. She took two side steps, blocking Professor Blue's and Rhyon's view, before grabbing his phone.

"Excuse me," she whispered.

Quincy let out a soft snore, and she noticed his ridiculously long lashes.

"Hello," she said a little louder, nudging his foot this time. He stirred, brows furrowed as he looked up at her.

"What's up?" Quincy asked groggily.

She held the phone out and said, "I found this; is it yours?"

He grabbed the phone, slid it across Professor Blue's desk, and the same warm smile she'd seen before spread widely across his face. She prayed it would become familiar.

"It's Blue's. He'd kill me if I lost it. Thanks."

"Avi," Rhyon called from behind. She ignored her.

"Oh, no problem. I assumed it was yours and didn't want you to get in trouble since we're not technically supposed to have our phones during the school day." She rolled her eyes internally at herself, but he just looked up at her, amused.

"We're gonna be late to College and Career Prep," Rhyon hissed. Avi waved her away, tight-lipped, and turned back to Quincy.

"'Preciate it," he said, standing. Quincy towered over Avi's five-foot-two frame as he adjusted the bag tossed over his shoulder. He stared at her openly. Curiously. Waiting.

Avi shifted on her feet, searching for words that wouldn't come.

And then his brows rose, and a smile spread across his lips. "You like a lot of different sci-fi or you're just a fan of *Lovecraft Country*?"

Avi squinted at him before remembering the notebook she held in her arms. The baseball card–like art on the cover showed Diana Freeman looking fiercely over her shoulder in overalls, with her new metal arm just peeking from beneath a brown overcoat. Paisli had gifted it to her the morning they left Sugah's for Briarcliff.

"Oh no, sci-fi's one of my favorite genres," she said excitedly. "*Stranger Things*, *Black Mirror*, Marvel as a whole, and anything written by Octavia Butler."

"Really?" he asked with wide eyes. "My cousin just recommended me this book called *Smoke Rises* by Alanna Ade . . . ?"

". . . Adebisi," Avi finished.

He snapped his fingers, pointing. "Yeah, that's it. I wasn't sure if I was gonna read it yet."

"Oh, you have to! It's long but doesn't drag and it's futuristic, but speaks heavily on climate change and war and the soldiers have bionic body parts. I finally got to the sequel last month!"

Rhyon's shoe tapped impatiently behind her just as a quiet beeping from the green watch on Quincy's left wrist dragged his eyes away. "I can't be late to Physics," he said, looking anxiously from his watch back to her. "But, imma check it out." He turned to walk away but hesitated a moment before flashing her another smile. "And thanks for waking me up, Dimples. See you around?"

Avi nodded eagerly, watching him jog out the room. Her "Anytime" came way too late as her eyes dreamily fixated on the door he'd just exited, thinking of how that went better than she could've expected.

But a second later, Rhyon grabbed her arm, practically dragging her out of the room. "Let's go," she whined. "We'll make a bad impression if we're late to the first class, and we only have seven minutes to get back to BP."

THE REST OF AVI'S WEEK went without any major hiccups. There were only a few run-ins with Fallon in French, and she managed to avoid any more social-ruining incidents like cutting across the grass. There *was* an unfortunate soup incident in the café on Wednesday that made a custodian give Avi a nasty side-eye. And she had almost given herself an asthma attack running to Orchestra with her violin on Friday morning after hitting snooze one too many times. But Kai's move-in day advice not to sweat the small stuff turned out to be most important in her new strides to let insignificant troubles go.

Such as the embarrassing amount of time she spent primping with her flexi-rod set and laying her edges on Thursday morning. When Rhyon knowingly asked, "Who are you all prettied up smelling like vanilla and sunshine for?" Avi claimed that every look she had was for her alone and that anyone else that wanted to enjoy it could. But the look she'd prepared (for no one in particular) turned out to be a waste because Quincy was a no-show in class. At least she got a pretty selfie from her fuss.

When Professor Lovette let the class out of English 9 early

on Friday afternoon, Avi went straight to her room to check her phone. There was a text from Antonio asking to FaceTime tonight. Also one from her mom, requesting more pics of Avi and her "new little friends" in their uniforms for her to post to Facebook. Lastly, Avi caught up with the forty-two unread messages from her group text with Belle, EJ, Moe, and Kai. She was apparently the only one too afraid not to follow the "no phone during school hours" rule.

Belle posted the PresCliff gossip page's latest update about a junior girl whose herb grinder fell out of her book bag on the first day of classes. A series of reaction gifs in their group chat followed before the last message.

Avi meet me and Jah at the cliff at 3:30?

KAI

Avi would have only been surprised if her godbrother was on time. So, she, Zazie, and Rhyon sat at a round table sipping on fruit smoothies and sharing a large order of waffle fries while they waited. The Cliff wasn't nearly as exciting without the music, free food, and student performances from the Organization Fair. But they quickly discovered it was still the center of student life for the two schools.

They were deciding what their weekend plans might look like when Kai dropped a green binder on the table and sat down across from them. A heavyset guy with green eyes, starter locs, and a bored expression sat next to Rhyon and side-hugged her. By now, they all knew Jasiri's father was G-Luck—record producer, songwriter, and a DJ who had headlined his fair share of blog posts. It was no wonder he and Rhyon knew each other. And from the gleam in Zazie's eyes, Jah was someone she wanted to get to know, too.

"Kai. Jah. This is my roommate, Zazie," she said, pointing before turning on him. "Why would you have us waiting for you for over thirty minutes? It's rude. And why didn't you answer your phone?"

A goofy smile spread across Kai's face. "Got distracted."

She pointed at the binder. "What's this for?"

"It's a binder."

"I know what it is. I asked—what are you looking at?"

Avi followed his gaze to find Fallon, Kieley, and a few other freshman girls from Hollingsworth. Fallon sat with perfect posture, smiling alluringly and batting her eyes at Kai. With narrowed eyes, Avi scooched to block his view and turned back just in time to catch Kai's arm as he readied to approach her.

"Nope."

"Why?"

Avi looked back again, but Fallon's attention was elsewhere. "I told you about the miniaturized bully competing for the creative-writing column. That's her."

"For real?" Kai's eyes widened, and then he leaned forward with a smile. "You didn't say she was pretty."

"Doesn't matter if she is. I forbid it."

Jasiri and Rhyon chuckled.

"*Forbid* it?" Kai gawked, and his face reddened. "You can't forbid me. If I wanna talk to her, I will."

"Not while I'm still breathing, you won't. Now, why are we here?"

Kai's eyes narrowed, and his nose flared. Avi sat up straighter, preparing for the inevitable yelling match.

But Jah jabbed at the green binder. "Might not be worth it, bro."

"You know what?" Kai exhaled, forcing a tight-lipped smile. "You're right. Because I need a favor."

Avi blinked at him. "A favor? You got a lotta nerve."

"Truce?" he asked, holding up his pinky. This was their white flag after years of dumb arguments. "C'mon, Avi," he pleaded. "I didn't know, and you started it."

Rhyon, Zazie, and even Jasiri agreed.

"Here. Let's call a truce, and I'll do your Algebra II homework for two nights," said Kai.

"Oh, you need that," Rhyon said.

Just last night, Avi had complained to Kai about how she was already struggling with the online homework and practice quizzes Blue wouldn't stop assigning. Forgetting this argument was worth two math-free nights.

She took his pinky.

"I'm running for freshman class president," Kai announced, and the sun shone off his peach-fuzzed lip. "But I need your help with some campaign stuff. Will you help?"

"Depends," Avi said with a raised brow. "Do you want help, or do you want me to do everything and slap your name on it?"

"A little of this. A little of that. Aye, have you noticed people around here are like super prepared for everything? That girl Thalia was handing out official campaign pins the other day, and one of the guys I'm running against posted an ad announcing his run yesterday. I feel like I'm already two months behind. If you help, it would be like you're my campaign manager."

Avi grinned. "I like the sound of that."

"No, I said it would be *like* it. Jasiri actually is."

Avi scowled as Kai pulled out a handful of ripped scraps and papers from the binder with his written notes and ideas and pushed them into her hands.

The group of five were brainstorming possible campaign slogans when Avi looked to see Belle a couple of tables over, surrounded by friends. She sat on Logan's lap as his large hand rubbed her thigh.

Avi still hadn't officially met Logan, but he was all over her sister's socials. Nevaeh, Adoree, Vannah, Logan, and two guys who looked like they could lead the O-line for a pro team guffawed at something they were watching when Avi finally caught her sister's eye. Belle stood, pulling Logan behind her.

"I see you're gettin' to it," Logan said to Kai as they reached the table. His toned arms bulged in his short-sleeve, blue-collar shirt. Unlike most of the guys at the Cliff, his tie remained in place.

"Man, I'm trynna catch up to you," Kai said, standing to dap him.

"Lo convinced Kai to run," Belle said excitedly. Her eyes were past dreamy, bordering on intoxication as she gazed at him.

Kai nodded like an eager politician desperate to make a good impression on the guy whose job he coveted. It was a wonder how quickly he could leave behind his typical nonchalance.

Avi looked at Kai with questioning eyes. They'd just talked

last night, and not once had he mentioned wanting to run for freshman president before twenty minutes ago—nor had he mentioned meeting Logan.

"Oh, yeah," Belle said, remembering why they came over. "This is my little sister."

Avi raised a hand to give a half wave, but Logan took it, squeezing too tightly.

"Nice to finally meet you, sis," he said as Avi took her hand back. She flexed it under the table. "Belle talks about you a lot."

Avi found that hard to believe. From her experience, the only person Belle always talked about was herself.

"Likewise," she said, hoping the smile on her face would be perceived as genuine. Not having thought to ask Belle what happened before now, Avi wondered what their father saw to persuade caution.

Belle used her hips to scoot Avi over, where she sat uncomfortably on the edge of the bench, trying her best to stay present in the conversation. Logan introduced himself to the table and soon set into a story about his father's watch party for King Bloom's latest comedy special. Zazie ripped her eyes away from Jasiri only to blush when Logan showed how thoroughly impressed he was that she had done her braids herself. Per his request, Belle promised to spread the word to upperclassmen about Zazie's hair-braiding services. He even made Jasiri stop looking at his phone and attend to the conversation after name-dropping some up-and-coming Atlanta rapper who happened to be a mutual friend.

Avi wasn't even slightly shocked to learn that Fallon was Logan's cousin. Annoyed, yes. Still, she was unable to keep the grimace off her face when he suggested setting something up for them to hang out. As if they were toddlers in need of a scheduled playdate.

What irritated her most was Belle's obliviousness. She didn't seem to notice that Logan monopolized the conversation, how he spun every comment back to himself or his need to share every opinion. If Avi was being honest, though, it was an ability that Belle and Logan shared. Belle was never as dominating, but the similarities were there.

Maybe it was their similarities that fascinated Belle, and that's why she hadn't stopped smiling since they sat down.

Never in Avi's life had she seen her sister's brash personality so subdued. Belle sucked up every word Logan spouted like her favorite juice. He seemed nice enough, but now Avi knew exactly where their father's annoyance came from.

9

ZAZIE, RHYON, AND AVI spent their Saturday morning in a reserved room of the three-story library, knocking out piles of homework. Considering it was the first week of classes, they'd assumed the workload would be lighter, but that wasn't the case. They twirled in low-back rolling chairs, scribbled equations with dry-erase markers, spread worksheets across the sturdy wooden table, and sporadically abused their professors' names.

First on the checklist was a page-and-a-half essay on "Defining Womanism as a Black Student" from Professor Akwi. Then all the odd numbers across three pages of Rhyon's and Avi's Algebra II book. A grammar revision worksheet from Professor Lovette. Two articles to read for US History+. And they all had foreign language assignments. Avi, French. Zazie, Swahili. Rhyon, Mandarin.

By noon, the trio was elated to greet the sunny day and leave their books behind. Belle and her co-captain, Vannah, led panting newbie majorettes on a run around the perimeter of the campus track with Fallon on her flank. Students littered the grass, shaded by tall cherry blossom trees, as they lounged on blankets with schoolbooks. It struck Avi as odd that she couldn't walk across the green grass without causing a commotion, but lying on it to complete homework was completely valid.

As Avi, Zazie, and Rhyon walked onto Preston's campus, beads of sweat forming on their foreheads, Avi thought of how grateful she was to have applied an extra layer of deodorant that morning. The next time Kai needed help with his campaign, he would have to come to them.

Newton Hall was the blue-brick freshman and sophomore dorm her brothers claimed was the best on Preston's campus. The tall walls of the lobby were covered in pictures of the dorm's step team, chess club, and resident honor society members. A golden trophy in a transparent case sat in the middle of the room on a stand that read 2021 DEBATE STATE CHAMPIONSHIP WINNER. The spacious common room, full of dark-blue couches, desktop computers, and a wide TV, was complete with a student-painted mural of Huey P. Newton. Preston students milled about.

At the entrance, a pimply boy who was supposed to sign them in hurriedly gave directions to the second-floor lounge and resumed his show. They trudged up two flights of stairs, huffing in the un-air-conditioned staircase.

"Z, I've been meaning to ask," Rhyon panted. "I know you have that nice camera, and I was looking at your photography page the other day. You're talented."

Zazie gushed, waving a hand. "Thanks! You wanna know if I can take those pics you need for your modeling troupe? I can do it tomorrow?"

Avi pulled the door to the second floor open and they rushed into the air-conditioned hallway.

"Really?" Rhyon smiled, pleasantly surprised.

"Yeah. I need to build up my portfolio, too. It's a win-win."

They walked past several open doors, trying hard not to peek inside. In one room, shouts echoed as guys gathered to watch a game of *Madden* on an illicit flat screen.

"Ooh, this one's Kai's," Avi said, pushing room 212's door open wider.

Zazie sighed as she walked into the room. "I'm underwhelmed."

Besides Kai's coveted signed LeBron jersey, a framed picture of himself as a baby with his parents, and the nerdy Star Wars figurines atop his three-drawer dresser, his side could be described as bland at best. Jasiri's hat collection lined the wall over his unmade bed, giving the room some much-needed oomph. Music equipment and comic books lay scattered throughout the room, along with smelly socks left where they were kicked off.

Rhyon looked at the pile of clothes on Kai's bed in distaste. "Neither of them even has a color scheme."

Avi shook her head. "Just a bunch of stuff that doesn't go together."

"Just like all of Kieley's junk."

"What makes y'all think a bunch of boys are gonna do over-the-top themes like 'pearls and sky blue with a dash of *Breakfast at Tiffany's*'?" Zazie asked with hands on the hips of her red denim skirt.

Avi held a hand to her chest. "You think my theme is over-the-top?"

"Or sunflowers. Or what was yours again, Rhy?"

"Posh," she said before giving in to her need to hang the rumpled sweater vests on hangers.

"Right. That," Zazie said, rolling her eyes. She ran her hands over a laptop sticker that said "LuckeyBeats" and flipped a switch on Jasiri's DJ control compact.

Avi plopped into Kai's rolling chair, knocking over a binder full of papers. "And what experience do *you* have with boys, pray tell?"

"Other than my third-grade boyfriend?" Zazie said. "Brother, cousins, uncles. The same as you guys." Jasiri's laptop screen lit at her touch, and she scanned the screensaver of him and his eight siblings.

Rhyon cocked her head to the side, exasperated. "Z, would you stop touching his things before something breaks? We already broke into their room, and Jah takes this DJ stuff seriously."

"How would I break something by pressing a couple of buttons?" Zazie asked, opening the top drawer to his desk. "I just need to find a conversation starter. He's cute. I'm cute. We gotta have *somethin'* in common."

Avi bent to restack the papers. "Well, Kai told me he said he likes your style."

"Guys, c'mon. This room is makin' me itch; let's go," Rhyon said.

They heard a sharp intake of air, and Avi turned to see Jasiri leaning on the door with his arms crossed over his Lakers jersey. He stared at Zazie's back with interest in his eye.

"Sorry," Avi blurted. She shot upright. "This is so intrusive.

We— Well, I remembered Kai saying this was his room number, and the door was open, so . . ."

"We got curious. No big deal," Rhyon said breezily.

"Curious, my ass." He sat on his bed, turning his attention back to Zazie, who stood looking caught with his headphones around her neck. "You can sit if you'd like." He motioned toward the chair. But Zazie showed no signs of hearing him. Avi looked from Jasiri back to her unblinking friend, waiting for someone to say something. Maybe, one of them could mention Jasiri's liking spree on Zazie's IG last night or the heart eyes he left under her most recent selfie with her Rottweiler, Fire.

"Actually," Rhyon said, attempting to save face, "we're supposed to be meeting Kai about his campaign stuff."

"He's in the second-floor lobby, right," Zazie said, pulling herself together. She took a seat. Not in the chair, but next to him on the bed. Jasiri grinned. "You guys go ahead. I'll catch up in a sec."

"Seriously?" Avi asked.

"Yeah. I'll be right there," she said, punctuating every word and turning from Jasiri again to give them a threatening *Get out before I hurt you* look.

They backed out of the room, and Avi pushed the door open wider as they left.

A door farther down the hall creaked open, and Kai stuck his head out, looking both ways before waving them forward.

"Go ahead," Rhyon said. "I'm gonna stay here and keep an eye on them."

AVI ENTERED THE STUFFY LOUNGE to see three desktop computers, four round study tables, and a whiteboard filled with unsolved chemistry equations. Kai shifted things around in a large cardboard box as EJ and Moe sat bobbing their heads to music coming from the laptop.

Avi leaned on EJ's shoulder to see the edited campaign flyer of Kai sitting at a teacher's desk, pointing at the camera with a stern look in his eye.

"No one needs to see your pink bra strap, and why are your jeans so tight?" Moe said without taking his eyes off the screen.

She hid the strap under her Dora Milaje tank top and looked down at the denim hugging her thighs. "They're comfy. And it's my body. Mind yours."

His nose flared, but he kept his comments to himself.

An array of sweets, stickers, and pins that said VOTE KAI sat outside the box in piles.

"My mom got excited when I told her I was running for president and overdid it," Kai said, answering Avi's mystified look.

When Rhyon, Zazie, and Jasiri joined them, tasks were assigned, Moe turned up the music, and they got to work. Avi and Rhyon eavesdropped as Jasiri and Zazie sat isolated at a table in the corner. The stacks of stickers and cookies sat forgotten beside them as they asked each other first-date questions like "Where are you originally from?" and "Favorite artist?" and "Top show to binge?" It was hard not to laugh out loud when Zazie tried her best to casually ask, "How willing are you to fight against the oppression of Black and Brown people, worldwide?" Luckily for Jasiri, he didn't miss a beat.

Moe and EJ were supposed to be brainstorming ideas for the creative direction in which they would shoot Kai's fifteen-second campaign video, but Moe couldn't keep his roaming eyes off Rhyon—not that she noticed. Avi had a feeling he hadn't quite figured out *who* she was yet, but the interest in his eye was more than plain curiosity.

An hour and a half after they started, Kai, Avi, and Rhyon stood at the dry-erase board trying to finalize a catchy slogan. They'd narrowed their choices from eight. But three options remained on the board.

Avi was thinking about how she would much rather be playing in traffic than still be a part of this conversation when she looked up to see Quincy stride into the room carrying a black basketball. The gym bag slung over his chest dangled with his chain as he bent to dap both of her brothers. She didn't need Zazie's waggling eyebrows or Rhyon's exaggerated bump on the elbow to know Quincy was there. How could she miss him? Effortlessly handsome, even in a plain white tee and red joggers.

Avi sidestepped behind Kai as Quincy dove into a conversation about some football game with Moe and EJ. He bounced the basketball from hand to hand under his long legs.

What was he doing here, and why was he so buddy-buddy with her brothers? Avi never caught what grade he was in, but if he was a TA, that meant he wasn't a freshman. Few things had occupied her thoughts (not to mention her dreams) besides Quincy since he missed class on Thursday. But it never occurred to her that she might run into him today.

"Would you stop?" Kai asked, shrugging Avi off. She

released her grip on the back of his T-shirt as he turned to face her, annoyed.

"She's hiding." Rhyon snickered.

Kai scanned the room. "From what?"

"I'm not hiding," Avi said unconvincingly. "I'm—I am looking for a different marker."

Kai thought of questioning her, but his disinterest quickly won out. "I'm callin' today done. Let's go with the top two slogans and go half and half with the posters." He moved suddenly to join the table, leaving Avi exposed.

Rhyon yanked at her hand, whispering. "C'mon, let's say hi."

"No! I'm not ready."

"You had no problem starting the conversation last time."

"That's because I spent the whole class psyching myself up," Avi explained. "Plus, that conversation started with him being unconscious. I don't have that advantage today."

Rhyon looked at her in disbelief before moving to sit with the boys. She patted the free seat beside her.

With a deep breath, Avi followed, wishing she'd tried to do more than a high puff to her hair that morning. She moved to sit in the chair directly across from Quincy, but his eyes were cast at his phone.

Say something, Rhyon mouthed.

Avi looked from Quincy to her brothers to Rhyon and shook her head.

Rhyon cleared her throat loudly. "So, did you finish the rest of that Algebra II assignment?"

"Huh?"

"I said, we had a lot to do for Algebra II on LionWeb. Did you finish yet?" Rhyon said through her teeth.

"Oh. Yep. Almost done," Avi muttered.

"I still don't know how you tricked the system into placing you in that class." Moe chuckled.

"I didn't trick anything. I'm in the class because that's where I belong," she said. It was a lie, but the last thing she needed was Moe making her look dumb.

"You're lucky they put you in Blue's class," EJ added as he stretched out in his seat. "You wouldn't stand a chance with Lester over at BP. She's tough."

The sound of Blue's name brought Quincy's attention to the conversation. He looked up, and recognition crossed his face. "Sci-fi, right?" he said recalling their conversation.

Avi gave a quick nod, smiling.

"Don't sweat any assignment Blue puts on LionWeb," he said, leaning forward on the table. "I check those."

Avi just grinned, suddenly unable to find working words.

That disarming smile of his was in full play across his lips as he stared directly into her eyes. "I just need your last name, and I'll look you up in the system."

"It's LeBeau," Moe and EJ said in twin flat tones before Avi could open her mouth.

Quincy's eyes dodged back and forth between Avi and her brothers for a comical amount of time. He pointed at her, eyebrows slowly rising as he peeped the familial resemblance.

"This is our *baby* sister, Avielle," EJ said.

"How do you know Q?" Moe demanded.

"From my Algebra II class," Avi said. She didn't appreciate the authority in his tone. "He's the TA, remember?"

Quincy sat back in his chair coolly. "Yeah, we had one class together. No harm, no foul." The smile he'd thrown her moments before was now friendly at best. "Nice to meet you, sis."

Avi gave him a tight-lipped nod, feeling all eyes on her. She looked at Kai, who was smirking at the end of the table, for a way out.

"Aye, Q," Kai said. "When are we supposed to meet the Carmichael hall guys at the court?"

"As soon as y'all wrap up here," Quincy said, eager to change the subject.

"**I GOTTA SAY**, I saw that going a lot of different ways, but I never expected *that*," Rhyon said, throwing a guilty glance at Avi's back.

Their walk from the disastrous campaign meet-up had been a quiet one as Avi stomped ahead of her friends.

She scanned her key to the front door of Hollingsworth, glaring at Rhyon.

"It was like a car accident," Zazie said, catching the glass door. "I couldn't look away even though I knew something terrible was about to happen. Your brothers shut that down."

"How would you know?" Avi snapped. "You were in the back wrapped up the whole time."

"Hey, I heard all I needed to hear and got my future husband's number at the same time. I multitask," she said smugly.

They passed by Housemother Lisa's office, and she handed them flyers for the upcoming Pizza Study Party.

"Honestly, it's my dad's fault," Avi said as they stepped on the elevator. "He's been training them as his little attack dogs our whole lives. Now, every time they get a whiff of something they don't like, boom"—she clapped her hands together, startling Rhyon—"my life is trash."

"How did you not know they were roommates?" Zazie asked seriously. "Didn't you look for his IG for like an hour the other night? They never posted him before?"

"I didn't even think to look at their pages," she whimpered. "Moe posted and tagged him five times last semester."

Rhyon shook her head. "Rookie mistake."

"In my defense, he didn't look like *that* last year. Summer did him well."

They walked down their hall to hear SZA blasting from Dove and Raquel's room. Ashia glanced up to smile at them, surrounded by books, having a study session on the floor outside her room.

"Look, I know that didn't go like you would've liked," Rhyon said as they walked into G-12, "but that doesn't change the way he was talking to you before your brothers swooped in and ruined everything."

"And that offer to make sure your grades look right," Zazie added as she bent to speak to her small potted peace lily plant. "That would've had my attention."

Avi plopped down at her desk, pouting. "But did you hear him call me 'sis'? He shoved me right into the friend zone."

"Sibling zone is more like it," Rhyon mumbled.

"I'm sure he did that to save face. It's against their li'l bro code," Zazie said wisely. "Guys aren't supposed to see their friend's sisters like that, especially not their kid sisters."

"I'm barely a year younger than them," Avi said, handing Rhyon her phone with @Know_Q2007's private page on the screen.

Avi turned to open her laptop, while Zazie and Rhyon argued about who could follow Quincy first without it looking too stalkery. She pulled up her Briarcliff email, sifting through the new messages. And then an email from Egypt popped up—with the subject line "Creative Column Finalists."

In a second, she scanned it, spotting her name in red, listed as a finalist for the column. Her computer chair hit the wall as she jigged, rereading her name on the screen. She was a finalist! Rhyon and Zazie rushed to the laptop to see what had Avi squealing as she hurried to call her mom. Not even Fallon's name alongside hers could ruin this moment.

10

WITH THE START OF OCTOBER, Avi felt like she was finally getting the hang of life at Briarcliff. She and Zazie found their rhythm, despite their differences. Avi was a night owl, not only because their massive loads of homework kept them up well into most nights, but also because that was when her words flowed best. At first, it irritated Zazie to have a noisy roommate so late into the nights, but Avi adapted by working by desk lamp, keeping her instrumentals to her headphones, and having her loud breakthroughs in the hallway. No one abided by quiet hours anyways.

Zazie, on the other hand, rose earlier than the sun most days. This was her time to meditate, edit photos, and recite her annoying positive affirmations to her reflection. Quickly Avi grew accustomed to finding random crystals under her pillows, hearing Zazie constantly cooing at her flourishing plant family, and having Zazie's braid customers in and out of their room.

Every Sunday morning they cleaned their room, but the ritual couldn't conclude until Zazie opened their windows and smudged the ground floor hallway, specifically the area outside of Rhyon and Kieley's room.

"By week's end, the energy around their door always has high levels of anger and intensity. Can't you feel it?" Zazie would ask.

Rhyon was endlessly frustrated with her living arrangements, only ever going into her room to sleep. After the first week, she moved her valuables (brooches, purses, shoes, and the Puerto Rican flag quilt her abuela hand-stitched) into Avi and Zazie's room. Rhyon wanted a normal high-school experience just like everyone else, but she was next-level spoiled. There were laughs when Avi and Zazie taught her how to do her laundry the first time. In turn, she taught Avi how to perfect her cat-eye and was helping Zazie improve her Spanish.

The schoolwork load was intense, but Avi managed well in every subject . . . except Algebra II. The class was fast-paced, but she knew that if she spoke to Professor Blue about her struggles, he would arrange tutoring with Quincy. Quincy was already ending every sentence he spoke to her with "sis" and keeping more than a healthy distance. The last thing she needed was him thinking Moe was right about her mistaken placement. On the bright side, he did keep his word about helping her out with online assignments.

Still, every meaningful conversation with him found a way to end badly. Like the day he walked in late as the class was paired up to finish a worksheet.

Avi and her assigned partner, Bernard, knocked the first three challenging equations out the way, but the last word problem (involving complex polynomial division) stumped them. Avi was about to raise her hand to call for Professor Blue's assistance when Quincy walked in. Avi waved him over.

"All right," he said, straddling a chair, "what do we have today?"

With patience and ease, Quincy explained the problem step by step, taught them how to properly check the equation, and caught their wrong answer to another question.

"Fifteen minutes," Blue said to the room from Rhyon's desk.

As Bernard read a hidden comic behind his textbook, Quincy readied to stand.

"Did you ever finish the book?" The words left Avi in a rush.

He sat with a smirk.

Somehow the conversation went from his rave review of *Smoke Rises* to them discussing how much smaller her hands were compared to his. Their hands lay side by side as they compared palm width and finger length. Avi took a chance and pressed her palm against Quincy's.

When their skin touched, her heart beat at triple time, but she liked the feeling—she liked the heat that seemed to radiate off him.

And then she glanced up, meeting his penetrating stare, and breathed, "You run hot."

Not a second later, Quincy not only pulled his hand from hers like she was on fire, but scrambled backward, muttering, "Let me see if anyone else needs help."

Avi stared at him across the room as he leaned over another student's desk, going out of his way not to meet her eyes.

The only time she could get Quincy out of her head was when she sat down to write. Since she received the email from

Egypt about her finalist position, she'd gone from planning and plotting details on her storyboard to obsessively writing and rewriting her newest short story.

It was a fantastical tale about a pair of supernatural siblings, willing to do anything and everything to save their kidnapped baby brother. She planned it so that her story would last for the next eight installments of the biweekly paper.

Her friends and Moe read the story and gave kind reviews, but Avi knew Belle would have the best idea of how the student body would receive her work. Belle agreed to look it over, but only if Avi agreed to guest star on her YouTube page for a sister tag video.

Avi arrived at the senior suites in Truth Hall that evening. Hollingsworth could only be described as raggedy in comparison. All suites were doubles, and they were roomier and had a common area. But the biggest plus was the lack of communal bathrooms; students only had to share with their roommate. After finding a used tampon near the drain in her favorite shower that morning, Avi was ready to trade anything to move into Truth today.

When she opened the door, Belle stood in her plush robe with her phone to her ear.

It's Logan, she mouthed.

Avi waved to Adoree, Cheetah Plans VP, and Nevaeh, who sat on the black couch in the common area watching *Insecure* reruns.

Belle's lavender-scented room featured black-and-white fur decor and a globe chair sitting in the corner. The wall opposite her bed held a four-foot-long corkboard with Polaroid pictures, Briarcliff Prep and Spelman College pennants, old concert tickets, a poster of prima ballerina Judith Jamison, and a quote that said "The grass is greener wherever I am."

Avi ran her hand over a large "Joie de Vivre" wall sticker before turning her attention to the twelve-by-fifteen canvas of Belle and a freckled Logan hugged up in front of a fountain. She grabbed the halfway-annotated outline of the poem "Sympathy" by Paul Laurence Dunbar from Belle's desk and fell into the rolling chair to wait.

". . . I'm gonna be here until dance practice at three. . . . Yes, Lo, I'm sure. . . . Mhmm, I'll call you back."

"He's super attentive," she said to Avi as she plopped back on the bed, almost landing on the white violin Grandma Rose had gifted her this past summer. Belle placed it back in the case.

"Sounds clingy," Avi said. "He needs to know where you are *all* the time?"

"It's what people in relationships do, Avi."

"If you say so. What's all this?"

Belle followed Avi's nod to the ring light and stack of unopened boxes on the desk.

"Products from different brands that want me to post reviews. Things get sweet when you reach 28K subscribers."

"Woowww. That's impressive."

"Right!" Belle said gleefully. "It's opened up a whole new side of YouTube for me. I think putting Logan on my last few vlogs helped me gain a couple hundred followers. We're givin' them that whole power-couple vibe."

"Power couple," Avi scoffed. "When did you guys get that title?"

"It's obvious, isn't it?" She shrugged. "But enough about my relationship. I wanna hear about yours."

Avi looked at her with bunched brows and her head at a tilt. "You wanna hear about something that doesn't exist?"

"Oh, but it does. I was at the modeling club's practice yesterday to help them with some choreo, and Rhyon told me about you trying to pretty yourself up for some li'l boy the other day. But I didn't catch his name."

"She talks too much."

"I like her."

"Because she's a good person or because of who her mother is?"

"Both for sure." Belle nodded. "More importantly, I've seen her dance, and she's skilled. When Vannah and I graduate, the Cheetahnaires are gonna need her. But stop trying to distract me. Who are you getting cute for?"

Avi stared down at her hands. "It doesn't matter. He's a little out of my league."

"Ellie, please. You are the league," Belle said with a dismissive wave. "We're not average."

"Okay, I'll tell you. But you can't say anything to the twins."

Belle's head cocked to the side. "Why would I?"

"Because it's Quincy."

She crossed her arms, lips pressed together. And then her mouth fell open. "You don't mean Q, their roommate, do you?"

Avi nodded, biting her bottom lip.

"Oh, I saw him yesterday," Belle said, getting excited. "We were in orchestra together last year. He's a little cutie now."

Avi didn't realize she cared before, but her sister's approval felt good. "Cute and nice and he's *so* smart, Belle. We even like some of the same books and shows," Avi gushed, and then her shoulders slumped, remembering how he scrambled away from her in class that day. "But Moe and EJ already got to him."

She told Belle exactly how everything had gone downhill in Newton Hall.

"That was uncalled for," Belle said with her bottom lip poked out. "Look, forget them. You're smart, responsible, and gorgeous. You can crawl out of the sister zone. It's all about what you want."

"What about what Quincy wants?"

"Eh, let's work with the idea that he doesn't know what he wants yet," she said, waving a dismissive hand. "What I'm saying is, if you want something, you don't just hope, wish, and stay up late thinking about it. I personally think Solange was telling us to *take* a seat at the table we want to be at. Not wait until someone invites us to sit down, ya know?"

Avi nodded.

"You gotta either make power moves or be content watching someone who had the nerve live the life you dreamed was yours."

Avi nodded again, but it all sounded a lot simpler than it was.

Belle had a point about being proactive about her wants, but what *did* she want here? For Quincy to notice her? Reciprocation of feelings? Or something more significant, like a relationship?

"We can figure out your plan of action later," Belle said, quelling Avi's thoughts. "The video won't take too long."

Belle forced Avi into a distressed denim jacket to coordinate with her own denim top with ruffled sleeves, "for the aesthetic." She began the video announcing her run for Briarcliff's Harvest Queen scholarship pageant before they answered questions from her subscribers.

"Are you guys mixed with anything?" Black and Black.

"Are you both close?" Yep.

"Is boarding school like Hogwarts?" No. And what does that even mean?

Then there were more trivial questions like "What's your sister's favorite food?" and "Who's more concerned about appearances?"

The video took longer to record than necessary because every couple of minutes, Belle would stop to reply to another series of Logan's texts. Avi would have assumed that between his duties as SGA president, basketball, and everything else he claimed to do, he'd have less time to text every moment of the day, but apparently not.

When they finished, Avi lay across the bed, scrolling through Twitter and pretending it didn't bother her that Belle was reading her story three feet from her. While she wanted to get proper feedback, this felt like some special kind of torture. Especially with the red pen hovering and Belle's audible "hmms" and "oohs."

Belle finally peeked over the paper, wiggling her eyebrows. "I love it!"

"Really?" Avi said. She sat up anxiously, and the bedsprings squeaked beneath her. "Do you mean that, or are you trying not to hurt my feelings?"

"Avi, this is something the entire school reads. And not just

BP students. Preston reads our paper, too, and regular people comment on the *Cliff News* website all the time. I wouldn't dare tell you this was good if it wasn't. And I think it is."

Avi beamed but caught Belle's smile falter when she looked down at the paper again.

"What?" Avi asked, jumping down from the bed. "Are there grammatical errors? I need it to be perfect before I turn it in. That Egypt girl is *wildly* serious about the paper. Her energy's very much like . . . Miranda Priestly in *The Devil Wears Prada*."

"Wow. That's spot-on. God, I love Meryl."

"I'm hoping she just acts like that because there's a high standard to the *Cliff News*, and she has to be cautious about . . ." Avi's voice trailed off as she noticed the disgruntled look on her sister's face. "She's a senior, right? Did she maybe mention me to you?"

Belle blinked. "No, we don't—"

"I tried to do that fake confident thing like Mommy said, but she didn't bite. Are you guys friends?"

She exhaled. "If I'm being completely honest—and I'm only telling you because I think you should know every possibility—freshman year, I thought we were friends, but it was a constant pissing contest. She got first chair for the flute in orchestra, I won one of the Winter Orchestra Showcase solo spots. She got top scores in our English class, I got top scores in Math and French. Eventually, we grew apart. But!" she added as Avi's eyes grew. "We're good now; that's long done and over with."

"You're sure?" Avi asked. She didn't need some silly "I'm better than you" rivalry to be the reason she lost this column.

"I'm positive! I'm proud of her accomplishments at the *Cliff*

News, and she was almost as proud of me for becoming dance captain as Nevaeh was." Belle bit her bottom lip. "Your real problem may be your competition."

Avi's head fell back. "I know you think Fallon's a great dancer and the Cheetahnaires have their own sisterhood or whatever, but she *sucks*, Belle. Like the girl's spirit is off. I promise if you let her get too close she'll stab you in the back."

"I'll worry about my back. What have you seen from her as a writer?"

"I haven't," Avi shrugged. "I'd assume she's pretty good, though. It came down to two sophomores and another freshman. Oh, and Egypt told me she was familiar with some of the other competition's work, I assume they had to be the sophomores. But we still beat them out."

"Well, watch your assumptions," Belle said seriously. She folded her legs beneath her, leaning forward. "Egypt was close with Simone Bane—she was the sophomore who lost to y'all—but she's also pretty close to Fallon."

Avi's head flew back. "Are you serious?!"

Belle grimaced. "Word is, both Fallon and Egypt were accepted to some four-week writing workshop this past summer. They got close, and Fallon told me she sees Egypt as something like a mentor. I haven't read anything she's written, but she must be genuinely good to have gotten one of the spots."

Avi exhaled audibly, trying to calm her nerves before she started to spiral. Belle stood, resting one hand on Avi's shoulder and raising her chin with the other. "Hey, Avi, you don't have to freak out. *You* got the other spot, without any outside advantages. You ask me? That's a pure talent type of situation you're in. And I mean, you're right about Egypt. She takes this paper seriously, and relationship or not she's going to vote for whoever submits the best work and makes her look amazing. I— Hold on."

Belle's phone was buzzing nonstop behind them. She picked it up and her nose flared in annoyance. But before she could begin to type, Adoree called her from their living room.

Alone, Avi grabbed a pen from the desk to read the notes her sister made, but Belle's phone continued to buzz on the bed where she'd thrown it. Avi crossed the room, reaching for it, hesitating just long enough to ensure no one was approaching the door. She didn't want to think about her chances of winning the coveted columnist position. And her curiosity demanded she see what the other half of this so-called "power couple" could possibly want now.

There was a missed call and text from Fallon:

> Wanna come get frozen yogurt with me later. I found this cute place close to campus.
>
> **FW**

A text from Paisli:

> I recorded a new song to post to my YouTube. Can you watch it first?
>
> **PAI**

And one from Logan:

> I don't care about that. Wear your hair straight for our date.
>
> **LO**

The phone buzzed again in Avi's hands.

I want you to stop hanging around Nevaeh anyways. I don't like her.

LO

Avi didn't know what they were talking about, but why did Logan think he had a say in how Belle wore her hair or which friends she kept close? Was it worth it to try and guess the password?

Slippers scooted near the door. Avi tossed the phone.

"All right," Belle said, striding into the room with Nevaeh by her side, "tell us everything you know about Q so far."

11

AVI DROPPED THE FIFTH POP QUIZ of the semester onto Professor Blue's desk at the end of class. Hopefully, all the extra studying she did last night would be enough to earn her higher than a C this time. At this point, Avi was convinced there was nothing worse than the feeling of not being able to understand something she put so much effort into. Then again, she still felt strongly that letters didn't belong in math in the first place.

Before lunch, Rhyon left campus for her therapy appointment, leaving Avi to walk to Preston and back by herself. She gathered her belongings from her desk, grateful not to have to listen to Rhy's usual after-quiz routine. First, she would try comparing their answers. Second, she would panic about not having had enough time to triple-check her quiz. Third, Rhyon would always sulk because she'd finally convinced herself she failed. But, of course, Rhy had never seen a grade below an A.

Avi pushed the heavy doors open, inhaling the fresh air of the warm autumn day and delighting in the crunch of each leaf under her brown Chelsea boots. It was almost too warm for the lavender sweatshirt she wore over her mustard-collared shirt.

As she leaned on the lion statue to yank up her knee socks, she heard a familiar voice call, "Where's your friend?" from the side door of Valintino.

Avi turned, putting a hand up to shade her eyes from the too-bright October sun. Through her squint, she saw Quincy jogging toward her, and her face split into a wide smile. As usual, his tie was missing, and a silver chain jumped on his chest.

"Rhy had an appointment," Avi said as he reached her. It was nice to see him after an unusually dull math class. With the absence of Rhyon's running commentary, Avi had found herself nodding off right before the pop quiz was announced. It didn't help that Quincy missed class again.

Quincy stood an arm's length away, hands strangling his backpack straps. "So you're gonna walk by yourself?"

"Back to campus? Yeah."

Two Preston students carrying a heavy grassland biome project walked toward them, and she and Quincy weaved apart.

"I'm shocked Blue let y'all out early," he said, nearing her again as he pushed up the sleeves to his admiral-blue Preston cardigan. "Where's your next class?"

"Wells in fifteen." Avi tightened her hands around the notebook she held to her chest, resisting the sudden, odd urge to touch his forearm.

"I'm headed over there, too. I'll walk with you."

Avi felt herself inflate and nodded.

"So, where were you today?" she asked as they strolled past the tall library.

"Oh, wow. Dimples is keepin' tabs on me after all?"

"Maybe I'm not, maybe I am. There's just one dimple by the way," she said, pointing to her left cheek. "Anyways, I did notice class was a lot quieter without you there."

His head fell back with a chuckle. "She's got jokes, too."

"She does." Avi grinned. "So, where were you, Quincy?"

"I needed to spend some time on my AP physics homework and asked Blue for the class off."

"AP Physics in tenth grade. So, you really are like a math whiz?"

He shook his head, scoffing. "I think what I'm good at is logic. I like problem-solving and making sense of things, ya know?"

"Yeah, I can get that. I can't get Algebra II, but I can get that."

They stepped off Preston's sidewalk and crossed the streets past Briarcliff's shining gold sign.

"You're not doing too bad from what I see," Quincy said as they swerved out of the way of a sprinkler watering the grass in front of Morrison.

"Then you must not have seen my other grades." Avi cast her eyes away from his, looking instead at the familiar faces of classmates passing by. She exhaled deeply. "I can usually make pretty good guestimations for the online work, but—"

"Your written homework isn't too bad, either."

"Oh, I didn't know you checked those, too. I guess they're

not too bad, but my quizzes usually are. And the first test was a complete flop."

Quincy ducked under a low-hanging branch. "So, you're worried about slipping behind?"

"That and the fact that we have another test in three weeks. And to be honest, stressing about this is taking away from time I could be using to revise my short story."

"I didn't know you write," he said, looking impressed.

Avi nodded enthusiastically. "That's how I make sense of things. But I won't be able to focus on that at all if I fail the next test."

Grades were posted online, and her parents checked for them regularly. Two weeks ago, Avi received a warning from them about not being able to participate in extracurriculars (including the *Cliff News*) if they saw anything below a seventy-nine on any future test. She already knew she was there for school. The annoying reminders weren't necessary.

He blew out his cheeks. "That's tough, but I'd say you have three options."

Avi looked up at him, listening.

"Option one," he said, holding up his long pointer finger. "You could just hope it gets better and keep studying on your own."

Studying on her own had so far led to two failed quizzes and a C on a test.

"Option two, you can go through Blue, and he'll fit you into my or one of his other TA's schedules three days a week. Part of his tutoring plan is mandatory extra online and book work. Not to mention, once-a-week check-ins where you have to go to his office to give him updates and get extra help."

Avi stopped in her tracks under the shade of a huge oak tree with few leaves still desperately clinging on to their branches. "Wait. Seriously?"

"Deadass," he laughed. "And anybody who receives less than a seventy-five on his test automatically has to do all that."

Avi pressed a hand to her head. She had to prove herself to Egypt, and her short story still needed work. "I don't have time for that. Wait!" she said, perking up, "You said three, right? What's my third option?"

"Option three. And in my opinion, this is the best. I could help you outside of all the official TA stuff. It would still probably need to be like twice a week, but it's a lot less pressure if you go through me instead of Blue."

He placed his hands back on the straps of his book bag, gazing down at her.

"That does sound a lot easier," Avi said, straining to keep her voice level. "But wait, don't you get paid through work-study for tutoring on that specific schedule?"

Quincy shook his head. "Don't worry about that. No, seriously," he said, holding up a hand to stop her objection. "I want you to be able to write if that's what you want to do. Plus, I make my real money cutting hair."

"Still . . ." She hesitated.

"Hey, I'm telling you it's not a big deal. But it's your choice, Avi. Option one, two, or three?"

She teetered on her feet, pretending to consider her options though her mind was made up. She held up three fingers. "But since we're not doing this the right way, you have to promise to tell me if you ever need help with a paper or something. Deal?"

Quincy took her hand in his, giving a very businesslike handshake. "Imma hold you to that," he said with a smirk. "I'll give you my number, and we can work around our schedules."

It was the combination of his wide smile and the sun glinting off his dark skin that had Avi's knees on the verge of buckling. She tried not to fixate on his piercing eyes or how her hand fit perfectly in his as they stood face-to-face.

Avi shook her head, remembering. "Oh, I left my phone in my room."

"Right, right. The rule."

Tragically, he let her hand fall and pulled his phone from his khaki pocket. "Here, put your number in, and I'll text you."

She saved her name under "Avi L" as they walked together around a crowd of students gathered near the bronze statue of the Briarcliffs. A stout guy in a Preston sweater vest stopped them to ask Quincy about one of their Physics assignments, and Avi sidestepped behind them, watching Kieley feet away on a bench with her head in a history book. As the two approached Wells, a small gust of wind shifted Avi's hair in her face.

"That's you?" Quincy asked.

"Is what me?" she said, trying to unstick her hair from her lip gloss.

His head cocked to the side in concentration as he inhaled deeply. "It smells like vanilla . . . and somethin' else?"

"Oh, that's my body mist and this new coconut hair fragrance I'm trying out. You don't like it?" Avi asked, suddenly self-conscious. She tried to sniff herself. "I might've put too much on."

"No, I like it . . . a lot." Quincy took a step forward, inhaling again with a curious look in his eye. "And I like talking to you, Avi."

She smiled up at him, dimple pushing through. Her heart hammered so loudly she was sure he could hear it. This time Quincy looked away first, caught off guard by the intensity of her gaze.

"Aye, Q," Moe called, making them both jump about a foot back from each other.

If anything, her brother knew how to ruin a moment.

Moe approached, smiling innocently at Avi before purposefully positioning himself between them.

"I thought you'd be at the field by now," he said, dapping Quincy before turning to Avi. "Dad said to call him when you get a chance. Why aren't you answering your phone?"

Avi's eyes turned to slits as she glared at him. He knew full well why she wasn't answering. "I don't have it on me."

"I'm just sayin', by now most freshmen forget that dumb rule. I ran into your roommate when I was passing Zody, and she had hers."

Avi shrugged and glanced over at Quincy. It didn't escape her that he was going out of his way to look everywhere but at her. She cursed her brother in her head, waiting as they picked up a conversation about their baseball coach.

"What are you still doing here?" Moe turned to ask her moments later.

Avi crossed her arms, snarling, "This is my campus. Why are *you* here?"

Moe's phone was in her face a second later. A selfie of him and Paisli the day before they left for school was his lock screen. "It's 2:57 p.m. I know you have class at three. Get outta here," he said, mushing the side of her face toward Wells. Avi's mouth formed a small *o*, and Quincy tried not to laugh as he looked between the two of them.

Why was it Moe's mission to make her look like a baby whenever they were in front of Quincy? Last week, at the Cliff, he'd found a reason to pull up her embarrassing school play pictures from three years ago, when she played "the wind." Now this.

Avi's nose flared as she turned sharply, allowing the sky-blue book bag on her shoulder to swing out and hit her brother in the side. Moe bent over, the wind knocked out of him. She knew she would find herself in a headlock later, but right now, it was worth it.

Avi waved goodbye to Quincy, who was doubled over with laughter, before prancing up the steps and walking into Wells. Despite her brother's sabotage, their conversation had gone better than she could have ever hoped. She really did need Quincy's help if she wanted to improve her grades and get her parents off her back, but it didn't hurt that her new tutor was the recurring guest star in all of her dreams. And not to be dramatic or anything, but it truly did feel like her hand belonged in his. That time in class, he'd pulled away so suddenly. Today, he allowed his touch to linger. This was progress.

Avi walked into College and Career Prep right on time, and she made a beeline toward the back of the classroom, where Rhyon and Zazie had saved her a seat. She had to tell them.

12

AVI ARRIVED TEN MINUTES before the start of the second *Cliff News* meeting. The first had been a general meet-and-greet before finalists were announced. Tonight, the small room was a lot less crowded, with only current members of the newspaper's staff and other hopefuls like herself.

Egypt stood at the front of the room, speaking in a low voice with the Vice President, Dawn, Fallon, and another girl Avi recalled seeing around campus—Janae or Janice, she couldn't remember which.

From a chair in the second row, Avi sipped from a water bottle and snacked on Cheez-Its. She'd been feeling considerably less hopeful about her chances after learning how close Egypt and Fallon were. Seeing them laugh together at the head of the room now made her insides twist. She was placing the unfinished crackers in her bag when she felt a tap on her shoulder from the row behind her.

"Avielle?" a girl with butterscotch skin, freckles, and rope twists said.

Avi nodded.

"I'm Cori Cortez, the senior editor of the *Cliff News*."

Avi's eyes widened, and she turned in her seat completely, returning Cori's broad smile.

"You wrote that satirical piece about Black fragility," Avi said pointing at her. "Oh, it was brilliant!"

Cori beamed, impressed that Avi could recall her writing from her name alone. "Funny," she said with a laugh. "I came over here to say the same about your samples. I was promoted a few weeks back and wanted to go around and personally congratulate all of our category finalists. But I also wanted to tell you that I had some personal say in hand-picking you, and that sci-fi essay of yours blew me away, girl!"

Avi almost teared up. She barely got a "thank you" out before a phone alarm began to ring in front of the classroom.

"If you ever think you need assistance or just someone to talk to, you can email me with questions whenever," Cori whispered as Egypt approached the podium.

Avi nodded gratefully, turning her attention forward.

"Greetings," Egypt said, smiling from the wooden podium at the front of the room. "My name is Egypt Mack, and I'm a senior from Boston, Massachusetts. As everyone knows, I serve as president of the *Cliff News*." She paused, looking around the room expectantly until Dawn broke into a round of applause.

Egypt introduced the rest of the club officers and then motioned to the back of the room when introducing the new faculty advisor. Avi's shoulders lifted when she saw Professor Lovette sitting attentively in the last row. When did she slip in? On the first day of school, Nevaeh told Avi and her friends that faculty advisors existed only to give help when requested or to stop the organization from flying off the rails. They kept order while allowing organization club officials to really lead. Avi caught Lovette's wink as she turned back in her seat.

The finalists for the advice, student sports, pop culture, and student life positions were introduced before Egypt turned to the creative-writing column.

"Fallon Walsh, a freshman from Milton, Georgia," Egypt announced. Fallon stood, giving a princess wave to the room. "And Avielle LeBoo—I mean LeBeau. A freshman from Upper Marlboro, Maryland."

Avi stood slowly, thrown off by the way Egypt had butchered her name, and gave a shy smile to the room. She sat again, listening to the explanation about all the finalists' columns being run in the October edition in three weeks. An email would be sent out the same day, allowing the student body to cast a popular vote for their favorites. The popular vote would then be taken into consideration as the club officers made the final decision.

At the end of the meeting, Avi walked around to officially introduce herself to the rest of the club officers. She had heaps of homework and was ready to leave, but she knew that's not what Belle would do if she were in a similar situation. This new approach of *taking* her seat rather than waiting to be invited spent a ridiculous amount of energy.

Avi scanned the room, looking for Egypt—the last person she needed to speak to—and spotted her hugging Fallon at the door. Avi approached her after she'd walked back to the podium to gather her things.

"Egypt?"

She looked up and actually smiled. "Oh, Avielle. Sorry, about before. I for sure know your name, but Fallon kept accidentally saying 'LeBoo' earlier, and I got all mixed up. Won't happen again."

Typical, Avi thought. She knew Fallon had been a little too quiet this evening. If it hadn't been at her expense, Avi could've almost found Fallon's little joke impressive. Almost.

"In other news," Egypt continued, crossing her arms over her chest, "congrats on getting that finalist spot." She genuinely seemed pleased. "Having two freshman finalists for this column is practically unheard of. Keep it up and make sure you have your short story in on time so Cori and I can send your edits by next Wednesday. Are you prepped to send?"

"I just have to do a final read-through," Avi said, nodding anxiously.

Egypt grabbed her bag and raised her phone to her ear, saying, "I look forward to being wowed," before marching out the door. Everything was always straight-to-the-point with her, but Avi was getting used to it.

When she'd walked into this room earlier, Avi had felt nervous knowing Egypt wouldn't be of much comfort or help. She was good at managing the *Cliff News,* but she wasn't a hand-holder. After meeting Cori and seeing Lovette, Avi felt renewed. She could win this.

TWENTY MINUTES LATER, Avi paced barefoot on her baby-blue rug with her Women's Studies notecards while Zazie snacked on a bag of Flamin' Hot Cheetos. She walked in and out of the camera, giving Kai a recap on FaceTime.

He smirked. "She got people to call you 'Avielle LeBoo'?"

"It was only Egypt and— Kai, it's not funny," she sighed into the screen. All her life, Avi listened to her Paum tell her about the significance of a name. *"Your name follows you. It gives people a taste of where and who you come from,"* he'd say. "God, I can't stand her!"

"Regardless, she's playin' in your face. You ever think she keeps messin' with you because of how easy you make it?" Kai offered. "Everything she does gets to you and she knows it. Makes it easier for her to throw you off your game."

"All I know is, she's literally the worst," Zazie interjected. "A self-absorbed narcissist with an imaginary crown on her head."

Avi pointed at Zazie. "That! That's what she is!

"A self-absorbed narcissist with an imaginary crown on her head who's successfully brown-nosin' her way to the top. Seems like she's got a plan. What's yours?"

Avi sat in the rolling chair, exchanging her notecards for her Algebra II notebook. "My plan is to outwrite her. That's all I can do."

The alarm on Avi's phone rang, and she checked the time. At this rate, she wouldn't get to bed until after two again.

"I gotta go," she said to Kai. "I have to start planning my bio project and finish my math homework."

"He still hasn't texted you yet?" Zazie asked.

Avi shot her an incredulous look, and Zazie's hands flew to her mouth.

Yes, it had been two days since she gave Quincy her number. No, he still hadn't texted her. If he had, Zazie would've been the first person to know, so why even ask that out loud?

"Who hasn't texted you?" asked Kai.

Zazie mouthed an apology. But there was no real use lying to Kai. He would be able to tell, and it's not like he was the type to run and tell her business.

"Quincy," Avi said, trying to be as nonchalant as him.

"That's new," Kai said with an arched brow. "Why are you texting Q?"

"For tutoring before the second Algebra II test. I can't get another C."

"And why is that a secret? You like him?"

Her scoff was too loud. "What? No! That's not it."

He glanced up from the paper on his desk with a chuckle. "And you couldn't ask Belle or Rhy or me for help?"

"Belle's busy with her pageant stuff, Rhyon's an angry teacher, and you're always distracted. Plus, our parents said to use the school's resources. It's not a big deal."

"Yeah, okay," he laughed, leaning back in his seat. "Keep telling yourself that and let me know exactly when Moe tries to murk you both."

Avi grimaced at the desk, tracing her finger along the ridges of the keyboard. Moe couldn't be mad at what he didn't know. There was nothing to tell anyway. Quincy hadn't shown up to class again on Thursday, nor had he been at the Cliff all week. Last night, she'd almost resorted to DM'ing him on IG, but Rhyon took her phone until she relented.

"New topic," Kai said, covering half the screen with his paper. "I just sent you the final version of my speech for tomorrow. Tell me if I need to change the way I say something. Z, can you listen, too?"

Avi exhaled loudly and opened her Briarcliff email on her phone. Before she could click on Kai's, another sent seven minutes ago caught her attention.

> **From:** Fallon.Walsh@BriarcliffPreparatory.edu:
>
> Can't wait until our columns are out for the public to judge. Hope you're ready!

13

THE LOT BEHIND the Lion Square academic buildings was roped off for the freshman election speeches and Harvest Queen contestant meet and greet. With another Friday evening rolling in, students were ready to socialize and bask in the seventy-degree weather.

Rhyon and Avi stood behind Kai's allotted table, handing out an array of sweets with the slogan "Level Up, Preston" and cutouts of his platform on little laminated sheets. Kai stood huddled on the stage, thirstily absorbing every word dripping from Logan's mouth.

Avi had her doubts about Logan, but she couldn't help being appreciative of the support he'd given Kai throughout the election process. He'd taken his free time to coach Kai on speech etiquette, posted and campaigned for him on all his socials, and really seemed to take Kai under his wing. It didn't even seem like this was all to look good for Belle anymore. When he moved on to another competitor, Kai wiped the sweat from his upper lip, took a deep breath, and pulled notecards from inside his blazer. He wanted this just as badly as Avi wanted the creative-writing column.

Thalia stopped by the table to thank Avi and Rhyon for their votes, as some guy scooped up three honey buns and pretended to read the handout Rhyon gave him. Kai walked up then, straightening his tie to congratulate Thalia on her win before asking Avi to walk around and hand out his tokens.

"For what?" Avi asked. "People have been coming to the table and taking your stuff with no problem."

"I can't because I have to read over my speech again before I go on, and it's only been people who can't vote that have been eating everything," he said, shooting an annoyed look at two sophomore girls who'd just taken drinks. "Here," Kai said, thrusting a shoulder bag full of sweets into Avi's arms. "You just have to give the Preston freshmen a drink or somethin' and make sure they know when the voting window opens and closes. C'mon Avi, please! Rhy's gonna stay here and staff the table. I need you out on the floor."

She rolled her eyes. "You better not mess up your stupid speech."

"Love you too," he called from behind.

Avi strolled the parking lot, bobbing her head to the music and handing out honey buns to students she could only assume were freshmen. Professors Blue and Lovette walked arm-in-arm amongst other teachers, monitoring students and handing out flyers for the new math team. Onstage, Headmaster Walsh made announcements no one paid much mind to as Zazie jovially snapped pictures of students for Photography Club. Nevaeh, Vannah, and Adoree popped up, holding number-four signs as Avi told two Preston freshmen about Kai's campaign. They pulled her away so they could record a Boomerang in their matching white "Belle 4 Queen" shirts.

Avi spotted Egypt talking to a group of Briarcliff and Preston seniors, with Cori by her side. She wore the same fitted white dress as the other Harvest Queen contestants and had a golden number two pinned to her chest. Avi walked toward them and dug in her bag for two waters, readying to say hello, but accidentally bumped into Kelby Shelton and two of his friends. Kelby was a well-known jerk, always doused in Axe body spray and overly full of himself.

Avi apologized and tried to move on, but he called her back, claiming to want to know more about Kai's platform. They were freshmen but close friends with another candidate. Still, she humored their simple questions. As Avi tried to move past them, she found Kelby's ashy hand wrapped around her own.

"How about this," he said suggestively. "Come to my room after this and you can earn his vote from me. Maybe we can watch a movie, and then whatever happens next, happens."

She snatched her hand back, turning sharply, only to hear him comment on her breasts when she was five feet away. She gave the can of soda in her hand a hard shake, fixed her face into a natural smile, and turned back to hand it to him.

"The voting window closes at midnight on Sunday," Avi said sweetly.

Kelby gave her another slow once-over before accepting the drink with a lick of his lips.

She squeezed between packs of students to get as far from Kelby as possible when Jordan, from French, called her name.

His broad shoulders provided the perfect shield. The can exploded on Kelby and his friends, splashing a few innocent bystanders in the process. She heard his loud gasp and roaring laughs just steps away.

Jordan guffawed. "Was that you?" he asked, spotting the cans in her bag.

"He deserved it. I promise," Avi said, peeking from behind him again. She smiled to herself, watching Kelby's furious eyes search for her in the crowd. "Here, take one. I promise I didn't shake it."

He took the drink, still laughing. "You probably lost Kai their votes."

"They're buddy-buddy with Austin, and he doesn't need their creep votes anyways. But I'm happy I ran into you."

"'Cause you're using me as a human shield?"

"Definitely that," Avi chuckled. "But do you believe Madame Delcour posted all that extra work on BriarWeb?"

"Yeah, she's wild. But the paper was a breeze."

"Of course you'd say that, Mr. French American Dual Citizenship. Who other than you would live in France for the first ten years of their life and then ask to be put in 101?"

"Harsh, LeBeau." He smirked. "I'm about to head out, but I'll look at your paper for you if you let me have a honey—" He stopped short of reaching in her bag. "Aye, Q, when can I get that cut, man?" he called.

Avi turned to see Quincy sliding a card out of his pocket as he walked toward them.

"Set an appointment on my Styleseat, and I got you."

Jordan nodded, pocketing the card. "I'll hit you up this weekend. Avi, email your paper and I'll look at it for you."

"I will," she said, tossing him a honey bun, "and don't forget to vote for Kai."

She turned, giving Quincy a tight-lipped smile.

"Avi," he said standing tall in his cobalt-blue sweatshirt and matching sneakers.

The sound of her name rolling off his tongue made her insides rise. Suddenly she couldn't remember why she was supposed to be upset with him.

"They got you campaignin' hard out here, huh?" he asked, flicking one of the "Vote Kai" pins on her "Belle 4 Queen" shirt.

She shook her head. "I was recruited to help do pretty much everything." She plucked a card from the stack out of his hands. "This artwork is nice," Avi said, looking up at him. "So, you're, like, official now?"

The white card read *QCutz*, with the Z tailing out into a pair of clippers.

"They came in the mail today," Quincy boasted with his hands stuffed back in his pockets. "My friend back home did the design. I just came up with the name."

"It's perfect," Avi said, flipping the card again. "I don't know how you find time to keep your grades up and run a small business out of your dorm."

He shrugged. "Everything here is about finesse. That and knowing when to say no. Otherwise, things get forgotten."

"I see. Um, is that maybe why you didn't text me about the tutoring?"

"What? No, I was handling some things thrown at me last minute, but I planned to text you tonight."

She looked skeptical.

"I'm serious. I can't forget about you, Avi."

She looked from his gorgeous smile to his honest eyes and knew that she couldn't stay mad at him.

Avi bit her lip, trying to hide her grin. "I'll be looking out for it."

The music died down as Logan approached the podium, the sleeves to his Preston sweatshirt pushed up to his elbows. He explained that each of the three candidates would have three minutes to speak before clarifying the online voting process.

Kai approached the podium, and every trace of his nonchalant nature vanished as he spoke with the confidence of a Carter and the reassurance of an Obama. When he wrapped, cheers sounded off before Austin took the stage.

Avi scanned the lot. "Do you know where my brothers are? I didn't think they'd miss this."

"EJ's probably somewhere with Noemie, and I was walking up here with M, but Coach Duke stopped him to talk."

She was about to ask him what position he played when a girl with stunning gray eyes, clear brown skin, and bouncy curls stood directly in front of her. Avi recalled seeing her at the Cliff with other Union Hall girls.

"Hey, Q," she said quickly, before turning and extending a hand to Avi. Avi shifted her bag and shook it awkwardly.

"I'm Keisha," she said with a silvery voice.

"Avielle. Nice to meet you. Is there something you needed?"

"Um, yeah," she said, shifting on her feet. "I see you're helping with Kai's campaign."

"Mhmm. Do you want a drink?"

"No—uhm. I noticed that you two are together . . . like a

lot. And I've seen you on his Instastory a few times, too. . . ." Her voice trailed off as she looked toward the stage where Kai sat listening to the third candidate.

". . . And?" Avi prompted. She raised a hand for her to go on, but Keisha just stood there, avoiding eye contact. Quincy shrugged. "I'm sorry, I don't know where you're going with this."

"This is so awkward," Keisha whispered, laughing nervously. "I've never come to someone woman-to-woman before."

Quincy covered his mouth, attempting to disguise his unmistakable laugh with a cough.

"I still don't understand," Avi said, squinting at them both.

Keisha crossed her arms over her chest. "Look, we've talked a few times, but Kai still hasn't asked me out. I'm guessing it's because you two are a thing."

"I— Wait, what?!?" Avi sputtered.

It was Keisha's turn to look confused. "No judgment, sis. Nowadays, girls don't mind being FWBs, and that's what the PresCliff page said."

"That was about us?" People around them shushed her as Headmistress Malone took the stage to speak on the history of the Harvest Queen Scholarship Pageant. She lowered her voice. "People are saying that here?"

"Yeah. My friend said she saw—"

Avi waved a hand to cut Keisha off. "Know what? I don't care what your friend thinks she saw. He is *literally* my godbrother."

Keisha looked doubtful. "So, you wouldn't mind if I asked him out?"

"I am telling you that something between Kai and me would be incestuous. He feels the same."

"Great!" She beamed. "I'm gonna ask him out. Do you have any more of those pins?"

As Keisha rejoined her friends, Avi said, "Can you believe her?" with a pout, turning to Quincy.

"I can," he said, still trying not to smile. "I was curious about your situation with Kai, too."

"There's nothing to be curious about. Our mothers are best friends and my family has called him my light-skin twin for as long as I can remember."

Quincy's smirk returned. "But you get that a lot?"

"We used to in middle school, but I didn't think people would make that stupid assumption here— Quincy, it's not funny." She pushed his elbow.

He tried to put on a serious face. "Okay, okay. I don't want to be one of those dumb people that makes assumptions about you," he said, cocking his head to the side. "So, tell me, what *is* your situation?"

"Well, my current situation is . . . single."

Quincy rubbed his chin, studying her. "I was hoping so."

Avi pushed her lips to one side of her mouth, trying to hide her grin. Since Quincy found out she was Moe and EJ's little sister, he'd tried to be standoffish. Recently, his actions seemed to hint that he'd at least be interested in a friendship. But that question? It felt like some of her wildest fantasies may not be as far-fetched as she'd thought.

Zazie popped up then in her *Protect Trans Kids* tee and camera asking, "Can I get a few pics of you two for Student Life Photography?"

Avi shook her head, but Quincy threw an arm around her shoulder. They posed for three pictures before Avi shooed her away.

"Make sure I get a copy of those," he called with his phone in his hands. "Hey, I have to cut a head in five, but I'll text you tonight. Oh, and tell Kai I said good luck." He turned to leave.

Avi found her fingers wrapped around his before she realized what she was doing. "What about you? Your situation, I mean."

Quincy flashed that disarming smile at her, saying, "The same as yours," before jogging off toward Newton Hall.

The dreamy smile on her face lasted long after he'd gone. It wasn't until the applause roared that Avi realized the Harvest Queen platform reveal had begun. She joined Zazie and Rhyon near the front of the crowd as the five contestants lined the stage.

Belle moved to the mic, flashing a dazzling smile as the crowd roared. Avi noticed a group of guys to her left whistling and stomping the pavement with approval. Farther to the left stood Logan, quietly viewing Belle with a critical eye.

14

"DOES YOUR STORY HAVE HEART? Duh. Dialogue on point? Absolutely," Professor Lovette said from behind her desk in a bright orange flare dress. "But am I actually there with your characters yet? I don't think so, Avielle. I mean, we're going on an adventure, so *take* me there!" She said this pointing past Avi as if her character's destinations lay somewhere right outside the door. "I wanna know what they're smelling, touching, feeling! And I mean feeling both physically and emotionally. Put yourself in your protagonist's shoes and imagine the lengths you'd go to get to one of your lost siblings. *Imagine* the emotional toll it would take to get them back." She handed Avi the marked-up physical copy of her short story. "You've only given us a peek when we wanna see it all!"

Avi nodded, trying not to feel too discouraged by Professor Lovette's criticism. It was wholly constructive, and her care was outrageously evident. Avi just wasn't used to getting so much feedback in one day.

Early that morning, the edits from Egypt and Cori popped onto Avi's laptop screen. She'd readily prepared herself for harshness so that every rude comment would roll off her back like water. And she was correct in the preparation. Avi didn't think that Egypt was trying to hurt her feelings, but she was a very straight-to-the-point type of person. When Egypt thought something was predictable, she said just that. Same could be said if she felt something Avi said was clichéd. There was no sugarcoating.

Cori's edits, on the other hand, were more Avi's speed, with suggestions to slow down the pacing in the beginning, dig deeper into the feeling of a character here, questions about whether the main character would really act the way they did, and a note to build up the tension in the end. At the end of her email, Cori asked Avi if she would mind sending the next two installments. That felt like a good sign.

After her last class, Avi was in her room working on Egypt's and Cori's edits when she got an email from Professor Lovette inviting Avi to come to her office hours for the feedback she asked for a week ago. It was intimidating, but her favorite part of writing was finishing that first draft and having the opportunity to revise and make her work better.

Avi grabbed the papers, with determination in her eyes, when her phone began buzzing in her pocket. The reminder said *Library in 10*. She'd been so caught up in her short story this evening that she'd forgotten that her first tutoring session with Quincy was nearing.

"Gotta go?" Professor Lovette asked.

"I'm sorry. I do."

"No problem, honey," she said scrolling on the desktop in front of her. "I can send you my additional notes and you can get to them when you have a chance."

Avi walked out of her office, double-checking her bag for

her math book and laptop and pulling out her warm vanilla fragrance for a last spritz. She checked her reflection in her camera, assuring that her twist out was still in place, and her lips were perfectly glossed.

Rhyon would kill her if she saw Avi in the vintage Morehouse sweatshirt she fashioned off the shoulder for what Zazie kept calling a "study date"—according to Rhyon, Avi should dress to impress, and this outfit wouldn't meet the expectations. But she didn't want to come off as trying too hard.

Minutes later, Avi was waving Quincy over to the high table on the second floor of the library. She tried to slow the fluttering in her heart when she saw his sullen expression turn to one of genuine delight as he laid eyes on her. She watched quietly as he unpacked his bag, pausing only to ask how her day went and what she felt she was struggling with.

There's nothing to be nervous about, Avi reminded herself. No big deal. It was simply a tutoring session. With a guy she couldn't keep her eyes off.

When Quincy finished setting up, they got straight to business. He gave Avi a series of practice worksheets to pinpoint her exact problem areas, all while maintaining a patient expression no matter how many times he had to repeat himself. While she worked, he suggested how she could improve here or pick up her pace there.

An hour later, Avi watched the night breeze rattling the high trees as the moon settled in its rightful place high in the dark sky. The hopeless practice sheet sat half done in front of her as Quincy browsed a shelf of books to her right. Aimless daydreams of a time when she would no longer be forced to take math and could write full-time consumed Avi's thoughts when she wasn't distractedly gazing at Quincy's back.

She glanced at the worksheet before placing a hand to her crinkled forehead.

"I don't get this word problem," Avi muttered into the silence.

Quincy turned, leaning over Avi as he placed a hand on either side of the paper. She inhaled. It was the end of the day, but he still smelled of fresh linen and body wash.

"You did everything right up until . . . step five. And then it looks like you kind of gave up."

Her head dropped with a thump.

"Can we please take a break," she said, her voice muffled by the table. "I don't wanna math anymore."

"Sure, why not," he said with a shrug, before dropping into the adjacent seat.

Because of Quincy's strict "no phone policy," Avi's phone had been left untouched since the beginning of the session. She unlocked it to see a missed text from her mom, two from Kai, and thirty-four unread messages from her group chat with Rhyon and Zazie. Avi skimmed through them, but she closed the text thread quickly when she saw questions ranging from *What are you wearing?* to *Are you in love yet?*

Quincy nudged Avi then, and a promo video of a cut he was prepping to post played on his phone.

She scrolled his cut page, clicking through the different pictures and videos of clean fades, line-ups, trims, designs, and shape-ups. He did them all.

"You're skilled," Avi said, bumping his shoulder.

"My grandpa taught me everything," Quincy said bashfully. "He owned a small shop in DC for thirty years."

"And this is what you want to do foreal foreal? Or is it a hobby," she asked, surveying him.

Quincy crossed his arms, slouching comfortably in his chair. "It's pretty lucrative, so I wouldn't call it a hobby. But my end goal is to practice as an OB/GYN."

Avi blinked, resting her cheek in her palm. Since starting at Briarcliff, Avi had met a lot of future lawyers, ballers, businessmen, artists, doctors, and general "millionaire" aspirations among the Preston students. A fifteen-year-old boy wanting to become a practicing obstetrician/gynecologist was . . . unique. A lot of what went on down there still left Avi uncertain and squeamish.

"And what made you want to get into that?" she asked with a squint.

He inhaled deeply like he'd explained this several times before. "Long story short, Black women are three times more likely to die in childbirth than white women. A lot of times, it's because they're not being listened to, or their pain is ignored until it's too late. I wanna be someone in the field who listens, and hopefully, I can make a difference, ya know?"

"Wowww," Avi said. "Color me impressed, Dr. McClain."

Quincy was unable to hide his bright smile. "Look at you, trynna make the kid blush twice in a day," he said, scratching the back of his neck.

"I'm serious, Quincy," Avi leaned forward and placed a hand on his arm.

She felt the energy between them shift, watching the earnest look in Quincy's eye. And she wondered if he could feel the sudden harsh pulse in her fingertips. Something about the fullness of his lips at that moment forced Avi to be still as the night. Scared that any wrong move might make him retreat. Frightened by the idea that they might never be this close again. Avi remembered to breathe then, and the smell of mint on Quincy's breath surrounded her. He leaned forward, and Avi tilted her head, meeting him halfway when—

Ding.

"Students, the library will be closing in thirty minutes."

The abrupt PA announcement brought Avi back too suddenly. She jumped, tipping her high chair too far back. Quincy caught her forearms, and she landed on her feet as the chair clattered to the floor.

"Thank you," Avi breathed. "That could've been ugly!"

Quincy nodded, releasing her to pick up the chair. When he straightened, she saw the wanting look vanish from his eyes.

"Hey—uh. Let's call it a day."

Avi didn't want their time to be up so suddenly, especially when they'd almost had a moment. But curfew was coming, and any reason to ask him to stay evaded her.

Quincy closed his laptop and stuffed his books in his bag, so Avi followed suit. Maybe she was imagining it, but it certainly felt like he was avoiding her eye as they walked down the steps together.

"I, um, appreciate you taking the time to help me," Avi said, squeezing the straps of her backpack.

Quincy smiled half-heartedly. "No problem. I think I know what your problem is, though."

"Seriously?! If you know what's wrong with me, then we can probably fix it!"

He smirked. "You're clearly intelligent, Avi. There's nothing wrong with you, besides your lack of confidence and obvious hate for the subject. You mostly know the correct steps and formulas, but you spend so much time second-guessing yourself that you don't even have the chance to get to the correct answer. So, your problem is obvious, right?"

"Yeah. Professor Blue makes the quizzes too hard and too long."

Quincy held the front door open. "Nah," he said, shaking his head. "You say you're not great at math because you don't know what you're doing, but I say you just gotta move faster and trust that you know the right thing to do. The next time we meet up, I'll take a different approach."

"Can that be this week?" Avi asked, hugging her arms to her chest. The cool autumn weather had gotten significantly colder while they were inside, and Avi was beginning to regret her off-the-shoulder sweatshirt with every new gust of wind.

Quincy nodded hesitantly, and Avi noticed the space between them as they stood leaning on opposite railings. She couldn't help feeling that the distance was purposeful, but at least he was looking at her again.

"Text me, and we'll figure out when. But it's getting cold. You should probably get inside." He nodded toward the cul-de-sac ahead of them.

Zazie would say that in an alternate universe, Avi got precisely what she thought she wanted tonight—her first kiss and a look other than unease in Quincy's eyes. Rhy would tell her that things happened the way the Saints planned, and there's no reason wishing on could've been's. Avi wasn't sure which she wanted to hear less.

She hurried past an arguing couple in front of Rashad Hall, feeling Quincy's eyes on her back as she pressed her ID to the sensor and waved him goodbye through the glass door. It was impossible to decipher the look on his face as he waved back. She stood there, watching until he disappeared around a corner.

15

AVI FOUND HERSELF in stunned silence in a boutique in Buckhead on Saturday morning. Belle emerged from the dressing room in a breathtaking burgundy fit and flare, with velvet fabric and a high-neck cutout. Weeks ago, she'd explained in detail her vision of a custom dress that would "make the audience want her approval." Based on the reactions from their friends, this dress would do that and more for the evening gown portion of the Harvest Queen pageant next month.

The group sat in a store in Lenox Mall later that day, picking an outfit for the talent segment of the pageant. The selection needed to be remarkable yet comfortable as Belle played her violin onstage.

Avi tried her best, but staying present on the small green couch proved close to impossible. They'd been judging outfits for the last hour and a half, and all she could think about was how awful her encounter with Quincy had been yesterday.

It was Preston's first home game of the basketball season, and students, supporters, and faculty alike had come out strong, filling the seats of Pollard Arena in the school colors.

The energy was high during the fast-paced game as the Lions defended their winning streak against the Silver Tigers.

Headmaster Walsh had lost all decorum as he'd attempted to coach Logan from the stands and eventually began running up and down the sides of the court with the players. Students even rallied in support when he got in a heated argument with one of the refs over a foul against the team's star player.

Avi had been rushing back from the bathroom to watch the band and the Golden Cheetahnaires perform their half-time floor routine when she ran into Moe, EJ, and Quincy. She could barely keep her eyes off Quincy in the denim jacket he wore over an olive green hoodie. But he'd barely spared a second look in her direction. Not that she'd dressed in her cutest butt-lifting jeans and tied-up Preston tee for anyone specific, she reminded herself. Avi had hoped for the best when they followed her back to their row, only for Quincy to say, "Excuse me, sis," as he passed the open seat by her to sit at the end of the stands next to Jasiri and Zazie.

She had her suspicions that he might be trying to put her back in the friend zone after their second tutoring session, but "sis" wasn't a term she'd been prepared to hear again. You don't almost kiss a person and then start calling them "sis." It was every type of wrong, and he knew it. Otherwise, he'd have met her eyes.

"Ellie, hello," Belle said, throwing a yellow bath bomb at her, forcing her back to the present. Avi just barely caught the caramel frap tipping out of her hands. "I said I think I'm going with this dress. What's your vote?"

"You spill it, you buy it!" Avi exclaimed, rubbing her arm where the bath bomb bounced off.

"Your vote!"

"I already told you I like what you're wearing," Avi whined. "Can we please leave now? I want a pretzel."

"And we still have to find our Halloween costume," Rhyon said, nudging Zazie awake.

Belle spun around, gazing at her reflection. "Like or love?"

"Love, Belle. Can this be over?"

"What's got you on edge, Baby LeBeau?" Nevaeh asked from behind a shoe rack.

"Nothing."

"This is her 'things are bad with Q' mood," Zazie yawned.

Nevaeh took a long sip from her macchiato. "I could tell it was about a boy."

"Me too," Belle shouted from behind the long green curtain, "but I was speculating. Nowadays, everybody else seems to know more about my little sister than I do."

Avi groaned. "What are you talking about?"

"I'm talking about the fact that Fallon, of all people, was the one to tell me that she saw you leaving the library with Q the other night. True or false?"

"Oop," Rhyon said, sitting up straight.

Avi still couldn't shake the feelings of betrayal about Belle and Fallon's burgeoning "friendship." Yeah, they were on the same dance team, but that didn't mean they had to parade around like they were running for Fakest Big Sister/ Little Sister Duo. Avi knew how important Belle felt family was in a relationship, but she still couldn't understand how she tolerated Fallon.

"Fallon is sneaky and evil, and you can tell her to keep my name out of her snake mouth."

Belle walked out of the dressing room with her pink sweater halfway on. "Spare me the drama. I mean, yeah, she's big-headed, and I've had to put her in her place twice already about who's captain, but she looks up to me. Plus, she can dance her ass off. I honestly thought you two would've clicked by now."

"It's hard to hit it off with La Diabla," Rhyon sang from behind a copy of *Vogue* magazine.

Belle rolled her eyes. "Why do I have to find out about you hanging out with Q past nine on a Wednesday from other people? Spill."

Avi told them everything that had happened since the first time he walked her back to campus. After their disastrous second session, Avi had avoided telling Zazie and Rhyon any details before rushing off to take an early shower. So it was no surprise that their ears perked now, as she shared how he'd sat across from her and avoided eye contact the whole session. Nevaeh's scoff was validating when Avi mentioned that she'd asked for a break after thirty-five minutes of studying and Quincy had opted to end their session instead.

"At least he walked you back to your dorm," Belle said.

Then Avi got to tell them of the "urgent" phone call that left her watching him jog toward Preston before they got to say their goodnights. She left out his latest "sis" comment from yesterday to save a bit of her pride.

"And I was looking at his phone. It didn't even ring." She pouted, slurping the last of her frap as they left the boutique, bags in hand.

"He's all over the place," Rhyon said, raising her red hoodie over her baseball cap and tightening the strings. That morning, two girls that looked to be at least eighteen had recognized her and bombarded her with compliments about her mother's modeling days. She'd been gracious and answered their questions, and had even posed for a picture, but she hated being approached by strangers.

"We're supposed to meet up tomorrow, but my hopes aren't high," Avi sighed.

"Why are you keeping so much from me all of a sudden?" Belle asked. She looked genuinely hurt.

"It's not on purpose," Avi said, looping her arm in her sister's as they drifted into a Sephora. "This is all new, not to mention embarrassing. Plus, you're super busy with the pageant. I wanted the chance to figure it out on my own, and it was kinda going well, but I messed something up."

Belle shook her head. "It wasn't you. It was the twins."

"I doubt Quincy would've told them."

"Of course he wouldn't," Nevaeh said knowingly. She held a display tube of body lotion to her nose. "This is like the ultimate betrayal of their little bro code. Tell me, why don't you want them to know you like Q?"

Avi sprayed a sample vanilla perfume on a blotter, saying, "Because it's none of their business, and they don't get to make my decisions."

"Exactly—good reason, by the way," Belle said, giving an approving nod to the scent, "but the situation may be more complicated for Q. He came close to kissing his best friend's little sister."

"That alone is enough to ruin their relationship," Zazie chimed from the Fenty Beauty section.

"And he's been doing all this behind their backs," Rhyon added.

"To top it all off, they still think of you as a baby." Belle shrugged. "Especially Moe—the little hypocrite. I know something's up with him and Vannah."

Rhyon leaned her head in between theirs with wide eyes. "Really? Isn't she a junior?"

"Yeah, but only because she skipped a grade in elementary. Here, smell this," Belle said, holding a new blotter to Rhy's nose. Rhy shook her head with a wrinkled face. "I thought so, too. Anyways, Vannah's gorge and smart, so I see why Moe is interested, but technically, he's still trying to do the same thing you are."

"Well, then, why won't Quincy just say so, instead of shutting me out?" Avi asked, annoyed. "It's immature." She inhaled deeply into the coffee bean canister to desensitize her nose. All the different smells were making her dizzy.

"Why don't you bring it up?" Nevaeh suggested.

That wasn't an awful idea. Unless doing so confirmed that Avi was reading too much into Quincy's actions. Or worse.

"What if he flat-out tells me he isn't interested?"

"Then he'd be lying, so you'd get a real tutor and move on," Nevaeh said sharply. "We don't deal with liars."

"Hey! He *is* a real tutor, and I don't want a new one."

Rhyon snickered. "Look at you, on the defensive."

"You know what? I don't want to talk about this anymore." Avi exhaled loudly. "Zazie, how are you and Jah?"

"Absolutely perfect," she said, walking to the register with some all-natural moisturizer in a basket. "Now, how are you gonna bring this up with Q?"

"I'm not," Avi said through her teeth. "New topic, please?"

"I heard the Preston/Briarcliff planning committee might

bring back the Sadie Hawkins Spring Formal," Rhyon said with a sly look on her face. "Do you think you'll ask Q?"

Avi dropped her head, but Belle cut in.

"We're not talking about him anymore," she said loyally. "Zazie, do you know when the edited pictures from the pageant shoot will be ready?"

THE GIRLS AGREED to meet up with Belle and Nevaeh in the food court, then went off on their own. They were standing in the Auntie Anne's line waiting for their orders when Rhyon bumped Avi's and Zazie's elbows, saying, "La Diabla y huelepedos. Two o'clock."

Zazie looked around; Avi tried to find a place to hide. She wasn't afraid of Fallon, but that girl possessed the ability to turn any good day all the way around, and Avi wasn't in the mood.

"No! *My* two o'clock," Rhyon said, nodding toward them. Too late—Fallon and Kieley had noticed them and were coming their way.

It was particularly irritating how everything about Fallon appeared flawless all the time, no matter the situation. Makeup perfect, not a pressed curl out of place, outfits consistently on point. That, apparently, was the life of a former beauty queen's daughter. It had to be exhausting.

"Avi, don't you look cute today," Fallon said. She gave Avi a slow once-over, distaste clear on her face as she took in Avi's pastel-blue-and-pink-striped sweatshirt, distressed jeans, and matching Uggs.

"Thanks. Talk to you later," Avi said, turning back toward the counter to grab her food and mustard packets from the cashier. She hoped Fallon would take the dismissal, but life was never that easy.

"Did Belle tell you we spoke about you the other day? She's a doll. You guys are nothing alike."

Avi whipped around. "Keep my name out your mouth."

"It was casual conversation." Fallon shrugged. "Too busy trynna clean up your short story to tell our sis about your late-night escapades?"

"One, she's not your sister. Two, I wish you'd mind your business."

"Oh, I'm sorry. I didn't mean to step on any toes. So, I shouldn't have told her that you and Q were all hugged up at the election last Friday, either?" She cocked her head to the side, feigning confusion.

"Wha-huh? We weren't hugged up, stalker. It was a picture, and we're just friends. Nothing more."

"Whatever you say, Avi." Fallon held up her hands in mock defense. "He is cute, though. Don'tcha think? I'll admit, I don't usually like my guys on the darker side, but I'd make an exception for this math whiz I keep hearing so much about."

"Your self-hate is heartbreaking," Zazie said. "He'd never be interested in you, anyway."

"And why not?" Fallon asked. As if she was incapable of believing there was a guy walking on God's green earth who wouldn't find her appealing. She flipped her curls out of her face. "I mean, it wouldn't matter to Avi, regardless. They're *just friends.*"

Avi surveyed her through narrowed eyes. "Honestly,

Fallon. I'd never be interested in anyone who'd still want to talk to you after you exposed your trash personality."

"That's rude."

"Why don't you take your fake-offended ass on and leave us alone?" Rhyon sighed, annoyed.

"Rhyon Bloom, is that you?" Kieley's voice boomed. She looked elated at the chance to finally jump in. "It's hard to tell, with your super-cute disguise on."

"Shut up," Rhyon hissed, getting in her face.

Zazie pulled her by the back of her jacket at the sight of a small table of boys egging for the girls to fight. Before long, phones would be recording. "Let's go," she said through her teeth.

"That's an awful lot of bags, Zazie," Fallon chuckled before they could walk away. "If I were you, I think I'd put all my spare coins toward tuition, maybe even room and board, not the likes of Forever 21 and Rainbow."

Zazie stepped in front of Avi and Rhyon, fist clenched as she tried to process the audacity. "No one's ever put hands on you before, have they?"

"It was an innocent suggestion." Fallon smirked.

"My backhand across your face won't be so innocent," Zazie snapped. Avi could see her rage, and moved between them.

Fallon laughed, but it wasn't as convincing with the menacing look coming from Zazie's usually sweet hazel eyes. "Let's go, Lee. My cousin's waiting, and things are getting a little too *Love and Hip Hop* over here."

A minute later, Avi sat on a bench between Rhyon and Zazie, munching angrily on a pretzel bite.

"You gotta stop feeding into her bull, Avi," Zazie said.

"Me?! You were gonna hit her!"

"Oh, I was, and I promise you one day I will—for the both of us," she said, smiling kindly. "But what y'all got goin' is different. She knows what she's doing and just how to get to you."

Rhyon sipped on her smoothie, saying, "If you ask me, she's intimidated."

"By me? Don't think so."

"She may write well, but connects helped her up. I don't think she expected you to be real competition."

16

"**I HATE YOU**," Belle grumbled to the piece of kale hanging off her fork.

They sat in the chaotic food court chatting across from a man in a bright purple suit and a woman with three wild kids screaming for ice cream. Fast foods from an array of restaurants filled their table, but Belle had chosen an organic pop-up handing out free wheatgrass shots.

Avi thought the dieting was ridiculous, but Belle was anxious about the pageant and had put herself on an even stricter food and exercise regime.

"You look miserable. Here," Avi said, dumping two sliced nuggets in her sister's salad bowl before she could refuse. "These won't stop you from fitting in your dress."

Belle's dimple deepened as she perked up. "Okay, but only because you made me. Hey, you never said when your short story's coming out in the paper."

Avi was grateful for the time she spent thinking of anything besides the creative-writing column competition. It felt all-consuming lately. Every Tuesday and Thursday she went to

Cliff meetings and had to watch just how buddy-buddy Egypt and Fallon were. Worse? She'd glimpsed just a page of the sample Fallon had submitted. Avi could no longer deny that Fallon had earned her spot as a finalist.

Still, Avi worked endlessly on her revisions—with Cori's help. She did so until her story was in its most pristine form, and she even took Cori's advice to volunteer wherever else the *Cliff News* needed extra hands. This meant any spare time was spent volunteering as a critique partner, beta reader, and occasionally on clean-up duty after meetings.

"Our columns will be in print this Monday," Avi said. "The popular vote ends Tuesday night, and they let us know which of us gets the position on Halloween. Cori says campaigning is frowned upon because we're supposed to let our work speak for itself, but you guys can remind people to vote when they get the email."

"We will," Nevaeh said. "FYI, my art show in Zody is in one week to the day and I expect to see each of your faces there."

Rhyon pulled out her tiny planner. "I'm having brunch with my dad that morning, but I'll be back right after to see the exhibit!"

Something across the food court drew Avi's eyes away from the conversation. She was surprised to see Logan standing there, scanning the crowd. She barely recognized him outside of his school uniform, but there he was, looking annoyed.

"Your boyfriend's looking for you," Avi said flatly.

The fork Belle was holding clattered to the table as she craned her neck. Upon sighting him, her nostrils flared, and her mouth went tight. "What is he doing here?"

"Since when do you not want him around?" Zazie asked.

"It's not that I don't want him around." Belle put the top on her salad and stuffed it in the bag, muttering to herself.

Nevaeh crossed her arms on the table with a quizzical look. "Well, he spotted you. Do you wanna go?"

Belle straightened, pushing her curls behind her ear. "No, of course not."

By the time Logan reached the table, the irritated looks on both of their faces smoothed over. He looked suave in a fitted gray sweater, and Belle was collected and smiling broadly when he greeted her with a kiss to the cheek.

"My cousin told me you guys met up earlier to hang out," Logan said, turning his charm on Avi. "It's nice to hear you guys are friends now."

Belle looked at her questioningly, and Avi gave them a swift nod. "Something like that."

Zazie scoffed and Rhyon gritted her teeth, but it would be a waste of time to keep arguing about Fallon. Especially if both Logan and Belle refused to see that she was an evil spawn.

"Babe, can I talk to you for a second?" he asked, taking Belle's hand and leading her a few feet from the table toward a tall green plant.

When they were out of earshot, Avi asked, "Nevaeh, do you like him?"

"I'm indifferent." She shrugged. "Dude is needy as hell, and they spend all their spare time together, but Belle swears he's her Prince Naveen. Anywho, I heard them arguing on the phone last night, so I know they're not on good terms."

Avi went back to dipping her fries but couldn't help remembering the text she read weeks ago on Belle's phone.

Logan hated Nevaeh and told Belle he didn't like them hanging out.

When Avi looked up again, Logan and Belle weren't by the plant anymore. She sat up in her chair, looking past a group of girls in Clark Atlanta University paraphernalia. She spotted them across the food court, under a sign pointing toward the restrooms. Logan's hand was clenched around Belle's upper arm as he dragged her along. Avi blinked to make sure she was seeing things correctly. Did he just . . . shove her around the corner?

She stood abruptly, ignoring the table's questions as she muttered "Excuse me" and squeezed past people standing in the way.

She walked into the filthy women's restroom, peeking under the stalls, but left after only seeing a little girl and an older woman near the sinks. Avi pressed her ear against the wooden men's door but was positive her sister wouldn't have gone in there anyways. So, where were they? She walked down the fluorescent-lit hallway, hearing her boots squishing on the tiled floor, until a sudden burst of muffled yelling came from the family bathroom at the edge of the hall. Avi edged closer.

"And then you go and turn off your location and purposely ignore my text and calls like I'm nobody," Logan yelled. His voice sounded rough—nothing like the calm, cool demeanor he always displayed for the student body.

But Belle's retort came even louder. "I told you I needed *one* day. *One!* And you couldn't even give me that!"

"Space away from me and with your hoe friend. I told you I don't like that—"

"Don't, Logan!" Belle was practically shrieking now.

"Aye, who the hell are you talking to?"

Avi knocked on the door, rattling the locked handle.

"It's occupied!" Logan's voice rang.

This time, Avi balled up her fist, banging on the door until it swung open. Logan stood feeling two feet taller, enraged with protruding eyes. And then he did it—the quick switch. His face transformed right in front of Avi from barely contained rage to the charming student body president that everyone adored.

"Hey," Logan said. The edge in his voice was gone. "Can we have like two minutes?"

Avi's eyes darted around the small room until they landed on Belle's back at the sink. Her reflection was calm, but her nose flared. "I came to talk to my sister, not you," she said, distrust masking her face.

The smile he held faltered for a moment, and there was an unsettling glint in his eyes that made her want to shrink.

Avi prayed she looked far more confident than she felt glaring at Logan, but he just chuckled. He turned his head to look at Belle, and Avi took the opportunity to slip under his outstretched hand and into the smelly bathroom.

With a disapproving look at Avi, he walked to the sink. "I gotta go, babe. Please, answer your phone later."

Belle let him tilt her chin up for a kiss before he swept out of the bathroom. She took a deep breath, put soap on her hands, and washed them slowly as steaming water gushed down the drain. Avi thought the tense air would leave with him, but here they were—clouded in it.

"Did he shove you out there, or am I seeing things?"

Silence.

Belle took a paper towel, somehow drying her fingers one by one in a hostile way. Avi could feel her heart beating in her ears now. She couldn't understand why it felt like she was the one in trouble.

"Fine," Avi said, daring to take a step forward. "Tell me this. When did we start letting boys with obvious anger issues tell us who we can hang out with?"

"You're following me and listening to my conversations now?"

"N-not on purpose," Avi stuttered. "It looked like something was wrong, and I—"

"And you wanted to be nosy because you don't have any real business of your own," Belle said, and then her voice lowered an octave. "You thought this was a good chance to get involved in mine, and that I'd be okay with that." Finally, she looked up, staring at Avi through the mirror.

"You should be okay with me wanting to make sure you're good. I'm your sister."

"And he's my boyfriend," Belle said with a tone of deadly calm. She leaned forward to apply gloss to her lips. "I'm a big girl, and I can take care of myself, okay? I don't need your saving."

Avi crossed her arms over her chest, unsure. "Belle, just tell me he didn't shove you."

She whipped around, swelling with anger. Instinctively, Avi took a step back from the finger in her face and the menacing look in her sister's eyes.

"Avielle, I'm gonna tell you this one time. I don't need you or your wild imagination in my relationship. You don't want the twins minding your childish business, and I don't want you in mine. So keep the drama to your little short stories."

Her words hit like a slap across the face.

"Fine. I don't want you in mine, either," Avi shot back, knocking her sister's hand away.

Belle adjusted the strap on her shoulder and snatched another paper towel. "Sounds good to me." She walked to the door but paused to glance back. "I don't want your friends in my business either, so keep it to yourself." Her eyes cut back to the door as she yanked it open.

Avi stood alone in the bathroom, hands trembling in anger, confused by the entire altercation. How exactly was she the bad guy in this? She came to help, but it felt like things were worse because she showed up. Maybe she had stuck her nose where it didn't belong, but what was her other option? Walk away and pretend nothing was happening in front of her? No, that wouldn't have felt right either. Maybe Avi hadn't seen correctly, but there was no denying what she heard.

17

THE FRESH MORNING AIR billowed from the open window in Avi's dorm as she reluctantly peeked out of her sleep mask on Monday morning. It was the day her short story would finally be in print in the *Cliff News*. The day people other than her family and friends would be free to read—and judge—the written piece of her that she'd handed over to Egypt. The thought alone was suffocating.

In hindsight, a place on the column didn't quite feel worth it. Especially after reading the (completely unnecessary) email from Cori reminding the finalists where they could pick up a copy of today's paper. That reminder had caused Avi to fumble desperately for the reviving pumps of her inhaler before seven a.m.

Rhyon pounded on their door while Avi was still in a zebra-print towel rubbing lotion over her legs. Zazie sat on her bed typing a petition for *Grown* by Tiffany D. Jackson as this week's book pick for English 9.

"Yes, and I'll send you a link to the site, Ma. Call you later," Avi heard her say into the phone as she opened the door. Rhyon walked right in fully dressed and made a beeline for

Zazie. She held a copy of the paper outstretched in her arms, hardly able to contain herself as she bounced in her boots.

The pencil Zazie chewed fell from her mouth as her face lit with glee. "Are you serious! They picked our picture?"

"They picked our picture *for the cover*," Rhyon squealed, turning so Avi could see. It was one of the pictures Zazie took of Rhyon back in September, so they could help build each other's modeling and photography portfolios. The photo itself was edited to show five images of Rhyon on one of the couches in Hollingsworth's main lounge, wearing a simple low bun, white skirt, lavender leotard, and pointe shoes as she posed dramatically.

Avi beamed at the photo as she tightened the towel around her. It was stunning. And the front page was typically saved for the best of the best photography and art submissions. This was a big deal. "When did you submit it?! And why didn't you tell me you were going to?"

Zazie bit her lip, grabbing the paper to view the photo and her and Rhyon's names captioned beneath. "It was my fourth submission. I didn't think it would matter," she whispered, staring at the photo with so much pride, it looked like she might burst into tears. "I gotta call my dad!"

"I already sent it to everyone I've ever known," Rhyon said, cheesing, as she fell onto Zazie's bed. "Oh, and Avi, your article's right on the second page, and—"

"Oh no, don't," Avi said, cringing. For a moment she'd actually forgotten that Rhyon was holding her work as well. She knew it should be a moment for them all to celebrate, but her nausea was back with a vengeance.

Most of Avi's morning was spent annoying Rhyon and

Zazie to new ends. Zazie didn't appreciate being told that the amethyst bracelet she'd let Avi borrow to calm her anxiety was useless after a mere fifteen seconds of wearing it. And Rhyon was sick of hearing Avi's far-fetched ideas that her writing would somehow be so terrible professors would band together to petition for her expulsion. But Avi's fourth pivot-and-scurry incident was the last straw. Every time Avi saw someone holding the paper—in the café, on sidewalks, and even once in the bathroom—she'd turn on her heel and hurry away. She all but fled in horror from the Johnson computer lab after seeing the October *Cliff News* edition on three students' screens. She would have to print her history paper on King Leopold II's cruelty another time.

She loved hearing all the positive reactions Zazie and Rhyon were receiving on their photo, but it wasn't until lunch when Avi heard a firsthand response to her own piece. Her favorite lunch lady, Ms. Bev, was a silver-haired woman known for speaking a mile a minute, remembering every student's name, and constantly fussing about whether everyone ate enough.

"Miss Avielle, I read your article in the paper this morning," she squealed as Avi's Cheetah card hung in the air, waiting to be swiped. "And I can't wait until the next one. Honey, ya know you had me after that fiery opening. Swear I was hooked just like my soaps, and you know I can't get enough of *General Hospital*."

Avi threw her arms around the bubbly woman. "Thank you, Ms. Bev," she sighed into her chest. "You don't know how much that means."

More of the same came throughout the rest of the day from

classmates and teachers. Headmistress Malone even stopped Avi on the way to French, confiscated phones banging in her custom bucket. She wished Avi good luck and gave her a link for an upcoming writing contest for teenage girls of color, hosted by a small publishing house.

As Avi walked down the hall, Paisli squealed with excitement from the AirPods in her ear.

"I just finished reading it," she said. "Avi, it was really fun! That other girl is okay, but she takes the horror too seriously, if you ask me. I'm gonna show it to my English teacher tomorrow, and maybe your article can count as one of our class's comprehension and analysis assignments. Then again, Mrs. Rue hates fun, so she'll probably say no."

Avi didn't know if it was because of the distance, but every day she wished Paisli were here with them. Antonio, too. Though he'd refused to read her story because, in his words, "it's too long and the print is too small."

"Thanks, Pai," she said making a kissy face at the camera. "That means the most coming from you."

Avi wished that she could be sharing this moment with Belle, too. But they weren't on speaking terms. When she wasn't thinking about her article, the moment Logan shoved Belle around that corner played on repeat. It made Avi want to reach out to her sister, but then she remembered how Belle acted after Logan left them, and was left pushing thoughts of reconciliation as far down as she could manage. It was a tortuous cycle.

Avi unlocked the door to her room and saw a clipping of her short story and Zazie and Rhyon's photo in individual frames hung on the wall. She felt her heart swell. Her words were in print for everyone to see, and the feedback didn't make her want to crawl into a hole and hide. The best part: Her best friends were right alongside her.

What had she been so afraid of this morning?

"**DO YOU *HAVE* TO** chew with your mouth open?" Avi asked, looking at Kai with disgust.

She was trying to focus on her assigned reading for Women's Studies, an article titled "The Roles of Black Women in Enslaved Communities," but thanks to Kai, their table was starting to sound like one of those mukbang videos Rhyon always raved about.

Study groups formed around them in the Cliff, and students socialized as band rehearsals, sports practices, and organization meetings let out.

Avi used her thumb to wipe a glob of honey mustard off Kai's left cheek, but quickly pulled back when she saw two kids at the next table gazing at them.

"We have to do something," she groaned. "People think we're dating again."

"Are you serious?!"

"Yes! That girl, Keisha, bombarded me at your election asking if we were friends with benefits."

"Disgusting." He shook his head, trying to clear images. And then his fingers snapped with an idea. "I'll post that throwback of us on the first day of daycare with 'My Godsister' as the caption."

Belle's picture came across Avi's buzzing phone then. She

took one look before pressing the red button, sending her sister straight to voicemail.

Avi hadn't spoken to Belle since she left her standing alone in the bathroom at the mall. They'd ignored each other on the ride home and continued avoiding each other in the hallways, café, and at the Cliff. Belle had even refused to acknowledge Avi when they were in the same locker room two days ago. But this morning, Avi received a text:

Voted for you ❤

BELLEY

She left it on read.

"What's that about?" Kai asked.

"Belle and her stupid boyfriend fought at the mall, and she took it out on me."

Kai shook his head. "I hope she doesn't mess it up with him. Me and Jah are going to his dorm tonight to watch the game. He's a good guy."

"No, no, no," Avi rushed. "Logan is the jerk in all this. He's always trying to tell her what she can do, and I think I saw him shove her on Saturday."

Kai dismissed that with a wave of his hand. "Nah, I know him. Lo wouldn't do that."

"I overheard them, and he was yelling at her." Avi wanted him to understand the severity of the situation without breaking her word. Belle was wrong about a lot, but it *was* her business. It wasn't Avi's place to tell.

"What? And she wasn't yelling back?"

"Yeah, but—"

"Couples fight, Avi," he said matter-of-factly, "You were ear hustlin', got caught, and now she's pissed at you. I can see why."

Avi huffed in exasperation. "You didn't see what I saw or hear what I heard."

Belle's face popped up again as the phone vibrated on the table. Avi flipped it over.

"If you ask me—" Kai started.

"I didn't."

"—I'd say you need to mind your own business and apologize to her."

Belle had been nothing short of cold toward her for the last four days. Now Avi was supposed to act like nothing happened? She refused to be the one crawling on hands and knees, begging for forgiveness.

"That's dead."

"Fine. Stay mad," Kai said, standing to discard his trash.

He came back to the table staring at his phone, his face moving from puzzlement to disbelief.

"What's wrong?" Avi asked, her thoughts already skipping to worst-case scenarios.

Kai thrust his phone into her hands. "What does that look like to you?"

There was a video on Crystal Thompson's Instastory that showed Crystal kissing Kai's cheek and the caption "He won!" The same video was posted on Twitter, too.

Avi chuckled at the dread on his face. "It looks like she's marking her territory," she said, patting his back.

Kai covered his face, and his voice came out muffled. "She said she wasn't gonna post it."

"What's the big deal?" Avi shrugged, mocking his nonchalance. "I mean, Keisha's gonna hate it, but I can tell from our Women's Studies class that Crystal's brilliant. Cute, too."

"It doesn't matter at all, because we're *not* together."

"Hmm," Avi said, squinting at the video. "I can't tell who, but one of you is confused."

"She is," he said through his teeth. "Can you do it, please?" He clasped his hands together, puppy-dog eyes in full effect.

"What? Oh, no. I'm not ending your situationship for you," Avi laughed. "Plus, there's a silver lining."

"What?"

"At least people will stop saying we're dating now."

18

PROFESSOR BLUE GAVE Quincy control of the last forty minutes of Thursday's class to put his teaching skills to the test. For once, Quincy's tie was on straight, and the sleeves to his collared shirt weren't rolled up to his elbows. Avi might have been happy that he was receiving this opportunity, but they weren't on great terms.

Over the last three days, Quincy had canceled four study sessions—including twice in one day. All last minute. Add in the fact that he was avoiding her in class, and Avi thought he was done with her completely. But no, this was worse.

The class was supposed to be a review for next week's test, but Quincy took it upon himself to use this time to torture Avi instead. She tried not to show her annoyance, but he literally called on her five times in twenty minutes. To top it all off, he showed no mercy, letting the entire class know exactly when and how she arrived at each incorrect answer.

Now, she glared at Quincy's back as he wrote two separate equations on the board. The first: relatively simple. The second: a challenge she didn't want to face.

"All right, does anyone want to volunteer?" he asked, holding two dry-erase markers toward the class.

The sounds of pencils scribbling and pages rustling filled the room as everyone avoided Quincy's eye. Avi, herself, worked on beating her score as she played *Block Dude* on her TI-84 Plus calculator.

"C'mon, don't all run up to the board at once," Professor Blue joked. "All right, Mr. McClain, feel free to pick two people."

"Last chance. No volunteers? Fine. Kalin, please do number one, and . . ." He scanned the room.

Feeling Quincy's eyes on her, Avi tried to make herself look preoccupied by glancing back and forth between her textbook and calculator. But it was futile; her name was the one that toppled out of his mouth.

Avi huffed audibly and smoothed her plaid skirt as she dragged herself to the dry-erase board. When Quincy held the blue marker out toward her, she snatched it from his hand.

They were still learning the basics of radical expressions, and this was far past that. Avi knew that an equation like this would only ever be a bonus question on Blue's test. And if it were, she would opt out of even attempting it to save herself the stress. Quincy knew that, too.

Avi looked back at Rhyon with panicked eyes to see her encouraging nod. She held her marker to the board, dropped it, and then held it up again only to repeat these steps twice more.

"Let's make this interesting and see if Kalin or Avielle can finish their problem first," Quincy said. "Guys, make sure to show all your work so the class can follow."

Avi glared at him out of the side of her eye, caught his smirk, and put the marker to the board without hesitation this time. The problem was eleven steps and came out as a funny fraction, but she managed to finish only seconds after Kalin. He went first, explaining how exactly he came to the correct answer as the class followed along. When Kalin took his seat, Avi coughed twice, to clear her voice. She explained her problem step by step, almost with ease, up until step nine. Then she had to pause.

"One second, I think I . . ." Her voice drifted off as she took a step back to reexamine the problem. Avi grabbed her calculator from her desk, plugging in the components while the class sat waiting.

Quincy raised his hands after a moment. "All right, guys, so this is what happens when we second-guess ourselves and don't leave enough time to check our work. Can anyone tell us where she went wrong? Rhyon?"

But Avi didn't give Rhyon a chance to speak.

"I can fix it myself," said Avi, looking past Quincy to Professor Blue. He nodded for her to go on. "I forgot to square the eight after I multiplied the coefficients of the inner terms." She picked up the marker to correct the problem and explained it as she wrote.

Quincy's brows lifted, and the corners of his lips tugged down. "Can you show us how to check the problem, too?" he asked just when she thought she was free to sit back down. Still fueled by frustration, Avi did so with ease.

When she finished, the bell rang, and the class began to pack their belongings.

"All right." Blue clapped to regain the class's attention. "Let's all give it up for Mr. McClain. No homework, but I'm expecting A's and B's. So study."

Avi stuffed her books and calculator in her bag before sweeping out of the classroom. Who did Quincy think he was, using her as an example? He knew this problem would come as a challenge to her, and he still went out of his way to quiz her in front of everyone. If that was how he was going to act, she didn't want or need his help anymore.

Rhyon finally caught up to Avi as she passed the Washington fine arts building.

"Did you guys have a fight or something?"

"'This is what happens when you second-guess yourself,'" Avi said in a deep, mocking voice. "Can you believe him, trynna embarrass me like that?"

"I don't think Q was trying to embarrass you. But to be fair, Kalin's problem wasn't nearly as hard." Rhyon grabbed Avi's arm, whining, "Why are you walking so fast?"

Avi slowed her pace. "Tell me what he was trying to do, because I'd love to know."

"Hey, I don't know what's going on in your weird relationship."

Avi stopped short. "There is no relationship," she shrilled.

"Oh wow. He's got you tight," Rhyon said, looking amused and alarmed at the same time. "Whatever's going on between you two isn't nothing. You have to admit that. Go ask him."

"No." It was like Rhyon hadn't witnessed everything in class. What about that would make Avi want to speak to him?

"Well, he's headed over here now."

Avi turned to see Quincy jogging to catch up to them.

She looked both ways, allowing a maintenance truck to pass before crossing the street. When she glanced back, Quincy and Rhyon stood where she left them, talking.

Back at Briarcliff, Avi stomped toward Wells. She couldn't stop thinking of the day Quincy walked her from Preston on this same route. The way he'd caught up to her and called her "Dimples." The way he'd complimented her fragrance and how he held her hand in his. Had that all been some kind of short-lived, purposeless nice-guy act?

The sight of Cori sitting on the bench under a leafless tree pushed the memories back where they belonged. Avi buttoned her lavender cardigan against the breeze and grinned when Cori waved her over. Professor Rae was always at least fifteen minutes late to College and Career Prep anyway, so there was no real rush.

Cori had been a real source of support for Avi since they met at the second meeting. In fact, just about everyone at the paper was overwhelmingly helpful. Avi desperately wanted to be a real part of their little family.

"How are you holding up in light of our little competition?" Cori asked with a mischievous look on her face. She flipped the long braids Zazie had done out of her face.

Avi laughed, letting her head fall back. "What kind of competition doesn't even let the competitors see what the votes are lookin' like? I mean, I'm getting decent feedback, but please give me *something*!"

Cori looked to her left and right for eavesdroppers but was more than glad to oblige. "Okay," she whispered, "I'm not technically supposed to say, but the popular vote is tilting in your favor."

Avi couldn't stop herself from dancing in her seat. Cori laughed.

"And what about the staff vote?" she asked, greedily this time. "I know you all's opinions are taken into consideration. I mean Egypt basically hates me if Fallon's in the same room, and it's hard to tell where the rest of the staff's feelings lie."

"Egypt does not hate you." Cori chuckled. "I think she can just see more of herself in Fallon."

"The bloodthirsty ambition, you mean?"

"Honestly, she can be sweet. A little overwhelming and insecure at times, but decent overall."

Avi pretended to zip her mouth shut and lock it.

"No, I'm serious," Cori giggled. "Egypt will always do what she thinks is right for the paper. Now, I can't speak for the rest of the staff, but you got my vote, LeBeau."

"Walk with me to the Cliff," Avi said, looping her arm in Cori's. "You just earned yourself a frap."

19

THIRTY-EIGHT PERM RODS. That's how many Avi put in the night before Halloween to achieve her favorite YouTuber CoiledCurls' "Perfect 4b Perm Rod set." Because of the weird positions she had to lie in to avoid messing up her hair, sleep hadn't come easy. Her alarm blaring forty-five minutes earlier than usual didn't help, either.

Avi flipped over in bed, only to see a text from Quincy delivered at four a.m. pop onto the screen. The sight of his name put an instant frown on her face.

Sleep crust fell from her eyes as she reread the message.

> My schedule's clear. Meet at the library for a session at 4:30?
>
> **QUINCY**

For a moment, she considered declining because of the stunt he'd pulled in class last Thursday, but she really could use his help. Even without face-to-face meetings, the video tutoring, math notes, and study tools he gave her were always helpful. Though she wouldn't admit it out loud.

Sure

AVI

She hopped out of bed, grabbed her bathroom caddy, and slipped into her blue robe. She sent a silent prayer that every curl was completely dry before placing the shower cap over her bonnet.

Avi didn't want to dwell on what had made Quincy text her at four in the morning—or deal with the disappointment of him backing out last minute again. Unreliability wasn't her thing, and there were more important, exciting things on her mind:

1. She would receive the final decision about the *Cliff News* creative column today.

The anticipation had Avi's stomach in knots all week. But she noticed that starting her day with fresh cantaloupe juice from Sugah's garden and Zazie's consistent smudging helped to shift her mood. She hadn't even needed to use her inhaler as a crutch this morning.

2. Briarcliff and Preston took Halloween more seriously than Avi ever had. She was maybe seven or eight the last time she remembered being genuinely excited about dressing up and going trick-or-treating. But here, students rattled on and on about outlandish costume ideas and Preston's Halloween party.

Avi bent in her fitted yellow tee to draw a black stripe under Zazie's left eye while Rhyon bobbed her head to "No Scrubs" in the mirror, adjusting her red Tommy Hilfiger boxers to show over her baggy black Champion sweats.

"C'mon, TLC," Thalia said, grinning from their door. She

had dressed as Katara from *Avatar: The Last Airbender.* "We're gonna take a ground-floor group pic."

The usually quiet, sluggish feel reserved for school mornings had been replaced with an air of fervor for the coming day. The morning sun streaming from the hall window provided perfect light as Easlyn snapped picture after picture of the floormates.

From their rooms to the lobby, Avi saw a Black Barbie, Penny Proud, Squid Game contestant 067, Wanda Maximoff, Lara Jean, and a trio from the penthouse dressed flawlessly as the Sanderson Sisters. They passed Housemother Lisa, dressed as a yellow M&M, as she reprimanded two students for their Hooters waitress costumes.

As they walked into the café, Avi felt suddenly grateful that Rhyon and Zazie had badgered her into dressing up. The detailed costumes their schoolmates wore were surprising. And impressive. Still, nothing could have prepared them for the number of girls dressed as the Cheetah Girls, either in the multicolored sweatsuits from the movie or decked out in cheetah prints and bodysuits. According to Easlyn (who was dressed as Thunder from *Black Lightning*) it was tradition to wear something cheetah-related at least once during your time at Briarcliff.

The morning announcements rolled out from the intercom, listing costume dress guidelines and the times for tonight's Halloween dinner, costume contest, and Preston's haunted trail. Avi sat at the long breakfast table, cutting into her waffle with a piece of bacon hanging out the side of her mouth when Zazie gasped with bulging eyes.

"What happened?" Rhyon cried as she and Avi peered at the screen hidden under the table. It was a throwback video of Q hitting a home run on his page.

"So what?" Avi shrugged. She took a swig of orange juice and regathered her utensils.

"Look at the comments, genius."

Avi looked through the first couple of kudos from his cousins and friends, even scrolling past one from Moe (@MorrisTheMogul) that said, *"We're gonna eat this szn, bro."*

It was the last comment posted four minutes ago that made Avi roll her eyes.

@FallonReigns: 😎 Check your DM.

Avi looked up at the table Fallon usually sat at to find her smirking. She seemed more sinister than usual, her *Purge* costume splattered with fake blood, slowly stroking the blade of her rubber machete. The theatrics were cute, but this only confirmed what Zazie and Rhyon said in the mall: Fallon was just as nervous about hearing the results as she was. Avi wouldn't take the bait today.

Rhyon snatched the phone to see the comment for herself. "Oh, she tried it." She leaned in, her raspy voice lowering an octave. "I say we get some of that tasteless stool softener and pour it in that bottle she's always carrying around."

Avi looked at her incredulously. "You wanna mess with her drinks?"

"Not enough to hurt her," Rhyon laughed. "Just to make her shit herself in public."

"No. We're not doing anything. They can have each other for all I care."

"Now you know you don't mean that," Zazie said, shaking her head. She thought for a second and then snapped a finger in the air. "Let's banish her! We just need an apple, mint leaf, a skewer and . . . somethin' else. I have to double-check the book."

"Banish her like how?" Rhyon asked, intrigued.

"Just like away from Avi," Zazie said. "What?"

"You're the one who told me not to let her get to me, so that's what I'm doing. Let it go."

Rhyon shrugged before delving into questions about the spell. Avi went back to her food. She was trying to keep her thoughts positive, but taming her imagination was tough. What did Fallon want with Quincy? And would he respond? Avi and Quincy didn't have any type of relationship, so it wasn't like he would be in the wrong. She had no right to be jealous, and it was more than apparent that he wasn't interested in her, anyway.

The first-period warning bell rang three minutes later, to Avi's relief. She stood, clearing her plate. She'd much rather stress about schoolwork and the *Cliff News* column contest than ever hear Quincy's and Fallon's names together again. Avi discarded her trash, adjusted her backpack, and followed two students dressed as crayons scurrying out the door.

"IF THERE'S NO Care with our Tender Lovin', how are people gonna know who we are?" Zazie whined as they walked out of their last class at three o'clock.

"Z, you're all types of wrong," Rhyon said, squinting at her with folded arms. "*TLC* stands for their names and Avi's wearing yellow, which makes her T-Boz. I'm Chilli." She gesticulated at her loose curls and red tee. "Do you even know who you are?"

"Yes, I know who I am," Zazie mocked, waving her DIY condom wrapper in Rhyon's face.

Avi had decided not to go to the Cliff with them. It was just going to be people parading around in their costumes—she didn't want to accidentally miss the exact moment Egypt's email popped into her inbox.

She looked at her phone, shaking her head. "It's already three. I promise I'll meet up with y'all at dinner."

For the first time, Avi risked the "no phones during school hours" rule—not that her professors cared. The day was full of class-related movies and unscheduled study halls where they were allowed to socialize for entire periods. Avi appreciated the break from academics, but she couldn't help but peek at her phone every five minutes for an email notification that never came. It was nonsensical, considering Egypt told them the email wouldn't come until after three, but the need to be sure was compulsive.

Avi reviewed the formula on the back of one of her study notecards as she turned the key to her door, dropped her bookbag, and plopped in her saucer chair. She figured if she distracted herself with the fear of failing tomorrow's Algebra II test, her nerves over the forthcoming news would settle. At least for a moment.

Just as Avi began reviewing her third notecard, the familiar ping of a new email rang simultaneously from her phone and laptop. Notecards flew in the air as she dashed to her desk.

Avi maximized the screen and clicked on the first notification, subject line, "*Cliff News* Category Winners." A picture of a girl with butterfly locs popped up first. The caption under her face read, "Brittany Baker, advice column." Avi scrolled quickly past the faces of the student sports, popular culture, and Briar highlights winners. Three more faces smiled at Avi before she saw it—Fallon's enlarged school photo. She tried to scroll more, but there was nothing left in the email. Avi deflated a little more every time she reread the caption "Fallon Walsh, creative-writing column."

No matter how badly she wanted to, Avi couldn't will the words to change, and the sight of Fallon's face soon became nauseating. She squeezed her eyes shut, resisting the immediate urge to cry as her chin dipped to her chest. If she'd just gone over her work one more time before turning it in, maybe things would be different. If she'd taken the time to put her nerves aside and really cozy up to Egypt like Belle suggested, maybe it would be her face and name being announced as the column winner. But it was too late for any of that now. All the worry, preparation, late nights, and stress had been for nothing. Everyone who had rooted for her would soon know it, too.

Avi wondered how disappointed her friends and family would be. It couldn't compare to how she felt about herself. Like the weight of her fallen heart held lead straps to every inch of her insides. The feelings came in crashing waves hitting like a repeated slap to the face.

Her father's face flashed in her mind. His undying support and belief that she could be the best. Her mother's hope that she would someday follow in her footsteps. Avi dreaded telling them. The idea of facing anyone right now was unbearable.

Minutes later, three soft knocks on the door startled Avi back to reality as she lay on her pillow.

"It's me," Belle's voice purred from the other side of the unlocked door.

The door creaked open as she walked in, still dressed as Normani from the "Motivation" music video.

Avi looked away, despising the look of pity on her sister's face.

"Are you—"

"How do you already know?"

"I ran into Cori at the Cliff," she said, keeping her voice soft, despite Avi's harsh tone. "Rhyon said you were here waiting on the word."

"I got it." She bit her bottom lip to stop the quiver.

Belle took two steps toward the bed and engulfed her sister in a hug. Avi accepted her touch at once, laying her head on Belle's chest. She inhaled deeply, picking up soft notes of cream from their mother's signature perfume.

Avi's exhale was audible. "I know it's stupid to be this upset over something as silly as a school newspaper. I just thought . . ."

"It's not stupid," Belle said firmly. "You put your everything into that story."

"And I still wasn't good enough." Avi leaned back, casting her eyes away from Belle's. "I can't take the pity in your eyes," she said, hugging her knees to her chest.

"Avi, I don't pity you . . . I pity that paper. I pity that Egypt didn't see how great you would've been."

"Well, that's obviously not the case. I could've—"

Belle held up a hand, and the look on her face made Avi fall silent.

"I can see what you're about to try and do to yourself. But, Ellie, the truth is, that sometimes things just don't work out. It's not always a legitimate call on your talent or your work ethic or your abilities. Sometimes, even your talent can't take you there when someone's pushing the door shut in your face, and sometimes you have to abandon Plan A and hope that Plan B or C will help you get to where you wanna be."

Avi shook her head. "That doesn't mean that I couldn't have done something better."

"Of course. There's always room for improvement, but you couldn't help that Egypt and Fallon were chosen for that fellowship last summer. You can't help that they became friends, and you can't help that friends tend to look out for one another."

Avi looked down at the chipped paint on her nails. "So you don't think I ever really had a chance at this?"

Belle took a seat on the bed, kicking her pink-and-white sneakers onto the floor. "I'm saying that you should consider every variable before you come down so hard on yourself. Look, I know for a fact that there were a lot of *Cliff News* club officers that liked your samples and *loved* your first column—I asked around. You were always in the running. But I did talk to Cori at the Cliff and the bottom line is, Egypt had the swing vote." Belle squinted at her, leaning in. "Do you get what I'm saying?"

Avi nodded. Logic told her that every word from Belle's mouth made perfect sense, but it didn't take away the sting of the outcome. Avi understood her sister's desire to give her a reason not to wholeheartedly blame her work and herself. But that didn't change the fact that she lost, and she needed time to learn to accept her failure.

Every day, Avi saw how committed Egypt was to her presidency. Upholding the *Cliff News*'s standard meant the world to her. On a personal level, Avi wasn't her favorite candidate. They all knew that. But if Fallon weren't qualified, it wouldn't be hers no matter what anyone thought. At the end of the day, if Egypt had truly thought that Avi's story was better, she would've won.

Hesitantly, Belle scooted closer, bumping Avi's shoulder. "What about us?"

Avi had almost forgotten about their fight, and she knew she didn't have the heart to keep it up. Belle heard about the column and literally rushed to her side. That's what mattered. It felt dumb now to have ever tried to push her away.

"I'm sorry for ignoring you," Avi said, holding her ladybug pillow pet to her chest. "You're right, I'm nosy—not Paisli nosy, but still. I couldn't help it when I thought something might be wrong with you. I don't know if you get what it sounded like, Belle. I would've tried to bust the door down if I had to."

Belle smiled, biting her lip. "I do know what it sounded like, but I promise we're good now." She held her right hand out, and Avi's eyes widened when she saw the glittering heart-shaped ring. "It's a promise ring. He was *so* sorry, but it was a huge misunderstanding. We both said things we shouldn't have. But I think he really loves me."

The ring was beautiful, but Avi was hesitant to believe that it was enough. "And what about you?"

"I loved him first," Belle said, staring at Avi. "Look, I get that you were worried, and I'm sorry, too. I shouldn't have treated you like that. But lately, it feels like you don't trust me anymore. You have to believe that I'm always gonna try to make the best decisions even if I mess up along the way."

Avi's head cocked to the side. "It's not you that I don't trust," she said meeting Belle's soft eyes. "I love that you're happy. And I do trust you. But Belley, I'll never not show up if I think you're in trouble."

"Me neither."

20

THE WORD PROBLEM in front of Avi made her want to scream. Instead, she scribbled nonsense to appear busy every time Quincy looked over.

Any feelings of betterment she'd gained from speaking to Belle vanished when she'd realized she was already two minutes late to her 4:30 tutoring session. Seeing Egypt in her purple Daphne costume on the way to the library didn't help.

To top it all off, when Avi reached their table, the first words out of Quincy's mouth were, "I usually cancel sessions after the five-minute grace period."

She looked at her watch—4:37 p.m.

Now, Quincy was becoming increasingly irritated with every incorrect answer Avi provided. The knowledge was there. They both knew that. But it was hard for her to pretend to care when all she could see was Fallon's smiling picture haunting the backs of her eyelids. She just wanted to sulk in bed.

With his back to her, Quincy dug through his bag for a new worksheet.

Avi took the chance to slip her vibrating phone out of her

black sweats. They'd been at it for half an hour, and she would only be a second.

There was a missed call from Grandma Rose—probably checking in about Avi's failure. And her group text with Rhyon and Zazie was going off.

She shot a quick text to quell their worries, only to find Quincy in his black Run-DMC Adidas sweatsuit, glowering. The gaudy golden chain swung, scraping the table between them.

"Sorry," Avi said. She stuffed her phone in her pocket and put pencil to paper, but the pressure of his glare stayed.

"You know I'm doing you a favor, right? The least you can do is not play around on your phone when my back is turned. And maybe even try when I put the worksheets in front of you." His nose flared as his voice hardened with sarcasm. "Or how about this. You could try showing up on time. That would be nice."

"I wasn't playing on my phone, and I am trying."

"Oh, really? Because I know what it looks like when you try."

"Yeah, really," she said, irritated. "And that was my first time being late. You're always late."

He leaned back, arms crossed. "I'm not the one who needs so much help."

"Quincy, I didn't ask you to tutor me. You offered."

"So that means you get to take advantage of the situation?"

Avi slammed her pencil down. It was hard enough right now not being curled up, hiding under her comforter. She didn't need his attitude. Balanced on the footrest on her chair, she met his full height.

"If you don't want to help me, I'd rather you say that, so I can find a tutor who isn't so bothered by my existence!" Avi threw the stack of worksheets in his face and hopped down from the chair.

"When did I ever say I didn't want to help you?" he asked, keeping up with ease.

"You didn't need to! It's obvious you don't want to be around me. You made three of our five sessions over FaceTime. You canceled on me four times last week, you avoid me on campus. And what was that stunt you pulled last week, trynna embarrass me in front of the whole class?"

"I wasn't trying to—"

"And now because I was two minutes outside your little grace period, I'm taking advantage of you?"

Ignoring the angry glances from Ms. Halgins at the librarian's desk, Avi stomped toward the first-floor staircase and swiped the ridiculous spiderweb decorations out of her way. Quincy's heavy footsteps clunked behind on the carpet.

"All right, I shouldn't have said that," he said, trying to reason now, "but what did I do differently than Blue in class?"

She turned sharply on the steps, listing his transgressions on each finger. "You called on me eight times. You made me come to the board when you knew I didn't want to, and then you tried to make an example out of me in front of everyone. Seriously, if you don't want to be here, it's not a big deal. There *are* other tutors."

Avi flew down the rest of the steps and entered the empty floor. There was nothing but private study rooms and overcrowded bookcases.

Quincy jogged to catch up and blocked her way into the

restroom. "It's not that I don't want to be here. I wouldn't have asked you to come if I didn't." His eyes pleaded for her to listen. "I want to be the one to help you, Avi."

She stood with her arms crossed over her chest, still hot. "Then I want you to be honest. I mean, I don't get it, Quincy." Her arms flapped up in exasperation. "You were sweet to me at first. Boosting my online work, walking me to classes, offering to tutor me. And then out of nowhere, you got . . . cold."

He rubbed the back of his neck, glancing around as if they were being watched. But the first floor was always the quietest, and given that it was Halloween, they were completely alone.

"I wasn't trying to make you feel some type of way. It—it's that . . ."

"What? You don't want to be around me?"

"No, I do."

"Why do you keep looking around like someone's watching us? You don't want people to see us together or something?"

Quincy pinched the bridge of his nose. "You're putting words in my mouth. I didn't say that."

"You're not *saying* anything." Avi urged him to continue with a hand, but he just stood there, unable to produce a coherent word.

She turned to walk away, but he grabbed her wrist.

"It's your brothers," he blurted.

"Huh? What does this have to do with them?"

Quincy looked at her incredulously, like the answer was hanging like a decoration from the ceiling between them.

"Can you imagine how mad they'd be if they found out I've been sneaking around with you?"

"Sneaking around." She squinted. "It's not like we've been hooking up. You're helping me prep for a test."

He shook his head. "It's the principle. I wasn't up front, so they won't see it like that. At least, Moe won't. Look, as long as I've known the twins, they've always been clear that family comes first, and now they're like my family, too. This would mess that up." He rubbed his forehead, like the stress of his guilty conscience would end him. "I convinced myself that helping you was innocent, and then . . ."

"And then we almost kissed," Avi finished.

She remembered everything Nevaeh and Belle said at the mall about bro codes and loyalty. The realization that his character flip really was because of the twins rekindled her anger. Why was this about them? She yanked her arm back out of his grasp, pissed.

"Fine." Avi shrugged. "I see no problem with how you're helping me, so let's stop sneaking around."

"What do you mean?"

"I mean, we don't have to do anything behind anyone's back." She pulled her phone out of her pocket. "Since this is such a moral dilemma for you and I couldn't care less, I'll post us on my Instastory right now. Better yet, let's FaceTime them!" She pulled up Moe's contact.

Before Avi could press *call*, Quincy snatched the phone out of her hand.

She gasped. "You *are* embarrassed to be seen with me!"

"You gotta relax!"

"I don't *have* to do anything," Avi sneered, backing him into a bookshelf as he kept the phone out of her reach. "Give it back!"

"Just hear me out. Please."

She lowered her arm slowly, adjusting her bright yellow shirt to cover her navel.

He took a deep breath. "Trying to kiss you was wrong."

"Because I'm their annoying little sister?"

"Because you came here that day for a tutor, not . . ." He swallowed. "I wasn't trying to make you uncomfortable, so I'm sorry about that."

Avi was confused. The last thing she'd expected was an apology for the almost-kiss that she'd wanted more than anything.

"Are you being serious right now?"

"Yes," he exclaimed. "I'm not supposed to see you like that."

"But you do?"

Quincy nodded, avoiding her eye again.

"I don't want that apology," she said, shaking her head, and concern etched his face. "You never made me feel uncomfortable. Not until you started being flaky and rude for no reason. And I did come for your help that day. But I'd be lying if"—she hesitated, trying not to lose her nerve—"if I said I wasn't hoping something more came out of it."

Quincy's eyes met hers, and the corners of his lips kicked up.

"I'm sorry for snapping at you like that. I don't know if you heard, but I was up for a column at the *Cliff News*. I put my all into it, but it still wasn't enough." She cleared her throat and bit hard on the inside of her cheek. "Anyways, I found out I didn't get it today, and—"

"Didn't get it?" he repeated.

"No, and that's why I was late." Before she could stop it, a traitorous tear fell down her cheek. She swiped it away with the back of her hand.

Quincy's voice softened. "I thought for sure that spot was yours."

"You read it?"

He shrugged. "You said you were a writer, and I was curious. Sci-fi is usually more my speed than fantasy, but I loved it. Plus, it was way better than any of the BS that usually comes from that column."

Avi laughed through her wet eyes. "You're just saying that because I'm standing here crying in front of you."

"I wouldn't lie to you, Avi," Quincy said firmly. "Look. After I realized who you were, it seemed smart to keep my distance. But that wasn't easy like I thought it would be. We like the same things, you're easy to talk to, and honestly, volunteering to tutor you was my way of getting your number.

"I liked spending time with you. I still do," he added. "But everything felt wrong after I lied to Moe about meeting up with you for our first session. I should've told you then that it would be better for you to find a new tutor, but I punked out and started canceling on you instead." He fiddled with his gold chain.

"And then when Blue asked me to teach. I thought it was a good chance to show you I was still trying to help. Avi, I swear I wasn't trying to embarrass you."

His eyes compelled her to believe every word that spilled out of his mouth. She felt herself softening.

"So, why'd you suddenly decide to text me this morning?" she asked.

Quincy shrugged. "I was up late working on a paper. And

then I checked my email and saw those photos Zazie took of us."

Avi smiled. "They came out so nice."

"And you looked pretty."

His words made her heart feel like a butterfly's wings were fluttering triple-time in its place. But any reply was stuck in her throat.

He bit the inside of his cheek. "Hey, I get why you're so upset. I mean, I've never been great with words, but even I can see your writing is special. I'm not sure what Egypt was looking for, but Avi, it should've been you."

Avi wasn't sure when she'd taken the steps to erase the space between them. She wondered if he was aware of the change in his dark eyes and how they lingered over her. Her eyes trailed down the features of his face. Seeing for the first time the healed scar on his forehead. Taking in his entrancing eyes. Appreciating the width of his nose and the fullness of his lips. She welcomed the spread of goose bumps across her chestnut skin as he tilted her head up with a soft touch to her chin.

The need to be nearer to Quincy and the fear of losing her nerve made Avi lean forward. Her breath hitched when their lips finally brushed. And she heard the sigh as he gently pressed his mouth to hers. Heart thudding, Avi followed the natural urge to lace her arms around Quincy's neck and feel the heat rising from his skin. She reveled in when he wrapped an arm around her waist, pulling her closer. In this moment, Avi could have found comfort forever. She'd imagined his lips on hers a thousand times, but reality beat out her imagination in every way.

It was too soon when Quincy pulled back, but she opened her eyes to find the warm smile she'd missed on his face once again.

"Here," he breathed, bringing the phone up to eye level, an arm still resting around her waist. "Do what you want. It was stupid to lie in the first place."

Avi rubbed her thumb along the screen. What she did and who she did it with was no one's business but her own. It should be her decision to let anyone know about whatever this was between them.

As Avi moved to put her phone away, it lit with a text from Rhyon:

> We're at Preston, are you still coming?
>
> **RHYON**

"The haunted trail is about to start," Avi said. She looked up to find Quincy still staring intently and blushed.

He held her hand in his. "Let's go."

21

Song

Lovely, dark, and lonely one,
Bare your bosom to the sun,
Do not be afraid of light
You who are a child of night.
Open wide your arms to life,
Whirl in the wind of pain and strife,
Face the wall with the dark closed gate,
Beat with bare, brown fists
And wait.

By: Langston Hughes

Minor setback for a major comeback, honey. Blessings on your test. I know you can do it! 🤗

MOMMY

AVI PRINTED THE POEM her mother had sent and tacked it to her corkboard before resuming the newest battle with her hair. She, Zazie, and Rhyon had stayed up until five the night before—a decision they all regretted.

Avi threw the wide-tooth comb down in frustration and went for a hairband instead. Her perm rod set was dead. Eco styler gel and a high puff would have to do today.

Zazie yawned widely from her desk chair. "If they were gonna let us stay out past curfew, the least they could've done was make today a half day. Starting at noon."

Rhyon snorted from Avi's bed. "If you and Jah hadn't been making out behind Jackson Hall all night, you wouldn't be so tired in the first place."

"Sis, I'm smitten with him. And here's a fact: I *will* have his kids one day. It's laid out in the stars." She spun in the chair, cheesing. "Avi, you're gigglin' a lot over there. If I'm not mistaken, you did your fair share of kissing last night, too."

"Right," Rhyon teased, "Miss 'I'm at the library to study.' Please! I knew it was just a matter of time before Q cornered you."

"Well, you were wrong." Avi smirked. "*I* kissed *him*." The phone lit, and her heart quickened.

> Good morning :) I'm not gonna be in class today, but I know you'll ace the test 👍
>
> **QUINCY**

And then, another.

> I don't think I said it yesterday, but you looked really pretty 😍
>
> **QUINCY**

"That goofy look on your face is telling me that text isn't from your mama," Zazie said.

Last night at Preston's haunted trail couldn't have gone more smoothly. When Quincy and Avi arrived at the spookily decorated, dim-lit gym, they were still holding hands. They went their separate ways, but not before Rhyon, Zazie, and Kai, who had dressed as Dwayne Wayne in retro flip-up glasses, saw Quincy whisper in her ear. Avi sauntered over to Dwayne, and her Chilli and Left Eye, with burning cheeks. It was like she was floating through her favorite dream.

She answered Kai's quizzical look and Zazie's and Rhyon's knowing laughs with a smug shrug. They would all get their answers, but she didn't want to discuss it there and chance being overheard. Seconds later, Fallon neared them with an intent look on her face, and Avi knew she'd made the right decision. They headed into the haunted trail, blissfully drama-free.

Students and teachers alike dressed as clowns, purgers, zombies, and mad scientists to terrify passers-by in the five-minute trail.

After they exited, Kai pointed at Belle and Logan making out on a bale of hay, Belle in his lap, the two of them decidedly flouting school policy.

"I guess they made up," Kai said, disgusted.

Logan wore a New York Giants jersey and jeans as a costume—minimum effort. Professor Taylor, Briarcliff's Microbiology teacher, bustled over in her blue galaxy-themed Ms. Frizzle dress shaking a pile of small pink papers in their faces. "I don't care about your positions," she reprimanded them. "Anyone can get these detention slips. Got it?"

Avi didn't see Quincy again until someone from the yearbook committee asked them to join everyone dressed in a nineties costume and pose in front of the stage for a group picture. Quincy and her brothers came over in their Run-DMC costumes—along with half of the student body. She posed for the photo with Quincy's arm draped around her neck, indifferent to whether the twins noticed.

Their night was full of laughs and firsts, and Avi was sad when it was over. Her lingering fear that Quincy's feelings may have changed overnight dissolved when she read his messages.

She responded:

Thanks 😘 You looked handsome yourself, Dr. McClain

AVI

before throwing her phone in her bag and heading out for breakfast.

22

THE FOLLOWING WEEK, Avi sat in her room, sifting through her Briarcliff email.

Picking up litter on the side of the road this Saturday for three community service hours: *No thanks.* Trash. Join the Cosplay Club for Wednesday meetings at two: *Hard pass.* Trash. Poetry Writing Contest for High School Freshmen and Sophomores: *Why not?* Starred. From Professor Blue—two homework passes for scoring over 85 percent on the second Algebra II test: *Finally.* Starred and printed.

From Fallon Walsh: "The Forgotten Road"—Second Draft.

P.S.: Don't hold back on your critique.

Not getting the *Cliff News* column she'd coveted was a major blow. Not to mention heartbreaking. But they were training new editors, and Cori had reached out to offer Avi a position. It wasn't where she wanted to be, but her father talked her into it.

"So what if this isn't your first choice? It's an opportunity to learn more about a different aspect of the paper," her dad had said as she sniffled into the phone. "And who knows, maybe one day because you're so well-versed, you'll hold the title of president of the *Cliff News* or even your very own organization. Success often isn't a straight line, baby."

Her father was right, so she sucked it up and accepted Cori's offer as soon as she hung up. Avi knew she'd much rather be writing for herself, but she couldn't deny that editing other people's work with Cori's required keen attention to detail was helping her learn to better pinpoint problems in her own writing.

Lucky for everyone, Egypt missed more meetings than she made because of Harvest Queen pageant preparations. Things went more smoothly when she wasn't there letting off steam through her usual harsh critiques or reprimanding the staff for not working endlessly harder or faster.

Fallon remained a consistent, unbearable pain, but they both had to act professional at *Cliff News* meetings. After all, as nasty as she could be, Fallon hadn't made the pick. Still, Avi had plenty of reasons to hate her aside from the creative-writing column. Like hearing through the rumor mill that Fallon still had her eye on Quincy. Thankfully, "The Forgotten Road" was Avi's first and last editing assignment for the freshman creative column. Cori picked up on their bad blood soon after pairing them up. She promised to assign any of Fallon's future work to other editors.

But today, Avi had to get through it. She'd been sitting at her laptop for an hour and a half, consumed with edits. First she read the piece through, then she read it again penning suggestions of where the story dulled, where she was confused, or when there was too much telling and not enough showing. Avi was on her third pass when the door handle jangled and then swung open.

"Do you always have to be late?" Zazie huffed, exasperated. She rolled Avi away from her laptop, chair and all. Zazie was already in her Cookie Monster onesie, with a night scarf on her head. "C'mon! You said you were coming upstairs thirty minutes ago."

Every Thursday night at eight, almost every resident of Hollingsworth gathered to watch the newest hour-long episode of *The Beholder's Beauty* in the main lounge.

"Sorry, I lost track of time. Let me send this to Cori and Fallon, and then I'll be ready."

Zazie tapped her foot loudly as Avi ran back to her laptop, sent the email, and wrapped her fuzzy blue blanket around her before they ran out the door.

The busy lounge was ridiculously crowded. Students from every floor were in their nightclothes, wearing scarves, bonnets, and face masks. Bowls of popcorn and chips were being passed around as Housemother Lisa paid the pizza guy and RS Marjani passed out paper plates. Rhyon lay across a bunch of blankets close to the TV, laughing with Thalia and Ashia.

"Where were you?" Rhyon asked as they took their seats. "The show's about to start."

"Editing an article," Avi said shortly. She pulled out her phone, scrolling through her screenshots. "Did you guys see this email from the BP Study Abroad Department?" She held her phone to them at full brightness. "A ten-day study abroad opportunity in Amsterdam for Briarcliff and Preston freshmen. It would be this summer, and we'd stay in a student hostel, learn about the language and culture, see incredible sights. They're picking fifteen Briarcliff freshmen." She put her phone down to count on her fingers. "All we have to do is get one recommendation letter from a professor, write a one-page paper on why we want to go, and pay a five-hundred-dollar deposit. Everything else—the room and board, food, etc.—is paid for by the school or alumnae donors. I forget which. And then we'd just need spending money."

"I'm in," Rhyon said without batting an eye.

"Five hundred dollars," Zazie exclaimed, drawing some looks. She lowered her voice, leaning in with a shake of her head. "It sounds cool, but that's a lot to ask from my dad."

Avi hadn't considered that. Her own parents would probably say yes as long as she had all the details. Sophomore year, Belle went to Haiti for a week, and last spring, she studied abroad in Paris.

"It is," Rhyon piped up. "But look at it this way. You charge, what? Forty dollars a head for braids? Do hair three days of the week and average one or two customers in those three days? You'd have the money in a month, tops!"

A shadow of a smile crossed Zazie's face.

"And that can be your spending money," Avi said, getting excited again. "I bet if we went around to teachers and faculty to wash their cars or babysit, they'd give us fifteen or twenty dollars here and there. The deposit's not due until late April."

"I'm not washing a car for less than thirty dollars each," Rhyon said, moving to flip her hair back before remembering it was tucked under her bonnet.

Avi rolled her eyes, turning back to Zazie. "What do you say? Are you in?"

Zazie's mouth moved from side to side as she thought. "I'd honestly much rather see Sierra Leone or Singapore."

"But," Rhyon urged.

“I’m in. Let’s do it!” Their excited squeals dissolved into laughter as Rhyon’s foot shot out and landed in a bowl of sour-cream-and-onion dip.

They were still laughing when Easlyn flicked the lights for silence and Housemother Lisa raised the TV’s volume. The show was about to start.

23

A TEXT LIT AVI'S PHONE as she strolled through the campus store's small hair-care section looking for her favorite leave-in conditioner. It was a reminder from Belle to be in the Angelou Auditorium by 1:45 p.m.

Since making up with Belle on Halloween, Avi had resumed her position as a full-fledged member of Belle's pageant team.

Be there in 20.

AVI

Avi huffed at the sad aisle of hair products, resolving instead to use some of Zazie's leave-in conditioner tonight. She sauntered over to the books and magazine section, running her hands over used copies of *Kindred* by Octavia Butler, *Odd One Out* by Nic Stone, and the most recent editions of *Sesi* magazine before looking closer at some of the newer releases. Avi picked one up, flipped the pages, and held it to her nose, inhaling the newness of a different story.

"Wow. You really just did that," said Quincy's bemused voice from behind her.

Avi jumped, a hand to her chest. "Where did you come from?" She snapped the book shut and held it behind her back like a stolen good.

He smirked as he approached her, and her shock eased. The days of awkwardness and avoidance were over. It was nice for Avi to finally relax around him. She was no longer worried about whether she was trapped in the sister zone or if they would ever be able to exist as friends.

"I saw you through the window," Quincy laughed. "You smelled that book like how they do in movies. I didn't know that was a real-life thing people do."

"Well, they do. Or at least I do."

She hugged the book to her chest and tried not to make her next deep inhale so obvious. Quincy always smelled so good, like laundry right out the dryer. He looked good, too, in his hooded green Helly Hansen jacket and black jeans. The heavy saxophone case he'd been carrying rested by their feet.

"You do it, why?" he asked, tugging the book out of her grasp and scanning the cover.

"I dunno. New books smell good to me."

"Okay." He nodded slowly. "And do you only buy the ones that smell good, or do you commit to buying them as soon as you've smelled them?"

"Ha-ha," Avi said, snatching the book back. "I'm gonna see if Cori will read it, too, so I can have someone to talk about it with other than strangers online. I think she mentioned liking dystopian before."

She walked toward the register with the book open to the author's biography. Quincy followed.

"You have to go to rehearsal today?" Avi asked, nodding toward his sax.

Last week, Belle had mentioned that the alumnae running the pageant were searching for students to perform during transitions. Wanting to stand out, Belle took it upon herself to volunteer EJ (who gladly took any opportunity to be onstage) and Quincy (who didn't mind).

"Yeah," Quincy sighed. "But they said rehearsal wouldn't be so long today. I was stuck in that auditorium for three hours yesterday. I forgot a cut appointment and had to give dude a discount." He shook his head, grieving the money lost. "You're going?"

Avi nodded and held up her violin case and a takeout bag. "Two of Belle's strings popped on her violin, so she's borrowing mine. And I'm bringing her a salad."

"Okay, we'll walk over together."

"Next," Lonnie said from the second register. She was a voluble girl on Rhyon's modeling team, and she always let Avi use her 10 percent discount.

"Hey, Lonnie," Avi said as they neared her station. "Just this book today."

Quincy wandered toward a spinner display full of key chains, pens, and gift cards, while Avi dug in her purse for her wallet. She held out the cash and found Lonnie looking at her with wide eyes and a suggestive smile.

"Is this the boyfriend people have been talking about?" she asked in a loud whisper.

As if Quincy wasn't feet away with perfectly functioning ears. Avi felt the heat in her cheeks at once.

"Will you lower your voice?" she said through gritted teeth. That was a conversation Avi and Quincy had yet to have, and the last thing she wanted was to come off as too eager. Even if she was. "No, he's not."

Lonnie mouthed *Sorry* as she bagged the book.

"One sec," Quincy said then before brushing past her toward the book section.

He showed no signs of having heard Lonnie. *Thank God.*

Avi took her receipt and waited at the door. Seconds later, Quincy came back holding a copy of the book she'd bought and walked to the register to make his purchase.

"If you wanted to read it, I would've let you borrow mine," Avi said as they exited the store to a mild breeze. She used her free hand to zip her bomber jacket halfway up.

Quincy tapped his finger to his head. "But if I read it at the same time as you, you'll have someone to talk about it with."

She hooked her arm through his free one, grinning up at him.

On the day of the Algebra II test, Quincy was waiting outside of Valintino to walk Avi and Rhyon to their next class. He'd done so every day since. His days were busy between cutting, tutoring, school, and now the pageant, but he was still making time to see Avi. It didn't go unnoticed.

Over the past couple of weeks, they'd discussed everything with one another. She learned that his favorite color was green, he could script the entire *Bad Boys* movie from memory, loved anime, played as a centerfielder on the baseball team, and—like Avi—he'd never been in a real relationship. She was glad to hear that he, his grandma, and his two younger siblings lived in an apartment building in District Heights, not too far from her own home. Quantrell, his little brother, was the same age as Paisli and Antonio and "a lot smarter than Quincy"—his words. And Quinn, his adorable seven-year-old sister, was the little girl missing her two front teeth on his lock screen.

They were passing through the shortcut behind the library when Quincy suddenly said, "So, I heard what the cashier said back there."

Avi stopped abruptly, cursing Lonnie in her head.

"I haven't been going around saying that," she blurted. "People talk, and rumors spread fast. It's like when people were saying me and Kai were going out until he started dating Crystal."

"Whoa, whoa, whoa," Quincy said with a laugh as he sidestepped two girls walking toward them on the sidewalk in tan Girl Scouts vests. "I just wanted to know . . . if you—well, what you thought about that."

If Quincy's skin weren't so dark, Avi would have seen the blood rushing to his cheeks.

She tightened her grasp on the violin case as she walked forward.

"Oh. It's not something we've talked about, and it would be weird to rush it. Right?" Avi chose her words carefully, but she still couldn't help feeling like she was stumbling over every syllable. "But I kind of like where we are right now."

Quincy nodded, seeming to digest her words as he held the door to the auditorium open.

Avi continued, "Later, if a title comes, then it comes."

"And how do we know when it comes?"

She turned to face him standing in the center of the Briarcliff crest on the carpet in the lobby. "When you ask me, of course."

Belle poked her head out of the middle double doors then, and their heads turned. "What are you guys waiting for?" she asked. "I'm starving. Come on!"

24

PAGEANT REHEARSAL was in full swing in the Angelou Auditorium. People ran here and there carrying costumes, makeup palettes, props, and sound equipment. Lamont, the rude junior who'd bothered Rhyon and Avi at the beginning of the year, sat on the steps of the stage with a microphone dangling from his hand. Dancers for the opening number stood onstage reviewing steps as one of Briarcliff's dance professors, Krista O'Jackson, clapped out three eight-counts to the beat of the loudspeaker. Rhyon whirled jovially in the first row, having the time of her life and seemingly oblivious to Lamont's unblinking stare.

"I asked you to stop twirling that microphone, Mr. Rodriguez. Master of ceremonies or not, you break it, you buy it," Jessica May said into her megaphone. Ms. May, the alumna director of the scholarship pageant, looked as stressed as the contestants as she barked orders in every direction.

"Let's try the yellow light for the opening dance instead," she shouted toward the soundbox. "And where are all of my talent transition acts? Oh, there you are! I have exciting news for you all, so don't leave rehearsal without speaking to me first. Okay, Professor O'Jackson, two-minute warning for your dancers! Contestant number four, your talent's up first. Five minutes! C'mon, people, let's move with purpose. The twenty-first is what? Two days away! We should be running like a well-oiled machine by now!"

Avi sat in a row near the back, tuning her violin while contestants Journey, Addison, Bailey, and Egypt filed up the aisle looking weary. Avi avoided Egypt's eye. Just yesterday, Egypt had bitten her head off in front of everyone for not turning in edits for the pop culture column. Avi triple-checked for the email Egypt swore she sent—then it turned out that Egypt had forgotten to assign Avi the column in the first place. An apology never came. What Avi did get was a curt email from Egypt with the pop culture column and two additional articles to be edited by the week's end.

As the door closed behind the contestants, Belle ran up the aisle half-dressed in her talent look.

"Is it tuned?" she asked, her voice frantic. "I didn't know I'd be called first."

Avi nodded and wiped a glob of ranch off her sister's cheek.

"You're a doll," Belle called, already running back toward the stage with her violin and bow in hand.

Rhyon jumped off the stage as Belle passed and plopped down into the empty seat next to Avi. Her hair bounced in a high ponytail and the back of her gray tank top was soaked.

"Sheesh. They're workin' y'all," Avi said.

"Not nearly as hard as the contestants," Rhyon breathed. "I don't know how they're keeping up. There are two dance numbers, plus the opening, the talent portion, the evening gown portion, and the questions—and they all have to look perfect while doing it. Nevaeh said she's been backstage since eight this morning helping Belle with everything. And this May lady is relentless; breaks are rare. I guess the twenty-thousand-dollar scholarship will make it worth it for the winner, but I don't think I could do it. At least not without my mom's glam squad."

Lamont walked center stage then to announce Belle, but he had to repeat his line four times before Ms. May approved of the way he said "applause."

"You didn't notice Creepy Eyes staring at you while you were dancing?"

Rhyon shook her head, annoyed. "I did, but maybe if I ignore the jerk, he'll get the hint."

The lights dimmed in the auditorium as EJ and Quincy exited backstage and took their seats in front of Avi and Rhyon. Belle's performance started slowly with what sounded like a mournful ballad before the background instrumentals of "Brown Skin Girl" began to play. And then, she killed it. Stagehands paused in their tracks to watch as Belle turned on the charm, playing her little heart out on the violin. The small choreography she'd added worked beautifully, and Avi knew it would get the crowd hype the night of the pageant.

When the song ended, Belle bowed, and the look of exhaustion returned to her face. She scurried to the edge of the stage speaking in rapid whispers to Ms. May.

When the lights flickered on, Avi rolled her eyes at the sight of Lamont sitting on the opposite side of Rhyon.

"Your sister's losin' it," EJ said, turning to face them in his seat. "You should've seen her yesterday. We were backstage, and she was laughing at this video I showed her. I turned my back for one second and boom, tears! Like for real boo-hooing."

"Why?"

"Absolutely no reason," he said in a hushed voice, like Belle might overhear him from the stage. "A minute later, she was on the phone fighting with Logan about something stupid."

"But it's not just her," Rhyon added. "Most of them are one lopsided eyebrow away from a full breakdown. I'm not going back there again."

"Me neither," Lamont chimed.

"I can't see anyone beating out her talent, though. She'll definitely win," Quincy said.

"Belle doesn't lose," Avi replied. "It's not her thing."

Lamont leaned forward in his seat. "I dunno. Egypt's spoken word about police brutality was pretty moving."

"Yeah, I guess I didn't hate—"

"And Bailey's dance is sexy as hell," he interrupted. "Rhy, did you see it yet?"

Avi hated Lamont being around almost as much as Rhyon did. He was so pressed to impress her that it was hard for anyone else to get a word in. And by far, his favorite person to cut off was Avi.

Rhyon's expression was suddenly severe. "Only my friends call me Rhy. Don't do that again."

EJ didn't disguise his laughter. "I see what Moe means about you now."

Avi narrowed her eyes between Rhyon and her brother. She was about to ask what he meant by that when they heard

Ms. May's megaphone. "Thirty-minute break, people," she announced. "And I mean *thirty minutes*. I want everyone back and ready to work at three o'clock on the dot."

Belle emerged from backstage again minutes later in baggy pink sweats. Without a word, she sat down, curled up next to EJ, and within seconds it looked like she was fast asleep on his shoulder.

"Q," Rhyon called. "Avi, Zazie, and I are applying to the study abroad trip in the Netherlands this summer. Have you gone anywhere with Preston yet?"

"Nah. And I don't plan to."

"Why not?" Avi asked, leaning forward.

Quincy turned to face her. "I'm not gonna willingly walk into a flying metal casket. I'm good off that."

"What about—" Avi began.

"I went to Iceland last spring break," Lamont said with a raised voice. "And this past summer my parents flew my fam out to the Hague for a week." He placed a hand on Rhyon's arm. "I'd be happy to tell you anything you need to know before your trip."

Rhyon moved her arms to her lap, not bothering to look at him. "I'm good. You're not the only one with a family that travels. Obviously."

Avi touched Quincy's shoulder, and he turned again. "Don't you wanna visit Jamaica one day and see all the places your grandma talks about?"

"Eh, maybe one day. But my pops said the flying caskets they use to get to the islands are even smaller."

Avi rolled her eyes. "I get that, but I still think Amsterdam is gonna be fun. Rhy, did you already start—"

But as if on cue (for a third time!), Lamont cut clear through Avi's question with one of his own. "Rhyon, did you know the Roman Colosseum is only a short—"

"Ease up, man," Quincy said, facing Lamont. "You're not the only one talking."

There was a stunned, awkward silence as Lamont held two hands up in playful defense. As if he hadn't been aware of what he was doing. "My bad."

Belle sat up from her phony nap, looking impressed as she met Avi's eyes.

Quincy nodded toward Avi, urging her to continue.

"Um, oh right. Rhy, did you start your application yet?"

Avi was too busy staring at Quincy to hear Rhyon's long-winded answer. Or Lamont's attention-seeking response.

Where did this guy, sweet as all get out and somehow . . . aware of how I feel, come from?

It wasn't until Avi noticed EJ glancing between the two of them that she was able to pull her gaze away. If EJ hadn't known something was up before, he knew now. The look on Avi's face made it plain as day.

AROUND FIVE, rehearsal came to an end. The guys snuck out an hour earlier, but not before Quincy handed Lamont one of his barber cards, saying, "Make sure you come see me before the pageant. I wanna get your fade straight." The remnants of the torn card lay balled up on the auditorium floor.

Later, Avi walked down the steps of the stage carrying her laptop and Belle's makeup bag. She spotted Rhyon near the back of the auditorium. Lamont was cornering her, and she looked ready to strike. Avi quickened her step.

"I said no," Rhyon growled.

"It doesn't make any sense." Lamont laughed sourly. "Look, I promise I'll show you a good time. Give me your number." He placed a hand on her hip.

"Hands off," Avi said as she reached them. She took the arm Rhyon was readying to slap him with and pulled her out of his grasp.

"Understand *this*," Rhyon snarled. "Even if I *were* into guys, you *still* wouldn't be my type. Okay? You repulse me." She pushed him out of their way, pulling Avi along as they walked out of the auditorium together.

"Do you think telling him that was enough to get him off your back?" Avi asked when they bounded down the steps to the lamp-lit sidewalk.

Rhyon shrugged and stuffed her hands in her coat pockets. Quietly, she said, "It's the truth. It should be enough."

Avi looked at her, shocked, but said, " 'No' should have been enough."

She hadn't known. How could she not have known?

"Well, maybe that's not the complete truth," Rhyon corrected. Her voice broke off in a whisper. "Bi would probably be more accurate."

"Okay."

"Okay?" Rhyon asked.

Avi nodded, looking her firmly in the eyes.

Rhyon tightened her arm around Avi's, exhaling deeply. Arm in arm, the two headed toward Hollingsworth.

25

FAMILY, FRIENDS, AND STUDENTS poured into the Angelou Auditorium for the scholarship pageant as the doors opened. Avi peeked from behind the purple velvet curtains to see Moe in the crowd fiddling with his camcorder. Noemie, Crystal, and Kai sat beside him on their phones, while Fallon stood a row ahead, recording a video with the Cheetahnaires in their matching "Belle 4 Queen" shirts.

Nevaeh pulled Avi back to the dressing room. It was full of pageant contestants and their people, plus Ms. May, who fussed into a headset. Avi and Nevaeh were Belle's people, helping with outfit changes, hair, makeup, pep talks. The whole nine.

Yesterday they gave the biggest pep talk so far—Zazie, Nevaeh, and Avi convinced Belle that her hair in its natural state would make a grander statement onstage. For the pageant, at least, Belle would rid herself of the flat irons and any additional heat damage.

Now, Avi stood in the busy dressing room, doing makeup flash tests as Nevaeh applied a soft body shimmer. Eyes closed, Belle attempted to steady her breathing and squeezed a blue lace agate crystal in her hand, as if it was her last hope. The sound of Lamont's irritating voice, welcoming the crowd and introducing the judges, couldn't have been helpful.

Before they knew it, the voices of Headmistress Malone and Jessica May rang in the mics, and a resounding "ding" echoed over the backstage intercom. Belle and the other contestants jumped like they were on fire, rushing to their positions and stretching in place. Three minutes to showtime.

Nevaeh and Avi watched backstage as Zazie snapped pics of the crowd and the judges' table until the curtains rose. She swiveled her camera, and the crowd turned their attention to the contestants and dancers frozen onstage.

The opening was phenomenal and had the crowd hype immediately. In no time, Belle was done with her intro, and Avi's throat felt raw from cheering.

The dressing room was now somehow even busier. The air held a competing mix of fragrances, sweat, and burnt hair as the girls changed outfits, warmed up, and rehearsed for the talent portion.

Nevaeh changed Belle's lipstick color while Avi used a ridiculous number of bobby pins to secure a curly ponytail to her hair. The harshest of hurricane winds couldn't make it budge.

Egypt paced behind Belle's station in a stunning monochromatic red suit, Dawn following with a blush palette. She would pause, consult her notecards, and murmur variations from a line of her spoken word, only to resume it all again a moment later. They heard Lamont introduce EJ, and the beginning notes of his cover of "Godspeed" by Frank Ocean came over the intercom. Mid-pace, Egypt's clacking heels came to an abrupt stop.

"That's not the song we agreed on," she shrieked, crumpling the card in her hand. "What is he doing?" Egypt demanded, whipping around.

Belle shrugged, looking deadpan as she glanced up at Egypt's reflection. "I don't know. But it's gonna be tough to follow that, huh?"

The silence, accompanied only by EJ's faint background singing, seemed to last a lifetime as Avi glanced from Egypt's enraged glare to Belle's calm grimace. The breath the dressing room collectively held was broken only by Nevaeh's sad attempt to hide her laugh with a cough. Looking as though she was about to erupt, Egypt shot out the room with Dawn on her tail.

"Why did EJ change his song?" Avi asked, placing spare bobby pins on the cluttered counter.

"He just *told* Egypt he would sing that negro spiritual she chose. We're shakin' the table a little."

Nevaeh snickered, "She was so pissed," with her head thrown back.

Avi took a seat in a free fold-out chair, her brows knit together. "What would he lie for?"

Belle's eyes fluttered. "The girl got in my face yesterday goin' on about how she's gonna crush me in this competition, and I don't take kindly to threats. Plus, I heard about her freaking out at you in that meeting. He's upstaging her on purpose."

Avi's eyes went wide.

"Don't worry about it. She's not playin' this clean either. Listen out for the Q-and-A."

After Egypt stumbled through her spoken word, a freshman girl did a short comedy stand-up before Addison's acrobatic routine. Then there was a baton twirler before Journey performed Taraji P. Henson's infamous bathroom monologue from *Hidden Figures.*

Belle was fine-tuning her white violin when Avi heard Quincy McClain being announced to the audience. With all the fuss of the day, it had completely slipped her mind that Quincy would be performing as a transitioner. Avi jumped from her chair and sprinted from the dressing room to watch from the wings.

A small smile played on her face as Quincy graced center stage in his well-fit brown blazer, button-up shirt, and jeans. The stage lights glared off the body of his sax as he raised the mouthpiece to his lips.

The notes were mellow, smooth, and sultry. It reminded her of the jazz they'd grown up listening to.

"It's 'Sara Smile,'" Belle whispered from behind. "I knew it would be the perfect opening when Q suggested it. He's good, right?"

That's an understatement, Avi thought. Watching Quincy play the sax was enticing. So much so that she was tempted to walk directly onstage. Too soon, it was over, and Avi was left gripping the curtain, praying that Moe's camera hadn't missed a single note.

Quincy walked offstage to applause, smiling broadly. "You liked it?" he asked tentatively, placing his sax in its open case.

Avi rose on the balls of her feet, placing her hands on either side of his face as she pressed her lips to his. "I loved it," she said when they broke apart.

Quincy's shock dissolved, and the corner of his mouth kicked up deviously. "If that's what you're gonna do, I'll play for you whenever you want."

She blushed, but out of the corner of her eye saw Belle's doe-eyed expression and Nevaeh's hands clasped over her heart.

"I forgot we were being watched," Avi began. Just then, Lamont ran between them and onto the stage with his microphone poised for a joke.

Belle pushed her shoulders back, phasing into her stage persona.

". . . Now please, let's give a warm welcome to contestant number four!" Lamont announced.

"Good luck," Avi whispered to her sister's back as she strutted onto the stage. Avi looked back to Quincy, moving to wipe her lip gloss from the side of his mouth. His warm hand wrapped around her waist, pulling her back to his side.

Belle met center stage in her tan thigh-high boots, matching corduroy skirt, and white off-the-shoulder sweater. The music began, and in seconds, the auditorium was on their feet.

Nevaeh tapped Avi's shoulder, suggesting that she and Quincy take their seats in the crowd. The only thing left was helping Belle get into her evening dress, and Nevaeh could handle that.

Avi led Quincy to the second row, where the crowd was settling down.

"Where did y'all just come from?" Moe asked as they took their seats.

"We ran into each other after his performance, and I told him there were empty seats out here with you guys. Problem?" Avi asked as she shimmied out of her black faux-leather jacket.

Moe looked past Avi to Quincy, who nervously said, "That's pretty much what happened."

It was obvious from his expression that Moe wasn't ready to let up. But before Avi could come up with a different distraction, Crystal touched her hand, whispering, "Cute shoes. Delia's Boutique?" After a moment, she felt Moe's uninterested eyes slide from her face.

The evening wear and question portion began as soon as Bailey finished dancing. Egypt glided onto the stage in a shimmery green form-fitting gown. Any confidence she'd lost from Belle and EJ's little stunt was back in full force as she gave an exceptionally well-informed, almost rehearsed-sounding response to Lamont's question about climate change.

Addison left near tears, realizing too late that she'd misunderstood her question.

During Journey's short answer, Quincy leaned toward Avi. "I wanna tell them tonight."

"Why?" she whispered, confused. Fallon glanced back at them, forcing Avi to fix her face.

"Because they should know. I think E already does."

Avi rolled her eyes, annoyed. "They're gonna try and ruin everything." Right now, it was just them, and Avi was enjoying the clarity of it all. It almost felt as if her brothers' inevitable bad reaction would sour them. "It's none of their business."

"—contestant number four, please come to the stage."

"You're the one who was gonna tell M on Halloween," Quincy said. *"'Better yet, let's FaceTime them,'"* he said, taking on a falsetto as he mimicked her.

Avi glared. "That's because you were pissing me off."

"—can we please have Belle LeBeau to the stage."

"Look, M already knows something's up, and I'm sick of lying about it. Avi, what are we hiding for?"

Her mouth opened and closed again. She wouldn't allow her brothers to hand out blessings or denials on her behalf. This was her decision to make, and she was happy with it. "I guess it doesn't—"

"Ladies and gentlemen, thank you for your patience," Lamont said into the mic. "I'm receiving word that contestant number four, Belle LeBeau, has dropped out of the running for this year's Harvest Queen Scholarship Competition. If contestant number five is ready, please come to the stage."

26

CONFUSED BABBLING broke out across the packed stadium as Avi scrambled out of her seat. In the hallway, with Kai, Quincy, and her brothers on her tail, Nevaeh marched toward them.

"What happened?" Avi asked.

"I was coming to ask you," Nevaeh said, running a hand through her hair. "After she came offstage, I helped her into her evening dress and took pics to send to your mom. She got a call and said she was gonna step outside because the dressing room was noisy, and then I heard the announcement when you guys did."

"She didn't come back for her clothes?" Kai asked.

Nevaeh shook her head.

"Was she upset when she left the room?" Moe asked with his arms crossed over his chest.

"No, she was happy to hear from them." Nevaeh took her phone out, saying she was going to call Adoree to see if Belle had come back to their dorm.

Rhyon, Zazie, and Vannah found them in the hall then, and Kai filled them in.

The phone rang twice in Avi's ear before heading straight to Belle's voicemail.

Avi turned back to her brothers. "She must've turned her phone off. I know it was charged."

"Our texts aren't delivering, either." EJ exhaled worriedly.

"Housemother Joyce said she didn't see her come in the building," Nevaeh said.

"Let's go check," Vannah said, already heading down the hall with Nevaeh. "She doesn't see everything."

None of this made sense to Avi, and the looks on Kai's and the twins' faces confirmed this was downright strange behavior for Belle. She'd wanted to win so badly. Rehearsed endlessly. Paused her involvement in Cheetah Plans and even let Vannah take over practices for the Cheetahnaires—all so she could focus on winning this pageant. Something terrible must have happened for Belle to up and quit without saying a word to anybody.

Avi scanned the faces around her, and it was suddenly apparent who was missing.

"Did any of you see Logan tonight?"

Everyone shook their heads.

"It's weird that he wouldn't be here to support her, right?"

Kai shrugged. "Yeah, I guess, but he's been swamped lately."

"Maybe you guys can check his dorm and see if she's there," she said to the twins. "Kai, Quincy, can you guys go check Preston's grounds, maybe the gym? The Cheetahnaires practice in their studio sometimes. Rhy, Zazie, and I can check the Cliff, our dance studio, and the senior benches."

They all went their separate ways to search for Belle. But

to no avail. After checking the Cliff and dance studio together, Avi, Rhyon, and Zazie split up to cover more of Briarcliff's grounds. Avi searched all the senior benches, the main student lounge, the chapel, the Cliff again, and even the locked doors of multiple office buildings just in case. After an hour, she found herself back at the auditorium during the judges' deliberation to search.

Avi was nauseous with worry, cold, and her toes ached in the stupid booties Belle had forced her into hours ago. She decided to go back to her dorm, put on a heavier coat, and change into flats before meeting up with her brothers again. They needed a new plan.

Avi was reading Moe's text saying that Logan was still nowhere to be found when she looked up to see him sitting on a bench adjacent to the closed Starbucks kiosk. He held his phone to his ear in one hand and a ruffled bouquet of roses in the other. Belle might have fully accepted his apology, but Avi still wasn't so sure. She'd been almost certain Logan had pushed her that day at the mall, but Belle swore she must've tripped. It wasn't like Avi went out of her way to avoid him, but their paths didn't naturally cross, and she was fine with that. But tonight she couldn't think of anyone else who'd have a better idea of where Belle might be. She took a deep breath and double wrapped her thin scarf around her neck before crossing the street.

Logan jumped out of his seat. "Avi," he said, and his breath fogged the air.

"Hey, um . . . You haven't talked to Belle, have you?"

He shook his head, concern etched over every inch of his face. "I've been looking for her everywhere. Someone told me she dropped out of the pageant, and now her phone is off. I checked the parking lot and her car is still here, but I can't . . ." He threw his arms up in exasperation. "Is she okay?"

Avi's shoulders slumped at his words. She couldn't still the tremor in her voice. "We can't find her either. I don't get it. When I left her backstage, everything was fine." She wiped at her nose with a gloved hand. "You haven't seen her at all tonight?"

Logan shook his head. "We got in a stupid fight before the pageant, and I told her I wasn't showing up. But that was a shitty thing to do to her, so I got these roses. Then by the time I got to the auditorium, Professor Lovette said she'd quit. I thought she was with you guys and ignoring me."

"She's not. We can't find her anywhere." A tear fell from Avi's eye and to her surprise, Logan pulled her into a hug.

"It's okay. I promise we're gonna find her, Li'l LeBeau." He held her at arm's length. "I'm gonna go check my dorm again. I gave her my spare key; maybe she's there."

Avi nodded, wiping her eyes clear. His hug—his words—were surprisingly reassuring.

"Here," Logan said, handing Avi his phone so she could put her number in. "Please, let me know if you find her first. And keep your head up, sis." He patted her arm once more and jogged off toward Preston, bouquet in hand.

Avi watched Logan disappear behind a corner and wondered if she had misjudged him after all. For the first time since they'd met, he seemed genuine and truly human to her. Not like he was hot on the campaign trail. She'd be sure to tell Belle how nice he'd been when they found her.

Avi scanned herself into Hollingsworth and walked down

the steps to the ground floor. She called Belle, but it went straight to voicemail again, and she jabbed the end button in frustration. She searched through her recent calls, thinking it was time to call her parents back. Maybe Belle had already called them.

Avi raised her keys to the door, but it was already cracked open. Zazie texted less than three minutes ago to say they were back in the auditorium, so it couldn't be her. With a finger, Avi cautiously pushed her door open wider, hearing sniffling coming from her side of the room. The powder blue comforter was lumpy, and a burgundy velvet fabric peeked out on the carpet below.

Avi sighed in relief and sunk to her knees by the edge of the bed. This close, she could hear her sister's quickened breath and sobs clearly.

"Belley," Avi whispered. "What happened?"

Belle gasped in a breath after every few words, trying to control her crying. "I'm so tired. I can't handle the high expectations"—*hiccup*—"and judgments from everyone anymore. I try so hard and still disappoint the people I love."

Avi pulled the cover off Belle's head to see a mix of tears and snot streaming down her face onto the sheets.

"I promise no one's mad at you. Everyone was really worried when you ran off like that. Why did you turn your phone off? I thought something bad might've happened to you."

"I didn't want to talk to anyone"—*hiccup*—"after I let everybody down like that. I thought you'd come back to your room."

"No one's let down," Avi repeated. She wet a washcloth in

their sink and helped Belle sit up, wiping her face. It was then that Avi noticed a purpling bruise on her sister's upper arm.

"I was rushing out of the back exit of Angelou and"—*hiccup*—"hurt myself," Belle said before Avi could ask. She leaned down with her face in her hands. Hair flyaways flew in every direction. "This dress is so tight."

"Why don't you take it off?"

The sound Belle made was somewhere between a laugh and a sob. "I can't reach the zipper."

Avi helped her out of the dress and texted her brothers, friends, and Logan to let them know Belle was okay. After a short conversation with their parents, Belle took four Tylenol PM and finished Avi's box of Cheez-Its. Then she was out. She slept through Tuesday classes and didn't leave Hollingsworth again until it was time to make the drive to Sugah's for Thanksgiving break.

With everything going on, it would be nice for them to get away from campus, even for a few short days. They could all use a break.

27

FOR THREE DAYS, they'd been in near bliss at Grandma Sugah's. Everything about the bright green house made Avi feel happy and at peace. The small but bursting vegetable garden in the front yard and the wraparound porch. The long yellow patio swing they'd carved their names in years ago. More tiny Black Jesus figurines than any of them could count. The shrine in the living room honoring Uncle Morris. The endless number of family portraits, random photos of Barack Obama, and purple, green, and gold NOLA decor lining the wall. And a cleanliness that only a grandmother could achieve.

The best part, of course, was being back in Grandma Sugah's presence. She was an intuitive woman with a radiant spirit, smooth rich black skin, and silver locs swinging down her back.

Avi hadn't realized just how much the "go-getter" vibe of the campus was affecting her day-to-day until she was back in the calm of her grandmother's house. But as much as she wanted to focus completely on resting before midterms began in the coming weeks, she couldn't completely let go. Not if Belle couldn't.

After days of Belle's detached attitude at Sugah's, she still refused to divulge the real reason she'd dropped out of the pageant. Avi knew her sister well enough to know that being exhausted wasn't the only reason. Belle spent most of their Thanksgiving break up under Sugah, helping her cook, tending to the garden, watching game shows. None of that was necessarily out of the ordinary. But Belle was also off social media, neglecting her vlog, and abandoning her phone for hours at a time.

What stood out the most to Avi was how Belle was going out of her way to ignore Logan's calls, texts, emails, and DMs. Since they'd left campus, he had even texted and called Avi several times. Each time, Avi did as she was instructed and told him Belle was busy . . . cooking . . . dancing . . . sleeping. Whichever lie came to Belle's mind first.

Avi tried to push answers out of Belle, under Quincy's suggestion, but no one could completely ignore and evade a person like Belle could. When Avi shared how kind Logan was the night of the pageant, Belle grumbled something about him being "a real Prince Charming" and made a flimsy excuse about needing to sweep the kitchen floor. Moe couldn't get her to talk about that night and neither could EJ—which was strange. Not even Antonio could coax out an answer, and she was typically the softest with him.

Eventually, Avi relented, taking Sugah's advice: "Go on and let her be. But don't stop being present."

Saturday came, and the sisters sat on Sugah's yellow front

porch swing, lounging comfortably in oversized sweatshirts. It was a breezy November day; the shy sun peeked from behind gray clouds onto the carved pumpkins in the front yard. Avi leaned against her sister's shoulder, rereading *The Everlasting Rose* as Belle stared intently at her laptop, editing an old violin cover. They heard a ball bouncing incessantly and a series of shouts about fouls from the backyard. Uncle Jovahn and the boys must have started a new game.

Suddenly, Belle snapped her silver laptop shut and spit, "I'm breaking up with Logan."

Avi closed her book, sitting up to face her. "Really?"

Belle nodded grimly.

"But I thought you said you loved him."

"I do—and I won't stop right away—but I'm learning that sometimes that's not . . . enough. Things got complicated fast. I wasn't ready."

Avi tilted her head to the side. "And he's not worth the complication?"

Belle didn't answer right away. She stared dead ahead at a bare oak tree, fiddling with her box braids. As a breeze shifted the leaves on the ground, Belle took a deep breath and said, "It's hard being with someone when everyone thinks they're God's gift to the earth. Especially when you've seen the real them."

"I only know he was never *that* great in the first place," Avi said with a snort. "I mean, yeah, he had his moments, but there was something in his eyes that day at the mall I still can't shake."

"What do you mean?"

"It was the way he looked me dead in the eyes after I

interrupted your fight. Like he was trying to force me to feel a way I didn't want to." Avi shook her head. "When I've done something shameful, it's always hard for me to hold eye contact." She shrugged. "I don't think he should have been able to look me in the eyes that day."

"That's because you're a good person," said Belle.

Avi's brows furrowed.

"Not that he's not," Belle added quickly. "It's just . . . you're right about that. He shouldn't have been able to look you in the eyes that day. Me neither, honestly."

"Maybe you can't tell, but I pay just as much attention to you as you do me," Avi said flatly. "I don't care how many times you say it. You're not like him."

Belle nodded, but disbelief lingered in her eyes. She leaned down, resting her head in Avi's lap. "I'm gonna do it when we get back."

28

AVI SAT ON THE BED in Aunt Naima's old room typing up her analysis report of Rhyon's pick for English 9, "Catch the Fire" by Sonia Sanchez. They were set to leave tomorrow afternoon, and Avi had left all her schoolwork to the last minute. Still, she was anxious to get back and see Zazie and Rhyon. It had barely been a week, but after three months of being with each other every day, this time away from their little family felt odd.

Belle sat at the desk, sympathizing as Paisli whined nonstop on her screen. Their mom was on a flight and she and Avi were standing in.

"You don't even get how bad it was! I was watching the whale show, because you know they're my favorite, and then when I stood, blood had stained my new white leggings and we were all the way at the touch tanks before Akari, of all people, told me," she sniffed.

Avi's head snapped up, "Akari, that girl you like?"

"No, the other Akari, Avi," she said sarcastically. "It was *so* embarrassing!"

"Hmm. Someone's snippy today."

"Pai, I'm sure Akari understands," Belle said gently.

"She wouldn't have *had* to be understanding if *somebody*, who I was with *all day*, had said something *first*," Paisli said, turning to glare at Antonio.

"Well, excuse me for not staring at your butt!" he shouted off-screen. "I gave you my brand-new jacket to cover yourself, didn't I?"

"After I begged, Tony!"

Avi's phone dinged with a text beside her just as they heard Moe yell, "What the hell, Avi?" from Jovahn's room next door.

told him. He's unhappy

QUINCY

She braced herself as he stormed into the room, followed by Kai (who looked like his favorite show was about to begin).

"Gotta go, Pai," Belle said.

"No, no! I wanna hear him yell at—"

"Who said it was okay for you to talk to Quincy, Avi? Is this why you've been blasting 'Sara Smile' on repeat for the last couple of days?"

"I did." She shrugged coolly. "And it's a great song."

He shook his head. "How long?"

"Only since Halloween, Moe. Can we be done now? I have a lot of work to do, and I don't have to explain myself to you." She grabbed her phone, but Moe snatched it out of her hands.

"No! We can't! Avi, you're practically a baby. I wanna know why you think it's okay to hook up with one of my friends. And why is everyone so calm about it?"

Belle rolled her eyes. "Calm down, Moe. They're not 'hooking up.'"

Moe's head snapped up. "Oh, so you knew, too?"

"Of course! And we didn't tell you because it's Avi's business, right Kai?"

Kai faced Belle slowly in open-mouthed disbelief.

Moe shot him a look of disgust before spinning around to EJ, who was standing in the doorframe. "E, this doesn't piss you off?"

EJ looked exasperated. "Aye, I don't wanna get in it, but it's not like Q's a bad dude, and she was bound to start dating eventually, M. Plus, you're trynna talk to . . ." His voice trailed off as he realized his mistake with scrunched eyes.

"To who?" Avi asked, sitting at the edge of her chair.

"Vannah," Belle offered.

Moe glared at his twin.

"My bad, man."

"If you can talk to Belle's friend, I can talk to yours," Avi said smugly.

"No!" he barked. "This is about you and my *old* friend. End it."

Avi chuckled, shaking her head. She knew Moe would try to make this all about himself. "Look, I dunno if you know this or not, but you're not Daddy. You can't tell me what to do."

"Yeah, I thought you'd say that." He nodded cleverly, pulling his phone out of his blue joggers. "We'll let him handle it."

Avi sat back on the bed, turning her attention to her homework.

"What's up, MJ?" their dad said cheerily from his screen.

Moe walked over to Avi, forcing her into the frame, too. "Pops," he said confidently. "Avi's dating Q."

He was only quiet for a beat before saying, "Yeah, I already know about their little situation. But I thought she said they didn't have an official label on it yet."

Avi snapped a picture of the exact moment Moe's smug expression fizzled. Under Belle's advice, she'd told her parents that she and Quincy had begun talking the day after they got to Sugah's. Her father wasn't as thrilled for Avi as her mom was, but they both agreed that he was a "nice young man" and told her to make good decisions. They'd talk more when they all returned for Christmas break.

When their father hung up, it was Avi's chance to show off as Moe exited with a new stony-faced resolve.

"I'm making this picture of you my new screensaver!" she said, laughing.

WELL AFTER MIDNIGHT, Avi took a break from writing her study-abroad essay to get a drink. She walked into the kitchen, where Moe sat eating an overflowing plate of Thanksgiving leftovers. His angry eyes stayed heavy on her as she opened the fridge and poured a glass of cranberry juice at the kitchen island.

"Do you wanna talk about it or no?"

Moe stabbed violently at the macaroni and sweet potatoes on his plate.

"Fine," she exhaled. "But don't blame Quincy. He always wanted to tell you. I asked him not to."

"Don't worry. I blame you."

Avi sat at the opposite end of the table, facing her brother.

"What's so wrong with us getting to know each other?" she

asked hesitantly. "If he was some jerk who dogged girls, or if he was disrespectful, I'd get it. But that's not Quincy. What's the problem?"

"You!" he said, and his fork clattered against the plate. "You're gonna find a way to get your feelings hurt because that's what you do. You build up how great things will be in your head, but you never prepare for the letdown. That's exactly what happened when you didn't get that column."

Avi grimaced.

"It doesn't help that you're soft."

"I am not," she said in an injured voice.

"I meant sensitive, Avi." He finally met her eyes. "You wanna care about everybody and stick your nose in people's business. Caring about people means caring about their problems."

"It's called empathy. Why don't you try it out sometime?"

"Quincy has real problems that you can't fix," he said seriously.

"I never said I wanted to fix all his problems."

"Not yet. There's too much shit going on in his own life you still have no idea about. He wouldn't even have the time to give you the attention you deserve." His eyes dropped back down as he moodily pulled the slice of cheesecake he'd been saving for dessert closer.

She leaned forward in her seat, beckoning his eyes. "M, whether you like it or not, Quincy says he likes me, and I *really* like him. I think it's sweet that you care because I honestly didn't think you did. But if you try to ruin this for me, I'm going straight to Daddy."

He folded his arms over his chest, looking as stubborn as a mule.

"Seriously, Moe," she whined. "Even EJ's being cool about this. For once, don't be an asshole and try to talk him out of it."

He took a long swig from his drink before grumbling, "Fine. Imma be watching the both of you."

Avi smirked, rising from her chair. "You do that."

"Do something stupid with him and I *will* find out," Moe called as she jogged up the steps. "By the way, I'm not talking to Vannah. But I am gonna ask Rhyon out when we get back next week."

Avi lost her footing, tripping up the steps.

29

FRESHMAN-YEAR MIDTERMS took a toll on Briarcliff students (and their sanity) as Christmas break slowly rolled nearer. School administration took steps to help students cope with the stress of exam season by extending library hours and adding open yoga classes in the gym. The Hollingsworth RSs even offered daily silent study breaks where they handed out fruit, coloring books, and crayons. Still, most students found ways to cope on their own.

Rhyon's Starbucks addiction kicked into hyperdrive, making her constantly jittery despite the bags forming under her eyes. YouTube mukbangs emerged as her saving grace during each of her scheduled ten-minute study breaks.

Zazie's coping method involved the constant muttering of positive affirmation mantras and obsessing over her plants. The accompanied overwatering resulted in the early demise of Tootsie Roll the Fiddle-Leaf Fig and a twenty-four–hour mourning period in which Zazie forced her floormates to participate.

Avi was an anxious ball of nerves, bringing her study guides, cards, and notebooks everywhere she went. Her daily consumption of chocolate Turtles and cream soda sky-rocketed, and she took random power naps wherever and whenever she felt even slightly overwhelmed.

The night before her last midterm, Avi asked Quincy to meet her and Zazie at the food truck Preston stationed in the Lion's Square for the week. Briarcliff offered students a food truck, too, but it was a plant-based option that didn't feed her craving for junk in this stressed-out state. Right now, she was in the mood for fried Oreos topped with powdered sugar.

Waiting in the long food truck line, they spotted Hazel, the junior girl Rhyon admittedly crushed on, sitting feet away on a bench. Her girlfriend sat on her lap, gesturing wildly in conversation.

"I see what Rhy means," Zazie whispered. "The girl is fine."

Hazel was Blasian, with a stunning white smile, absurd jawline, and wavy hair in a top knot with a crisp undercut.

Jasiri looked at Zazie with raised eyebrows.

"What? I can't make an observation?" She laughed, leaning into him.

"She is really pretty," Avi agreed, looking curiously at the girl's undercut. She wondered if Quincy was her barber, but turned quickly when Hazel's girlfriend caught her staring. "I wish she was single," she muttered, thinking of Moe's comment about Rhyon.

Rhyon was picky and rarely admitted interest in anyone, so Avi was shocked by her reaction when she'd tried inconspicuously to ask if she'd say yes if Moe asked her out.

Her lips had gathered at one side as she considered. "I don't know if I'd say yes, but I definitely wouldn't say no."

"Huh?"

"Why, did he say something?" she'd asked, lifting an intrigued brow.

Avi wondered if Moe would make good on his threat.

She felt a finger poke into her side and giggled like the Pillsbury Doughboy, whipping around to see Quincy carrying his backpack and a beat-up barber's case.

Avi hugged Quincy, pulling him to the side before he had a chance to greet Zazie and Jasiri.

"How was M today?" she asked tentatively.

Quincy and Moe's relationship had been rocky since Quincy admitted the truth about him and Avi. This left EJ to play referee in the room they all shared. Avi wasn't thrilled to be the reason for the tension.

"Still pissed that I lied but he doesn't *hate* me. Aye, I'm feelin' this hairstyle," he said, changing the subject. He stretched random out-of-place strands from her poorly done bun and watched them coil up again. "What's it called?"

"You think you're funny," she said, swatting at his hand. "It's called the 'midterms are kicking my butt, and I haven't had time for myself' look."

Quincy gave her a slow once-over. "You look good to me."

Avi blushed, glancing unbelievingly at her Dunder Mifflin sweatshirt and pink thermal leggings. It was a sweet lie to tell.

"Speaking of midterms," he continued, "are you done yet?"

"Nope. I have Women's Studies tomorrow and then I have to start packing because we leave on Saturday. Do you think we'll get the chance to see each other during winter break?"

"If you wanna see me, let me know and I'll be there. But I'd like to see you tomorrow, too."

"I'm free after three. You wanna meet at the Cliff, or—"

Quincy shook his head "No. I meant we should link off campus."

Her head tilted to the side. "Oh. Like a date?"

"No. Not *like* a date. A date. We can catch a movie in Atlantic Station. And I don't know how to, but there's an ice-skating rink set up if that's something you're interested in."

Belle always spoke of how beautifully Atlantic Station was decorated for the holiday season. Christmas decorations, restaurants, ice skating—the whole nine.

"I'd love to go on a date with you, Quincy."

Avi watched as her favorite smile spread across his face, melting her insides.

"I'm late for a tutoring session with a new student, so I have to run. But I'll call you tonight?"

Avi nodded, her smile just as bright as his. He leaned down to kiss her cheek before jogging off.

30

WOMEN'S STUDIES PROVED to be the hardest of Avi's midterms by far. Thirty-five multiple choice. Ten short answers. Five paragraph-long responses.

At three o'clock, the class filed out, handing Professor Akwi their exams as she smiled pleasantly, saying, "Have a beautiful break." As if she hadn't just done everything in her power to take them out.

Back in the light of the cold December sun, Avi checked the Briarcliff app on her phone, assuring that her campus leave tonight was approved by her parents and Housemother Lisa.

Avi and Zazie saw Rhyon off to her dad's place in Atlanta before heading to their nail appointments in Rashad Hall with a sophomore named Taylor. Easlyn swore by her talent as the best gel manicurist on campus. Typically, the roommates would prefer to paint each other's nails, but these were special circumstances: Avi's first date and Zazie's first dinner with Jasiri's family.

With less than an hour before she needed to meet Quincy, Avi held the curling iron to her head with one hand and scrolled through her Instagram feed with the other. There was a boomerang with her mom and Godmommy Char posing in the lobby of their office. A picture of her cousin Bryce and his boyfriend gazing into each other's eyes. Thalia's newest freshman council flyer for next semester's feminine product fundraiser. Fallon in her Cheetahnaire uniform, executing a flawless toe raise. And then a new picture of Belle posted by Logan.

Weird. Avi was with Belle last night after she finally gathered the courage to end things with him after two tries. According to Belle, he'd been dejected and wouldn't say much, but had nodded an "okay" when she asked if they could still be friends. So why would he post this off-guard picture from a date almost two months ago?

> **@Logan__Walsh22:** The past few months with you have been nothing short of perfect. I wouldn't trade what we have for anything. Through our fights, disagreements, good and bad times, you've stayed by my side. I know now that I would never have to think twice about you having my back. The future can only bring greatness on this ride together. I'm proud to be stuck with you forever 😍 💍

The comments overflowed with sentiments like "You two are perfect together," random love-related emojis, and one that read "I knew you two would work it out" from @FallonReigns.

Avi accidentally grazed her finger on the blazing plate and shrieked, startling Zazie, who was on the phone asking last-minute questions about Jasiri's family.

"Are you okay?" Zazie asked as she jumped from the bed.

She was fully dressed in an olive-green pinafore dress and white knit sweater.

Avi waved her hand frantically, nodding toward the phone. "What does that look like to you?"

Zazie scanned the caption. "It doesn't sound like a moving-on post."

Belle picked up after the third ring, her hair disheveled as she squinted at the bright screen.

"What's up?" She looked over at the clock on her bedstand. "Shouldn't you be heading out for your date? Your hair isn't done. And what are you wearing?"

"That pink corduroy skirt I took from your closet last week, a white long-sleeve scoop-neck top, and my beret. I'll send you a pic when I'm dressed. Hey, did you see what Logan posted?"

"No," Belle said, rubbing crust out of her eyes. "What is it?"

"A picture of you with a non-break-up-y sounding caption."

Belle paused the call and Avi heard her loud exhale after a moment.

"When did you guys make up?"

"We didn't. He's being difficult." Belle's face reappeared, looking indifferent. "Don't worry about this, okay? I'll handle it. Finish getting ready and have fun."

"Okay," said Avi hesitantly. "Are you sure you're good?"

"I'm fine. Focus on you and be ready when the final shuttle comes to pick y'all up, or they'll suspend your privileges and give you detention at the start of the spring semester. I gotta go, but don't forget to take a first-date picture. They're super important!"

"I guess it's not a big deal?" Avi shrugged, turning back to Zazie.

"Maybe? The hopeless romantic in me is like, 'Aww he's fighting for their love.' But at the same time, she seemed pretty serious about breaking it off. Maybe he should respect that?" She grabbed the hot iron from the desk. "Here. I'll curl the rest for you."

31

QUINCY AND AVI strolled up a sidewalk of Georgia's Winter Festival, sipping hot cocoa and stealing nervous glances at one another. When she'd met Quincy in the lobby of Hollingsworth, he proposed a change of plans, having heard of the festival from some upperclassmen. Avi promptly agreed, making sure to change the destination in her app to inform Housemother Lisa and her parents of her new plans.

The festival was far better than Avi could have ever imagined. Sparkling lights dangled between light poles and twinkled on fir trees. A live band played on a round stage as a sultry woman in a Chaka Khan wig crooned "Santa Baby" into her microphone. Small children ran about, joy lighting their eyes as they waited to tell Santa this year's wish list. In tents stationed around the park, vendors sold trinkets and snacks like frosted sugar cookies, chocolate treats, and eggnog. The only thing missing was a dusting of snow.

Everything was so perfect, Avi didn't even mind the overwhelming number of their schoolmates among the crowd of locals and college students.

Side by side, they exited one of the handmade holiday jewelry tents, and Quincy asked, "So, when do I get to read the rest of the story?"

"I stopped reading that so I could study for midterms. Are you almost finished?"

"What? No, not the one from the bookstore. I meant your short story. You never said what you were gonna do with it next."

"Oh, that," Avi said airily. "After I didn't get picked, I still felt like I had no choice but to finish it. So, I did."

"What do you mean?"

"The characters in my head sometimes feel so real that I have to get them out. It's like they don't belong in there anymore. I was always planning what would happen next and dumping ideas in my notebook." She gazed over at couples cozied together on log benches, watching *It's a Wonderful Life* projected on a big screen. "Anyways, I ended up finishing the next seven-ish installments. It's really bad, but it's resting peacefully, unedited, in the top drawer of my desk."

Quincy's left eyebrow arched. "And you're okay with no one ever reading it?"

"Finishing is how I made my peace with it." She shrugged. "But you can read it if you'd like."

He took another sip from his cup. "I would. And maybe other people would, too. You could try a blog or that fan-fiction website my brother's always on. . . ."

"Wattpad?"

"Yeah, that," Quincy said, snapping his fingers. "More readers."

Avi smiled at the idea as they inched toward a loud crowd of people watching a high-energy game of musical chairs. She hadn't given her short story much thought since she finished it. But maybe Quincy was right. The *Cliff News* wasn't the only way to reach an audience.

"I'll think about it," said Avi. She smiled at his skeptical look. "Really, I will."

The watching crowd burst into laughter then at the sight of a little girl in a pink peacoat pushing a guy in a Morehouse varsity jacket off a chair to secure her seat at the end of "Jingle Bell Rock."

Ten minutes later, Avi found herself in a competitive game of reindeer ring toss. They'd watched the first raucous game together, and when the attendee asked for volunteers, Quincy shouted Avi's name, pointing wildly at her until the small crowd around her also urged her on. By chance and sheer luck, Avi was the first to get five rings around her reindeer's antlers and was awarded a palm-sized white teddy bear key chain.

"I'm impressed," Quincy said, his bottom lip sticking out amusedly as they exited the tent.

"That I won?"

"Yeah! I've known you have no real coordination ever since you almost fell out of that chair at the library."

Avi went to push his shoulder, but Quincy caught her gloved hand mid-swing. In one move, he'd interlaced their fingers and positioned himself in front of her on the sidewalk.

She was always so caught off guard by the intensity of his dark eyes. Before him, she hadn't known that black eyes somehow possessed the power to be as electric as the brightest shade of green. It was alluring. Disarming.

Quincy looking at her like this sent chills down her spine that had nothing to do with the dropping temperature. It was like she was the only person around, even in this crowded park. Like she was the only girl who could hold his attention. She wanted to be. It had been almost a month since they spoke in the bookstore about making their relationship official. Back then, Avi was unconcerned about a title. But now, when Quincy stared at her like this, she couldn't help but wonder what he was waiting for.

Avi took a step forward, inhaling the smell of peppermint heavy on Quincy's breath.

He held her wrist, watching the rose gold "A" charm dangle. "You wear this a lot, huh?"

"Only every day."

"Hmm. And it goes with your skirt," he said, brushing a hand against her hip. "I like pink on you."

Avi looked up at him, her head cocked to the side with a smirk. "What? Are you trynna make me blush?" she teased.

He shrugged. "I like it when you smile."

She felt like she could almost see the question forming on his full lips when a voice cut so bluntly into the moment she thought she would scream.

"Well, isn't this cute."

Avi whipped around, already irritated. Of all the places Fallon could be, she had to be here. In this very park. Making a conscious choice to interrupt them.

She approached wearing a leather jacket, sweater dress,

knee-high boots, and a sly smile. Avi silently dreamed of the power to close her eyes, click her boots three times, and wish Fallon away.

Instead, she forced a smile on her face. "What do you want?"

"With you? Nothing. I get to see you all the time," Fallon said as she reached them. "I came to say hey to Q. You know, he's a surprisingly difficult person to get an appointment with. But since I have his number now, I assume it'll be easier to keep in contact. DMs are always so messy."

Avi turned to look at Quincy and then back at Fallon.

"What's up?" he asked, sounding unsure.

"Quick question." Avi held up a finger to quiet Fallon's response. She scratched her forehead, saying, "Why do you have each other's numbers?"

"She's the new student I told you I was meeting up with for tutoring yesterday."

Avi bit the inside of her cheek, trying to force herself not to say the wrong thing. Yes, he'd told her about the new student, but omitting that it was Fallon felt intentional. She squeezed out a tight-lipped "Interesting."

"Yeah, it is," Fallon laughed. "It took *forever* to get our schedules aligned, but I was determined. I've had to teach myself the material for Chem all semester, and I got sick of it. But everything's good now. I don't know about you, Avi, but my reception to new information is *always* better when my teacher is easy on the eyes."

Quincy was at a loss for words, a bewildered look on his face as he looked between the two.

Avi crossed her arms. "What's your problem with me?"

"*Problem?* I dunno what you mean," Fallon said, looking

affronted. "We're friends. Like how you and Quincy are *just* friends. At least that's what you told me."

"I know what I said then. Now I'm telling you things have changed. So relax."

"Oh, so you guys are official now?"

"That's none of your business."

Fallon chuckled. "I'll take that as a no. If I were you, I would get on it. It'd be a shame if someone snatched him up while you were dragging your feet." She reached out to touch Quincy's arm, but Avi smacked it away.

"Watch it, LeBeau," Fallon said, a finger pointed at Avi's chest.

"Watch yourself."

The smug smile crept slowly back across Fallon's face as she looked at the silver watch on her wrist. "I gotta get back to Stephan, but we'll chat later. Maybe tonight, back in Holli. Q, I can't wait to start our sessions up again after winter break. But watch your phone. I may text you before then."

Avi watched with narrowed eyes as Fallon scurried across the street, handbag swinging at her side.

"Damn." Quincy whistled. "That's wild, 'cause she was really nice yesterday."

Avi turned on him, her voice sharp. "Why didn't you say you were tutoring her?"

"I didn't have a choice, Avi. *She* went to Professor Ivy, and I was assigned to her. And you never told me this thing between you two was that serious," he said defensively.

"Well, it is. That girl is poison. God, I can't believe I let her egg me on like that again." Since that day at the mall, she'd been better about not getting into it with Fallon, letting all her slick comments in *Cliff News* meetings or class go in one ear and out the other. But now she was crossing a line.

Quincy placed his hands on her shoulders. "Okay, it looks like tutoring her is gonna be a problem, so I'll request to be taken off her case. Easy."

Avi shook her head, arms crossed stubbornly over her chest as she pouted. "It's fine," she lied. "I don't mind."

He scoffed at her sad attempt at maturity. "She mentioned you like five times yesterday. I should've known somethin' was up."

Avi evaded his eyes, but he touched a finger to her chin, taking her hand in his. "Hey, that was one thing. We still have the rest of the night, okay?"

Avi nodded and let Quincy lead her toward the round stage for the start of the light show.

She could pretend like Fallon never happened. Go on as if their perfect night had no hiccup. Avi shook her head, washing that part away.

The area by the stage was crowded, but Quincy snagged two seats near the front. Children sat on their fathers' shoulders, and to Avi's left, two Preston guys giggled with their heads together. When a festival photographer asked to take their picture, Quincy placed his arm on the back of her chair. Avi leaned into his chest, watching as the presenter ran onstage, urging crowd participation for the show.

"When I say, 'whatdayathink' y'all scream, 'Do it, Bobby K!'"

Two seated blurs, sharing a kiss on the opposite side of the stage, caught Avi's eye. They were far away, and she was still fairly new to contact lenses, but there was something undeniably familiar about the couple. Avi blinked hard, attempting to focus her vision on them.

Smiling, Quincy leaned forward. “Is that Moe and Rhyon?”

THE TWO COUPLES stayed after the show ended. Avi knew it was bound to happen, but she at least thought Rhyon would tell her.

“He didn’t call until after I left,” Rhyon said. “I went home, showered, got dressed, and met him here only like thirty minutes ago. I was gonna tell you tomorrow.”

Their conversation had gone better than Moe and Quincy’s.

“What the hell?” said Moe. “You said you were taking her to a movie. What are you still lyin’ for, man?”

Quincy rolled his eyes, stuffing his hands in the pockets of his jacket. “Nobody lied. We were, and then Jerome told me about this festival, and it was a better idea. And didn’t *you* say you were taking Rhy ice skating?”

Moe sighed. “I was . . . and then I ran into Jerome.”

Now, Avi and Rhyon stayed in their seats while Moe and Quincy walked across the field to a food truck selling burgers.

Rhyon snacked on popcorn, looking enraged as Avi told her about the encounter with Fallon.

“Oh, she’s tap dancin’ on the line!”

“Right,” Avi said grabbing a handful of Rhyon’s popcorn. “The worst part is that I thought he was gearing up to ask me to be his girlfriend before that walking, talking irritant interrupted us.”

“The night’s not over. Maybe he still will.”

She shook her head. "I'm having a good time, but the night's low-key tainted. I dunno, maybe he's not interested in making it official anymore."

"Maybe you should be a little more proactive," Rhy said, wiping her hands on a napkin so she could adjust the pearled strawberry brooch attached to her sky-blue cape. "If Hazel were single, I'd ask her out."

"What about Moe?"

"Oh, we're not serious. Like, we both think the other's attractive, but this is more of a . . . friendship outing."

Avi watched as the boys approached them, holding trays with their food. She considered Rhyon's suggestion. For some reason, it had never occurred to her to ask him. Quincy had made it clear that he was interested, and he'd brought up labels first—even asked her what he needed to do. What was the holdup?

Then again, it was only their first date. Was she rushing things? No . . . beyond the timing, something didn't feel right. Avi couldn't shake the feeling that there was something else holding him back.

32

BEING BACK IN MARYLAND felt like a dream. Avi realized how much she used to take for granted—the comfort of her full-size bed, being able to take showers without flip-flops, waking up without a blaring alarm. And not having to worry about someone stealing her clothes out of the dryer (other than Paisli and Belle).

At least it felt that way for her first two days back. Too soon, she found herself back on dirty-dish duty and their bathroom/kitchen cleanup rotation.

Days before Christmas, the LeBeau girls put the finishing touches on their tree as *Dr. Seuss' How the Grinch Stole Christmas* played on the TV. The electric fireplace roared behind its glass case as their mom tried to mediate Belle and Paisli's annual argument over which of their personal ornaments would be placed dead center on the tree.

The Grinch was modeling clothes in his mirror for the Whobilation when they heard the front door open and Moe's and Antonio's voices echoed in the foyer. Avi tuned them out as they discussed whose ball was the fastest at the batting cages. Until she heard Antonio ask, "Q, what's your position in the batting lineup?"

To Avi's surprise, Quincy responded, "Fourth."

She jumped up from the family room couch, skidded through the kitchen in her fuzzy fur socks, and regained her composure before turning the corner into the foyer.

Quincy paused while removing his jacket and smiled brightly when he saw her.

"Hey," he said.

"Hi," Avi panted. "I didn't know you were coming over."

She glared at Moe removing his boots.

"It was a last-minute decision," Quincy said. "But I wanted to see you since I was around your way."

From her peripheral, she could see a cluster standing in the kitchen. "It would be less weird if you guys just came out," she called.

Quincy's expression warmed when Toni, Belle, and Paisli rounded the corner. Avi wished she could wipe the cheesy grins off their faces.

"Quincy, it's so good to see you again," Avi's mom exclaimed as she embraced him in a tight hug. She held his face in her hands. "I hope life's treating you well. Did you like the care package we sent through the twins?"

"Yes, ma'am. Thank you again for that."

Belle was about to say something when Paisli stepped in front of her, extending a professional hand. Quincy smirked, taking it.

"I'm Paisli," she said with a devious grin. "Did you know Avi watches that video of you playing the saxophone before she falls asleep every night?"

Avi inhaled sharply as Moe snickered and Belle slapped a hand over Paisli's mouth.

"We're gonna give you guys some privacy," Toni said, throwing a stern look at her youngest daughter.

They retreated into the kitchen—except for Moe, who took a seat on the stairs.

"Can we help you?" Avi asked.

"He said he has something to give you. I'm curious."

The sounds of their mom reprimanding Paisli in the kitchen stopped abruptly. "Morris, find some business of your own or come unload the dishwasher now!"

"Fine," he muttered, standing. "I don't wanna watch y'all bein' gross anyways."

Quincy waited for the basement door to click shut behind Moe before asking, "Is there somewhere we can talk?"

Avi grabbed his hand and started toward the steps. "Sure, we can go to my room."

Hesitant, he pulled back, whispering, "You don't think that's gonna piss off your mom?"

"What? No. She likes you. Plus, we're just gonna talk."

"I don't want them to think . . . ya know."

"It's not that big a deal, Quincy."

"But it is," her mom's voice called threateningly from the kitchen again. "You better listen to him!"

She doubled back down the steps and grabbed her bubble coat from the open hallway closet. "Outside it is."

On the front porch, Avi wrapped her scarf around her neck and sat next to Quincy.

"It's nice to see you. I thought we'd get to hang out more over the break."

So far, Avi's requests to see Quincy had been met with responses about his father "being back" and "dealing with him." Whatever that meant.

Quincy cleared his throat. "Yeah, my house has been . . . hectic."

Avi pulled her knees up to her chest, leaning forward. "Everything okay?"

"Just another one of my dad's episodes. We're—" He paused, taking in her face. "What?"

"Nothing," Avi said airily.

"Nah. You got that look on your face," he chuckled, scooting closer to her on the step. "What's up?"

Avi considered her question for a moment, unsure if they were in the invasive-personal-question-asking stage of their relationship. Still, good friends tended to know personal things about each other, and they were more than that.

"I just remember you saying that your grandma raised you, Quintrell, and Quinn."

"Yeah."

"But you also said your dad is sometimes around, but not a lot. And you mention these episodes he has, but what kind of episodes are they? And you've never really said where your mom is either."

Quincy looked taken aback. He stretched his legs on the steps and stared toward the cars in the driveway.

"I'm sorry, that was a lot," Avi said. "I have easier questions. What's your favorite song right now?"

"No, it's fine," he said, though his smile was hollow. "You remember when I said I wanted to be an OB/GYN?"

Avi nodded.

"My mom, Cynthia, is the real inspiration behind that. She had a healthy pregnancy with Quinn, and when it was time, she went to the hospital. But there were complications. She had to have a C-section. Quinn was born healthy, but then . . . while my mom was in recovery, her blood pressure plummeted, her heart was racing, and my grandma said she was complaining of sharp pains in her stomach. It was eight hours before her doctors finally listened and took her back into surgery."

"Eight hours . . ." Avi repeated, her voice strained.

"Yeah. She was hemorrhaging; all the signs were there. She told the nurses something was wrong. And my dad begged the doctors to do something sooner, but by the time they acted, it was too late. They didn't listen, so she died on the operating table." Quincy cleared his throat again and ran a hand down his chin. The pained look on his face aged him.

"My dad never really recovered after she died. Clinical depression. He'd be in a room with us, but not really. He would only come back to me when he played the sax. I ended up loving it, too, but I only learned to play so he'd talk to me again. And he did. For a few weeks, he was back. Then one day he was on his way to work, and there was a bad car accident. The painkillers for his injuries were prescribed, but they made him feel better than the antidepressants ever did, so . . . he didn't stop taking them." Quincy shook his head, exhaling slowly with a fidgety hand on his chain. His eyes landed on Avi again, and she was surprised to feel his thumb swiping a tear on her cheek.

"I didn't— I wasn't expecting . . ." Her voice trailed off.

"But, happy endings." He shrugged. "We're good now. My grandma's got us, and I got them."

Avi nodded, but that level of responsibility sounded like it would have been enough to crush her. She didn't understand how he could bear it—losing two parents, even while one was still alive. It wasn't fair.

"I can't wait to see what you do in the field, Quincy."

"C'mon." He smiled, grabbing Avi's hand. He stood, and she followed. "I didn't come here to try and depress us both. Lighter subject," he said with an eyebrow cocked. "Do you really watch that video of me playing 'Sara Smile' every night?"

Avi rolled her eyes toward the cloudy evening sky to avoid Quincy's smug look. "I can't believe her. Paisli will say whatever it takes to get the attention she wants."

"So, she was lying?" he asked with a knowing smirk.

Avi barely suppressed a laugh. "You said you wanted to talk. What about?"

"Right. Right." Quincy dipped a hand in his olive-green coat pocket. "Do you remember what Fallon was saying on our date?"

Her face fell. "Ugh. I've been trying to erase the memory of her from that night."

"Yeah, but something she said has been bothering me."

Avi squinted, trying to remember what specific awful thing he was referencing.

"She asked if I was your boyfriend, and you didn't say yes."

"Oh," Avi sighed. Fallon's nasty comments about their relationship status (and "snatching Quincy up") rushed back.

"Well, we talked about it before and said we'd be friends until it felt right."

"And we text, talk, and hang out all the time. I think we got the friend thing down."

A smile began to stretch across Avi's face, but the corner of her lips fell. "Wait. I don't want Fallon to be the reason—"

"She's not the reason for anything," Quincy said, taking a step closer. "I took a minute because I needed to be sure. It's hard for me to let people in if I think they might up and leave. But I'm sure about you now," he said, nodding. Quincy looked nervously at her as he pulled a tiny velour box out of his pocket. "I was just waiting for this to get here."

Avi felt her heartbeat quicken.

"I wish you could see the way your eyes lit up when you first saw me walk in the house. You do that every single time you see me. I don't want that to change."

He held the box out, and Avi didn't hesitate to pop it open. Inside was a small rose gold charm, a perfect match to the bracelet she wore on her left wrist. She'd bought the bracelet and lone "A" charm last year with her graduation money. This charm, in the small box Quincy handed her, was a "Q."

"You said a title wouldn't come until I asked you," he said timidly. "So . . . this is me, doing that."

Avi touched a finger to the shiny charm and then looked up at Quincy, mouth agape.

"You wear the bracelet every day, so I thought you'd like it," he added hesitantly. He stuffed his hands in his coat pockets, becoming increasingly nervous as the silent seconds stretched. "So, what do you say?"

Avi flung her arms around his neck, the force knocking him

back a step. "I'd love to be your girlfriend," she squealed in his ear. She pulled back, giving him a quick kiss on the cheek.

With a smile just as bright and wide as Avi's, Quincy took the charm, attaching it to the bracelet as he gently held her wrist. The "A" and "Q" shone side by side, her bracelet now a shimmering reminder of their relationship. She promised never to take it off.

33

AS CHRISTMAS ROLLED IN, family poured into the LeBeau home. They celebrated with festive music, plentiful food, and boisterous card games. Late Christmas night, Avi awoke on the couch to the sounds of Kai's snores, Belle's happy tears, and delighted shrieks from their mom and Aunt Char. A neighbor had delivered the powder blue Spelman acceptance packet that had mistakenly arrived at her house days ago. A new round of celebrations lasted well into the early morning.

Two days before the girls headed back to Briarcliff, Paisli forced Avi and Belle to do a new sister tag video. "This one will be true to its name," she'd declared, annoyed at having been left out of the last one.

Paisli was listing her fifth answer to "three things about Avi that annoy you" when the doorbell rang three times. With their parents out on a date, the LeBeau siblings were left to decide door-answering duties through what was essentially a game of "not it."

EJ's voice sounded from the intercom in Avi's room. "Somebody go answer the door. I'm busy."

"We're recording a video," Belle said, pressing the talk button. "Where's Moe?"

"Shower."

"Antonio, get the door."

The bell rang again, and Avi opened the home security app on her phone.

"Why? It's for you," Antonio said.

"He's right," Avi said quizzically. "Logan's outside holding white flowers."

Belle rushed to the phone to see him standing there for herself.

"I thought you weren't speaking to him. Why'd you invite him over?"

"I didn't. I thought he was in Georgia," Belle said, looking dumbfounded. "I don't even remember giving him our address."

Avi's eyes darted to her sister. Despite the fact that Belle had removed photos of him from her social accounts *weeks* ago, Logan still refused to do the same. The number of calls, texts, and emails from him also increased in outrageous volume with each passing day. More than once, Avi had caught Belle looking through old pictures or rereading his one-sided text thread.

The bell rang twice more.

Paisli popped out of her seat, dragging Belle toward the door by her sweater. "C'mon, I wanna see his freckles up close."

"No, you can't!" Belle said sharply.

"You said I could on the phone," Paisli whined.

"That was *before* we broke up."

"What happened between you two?" Avi asked. "Did he cheat or something?"

Belle's jaw clenched like she was trying to chew through a rock.

When the doorbell rang a seventh time, it was Moe's irritated voice they heard over the intercom. "Do you want me to tell him to go away?" he asked.

Belle bit her bottom lip, thinking. She pressed the button again. "No, I got it."

She flew out of the room, and her sisters followed. Avi stopped Paisli from following Belle down the steps, despite her protests.

In the foyer, Belle smoothed down her hair and took a deep breath before wrenching the front door open. "What are you doing here?" she growled.

Logan stood there wearing pitiful puppy-dog eyes. "If you read my text, then you would've known I was in your city for my uncle's New Year's Eve party."

"That still doesn't explain why you're *here*."

"Babe, give me five minutes to explain. Please."

Belle crossed her arms, contemplating. "You have three."

Logan was about to step inside, but she pressed a hand to his chest. She looked back at Avi and Paisli with a reassuring smile before joining him outside and closing the door.

Avi wanted to watch through the live security feed almost as much as Paisli did. But after their last argument, she'd promised Belle to trust her more. She liked where they were right now, and if trusting Belle meant giving her privacy, then she could do that. Defeated by Avi's threats to tell their parents if she snooped, Paisli resigned to glaring at Avi and scrolling through TikTok.

Ten minutes passed, and they heard the front door shut. Feet pounded up the steps past Avi's room as Belle flew straight to her room and slammed her door.

Avi knocked three times before Belle's muffled voice yelled, "Later!"

She shrugged at Paisli. "We'll finish the video later."

WELL AFTER MIDNIGHT, Avi walked around her room repacking her suitcase for the trip back to Georgia. She didn't want to hear her mom's inevitable lecture about how Avi always waited until the last minute to do everything.

"We wear uniforms," Quincy teased from her laptop screen. "Why do you need that many clothes?"

"Because you never know what might come up. Why do you need so many sneakers?"

"I actually wear different shoes every day."

Since they'd made their relationship official, Quincy was around a lot more. It was lovely having him over for dinners, a movie, or just to lounge on the couch, talking about books, music, and just about anything. And they FaceTimed every night.

An angry off-screen voice said, "Child, I know you don't think you're gonna leave these dishes in my sink overnight."

Quincy sighed.

"You better go do what your grandma says." Avi laughed.

Smirking, he stood and headed for the kitchen. "I'll text you when I'm done, Dimples."

"Quincy!" his grandmother yelled.

"Gotta go."

Avi exited the app, staring dreamily at her laptop's wallpaper, a photo of the two of them at the Winter Festival. She placed a final top in her suitcase, zipped it, and climbed into bed, cuddling her pillow. The wind and rain beat relentlessly against her window, making it rattle as she yawned and rolled over to check the clock on her nightstand: 1:42 a.m. She was exhausted, but she didn't want to miss Quincy's goodnight text.

Absentmindedly, Avi stroked her thumb over the "Q" charm as she had hundreds of times since he'd attached it to her bracelet weeks ago. It was almost scary how much Quincy was beginning to mean to her. She wouldn't quite describe it as being in love. That was a phrase she currently reserved for her parents. Perhaps "puppy love" was more accurate. Still, this feeling wasn't one Avi could ever imagine being short-lived, and whatever the word, Quincy was inspiring an embarrassing amount of sappy poetry on her part.

The conversation they had when Quincy asked her to be his girlfriend replayed in her head on an endless loop. Avi wished she could remember everything he'd said that day, word for word. Or even watch it again, as she did with all the videos they'd made in the past few days.

And then Avi remembered—she could! Or at least, she should be able to watch parts of that day on their home security footage. They'd been right outside the front door. Avi scrolled back to late December on her app, and there it was. Yes, the sound was janky, but it was something.

The moment had been recorded in several clips. Avi replayed the one of Quincy taking her hand after he shared his story. And the clip when he attached the charm to her bracelet. Finally, there was a video of her throwing her arms around his neck in a hug.

It was way past three when Avi finally decided to go to sleep. Quincy had texted her an hour ago, but the excitement of discovering the videos kept her wide-awake. Avi saved them to her phone for future viewings and scrolled in the app to see when exactly her parents got home from their date earlier. But something odd jumped out at her. The timestamp was 8:45 p.m. today, and it was dark out, but the thumbnail clearly showed someone standing over something . . . or rather some*one* crumpled on the ground. Avi clicked on the image.

It was Logan stepping over Belle as she gasped for air. Holding her breath, Avi closed that video and scrolled to the first clip, beginning when Belle followed Logan outside. It was impossible to hear what they were saying because of the wind, but the conversation in the first few clips seemed calm. And then, Belle was gesturing broadly with an accusatory finger in Logan's face. In the next video, Logan was yelling, too. Suddenly, he grabbed Belle's forearms, yanking her toward him.

Avi's hands shook as she loaded the next clip. Logan faced the camera with a hand covering his mouth, and his eyes were shut tightly. His anger radiated from the screen as Belle spoke with her hands held out cautiously. Without warning, Logan turned sharply, wrapping two hands around her neck. Avi felt light-headed as she watched this pixelated Logan choke her sister. Belle scratched at him. His hands. His arms. His face. But he only let go when she toppled down the steps. The last clip was the first Avi had found: Logan stepping over Belle as she coughed and sputtered, trying to regain her breath. He walked back to his truck without even a second glance.

Avi sat mortified as she struggled to fill her lungs. As if *she* was the one who had been choked like a rag doll. The Chinese takeout she'd eaten earlier churned in her stomach, and it wasn't long before she felt an acidic burn at the back of her throat. She ran to the bathroom, emptying her guts in the toilet. Moments later, Belle's door flung open, and she crouched over Avi, patting her back.

"I told you the ice cream and lo mein would be a bad mix," Belle said groggily.

Avi stood weakly, and the room swirled as she gripped the sink. She grabbed her toothbrush, weakly going through the motions as tears spilled over. Belle left the bathroom, returning shortly with a cold bottle of water as Avi placed her toothbrush in the holder.

Belle sat her down on the edge of the tub and forced her to drink half the bottle before saying, "Talk to me."

Avi stared at her sister as if she was seeing her clearly for the first time in months. The arguments, the obsessive texts, the avoidance—and now the stalking—suddenly made perfect sense. But Avi never imagined things would go this far. How could this have been happening right in front of them? How come no one knew? Why didn't Belle ask for help? Avi's eyes fell to her sister's neck. The shadow of a bruise peeked out under her jaw. Almost completely covered by concealer.

"Why are you wearing a turtleneck to bed?" Avi asked.

She shrugged. "My room is cold. You know that." Avi heard the hoarseness in her sister's voice.

"Belley, why are you wearing makeup at three a.m.?"

This time, Belle's eyes dropped. "I'm practicing for a new video," she whispered.

"Say it again and look me in the eyes," Avi demanded.

Silence.

"What happened with Logan today?"

Tears slid down Belle's face as she fidgeted nervously.

"Has he done that to you before?"

"Done what?"

Avi scoffed. "The front porch camera caught it all! Why is this happ— Where are you going?!"

Avi followed as Belle raced out of the bathroom, down the steps, and through the foyer, skidding to a stop in front of the security panel in the kitchen. Her nails tapped rapidly on the screen.

Belle started the fifteen-second video of Logan facing the camera. They both flinched when his hands wrapped around her neck.

"No, no, no," Belle muttered, and her nails tapped again as she prepared to delete the video.

"What are you *doing*?" Avi yelled. She pushed Belle to the side, anchoring her body in front of the panel.

"Shut up before you wake the twins," Belle hissed, casting a nervous glance toward the basement.

"You can't! Daddy said the videos disappear forever when you delete them from the panel."

"That's the point," Belle said through gritted teeth. Belle shoved Avi to the side and began tapping the screen again.

One video gone.

Avi knocked her down, trying to recover the video, but Belle tackled her to the ground. They wrestled, elbows and knees flying as each tried to make it to the panel and block the other. Finally, Belle overpowered Avi, straddling her and pinning her arms over her head.

They both panted as Avi struggled to break free.

"Calm down," Belle whisper-yelled.

"What's happening to you?! Why didn't you *say* something? I could've—"

"Could've what? Told Mommy and Daddy?"

"Yes!" Avi cried. "They can *help* you. That's what they do. And we need those videos. They're evidence."

"I don't need evidence of anything. He already emailed my old account and apologized. He said that I was right about us breaking up. The pictures on his Instagram are gone. The tweets are gone. Logan has accepted that we're over. For real this time."

"And that makes what he did okay?" Avi shot.

"No. Nothing makes it okay. But it doesn't matter anymore."

"He doesn't get to show up to our house, choke you out, and think his apology makes everything better. You can't let him think that's okay!"

"Those videos could *ruin* his *life*," Belle said sharply. "He could get expelled from Preston. They could rescind his college acceptances. All over something that's over."

"Who cares?"

"I do," Belle said with a pained look in her eyes. "You don't understand."

"You're right—I don't," Avi said, breathless. "Make it make sense, or I'm gonna scream."

Belle released her grip on Avi's arms and leaned back, looking resigned. "What you saw was the worst of it. Logan has had a lot of awful moments, but they weren't all bad. There's a lot of good in him, too."

Avi sat up on her forearms, panting. "Are you being serious?"

"I am. He hasn't convinced me to think I deserve what he's done, Avi. I don't. No one does." Belle sighed and closed her eyes. "But at the same time, I've messed up a lot in our relationship, too."

"That doesn't make throwing you around right."

"It doesn't, but you have to try to understand. If you tell, it wouldn't just be something Mommy and Daddy and his parents try to settle. Our schools would be involved. The police would be involved. And word spreads fast. Everyone would know! My friends, our classmates, professors."

Avi's eyes bulged out of her head. What did any of that matter? "Is that more important than you getting help?"

"Yes—I mean, no. I—" Belle swallowed hard, swiping at a fallen tear before she could look Avi in the eyes again. "I can't take people knowing how stupid I was. Or worse, calling me a liar. I don't want to feel their eyes on me, and I don't want to deal with the fallout."

"What *do* you want?" Avi whispered.

"I want to graduate in May and go to college in August. I want to move on and pretend that the bad parts didn't happen. This is my chance to do that," she sniffled. "It's finally over,

Avi. I'd get it if we were still together. Or if I was in danger, but he finally gets that it's done. If you tell Mommy and Daddy, it's not done. Everything is gonna get harder and more complicated. *I* got myself out of the relationship," she said, jabbing at her chest. "It should be my decision how things are handled. Ellie, look at me. Logan tried to control me for months. Please don't take my chance to move on away from me."

Avi couldn't think of a good comeback. The last thing she wanted to be was like Logan. In her opinion, he deserved far worse than expulsion or jail, but Belle was right. That wasn't her decision to make.

"Fine."

"No. You have to promise me."

Avi bit her bottom lip, considering the ways this could all go to hell, but the pained look in Belle's eyes made the words "I promise" slip out of her mouth before she knew if she believed them.

Belle exhaled in relief and climbed off Avi. At the panel, she scrolled through the clips, permanently deleting them all. The only one that remained was of Logan coming to the door and ringing the bell.

Avi sat against the wall, hugging her knees to her chest, unable to stifle the constant flow of tears as her mind raced.

How could Logan have been doing this to Belle for *months* without her noticing? Avi knew Logan seemed a bit off, but in that video, he was unhinged. Was he already hitting her that day at the mall? That bruise on Belle's arm the night of the pageant . . . did he do that, too? He had to have. What would EJ do if he'd found the videos? Moe? What if Logan changed his mind again? What if Belle did? Avi wanted to say a lot. She had a million questions. But the first words that spilled from her mouth were: “This doesn’t feel right.”

“Maybe not right now,” Belle said, kneeling. “But it’s what’s best for me. Ellie, no one’s ever trusted me like you do.” She pushed a strand of hair behind Avi’s ear and pulled her to her feet. “It’s late. Let’s go to bed.”

34

AVI SAT IN WOMEN'S STUDIES drifting in and out of the conversation about portrayals of Black women in the media. It wasn't that she didn't find the topic (the Mammy archetype, how she came to be, and why she persisted in everyday media, life, and perception) interesting. But before class, she'd found her sister in the bathroom by the Cliff, crying.

The spring semester started two weeks ago, but Belle was still having a hard time adjusting. It was confusing. When this all started, it was Belle who was adamant about them breaking up. She was the one who was avoiding his calls, refusing to accept his sad apologies, and telling people they were over. But something changed when they came back to school. Logan acted like she didn't exist, and it messed her up.

Ignoring Avi's and Nevaeh's protests, Belle stepped down as co-president of Cheetah Plans just three days after their return, and it had been weeks since she recorded a video for her channel. Turns out, if it didn't have to do with dance or her schoolwork, it no longer mattered.

Avi's own responsibilities were beginning to slip between her fingers. If she wasn't late turning in a class assignment, she was apologizing for subpar editorial work at the *Cliff News*. She knew it was bad when Cori pulled her aside at yesterday's meeting.

Cori had walked up to Avi as she was gathering her things to leave, holding out a soft blue spiral planner. "I thought you might be able to use this."

Avi already had a planner, but she accepted it with a soft exhale. "Thanks, Cori. And thank you for covering for me with Egypt."

"No problem," she said with a shrug. "I just noticed how spaced-out you've been. Is everything all right?"

For a moment, a pang of guilt engulfed her as she held back the truth. It was the same feeling she had at the Cliff on their second day back when Quincy asked if she was feeling sick after she'd seen Logan pass by laughing with two friends. And again three days ago when her father had asked "What's going on with you?" for the fifth time since they'd returned to campus.

"I'm okay." "I feel fine." "Everything's all right." She'd lie, cutting off the conversation because she was sure the truth would come toppling out if she didn't.

The one thing Avi did do right was turn in her poetry submission to Professor Lovette for the special Black History Month edition next month. In early December, she'd been grateful to receive the email from Lovette urging her to enter the poetry competition. It had felt like a brand-new chance. But when she sat down to finish it last week, she ended up with the angstiest piece she'd ever produced. Luckily, the subject matter (the Sixteenth Street Church Bombing) needed no shortage of angst.

If Avi was being honest, her schoolwork, the paper, and her writing all felt a bit inconsequential at the moment. And, sure, it was troubling that Belle hadn't picked up her violin in weeks and was slowly dropping things that used to mean the world to her—but at least that asshole wasn't back in the picture.

Images of Logan choking Belle seeped into Avi's every thought, every memory. She couldn't even escape them in her dreams. She had a reoccurring nightmare of Logan beating the crap out of both of her sisters in turn. No matter how loudly she screamed or how hard she hit the glass that separated them, he never let up. But the dream always ended the same: Eventually, the glass would break, and she'd have the attention from Logan she'd so desperately wanted moments before. Only then did Avi realize she should've run to get help when she had the chance. She'd startle awake just as he'd turn and reach for her.

Zazie nudged Avi's elbow, and her pen dragged across her color-coordinated page of notes. Avi glared at Zazie, who nodded toward the front of the class. Everyone was staring at her, including Professor Akwi.

"Ms. LeBeau," she sighed with folded arms. "I'm going to have to ask you to pay attention for a little while longer. Everything we're covering will be on the test on the twenty-fourth."

Avi bolted upright in her seat. "I apologize. It won't happen again."

"Class, the next time we meet, we'll be discussing the Sapphire, aka the Mad Black Woman image and analyzing the lyrics to Solange's 'Mad,' as well as the character Cookie from *Empire*. Come prepared with examples. The assigned reading will be posted on BriarWeb. And ladies, it is expected that you *complete* the reading before class—don't just skim through. In addition," she said, turning to stare at Avi over her black-rimmed frames, "Ms. LeBeau will present us with her findings of a relevant scholarly article to kick off the discussion. You're dismissed."

Avi kept her eyes down, attempting to school her face into some semblance of respect. She stuffed her books in her bag, yanked on her coat, and readied to follow Rhyon and Zazie out of the room when Professor Akwi cleared her throat.

"Avielle, I understand that things outside of class preoccupy us, but I will have to ask that you try better to keep your mind out of the clouds, as I've noticed that's where you've been lately." Avi opened her mouth to reply, but Akwi held up a hand. "I don't want your excuses; I need your attention. Make sure the article is a good one."

Avi nodded and took Professor Akwi's silence as a dismissal.

In the cafe, Avi slid her tray through the pizza line, trying not to think of her growing pile of homework or the two articles Cori sent for review last night.

"Where'd Zazie go?" Avi asked when she reached their table.

"Motherland United lunch meeting," Rhyon said, scrolling through her favorite style influencer's TikTok. She scooped a spoonful of stir-fry in her mouth. "Hey, do you wanna hang out later with your brother and me? We're meeting up in Newton after the last bell."

One thing that proved to be true: Neither Rhyon nor Moe took the other seriously. Rhyon remained adamant that she was far too busy with her modeling group and schoolwork to have a boyfriend—especially when she still had her eye on Hazel. This was perfect for Moe, who had ended things with Vannah because she kept badgering for a relationship. He wasn't the type to be forced into a commitment.

"You guys are gonna hang out or spark?" Avi asked.

"Both, probably," Rhyon said mischievously. "Come with. It's Q's room, too, and I feel like I see him more than you lately."

Avi knew Quincy had to tutor someone and cut three heads before the night was over. Their conflicting schedules didn't leave them nearly as much time together as she'd thought. Already, she craved the time they'd spent lounging around on her couch during Christmas break. Life was simpler then.

She caressed the charms on her bracelet between her fingers. "He'll be in class tomorrow, and we're supposed to hang out this weekend. Seeing him on FaceTime tonight will have to do." Avi waved at Crystal, passing by with a group of Union girls, but she pretended not to see her. Rude. "Plus, I'm going to Belle's so she can look over my French homework, and I have to start the Bio project you finished last week."

"I told you to come with me to the library," Rhyon sang. "When you're done babysitting Belle, come join."

"I'm not babysitting. I'm making sure she's safe." Avi took a huge bite of her pepperoni pizza, fending off Rhyon's attempts to pour hot sauce on the slice.

"And what could hurt her on campus?"

"I meant making sure she's okay. The breakup was tough."

"Yeah, I guess." Rhyon shrugged. "I saw her going into Chisholm yesterday—and don't get me wrong, you know I love your sister—but baby girl looked rough." Her face brightened with a thought. "Hey! Maybe she could talk to my therapist. At first, my mom sent me to Dr. Cashmere when my dad started impregnating every IG model with a cute face and fat ass, but now I go because I like talking to her."

"How is your dad?"

"Clingy and overconcerned with my affairs," she said, waving her hand. "Avi, Dr. Cashmere specializes in all the teen issues, including dating stuff. I honestly wouldn't have even tried to speak to you the day we met if it weren't for her. Plus, she's relatable as hell."

Avi considered that. Belle talked to her almost every day about the breakup and mentioned being overwhelmingly sad. But there was only so much Avi could offer back. A professional might know how to raise Belle out of this funk. "You know, that's not a terrible idea."

"I don't have bad ideas," Rhyon said, brushing some food off the Chanel brooch on her sweater vest. The passing period bell rang, and chairs scraped the floor as students headed to fourth period. Rhyon nudged Avi's arm. "Hey, I know a lot of what goes on stays between you two. But if you wanna talk for real, tell me. Okay?"

Avi smiled gratefully, and they rose with their trays. "I'm good. But I do want Dr. Cashmere's info. In the meantime, focus on your boyfriend," she teased.

Rhyon rolled her eyes.

35

THE *CLIFF NEWS* had one of its most productive meetings on Tuesday night. Writers gave updates and consulted Cori and her editors on pieces. Near the end, there was an exciting brainstorming session for the March "Spring" edition. And the best part was that Fallon never bothered to show up.

Afterward, Avi met Belle in the gym as she wrapped up in one of the reserved dance rooms.

"Where's Vannah?" she asked, leaning on the doorframe.

"She couldn't make it, so Fallon offered to come instead. She just left like five minutes ago." Belle yanked her Preston sweatshirt over her head.

So that's why she missed the Cliff News *meeting.*

"What are you doing here?" Belle asked.

"I was next door in Eckford for my meeting and thought I'd walk with you back to our dorms," Avi said, trying to sound casual.

Belle flicked her eyes downward and let out an irritated sigh. Avi knew what it meant.

I'm fine.

I don't need to be watched.

Truth is three hundred feet away. I don't need an escort.

Avi had heard it all before and she didn't mean to be overbearing. She just so happened to know Belle's strict, rarely changing schedule by heart. Plus, she really was right next door.

To lighten the mood, she said, "Egypt assigned me an article on her called 'Life After the Win: Second Runner-Up, Egypt Mack.'"

Belle guffawed as she packed her gym bag. "You're kidding?"

"I wish. It's standard that Journey gets the cover because she won. But Egypt is allowing one page for herself—and she has to let Bailey have one, too, since she was the *first* runner-up. Egypt's been . . . off with me ever since you and EJ pulled that stunt on her at the pageant. I'm like ninety-three percent sure she was trying to be mean when she asked me to write hers in front of everyone. Even said that I've 'worked hard despite not winning the exact position I wanted,' and 'that deserves attention.'"

"Huh. That's her exact reason for thinking she deserves her face in the paper. So predictable. But I'm sorry she's taking that out on you. Are you good, or should I—"

"Nope. I don't think anything you'd say to her would help my case."

Belle swung her bag on her shoulder, following Avi out. "Hey, have you talked to Pai lately?"

"Mhmm, she's psyched she was cast as the lead in their school play . . ." Avi trailed off as Belle's face dropped. "I'm sure she was gonna tell you," Avi added.

Belle shook her head as they headed down another flight of stairs. "Antonio told me an hour ago, but I haven't talked to Paisli since we left for Georgia. She never returns my calls, and all I get is one-word responses to my texts—if she even bothers."

Belle looked genuinely hurt, but Avi shrugged.

"Paisli's twelve. She's all over the place. You probably took a sweater she wanted to steal from your closet." Avi snapped her fingers, remembering. "She was pissed we never got to finish the sister tag video. That's probably it."

Belle's nod was unsure. "Yeah, that makes sense."

Avi felt the cold hit her like a brick wall as they walked out of the building. She stuffed her gloved hands in her pockets, scanning the sky for signs of snow.

"More importantly," Avi said, "Mommy keeps calling me about you. If you didn't want her to know something was up, you never should've quit Cheetah Plans. That was like your baby."

"Adoree has it covered. It's not that big a deal."

Avi sighed. "I'm not good at this. I've never had to keep anything serious from them before."

"You sure kept quiet about Q until you were ready."

"This is bigger than that and you know it. Belle, yesterday Daddy told me he knows something's going on with me. Again."

That got Belle's attention. "Seriously? He told me he could feel my spirit was off this morning."

"See! If you don't stop moping around, they're gonna fly down here."

"I'm not moping."

"I'm sorry," Avi scoffed. "Is *sulking* the right word?"

Belle glared at her. "I'm allowed to be sad."

"Yeah, but you haven't been yourself in months. People notice." Belle tried to put her AirPods in, but Avi grabbed her wrist. "The breakup should be the least of your worries. You went through something worth talking to a professional about."

Belle yanked her hand away and stomped onto the sidewalk toward Truth.

Avi rolled her eyes and walked left toward Hollingsworth. Every time she brought up therapy with Dr. Cashmere, Belle got angry again. She had a fair point: "I don't turn eighteen until April. Anything I disclose about Logan, she'd tell."

That's what Avi wanted. Belle argued that as annoying as she was, Avi "just being there" helped a lot. But it couldn't be enough. They needed their parents in the loop.

But she gave Belle her word that night, and that had to count for something, too . . . didn't it?

As Avi dug her key out of her bag, she heard voices behind her. She turned to see Logan standing just feet from Belle on the lawn in front of Truth.

Heart racing, Avi sprinted to them, positioning herself next to her sister. "It's almost curfew. Why are you still on our campus?"

The pitiful look on his freckled face was the same one he wore the night of the pageant. But it wasn't fooling anyone this time.

"Belle, I just wanted to ask if it's all right for us to talk."

"No, it's not," Avi barked. "And it's weird that you keep popping up when you haven't been invited."

"Babe, please," Logan pleaded, looking directly into Belle's eyes. "I know I've been ignoring you, but I don't know how to do this space thing, and things are tough for me right now. I've been waiting out in the cold for you for forty-five minutes. Can't we talk?"

He took a step forward, but Avi moved directly in front of her sister. "No!"

Belle touched her shoulder. "It's okay. It'll only be for a minute."

"What?" Avi turned to her, outraged.

"Give us a second. Please?"

"You want *me* to leave?!"

"No. Wait at the bench." She pointed at the one their parents sat on the day they dropped them off. "I'll be right over," Belle said, nudging Avi away. Eagerness gleamed in her eyes.

As Avi sat fuming on the bench, she heard bits and pieces of their conversation. Belle asking Logan how he was. Him saying, "I miss you." Her not returning the sentiment but smiling at his words. The wind began to whistle, and Avi missed more and more, but she saw Belle take a step closer and inhaled sharply when Logan took her hand. She waited for Belle to yank it away, but she didn't. Avi could hardly believe her eyes. She was looking at Logan the way she had when they first started dating. It was sickening.

Three minutes passed, and Avi had had enough. As she stood to interrupt, she saw Logan move to walk away. Before he could, Belle pulled him back and into a hug. Avi lowered onto the bench, watching them hug for four whole Mississippis. With a nod and a smile, Logan finally turned to walk away.

Avi stood, heading straight for Hollingsworth with her ID in hand.

"Wait," Belle shouted. She ran to catch up. "Don't you want to know what he said?"

Avi gritted her teeth. "I don't care what he said, and you shouldn't, either. He's stupid."

Avi scanned her card, but Belle blocked the door with her foot.

"Everyone makes mistakes, Avi. I can't spend the rest of my life hating him."

"I can!" She tried to pull the door again, but Belle's boot stood firm. "And 'a mistake'? He treated you like trash," Avi said. "I can't believe you're even speaking to him, let alone allowing him in your space again. I'm spending all this time trying to make sure you're okay, and you're out here hugging him like—like nothing ever happened!"

"I'm not acting like nothing happened," Belle said, injured. "I lived it, okay? And I never asked you to watch me every second of the day."

"You not asking doesn't mean you don't need me."

Avi scanned the door again, and this time Belle moved when she wrenched it open.

"And I'm not gonna stop, either," she added. "So get used to it."

Inside, Avi stripped off her gloves and scarf as she walked into her room.

Zazie peeked at her over the latest copy of Preston's newspaper, the *Lion Times*.

"You good?" she asked as Avi slammed her bag on the bed, struggling with the buttons on her coat.

"Oh, I'm peachy. Just sick of human beings. Also, I realized I forgot to finish Lovette's reading, and now—"

Avi looked up at the newspaper in Zazie's hands, where she saw the cover: Logan, holding his college acceptance packets in one hand and a briefcase in the other. She'd heard that he was getting a feature to help his stand-up-guy image, but seeing it in their room was too much.

She pointed an accusatory finger at the paper. "Why do you have that?"

"Oh," Zazie said guiltily. "They were handing them out in the Cliff."

"And you thought it was a good idea to bring his negativity into our positive home?"

Zazie closed the paper and stood. "I'm thinking something else may be bothering you. This is a whole new level of drama."

"It. Is. Not. Drama," Avi said, finally getting her coat unbuttoned. "You brought evil in our room, so pull out the sage and start cleansing from scratch."

Zazie plopped down on Avi's bed, unconcerned by her hysterics. "This stuff with your sister is really getting to you. Was it that bad?"

Avi nodded with her arms folded over her chest.

"Forget I ever brought it in here," Zazie said. She balled up the paper and shot it into their small wastebasket.

"Thank you," Avi huffed. She took a seat on the bed, too.

And then Zazie rushed over to retrieve the paper out of the can.

"Girl, I forgot for a second," she said, smoothing Logan's face on her desk to refold. "Paper gets recycled. Don't sweat it. I'll take it out tomorrow."

36

MY DAD, Kai mouthed with the phone to his ear. He waved Avi in and turned to his disastrous room.

"Hey, Uncle Algee," Avi shouted near his ear.

The distinct odor of dirty socks and something spoiled hit her nose as she kicked a path through the clothes and empty plastic bottles on the floor, placing a bag of sweets from Sugah on Kai's desk.

A fallen frame showed Uncle Algee and Aunt Char standing against a sunset backdrop. In the photo, Algee stood broad-shouldered in his state-issued sweatshirt and pants, an arm wrapped around Char's waist. Kai took mostly after his mom, but from the picture, Avi recognized his dad's smile, Dumbo ears, and dignified stature.

Avi placed the picture upright before taking a crusty bowl sitting on Kai's keyboard to the sink. She waited on the unmade bed, opening her laptop to an email notification from Cori calling for all last submissions for the BHM poem feature. Avi sent a quick prayer, hoping that what she'd submitted was good enough. Then she opened Word and tried (for the third time that day) to write something about Egypt that didn't sound robotic. She wished that she had declined the article, but this was the first chance Egypt had given her to write, and maybe even to prove herself. Even if it was given out of petty spite.

Kai told his dad about his latest proposal to get Jakobi Lee, a former-inmate-turned-prison-abolitionist, to speak to his Pre-Law Club before finally hanging up the phone and biting into a cinnamon roll.

"It's ridiculous that you guys live like this," Avi said without taking her eyes off the screen. "Now I understand why Jasiri's always in our dorm. Crystal knows you don't clean?"

He shot a little orange ball into a plastic backboard hanging from his closet. "I never let her come over. But that's irrelevant since we're—" He ran a long finger across his neck like a knife.

Avi snapped her laptop shut. "Since when!"

"Like three days ago."

"Are you serious? We talk every day. Why didn't you say something?"

He shrugged indifferently. "Forgot."

"And you don't seem very heartbroken, either. What happened?"

"Man, I couldn't look in another girl's direction without her accusing me of doing something I didn't do. And she's had an attitude with me ever since we got back, but she wouldn't say why. Then randomly she texted me this long paragraph about how pissed she was that I spent so much time at your house during the break."

Avi rolled her eyes. "I knew she gave me a nasty look the other day."

He pretended to cross someone up and threw the ball with a jump. "I was starting to get sick of her anyways. She thinks she knows everything."

"Yeah. You're usually the know-it-all in relationships, but I've seen her in class. She's way smarter than you."

Avi pulled her phone out to see if she'd missed Quincy's text. He was supposed to tell her when he was done cutting hair so they could hang out this afternoon—still nothing. But Belle finally responded to Avi's "wyd" from forty-three minutes ago.

> Headed to the gym with Vannah, Kennedi, and Fallon to work on choreo.
>
> **BELLEY**

"I forgot," Kai said, peeking at her phone. "Logan asked if Belle was talking to someone new."

"You still hang out with him?"

"Mm-hmm," he grunted, staring at his phone now, "that's my boy."

She swallowed what she wanted to say. "It's none of his business. Plus, I saw them talking yesterday at the Cliff. He could've asked her then if he cared so much."

"Why are you stalking them?"

"I'm not," Avi said defensively. "I just don't see any reason for them to talk."

"That's because it's none of *your* business. I don't get what your problem with Logan is. He's been helping me with my presidency from the jump. Got accepted to Howard, Cornell, and Morehouse—and he just had an interview with some important Princeton alum last week. The man even put me on with his shoe connect. And still, from day one, you've hated him for no reason."

"I have my reasons."

"Yeah, okay," Kai chuckled. "What are they?"

Avi wished she could wipe that smug look off Kai's face and tell him the truth. And for a moment, she did consider telling. It was Kai, after all; he'd kept as many of her secrets as Belle had over the years, if not more. If Avi made Kai swear, she could almost guarantee that he wouldn't say a word. Maybe if she hinted toward the truth . . .

Avi's phone buzzed, dragging her out of her thoughts.

I'm done. Do you still wanna hang out?

QUINCY

Avi looked from her phone to Kai and back again. She would keep her mouth shut for now.

"I have my reasons."

"Whatever," Kai said, sliding the closet door open and grabbing a pair of black-and-red Jordans. "I'm about to go shoot hoops with your 'mortal enemy' at the court."

"You think you're funny, but I'm serious." Avi snatched up her bag. "I'm telling you, as your godsister, that your 'friend' is a bad person. That should be enough."

"C'mon, Avi. I was playing with you," he called as she slammed the door behind her.

37

AVI WALKED DOWN the fourth-floor hallway until she saw the room that Quincy and the twins shared. The door was cracked open. She approached slowly, praying neither of her brothers was home. Noemie told her that she and EJ were visiting the Georgia Aquarium this afternoon, and she knew Uncle Jovahn was supposed to pick Moe up to attend some “Big Brother Luncheon” hosted at Morehouse.

Avi peeked in to see Quincy alone in the room. His bare back was to her as he polished the saxophone on his desk and bobbed his head to music streaming through his black wireless headphones. She pushed the door open inches wider and knocked twice. It wasn't until her second round of knocks that Quincy moved the headphones back.

“What's up?” he asked without turning.

“I was wondering if you're too busy to hang out with me?”

Quincy swung around in his chair at the sound of her voice and crossed the room. She took a step in to meet his embrace.

Her mother had once compared the honeymoon stage of a relationship to waking up on Christmas morning and seeing the present you've been praying for. But Avi couldn't quite imagine there ever being a time where she wasn't excited to see Quincy. Every time he smiled, she still felt trembles in her heart.

"You didn't say you were coming over," Quincy said as she loosened her arms from around his neck and walked fully into his room for the first time. The door clicked shut behind them.

"I was downstairs to give Kai the cinnamon rolls Sugah made for brunch, but he got annoying quick, and you texted me just in time. So I thought I'd come see you instead. Unless you mind?"

Quincy shook his head but ran a nervous hand over his durag. "I would've tried to straighten up a little if I knew you were coming over. That's all."

Avi scanned the room. Besides a few clothes strewn around, random books lying about, and two unmade beds, their room was fairly clean. Their mom never played about living in filth, and it looked like her rules stuck better with the twins here than it did at home. Though Avi knew their mother wouldn't love the faint earthy smell.

"Let me grab a shirt," Quincy said, pulling a white tank top out of a drawer.

Avi tilted her head to the side playfully. "What? You're shy now?"

A coy smile danced on his lips as he pulled the shirt over his head.

She watched unashamedly until Quincy took a seat on the edge of the bed. Avi turned her attention to the room.

The triple was slightly smaller than Kendall, Deloris, and Neila's in room G-3 of Hollingsworth, but it still had the standard sink, wall dividers, closet, bookshelf, desk, and chairs.

Avi grazed a hand over the sax lying on the desk and then picked up the framed picture of his mother smiling broadly with a breathing afro and a notable gap between her front two teeth. Avi marveled at the strong resemblance to Quincy's sister. Though all the siblings shared their mom's piercing black eyes, Quinn was her mother's twin. Atop Quincy's bookshelf sat his baseball glove and the thrifted barber case Avi had given him for Christmas.

"When do you guys start practices?" she asked, slipping the glove onto her small hand.

"We were supposed to start this week, but it's still too cold out. Coach will probably have us using the feeder and lifting for the next two weeks." He leaned forward, not moving his midnight eyes from Avi. "Are you gonna come to my games?"

She placed the glove back in its spot. "I wouldn't want to be anywhere else, Dr. McClain."

At his night table, Avi grabbed his glasses case and popped it open to reveal the black-rimmed reading glasses she never saw him wear outside of FaceTime.

"Hey, how'd your English essay go?" she asked, sliding the frames onto his face.

Quincy's smile fell as he reached beside his bed and dug through his book bag.

"I meant to ask if you would look over it for me."

He handed her a five-page paper titled "The Great Debate: The Ideologies of Booker T. Washington v. W. E. B. Du Bois" with a red C- at the top.

"Professor McKnight is giving me until next Friday to resubmit, but I'm not great with words, and my grade will drop to a B if I don't rewrite it. Will you help me?"

A sly smile crossed Avi's face. "Talk about things coming full circle. You're bad at something?"

"I don't know if I'd say I'm necessarily bad at it. But McKnight thinks I suck at persuading my readers."

"Hmm. Whose side are you really on? Du Bois or Washington?"

"Ida B. Wells."

Avi looked at him with raised eyebrows.

"Plus," he continued. "Writing is your thing, and you're better at it than me."

"That's what I like to hear," Avi said, plucking a pen from his desk.

She was three minutes into reading Professor McKnight's written comments when her phone vibrated in the pocket of her pink cardigan. She read the text and turned back to the paper, annoyed.

"Who was it?" Quincy asked, seeing her irritation.

"Fallon. She wants to know when I'm free to meet for this stupid French project. The only reason Madame Delcour put us in a group is because she knows we can't stand each other."

"You're not gonna respond?"

"Not now," Avi huffed. "I'd honestly do the project by myself and stick her name on it if it meant we didn't have to speak."

"You're that good?"

"I'm decent."

"But not fluent?"

She scoffed. "In French? It's still my first year!"

"So what?" Quincy reached for her cardigan, pulling her

from the desk to stand between his legs. "You said it was your best class. I wanna hear you say something in French."

He looked up at her through his too-long eyelashes, waiting as she ran through all the simple phrases she knew. And then she remembered the black-and-white silent film they'd watched a week ago in class. It was about a woman who wrote letters to her love, even after he died in World War I. One phrase from the woman's last letter stuck with Avi.

"Je pense toujours à toi," she said in her best accent.

"What does that mean?"

Avi stared back into his dark eyes and said, "I always think about you."

"Oh, yeah?"

She cupped Quincy's stubbly chin in her hands before angling down to kiss him softly on the lips. Each kiss with him felt like their first. Enchanting. The stuff out of fairy tales, for sure. Avi let him pull her onto his lap as he kissed her more fervently.

There was a knock at the door. He pulled back, lips pursed in annoyance.

"What's up?" he asked in a raised voice.

"It's Dylan," said his RB from the other side of the door.

Avi scooted back off Quincy's lap and sat cross-legged next to him on the bed.

"Come in!"

Dylan, a stout, fair-skinned senior with locs, walked in the room. His eyes flitted momentarily between the two. "Hey, man. Patrick told me you were in here. Can you line me up real quick? I got an interview in an hour."

"I would, but my girl's here," Quincy said, nodding toward Avi.

She stood, grinning as she gathered her things. "It's okay. We can meet up later."

Quincy grabbed her hand, pulling her back down. "Stay. Give me twenty minutes."

Avi nodded and picked up his essay and her pen as Dylan took a seat in one of the rolling chairs.

"Thanks, man," he said. "I appreciate it."

"Don't mention it," Quincy said, but Avi heard an edge in his voice. He pulled his case down from the shelf and tossed a cape at Dylan.

"Hey, uh. Just so you know for the future. The door's gotta be open if girls are in here."

Quincy's arms dropped as he looked sideways at his RB. "Do you want your hair cut or not?"

"Yeah, yeah. My bad," Dylan said hurriedly.

38

THE PROJECTION SCREEN showed a photo of Whoopi Goldberg as Miss Celie as Avi closed out her presentation on *The Color Purple*, focusing on the themes of the novel:

1. The importance of female relationships.
2. The lasting emotional, psychological, and physical consequences of misogyny and racism.
3. The disruption of traditional gender roles.

In her accompanying report, Avi focused on the controversy concerning how Black men were depicted in the book and movie. Her stance was that Alice Walker had every right to write the truth about how Black women post-slavery often suffered at the hands of not only white men and women, but Black men as well.

When the time came for Avi to submit her project proposal to Lovette, she'd only seen the movie once, and she'd mainly picked the book because of how much she loved the Broadway soundtrack her mother blasted at the start of every road trip. While reading and doing the report, though, she was surprised at just how relevant it turned out to be.

"Your premise is intriguing and ties in superbly with the conclusion," Professor Lovette said. "I look forward to reading your report. Now—wait a second! Before you take a seat, does anyone have questions regarding Ms. LeBeau's presentation?"

Avi exhaled in relief when no hands budged. She turned to exit out of her PowerPoint when a girl named Maya spoke up from the front row.

"To play the devil's advocate . . . I kind of see where they were coming from. I haven't finished the book yet, but I've seen the movie, and it seems like Black people should have been fighting for each other. Not racing forward to tear one another down. Didn't white people already do that?"

"Right," Kieley chimed from her seat near the back. "It's like how sometimes things are family business. Let's keep our issues private and present ourselves as a united front. Otherwise, we won't progress."

"Those aren't questions," Avi stated plainly.

"No, but it is a learning opportunity," Professor Lovette said. "We use our hour here to teach one another and better understand different points of view. Miss LeBeau, defend your stance."

"Okay," Avi said with a deep breath as she gathered her thoughts. "Well, to relate those statements to the book, Miss Celie's constant internal struggle and the reason she remained stagnant so long was because of her silence and inability to fight back. Whenever Shug Avery could, she fled her situation so she wouldn't have to fight. Sophia couldn't stop fighting physically or with her tongue, and it got her hurt, but her fight was still important." Avi looked hesitantly at Professor Lovette, who nodded for her to continue.

"Professors Lovette and Akwi have been teaching us about intersectionality all year. As Black girls, there will never be a time when we're Black and not girls or girls and not Black, and those are only two of our identifiers. One isn't more prevalent than the other. And I think it's wrong for anyone to try and make any of us choose which identity we want to represent or defend when they exist at the same time."

"I hear you," Maya said as she sat up, intrigued by the conversation. "But I still think that's our problem. The majority of white women stick behind their men, no matter what. Their voting is basically united, and so are many of their beliefs. That's why they're so strong, collectively. And that's why white supremacy still affects our daily lives."

"By 'sticking behind,'" Zazie said with finger quotes, "do you mean upholding racism and misogyny? Because that's what's happening."

"'If you can only be tall because someone else is on their knees, then you have a serious problem.' Toni Morrison said that," Rhyon added, pointing toward the exact quote on Professor Lovette's wall of wisdom.

"Exactly," said Sheritta, who sat right next to Maya. "In that example, Black women would be the ones on their knees, right? Why should we be so pressed to stick behind men or women who wouldn't even do the same for us?"

"You sound like a typical man-hater," Kieley spat.

"Really?" Professor Lovette asked. "Because what I'm hearing her say is *accountability*. I agree that we should be able to hold not only other women accountable, but our male counterparts as well."

"My grandma always said boys gon' be boys, but it's up to

me how I'm gonna react and if I'll let it affect me," said a girl named Jocelyn.

"Thinking you have a choice in whether or not racism and misogyny will affect you is wishful at best," Professor Lovette said, looking sadly at Jocelyn. "And all respect to your grandmother, honey, but therein lies the problem. What if I told you 'boys gon' be boys' quickly turns into 'men gon' be men'? And what if I also told you that this happens because, from an early age, little boys are given that easy excuse—while little girls are handed the responsibility?"

Professor Lovette stood from her blue swivel chair with clasped hands, and Avi took that as her cue to sit. "All right, class. Your book report on *The Color Purple* is due by 11:59 p.m. on Sunday night. If you can pull out your language books, we'll spend our last fifteen minutes discussing the structure of an argumentative essay."

39

Four little girls with ponytails and curls
Went to church to learn of His word
But what they endured could not have been predicted
Smoke filled the air, panic rose
They were blown away and their spirits lifted
Cruel beyond means, these girls were killed by a foe
The KKK succeeded with the help of Jim Crow . . .

APPLAUSE FROM the *Cliff News* staff roared around Avi as she smiled bashfully from her seat. Her Black History poem "Four Little Girls" was a hit, according to the numbers. In a week, the poem had received the most comments and re-shares on the paper's website since the beginning of the new year, followed closely by Aubrey's article "10 Signs You Go to a HBBS."

Fellow freshman editor Brittany hugged Avi from the side as Cori asked her to come to the front to read her poem aloud. Fallon sat in the front row, refusing to acknowledge Avi's existence. Egypt was doing much of the same. If Professor Lovette hadn't put Cori in charge of the special Black History edition of the paper, Egypt would never have allowed Avi's poem to make the final cut. The only thing keeping her silent in her seat now was the Harvest Queen cover story.

Avi couldn't deny how great it was hearing good things about her poem around campus. But nothing felt as amazing as seeing her words in print again.

She floated on cloud nine as she and Brittany hurriedly cleaned the small spread in the back of the room while people bundled up to head out. She would need to leave soon, too, if she was going to make it on time to Rhyon's modeling troupe showcase in the courtyard. Avi and Brittany picked up trash in between chairs and talked about their Valentine's Day plans. Brittany's friend, a member of Cheetah Plans, was hosting an outdoor movie in the courtyard to give an option to those who didn't want to attend the dance.

It was perfect. Avi and her friends could go as a group, and she was sure Quincy wouldn't mind Belle tagging along.

"I have a ton of AP English homework, so I'm about to head out," Cori said. "But I want to ask how it feels to be on the writing side again."

"Amazing," Avi gushed. "This opportunity means the world to me."

"We went through the usual submission and picking process. You earned it!"

"Please," Egypt scoffed from the podium.

Avi cut her eyes toward Egypt but went back to cleaning.

"Don't let the childishness get to you," Cori said in a raised voice. "She's a little salty about the positive feedback you're getting."

"*Salty* is never the word I'd use to describe myself," Egypt said, resting her chin in the palm of her hand. "As a matter of fact, I never did say congrats about your poem's reception, did I? It was endearing."

"Thanks," Avi said, quickly stacking the remaining cookies on a napkin to bring to Quincy. She didn't want to give Egypt a chance to bring her down.

"To be honest, it's the exact kind of thing the student body needed to read."

"I agree," Brittany said, leaning on the broom she held. At least she was genuine.

"Can I ask you just one little question?" Egypt said, walking out from behind the podium. "And you have to promise to answer honestly."

"Egypt," Cori said with caution in her voice.

"No, it's fine," Avi said. She placed the cookies neatly in her bag and turned to face her. "What's your question?"

"How much help did your mom give you?"

Brittany's mouth fell open with a gasp, and the broom smacked the ground.

Avi chuckled. "I didn't receive any help writing my poem."

"Hmm. I heard through the grapevine that that's not entirely true." Egypt shrugged. "If it *is* true, I'd hate for this to get out and tarnish the integrity of the *Cliff News*."

Avi sighed. "That won't happen, because *I* wrote it. I'm not sure who your source is, but they're lying to you, Egypt."

She scooped up her notebook from the desktop and unzipped her bag. This was silly, and she was ready to go.

"Well, then, I'm actually proud of you," Egypt said, crossing her arms over her sweater vest. "There are a lot of people who don't have the nerve to stick things out when times get hard."

Avi's head cocked to the side. "And what does that mean?"

"Just that I wasn't sure if quitting at the final hour was a *family* trait or strictly how your sister handles things."

Avi could hear the blood rushing in her ears as she tried to process Egypt's words, but Cori spoke first. "Okay, that's enough—"

"Then again," Egypt continued, raising her voice an octave, "it may have been that she could see the end of her little relationship in plain sight, and it was all too much to handle. I get it. We've *all* seen Lo get around. But I think it's sad when girls depend on a guy for their happiness. Don't you agree?"

Avi's eyes narrowed, and she swallowed hard, resisting the sudden urge to jump over the table and tackle Egypt.

"You know what?" Avi said, slamming her notebook on the table. "If you wanna attack me because you're mad that I can produce content our classmates like, that's fine. But that's the *last* time you bring my sister into it. She dropped out of the Harvest Queen pageant, and you *still* found a way to lose. Get over it. Because this bitchy mean-girl act is pathetic."

"Who the hell do you—"

"No, Egypt," Avi said, holding a hand up. "I'm done pretending to care about what you have to say." She threw her bag on her shoulder and turned toward the door in one swift move. "You win, okay? Cori, I'll forward all of my finished assignments to you so you don't fall behind, but after that, I'm done."

“Avi, don’t—”

“I quit.”

She strode out of the room, not bothering to look back at Egypt’s stunned expression.

40

"**MS. LEBEAU**, may I have a moment of your time?" Professor Lovette said as the class began filing out of the room. She leaned on the front of her gray desk, just as Avi had seen her husband do a thousand times in Algebra II.

Avi knew that her favorite professor wanted to discuss her abrupt departure from the *Cliff News* yesterday, but she didn't want to hear it. "Actually, Professor Lovette," she said, inching toward the door, where Rhyon and Zazie waited. "I *really* gotta get back to my room so I can start my history homework."

"Uh-uh. Take a seat," Professor Lovette ordered. "Ms. Bloom, Ms. Lewis. She'll catch up with you later."

Defeated, Avi dropped into a seat in the front row. "I'm sorry, but nothing you can say will convince me to rejoin the paper."

"And I wouldn't ask you to."

Avi's brows lifted, surprised.

"I know what Egypt said, and I hear she's been giving you a hard time. She'll be dealt with. But I need you to tell me—what's next?"

"Huh? Next for what?"

"You've been down lately. I've noticed, and I've asked you a thousand times to talk to me. You say you don't wanna talk about it? Fine. But if you're determined not to accept outside help, then how will you help yourself?" She tilted her head, scrutinizing Avi. "Even when you were ridiculously busy with editing, you showed up to work—and did so enthusiastically. Now, you've decided that chapter's closed. So, what is it that *you* can do to lift yourself up again?"

Avi opened her mouth and closed it again. For so long, she'd dreamed of writing for the paper. That didn't work out, so she began editing for the paper. It was consuming, and she'd loved it, but now that it was over . . . She shrugged. "I honestly don't know anymore."

"And that right there is my problem, Avielle."

Avi sulked in her seat. "You know, you sound more like my dad every time we talk."

Professor Lovette threw her hands up dramatically. "Oh no," she gasped. "Another adult who cares about you reaching your full potential! *Oooh, scary!*"

Avi glared.

"Watch those eyes," Professor Lovette said pointedly, taking the seat beside her. "Look, honey, you told me before that you're never happier than when people are reading your work, and I saw your face the moment you got word that your poem was picked. How do we get you back to that? How do you find a new audience?"

Avi gazed down, fidgeting with the A and Q charms dangling from her bracelet. She bit her lip, sad that she couldn't give an answer. "I genuinely don't know, Professor Lovette. I can't go back to the *Cliff News*, and that's the only place where I've had readers outside of my family and friends before."

"Wattpad," Quincy said, strolling into the room. Avi turned with furrowed brows to see him carrying two stacked brown boxes. He placed them on the desk.

"Blue asked me to drop this off to you before practice," he said to Professor Lovette.

Lovette nodded slowly, a huge grin on her face. "Wattpad's smart."

Quincy leaned on her desk, smirking, too. "You said you'd think about it before. Maybe now's the time?"

Avi had said that the night of their first date. But she hadn't had a chance to consider it since. Now, she had nothing but time. She could edit her short story, and then she could set it free to be read. She looked at them both, a smile spreading across her face. "Maybe it is."

41

ZAZIE WOVE KANEKALON HAIR into Ashia's head as she sat in a computer chair in G-12, flinching and frowning at every tug and pull.

"Beauty is pain," Rhyon remarked, sucking hair scraps into her handheld vacuum.

"Yeah, especially when your hairstylist is heavy-handed on purpose," Ashia muttered.

"Pop a Tylenol or three and stop whining," Zazie said. "Didn't nobody tell your tender-headed self to come ask for last-minute jumbo braids *on* Valentine's Day."

Zazie had offered to do Ashia's braids yesterday, but her nerves wouldn't allow her to sit still. Easlyn and a group of the ground-floor girls had stayed up late last night in the lounge, helping Ashia plan how she would ask London, a girl who lived on Hollingsworth's third floor, to the dance.

To Ashia's surprise, London had said, "I was just about to ask you!" So right after classes, she'd come to G-12, begging Zazie for braids.

Their door stood wide open, so they could see girls walking

back and forth in various stages of frenzy as they readied for tonight's dance in Briarcliff's gym.

Najah sat on the floor of the room painting Meme's toenails. Thalia, on the other hand, lay across Zazie's bed, with a heating pad on her stomach as *WandaVision* played on her laptop. She would be accompanying their group to the courtyard movie at six.

Avi had her reservations about she and Quincy missing their first dance. But watching her floormates run around in a tizzy made her feel they made the right choice.

So far, her day had been nothing short of calm and lovely. Cheetah Plans placed pink, red, and white decorations all over campus. Members of the Briarcliff Prep Glee Club performed sing-a-grams for unsuspecting students. And during lunch, Professors Blue and Lovette posed for yearbook pics in their matching pink suits as students fawned.

Then, as Avi walked out of her last class, Quincy popped up to gift her a single baby-blue rose held in the cutest round white box.

"The flower lasts for a year," he said when she kissed his cheek.

One by one, he was checking off all her firsts: kiss, jewelry, flowers.

Now Avi was at her desk, snacking on the heart-shaped box of chocolate Turtles her father sent and scanning her Wattpad profile.

An hour after Quincy and Professor Lovette sparked the idea, she'd made a profile and uploaded the first part to her short story. She'd worked through the night to perfect the second part and uploaded it right before her eight o'clock class the next morning. When she opened her laptop that evening, she already had thirteen reads and four comments from readers anxious for part three. In a day that was up, too. Avi loved that readers could reach her so directly—at least the kind ones. And her small following renewed her passion for creating in a moment when she'd feared it might be stunted for good.

Avi pulled up her partially edited part four to give it a quick look, just as Belle walked into the crowded room in a Spelman sweatshirt singing, "Everybody say hi to my viewers for my special Valentine's Day vlog!"

Ashia hid her face and hair from the camera while Zazie gave a dazzling smile and shamelessly plugged her father's restaurant.

"Ooh, is this what Q gave you?" Belle asked. She scooped the round box that was sitting on Avi's desk into her hands and held it up to the lens.

Avi blushed at the camera, grabbing for her flower. "Yes, and I liked it where it was." She placed it carefully back on her desk. "We're not leaving for another hour. I thought you were gonna meet us there."

"That's why I'm here," Belle said, dropping the camera to her side. "I'm not going with you guys to see the courtyard movie."

"Why not?" Avi asked through a mouthful of chocolate.

"Don't you think it would be kind of sad for me to third-wheel on my little sister's first Valentine's date?"

"It's a group thing, so you wouldn't really be third-wheeling."

Belle frowned. "And all of you have dates?" she asked the other girls.

"No, but we're going to the dance," Najah said.

Ashia winced in the chair, glaring back at Zazie. "Me too. I'm going with London."

"Zazie's with Jah, of course," Rhyon said. "But Thalia and I don't have dates."

"What? Moe won't be there?" Belle asked with a smirk.

"Just because we're both in the same space doesn't make him my date."

Zazie snickered. "Yeah, right. If y'all aren't boo'd up by the end of the night, I'll give you a hundred dollars."

"See, that's another thing," Belle said, wrinkling her nose. She propped herself comfortably on Avi's desk. "No offense, but you're all underclassmen, and everyone at the screening probably will be, too."

"And what's wrong with us?" Thalia asked, completely offended.

"Not a thing, but I'm a senior. I'd be out of place."

"But being by yourself on Valentine's Day isn't cool either," Avi said. "Maybe Quincy wouldn't mind if I didn't go."

"What?" Rhyon and Meme said together.

Shocked and annoyed looks came at Avi from every direction. It was like she'd just committed to throwing her firstborn off a balcony.

"Girl, be serious," Zazie said without looking up from the braid she was installing.

"He would, and I'm not letting you do that," Belle said. "Plus, I won't be alone. I'll be with Adoree."

"What about her boyfriend?" Ashia asked.

Belle leaned in, and everyone's ears perked up. "Y'all didn't see the PresCliff's latest post?"

Zazie's mouth dropped open. "You're saying that was true?"

"What's true?" Thalia asked.

"Her jerk boyfriend broke up with her two days before Valentine's Day," Belle said. "And now he's taking Wynter to the dance—ya know, that cheerleader. And to make matters worse, he gave Wynter the heart necklace he took back from Adoree, and the girl's been wearing it faithfully."

"You're lying," Rhyon exclaimed.

"Not. And Adoree's birthday's next week, so she's a mess. Anyways, we're gonna stay in, eat Talenti and rewatch season two of *Dear White People*."

"That's a pretty good excuse," Avi exhaled, but she looked at her sister with a squint. If anything, Belle knew how to put on a brave front. "And you're sure you're good?"

"I'm fine," Belle said exasperatedly.

She picked her camera back up and smiled in the lens.

"I have my friends and my viewers to keep me company during this god-awful holiday," she said and jumped off the desk. "Have fun, and make sure you guys document the night. I wanna see everything later. But now, I gotta go take pics of EJ and Noemie to send to Mommy." She whisked out of the room. "À bientôt!"

42

MIDWAY THROUGH THE SCREENING of *To All the Boys I've Loved Before,* Avi glanced around at her classmates. Belle was wrong. There were kids from every grade scattered in the grassy courtyard behind the library, bundled up and cozy. Not to mention teachers and faculty watching them closely.

Jasiri and Zazie snuggled up on their blanket, paying more attention to each other than the movie. To Avi's right, Kai poured the remainder of Thalia's sour gummy worms in his mouth. She shoved him off her blanket despite his whispered protests. Moe lay across his blanket as Rhyon leaned on his back. *Bet lost.*

Avi looked over at Quincy, who was entranced by the movie, as he took a sip from his orange soda. She bumped his shoulder, holding a bag of white cheddar popcorn out to him. He took a handful, but not before he pulled her blanket over, closing the small space between them.

An hour later, at the gate, the track coach, Professor Orchid, had to physically separate Zazie and Jasiri, announcing, "All right, everyone, as cute as y'all are, this isn't the last goodbye.

Preston underclassmen, you know curfew was already pushed back. It's time to go!"

Avi graciously accepted Quincy's kiss on her cheek, knowing that prying eyes were everywhere. She wasn't quite ready to display affection like Jah and Zazie. But Moe's and Rhyon's dry nods goodbye wouldn't have sufficed either. With a final hug and promises to call later, Quincy stepped off Briarcliff's sidewalk as Professor Orchid ushered a crowd of Preston students onto their campus.

As the girls passed the gym, Avi stopped smelling Quincy's blue hoodie long enough to tell them that she was going to pass by the Cliff vending machines to get a drink. Zazie and Rhyon rushed to the sushi spot before the grumpy manager could close the gate.

Up the sidewalk Avi strolled, looking doe-eyed at the selfies of her and Quincy from tonight. Juniors and seniors dressed up from the dance littered the Cliff. They held hands, laughed, and kissed. Some were so bold with their PDA they made Avi blush and look away.

She checked her watch, slipping two dollars into the vending machine. The extra half hour upperclassmen got for curfew was unfair, but almost up. She grabbed her cranberry juice and Cheez-Its from the slot, and out of the corner of her eye saw movement on a senior bench—the one under the pavilion.

Hearing familiar voices, Avi peeked from behind a pillar and saw her sister and Logan sitting close together. Too close. His head was hung low, and Belle was wiping tears from his face. Logan took her hand, and Belle angled his head to hers. Before Avi could squeak out a sound, they were kissing. She stood out from behind the pillar, dumbstruck. A small pop from the Cheez-Its bag she squeezed sounded off, but they didn't hear.

Avi had known they were back on speaking terms, but Belle assured her it was nothing more than amity. But this was more than that. It was passionate. Desperate.

Housemother Joyce walked into the Cliff, talking through her megaphone.

"Curfew is in five minutes." Her voice blared, and everyone cringed. "Anyone I see past curfew without a Briarcliff student ID will get written up. Up and out," she said, steering students along.

With a final kiss, Logan left the Cliff. Belle was so busy staring goofily at something on her hand that she walked right into Avi.

"Oh, hey," she said, her voice much higher than usual. "I was about to call and ask how the movie went."

Avi stared at Belle with a ferocity she'd never felt before.

"Fine," Belle sighed. "How long have you been standing there?"

"Long enough. What was that?"

"Nothing really," Belle said, biting her lip. She held up her hand, wiggling it in Avi's face, the promise ring glinting on her finger. "Just us getting back together."

"Wait! What?" Avi sputtered. It felt like she'd gotten the wind knocked out of her. Sweat gathered on her forehead, despite the cool night's air. "You're kidding, right?"

"No! We've been talking more lately. Neither of us liked how we ended—or how we were apart. This is a chance for us to do it right."

"You didn't like how you guys ended last time because *his hands were around your throat.*"

"Avi, you said you wanted me to feel better, and I have been. But only after Logan and I started talking again."

"I wanted you to talk to a therapist! What's wrong with y—" A coughing fit muted Avi's words, and she bent over trying to regain her breath.

Belle's smile faded. "This is something I want. I thought you'd be happy for me."

"Happy for you—what is there to be happy about? Belle, I'm devastated." Looks from passing students forced Avi to lower her voice as Belle pushed her toward the pavilion. "The Logan that traveled hundreds of miles to choke you is the real him. Not that actor who cried here tonight. But now you got an apology and that tired ring, and everything's good?"

Belle shook her head skyward, arms crossed. "I'm not gonna sulk about what happened forever. I forgave him, and it's time for you to do the same."

Avi paced for a moment with her hands on her chest. It felt like her heart was trying to claw its way out. When she looked at her sister again, it was with disbelief. Belle's face held a new, stony resolve.

"Tell me this is some sick joke to ruin my night. Please. Because it's working." She bent over again, hands on her knees as she coughed. Any gasps of air she did manage were painful.

Belle pressed a hand to her back. "You're gonna give yourself an asthma attack if you don't stop freaking out over nothing."

Over the pounding in her ears, Avi heard Belle digging

around in her bag. A second later, she pushed Avi's spare purple inhaler into her hands.

Avi took a long drag, panting. "It's not an asthma attack . . . it's a panic attack."

With another puff, she squeezed her eyes shut, trying to ignore the pain in her chest and concentrate on breathing instead. When she opened her eyes, Belle stood over her with concern etched across her face.

"The only reason I agreed not to say anything was because you promised you two were over for good. If you can't keep your promise, then why should I keep mine?"

"I swear if you open your mouth, I'll never speak to you again." Belle's tone was harsh, her expression deadly serious.

Avi straightened her back against the wall, unable to hide the hurt on her face as she looked her sister squarely in the eyes.

"You would stop speaking to me over him," she whispered. "He's worth that to you?"

Belle's lip trembled, and she looked toward her feet. "I love him."

Avi threw her hands in the air. "Three months ago, you said that wasn't enough! But things have changed now, huh? Fine. We don't have to speak anymore."

"What is that supposed to mean?"

"It means that if you can put Logan before me—and yourself—then you can have him. But you're gonna be stupid by yourself this time." Belle reached for her arm, but Avi wrenched it away. "No. I'm not gonna help you run back to someone who hits you!"

She spun to leave—only to see Zazie and Rhyon standing frozen with matching looks of horror.

"He what?!" Zazie actually shouted from the edge of the pavilion.

Rhyon's troubled eyes moved between them. "This is the secret?" she asked, her voice strangely airy.

Belle moved forward, shaking her head, but Avi met her friends' eyes intently. "Yes." She needed them to know.

Housemother Joyce turned the corner before Belle could start yelling. "Clearly, I wasn't heard," she said observing them all with a stern eye. "Curfew is now—and it already passed for underclassmen."

"But—" Avi started.

"Miss LeBeau, please don't make me write you up. The three of you to Hollingsworth. Now."

The four of them began to walk, and already Belle was pulling at Avi's arm. "Older Miss LeBeau, fall behind," she said, making them pause. "We need to discuss these late-night choreo sessions you're holding in the lounge."

Avi took the chance to speed ahead of Belle and her friends, marching from underneath the pavilion. She was upset with Housemother Joyce's interruption, furious with her sister, frustrated that she would have to explain everything to Zazie and Rhyon when they got back to Hollingsworth, and terrified at the realization that they were back to square one.

"Avi, can we talk about this later?" Belle shouted when they were feet away, interrupting Housemother Joyce mid-sentence. Her voice was desperate.

Avi shook her head, not bothering to look back.

43

TWO OUTFIELDERS COLLIDED with their heads held heavenward on the baseball field. The soaring ball was lost to the crowd in the sun, but Quincy ran at full speed, glove outstretched. He caught the ball, did a one-eighty, and launched it toward the bases. The Lions' team captain caught it, tagging out a Red Badger as he slid toward home plate.

Avi jumped up and down, cheering in her DIY #8 jersey with the rest of the crowd.

Though Moe had played baseball since they were toddlers, Avi had no real interest until recently. This season, she hadn't missed a single home game. Still, it was hard for her to tell if she really enjoyed baseball or if she just loved watching Quincy play. It was almost as exhilarating as watching him play his saxophone. Almost.

Avi was busy staring at Quincy in the dugout when Moe hit a home run. This time, Rhyon was the first on her feet, outcheering everyone in the stands.

Zazie guffawed. "I can't believe you wouldn't let me paint his jersey number on your cheek."

"What? I can't be happy for my friend?" Rhyon asked, quickly taking her seat.

During the seventh inning, Belle and Logan walked up the bleachers hand-in-hand, smiling and nodding at people in the stands like they were Meghan and Harry. Avi pretended not to see Belle wave. She ignored the sad look in Belle's eyes when she turned to sit down on the bleacher, rows in front of them. Ever the actor, Logan placed an arm around Belle's shoulder, and she leaned into his chest.

The two were back to posing as Briarston's Best Couple, which apparently meant never being apart. Whether they were between classes, at lunch, or attending games, plays, or literally any campus event, they were arm-in-arm. Without fail.

"How long do you think you can go without speaking to her?" Zazie asked.

"I spoke to her at lunch yesterday."

"It's true. I was almost shocked, and then I remembered their parents' weekly check-ins," Rhyon huffed.

Avi pulled her denim baseball cap down to shade her eyes, watching the Badgers coach motion wildly to his pitcher. "As long as she's with the creep, I have nothing to say to her."

Zazie sighed, casting a sad look at the back of Belle's head. But all Avi could see was Belle's freshly straightened hair. Had she straightened it because *he* told her to?

"Maybe she wants to apologize," Zazie suggested.

"I don't want an apology," Avi hissed. "I need her to wake up!"

After they learned the truth, Avi made them swear to keep

Belle's secret. They'd only overheard the very end of the conversation, but it was enough. Rhyon and Zazie didn't make her feel like she was overreacting, or sensitive, or meddling where she didn't belong. For hours, they listened to her rage—and often joined in.

Still, Rhyon and Zazie made it clear they didn't agree with Avi's decision to shut Belle out. Avi had to admit, ignoring her sister hadn't gone the way she thought it would. The plan was to give Belle nothing, and eventually, she would snap to her senses and dump Logan. But here they were—late March and the two hadn't had one conversation of substance since that night. Not that Belle didn't try, at first. But lately, even the texts had stopped trickling in. Avi pretended it wasn't affecting her, but she couldn't trick herself.

"You can't ignore her forever," Zazie said, bumping Avi's shoulder. "I know it's hard, but other than Logan, you're the only person Belle has to talk to about this."

"What if she needs you?" Rhyon asked.

"If she needed me, she'd come to me."

"She didn't before. Why would she think she could now, when you won't even look her way?" Rhyon asked, with a sharpness in her voice.

"I don't wanna talk about this," Avi said, standing. She headed for the bathroom in the tunnel under the bleachers.

It bothered her how right they were. Sure, Belle looked perfectly happy with Logan, but what if she was hiding scratches and bruises all over again? What if she was dealing with this entirely alone? Avi was the only person Belle used to confide in, and now she didn't even have that. Come to think of it, Nevaeh and Belle were rarely together anymore either. They'd been best friends through everything way before Logan entered the picture. What could make them part ways?

Avi dried her hands with paper towels, lost in the possibilities. When she yanked the door open, she yelped, jumping back a foot. The devil himself stood waiting for her.

"Sorry," Logan said, propping the bathroom door open. "I didn't mean to scare you."

Avi's eyes darted around the room. The only exit was past him.

"Can we talk for a second?" Logan asked. He stood with his hands in his pockets, a meek look on his face.

Avi wanted to punch him.

"About what?" she asked, sidestepping him. She knew being trapped in the bathroom alone with Logan wasn't smart. She headed closer toward the bleachers where her screams could at least be heard.

Logan took three long strides and positioned himself in front of her again. "Belle."

Avi crossed her arms, her heart beating so loudly she was sure he could hear.

"What about her?"

"Look, I know you've never really liked me, so this is a long shot, but she's messed up about you guys not talking. Would you consider sitting down and having a conversation to clear the air? I'll set it up, all you have to do is show up."

Avi narrowed her eyes at him. "It made sense when she sent Kai and Rhyon, but *you*? Belle thought sending *you* was the way to get us to talk?"

"Of course not." Logan shook his head. "I'm coming to you on my own because I know how upset she is about your situation."

"But you do know why we're not speaking, don't you?"

His eyes cast down.

"I thought so. If you want us to talk, then it's simple. Break up with her."

Avi tried to move around him, but he blocked her path.

"I think you know that wouldn't help anything," he said with a look of almost-believable confusion. "She's your sister, and you can't even put your petty feelings aside for a couple of minutes to make her happy?"

"Feeling like my sister deserves someone who won't put their hands on her isn't petty," Avi retorted.

Logan blew his cheeks with a long exhale. "That was a mistake, and—"

"Weird. You say that like you only did it once."

"Look," he huffed. "I heard you got kicked off the *Cliff News* last month. I could talk to Egypt and maybe arrange something. But I need you to help me out with this first."

Avi arched her eyebrow, scoffing. "First, I didn't get kicked off—I quit. And my answer is no, to both. Now, if you don't mind, I'd love to get back to my boyfriend's game. Please move."

Logan stared down at her, surprised at her refusal. He stepped out of her way with disdain in his eye, and a smile that sent ice through her veins crept across his face.

"Go ahead and watch the rest of your little boyfriend's game," he said as she passed. "And Avi," he added when she was feet away. "Have a good day. I know Belle and I will."

Avi couldn't control the shiver sent down her spine as she turned back into the warm, natural light of the day, leaving Logan behind in the shadows.

44

AVI DRAGGED HER MOP across the floor of the women's bathroom in Zody, cursing every bit of Fallon's existence. When she'd been called into Housemother Lisa's office last night over the dorm's intercom, she assumed it couldn't be anything serious. Even when Easlyn pressed play on the video Avi posted of her playing *Mario Kart* with Quincy in his room, she didn't see the point they were trying to make. The second time Housemother Lisa played the video, Easlyn pressed pause where it showed the Kobe poster on the back of Quincy, Moe, and EJ's shut door.

Automatic violation. Automatic detention for a first offense "of this magnitude."

Avi asked how Housemother Lisa got the video, but neither she nor Easlyn would disclose their source. She already knew, anyway. She and Fallon had spent the night before arguing about their French project. One insult flew after another, and then Avi announced to everyone in the hallway that Fallon had walked into French the day before with the back of her skirt tucked into her panties. With narrowed eyes, Fallon had silently backed into Kieley and Rhyon's room. Avi knew she was up to no good but shrugged it off. Of course Fallon had screen-recorded Avi's story from over a week ago and saved it for an opportunity like this to strike back.

As if getting bathroom-duty detention wasn't bad enough, Belle was there, too, restocking the bathroom's paper towels. Apparently, she'd gotten smart with Professor Lou when he tried confiscating her phone on her way to Home Economics. Mr. Lankin, who handed out detention assignments, thought he was doing them a favor when he assigned them to clean the four bathrooms in Zody.

"Oh, are you two sisters?" he'd asked. "Okay, I'll pair you off together, but don't spend all your time gabbin'. Those floors and bowls need to shine. Otherwise, I'll see you both back here tomorrow." He'd pushed a sanitation cart into their hands. "Don't look so sad. The time will fly."

He was wrong. It was Saturday morning, and they'd been cleaning for two hours already with lots to go. Avi had a lot more free time now that her *Cliff News* dreams were buried, but her homework pile was always increasing. Plus, she was trying to plot a new idea to eventually post on Wattpad. Why couldn't this be a regular high school, where detention meant you had to sit quietly and reflect on your wrongdoings?

Belle sighed loudly, as if Avi needed a reminder that she was still there. For the first hour, she'd tried starting random conversations.

You know Mommy's pissed at the both of us, right?

I finally finished your entire short story. Your last part had over a thousand reads!

Paisli actually called me back yesterday.

Are you gonna stick to uploading poetry now? I think that's a good idea.

Avi had ignored her while they cleaned the two women's bathrooms. Now they stood in the first men's restroom, utterly offended by its disgusting state.

Avi jumped right in, plunging one of the toilets, but the smell was outrageous.

"Here, let me do it," Belle said. She held out her gloved hand for the plunger. Avi's eyebrows bunched in confusion until Belle placed the plunger back in the cart, opened a compartment, and pulled out yellow caution tape instead.

The dust masks muffled their laughs.

Belle went back to mopping, and Avi abandoned toilet duty completely for the Clorox spray and paper towels.

She wiped the counter in circles, stealing glances at her sister. Finally, she said, "You know, when Zazie went and destroyed those Preston signs of that old revolutionary who turned out to be an admitted rapist, Headmaster Walsh tried to get her suspended. But Headmistress Malone stepped in and assigned her to the campus greenhouse instead."

Belle's hands slid down the mop's handle. "They seriously let her spend two weekends watering flowers and breathing clean air while we got stuck cleaning filthy bathrooms."

"I mean, she did have to handle manure for some of the plants, but she loved it. Says she's gonna have a farm when she gets older now."

"Well, if she wants, there's a whole lot of fertilizer in these toilets."

Avi's face scrunched. "Mr. Lankin can forget it. That toilet needs a plumber, not me." Her head dropped back as she leaned against the sink with folded arms. "This is such a waste of time. I need to go over the study packet Nicole gave me. Finals are right around the corner."

"Nicole? What happened to Quincy?"

"We can't focus when we're together anymore. When my grade started to slip again, Blue personally called Daddy."

Belle laughed as she scooped up toilet paper rolls to put in the stalls. "Did you know they were friends at Morehouse in the nineties?"

"Not until after the call."

It was silent again in the restroom. But not the uncomfortable kind they'd faced all morning. Belle pulled her mask from her face and leaned on the counter by Avi.

"Hey," she started hesitantly. "Next month I'm taking my grad pictures. I was actually thinking of asking Zazie to take them for me. Those pageant pics she took were stunning."

"She'd love that." Avi smiled, pleased that Belle was seriously considering Zazie. "How many outfit changes were you thinking?"

"Three. A Briarcliff shirt, a white dress, and my Cheetahnaire uniform with the gold fringes."

Avi already knew about Belle's photo shoot—and that Belle was going to invite her. Last night, Avi's mom had kicked her guilting up a notch. "No matter what's going on between you two, family comes first," she'd said. "You two need to work out whatever it is you have going on. Because at this point, I'm annoyed. Belle said she wants you there. So show up!"

It had been almost two months since Avi and Belle held an actual conversation. Sure, it was mostly about nothing. But at least they were talking. In all their lives, the longest she and Belle had gone without speaking before this was two weeks (over a broken necklace). That time, Sugah had locked them in a room until she heard conversation. She'd forgotten how much she missed her sister. Maybe they could find their way back to one another today.

"Yeah, I'll come," Avi said. She pulled herself onto the counter to sit.

Belle looked taken aback, but she smiled as she stripped off her gloves and dropped them into the trash can. "Seriously?"

Avi nodded. "I was scrolling on Twitter and saw this one girl's senior pictures. She was wearing this shirt that said something like 'Headed to Hampton U' with this cute anchor on it. Here, let me see if I can find it." Avi held the picture out to Belle, who gave a half-hearted smile. "You could get one custom made or ask Mommy to send one of her old Spelman shirts. They count as vintage."

Belle crossed her arms over her stomach, looking dejected.

"You don't have to do one in the shirt." Avi laughed. "It was a suggestion."

"A good one. But I don't know about Spelman anymore." This was news to Avi.

"What don't you know?"

"College decision day is coming, and it turns out NYU has a great dance program. Business, too. I think I'd do well there."

"Hold up. NYU? Since when was NYU seriously on the table? I thought NCAT was your second choice. And last year you said you were going to an HBCU regardless because of their dance team opportunities." And then a lightbulb clicked.

Avi hopped down from the sink, looking Belle in the eyes. "He chose Princeton, didn't he?"

"And he got a scholarship," Belle said, attempting to look bright as she ran her fingers up and down her arms. "This way, we won't have to do that whole long-distance thing. I just need a little help with something." Avi could hardly believe her ears.

"What now?"

"Figuring out how exactly I'm gonna tell Mommy the new plan so she won't freak out."

"And this was your idea?"

"Yeah."

"You're lying." Avi stomped her foot in frustration. "He's still controlling you. He's still making your decisions."

Belle huffed. "We're better now than we ever were before. Logan has changed, and I trust him. If you would give him another chance, you'd see it for yourself." She grabbed Avi's forearms. The look in her soft brown eyes was desperate. "Come back with me to my dorm, and we can—"

Avi ripped her arms out of Belle's grasp. "I'm not coming to help you make a plan to ruin your life even more!"

"Excuse you?"

"Belle, this is exhausting. Aren't you tired?" she asked, her voice cracking. "I mean, this literally goes against everything Mommy and Daddy have ever taught us. And he's somehow even got you lying to yourself. You went back to straightening your hair every day! Don't think I didn't notice. And now you're changing your college decision? I— You know what? If you wanna see if he's changed, stop asking and *tell* him what your next step is gonna be. It's still *your* life."

Belle shook her head. "We've already made the decision. This is what couples do, Avielle. They take each other's feelings and wants into consideration."

Avi was so sick of hearing "that's what couples do" as an excuse to cover for Logan.

"Quincy has never tried forcing me to do something he knows I'd hate just so he can feel good about himself. Tell me one sacrifice Logan has made for you."

Avi waited, but Belle didn't say a word.

"That's what I thought," Avi said. "God, I never thought you could be this stupid!"

She said it with intended malice, and the effect was immediate. The fury that had been in Belle's eyes evaporated. Now, her expression showed only the most profound hurt.

Avi knew she should apologize, but the words wouldn't leave her mouth. The moment stretched uncomfortably then snapped. Belle seemed to make a decision before squaring her shoulders and marching out of the bathroom without another word.

45

WHAT BEGAN AS a study session in the lounge for the girls' upcoming biology final became a fiasco. An hour into reviewing Rhyon's self-made *Jeopardy!* game, Jasiri texted Zazie to see if he could swing by, and he and Kai showed up with their books, hoping to weasel a free Spanish lesson out of her. Thirty minutes later, Moe, EJ, and Quincy arrived empty-handed, having seen them all studying on Ashia's Instastory.

They somehow went from discussing the importance of ATP to having a heated debate on the top ten Disney movies of all time. Moe took it upon himself to erase Thalia's bio definitions from the dry-erase board to make room for their ranking system.

"Wait a minute. Are you seriously trying to put *Beauty and the Beast* anywhere near *Coco*? That's not okay," EJ said, plucking the marker out of Ashia's hand.

"He's right, Shi." Rhyon shifted herself forward on a plush purple beanbag. "Now, if we're being serious, then everyone knows *Aladdin* deserves to be in the top five."

"What?" Jasiri exclaimed. "The music doesn't even slap in *Aladdin*. *Mulan* had 'Be a Man,' and 'I Just Can't Wait to

Be King' puts *The Lion King* at number two. I'm not hearin' anything less."

"If we're talking music, then *Moana* deserves a top spot. 'You're Welcome' is a bop," Kai added.

Quincy stared at the board as if it were an impossible equation. "Sure, that's a contender, but I won't fake like I didn't shed a tear when Ellie died in *Up*, so where does that one go?"

Moe stood, shaking his head incredulously. "So, we're all gonna sit here and act like *Monsters, Inc.* doesn't exist? *Toy Story 3*? *The Incredibles*?"

"And what about the first Black princess, Tiana?" Thalia asked.

"Hey! We're all forgetting a top nominee," Zazie shouted. Her red marker squeaked on the whiteboard as she wrote *Wall-E* in all caps next to the number one slot. Loud groans and rebuttals sounded off around the room.

Avi needed to study, but she was grateful for this distraction. Belle had left an irate voicemail on her phone after their argument that morning in detention, going on and on about how Avi had no right to judge and telling her that she would be waiting for an apology. The other option included being ignored for eternity.

It was dramatic for sure. But the fact that Belle could rage this way over Logan was disconcerting. Plus, it would be a cold day in hell before Avi apologized for being right. In hindsight, she could have said it more tactfully, but Belle didn't seem to respond to subtlety anymore. If she was willing to give up her dream school for Logan . . . Avi was scared to think of what else she'd do.

Ten minutes later, they were all seated quietly, debate forgotten. Rhyon couldn't let it go when Moe and Thalia admitted they'd never seen *Finding Dory*, so she loaded up Disney+ and cut the lights. Quincy dropped on the couch next to Avi, startling her out of her thoughts as the movie began.

He scooped the textbook out of her lap. "You either don't have an opinion about the top movie, or you're really into bio all of a sudden."

"*Inside Out* is number one. No questions about it." Her finger hovered over the block button on Belle's contact info.

"Huh," Quincy grunted. "I forgot about that one."

"Shhhhh!" Zazie hissed.

Quincy glared but lowered his voice. "I'm guessing detention with your sister wasn't fun?"

"I'm honestly still trying to understand how *you* got a formal warning, and *I* ended up plunging toilets in Zody for three hours."

"Different schools, different rules," he said, smirking. "That's why you're so quiet?"

"Nope. It's the usual." Avi clicked on the voicemail and handed Quincy her phone to listen.

"Sheesh." He whistled. "I didn't know Belle used words like that."

"Turns out I can draw out the worst in her if I try hard enough."

"You know, you worry about their stuff all the time," he said, nudging her shoulder.

"Do not."

"Do too. Your people are gonna make mistakes. That's

life." He leaned back on the couch. "Get this. Every day, my dad wakes up and decides to be a shittier person than he was the day before. And succeeds."

Avi's eyes moved from her phone and landed on Quincy's indifferent expression.

"But you love him. How are you not worried every day?"

"I am." He shrugged. "But when I was eleven, my grandma said, 'Bryan's gonna do what he wants to do, the same way life is gonna do what it wants to us.' Can't control either."

"Life or people," Avi whispered.

"Yep. But at the end of the day, you can't fold when things get tough."

She stared down at her fingers. "Sometimes, you talk about him and it doesn't even sound like your story. It's like you're telling me something you heard from someone else. Maybe you're too far removed from your dad's issues?"

Quincy shrugged again, but not with convincible nonchalance. "The other option is to sit in it. Cry and complain. I'd rather find the solution."

"Not everything's as simple as a math equation."

"Isn't it, though? Me, minus him, equals a happy life."

Avi shook her head, not wanting to push him or say out loud how unhealthy that option sounded. Was that the point one arrived at when all other options were exhausted? It surely wasn't healing. Avoidance, maybe? Perhaps in Quincy's case, avoidance allowed him peace, even if it wasn't sustainable.

Avi turned to him with her elbow propped on the couch's back. "Okay, so tell me then, O Wise One. How do I not worry constantly?"

Quincy turned her phone off and plugged it into the outlet behind the couch. "Don't touch it for one hour."

She sunk into the cushions with a pout. "I've seen this movie a million times; it's not a good distraction."

He thought for a second and then said, "Oh, the people from the Sky Zone in Bowie called back. I got an interview when school lets out."

"For real?!" Avi squealed.

"Shh!" It was Moe this time. For someone who'd fought against watching the movie in the first place, he seemed awfully entranced, concern for Dory's well-being clouding his face.

To no surprise, Avi felt refreshed after an hour without her phone. Even so, the space that Avi could put between herself and Belle was different from the space Quincy required between himself and his father. He was shielding himself from a different type of pain. The idea of putting up a wall that high between herself and Belle was unfathomable. But if she couldn't stop Belle from choosing NYU, she may as well begin laying the bricks herself. She turned her phone back on.

Messages from Belle flooded in one after the other.

I thought about it. I'm gonna tell him I don't want to go to NYU.

5:12 P.M.

Plz come

6:04 P.M.

In me room

6:04 P.M.

am sassy

6:12 P.M.
BELLEY

Avi reread the messages three times. She was glad Belle was starting to come to her senses, but it was odd for her to use shorthand, even in text. And what did "am sassy" mean? She looked at the top corner of her phone—6:33 p.m.—and grabbed her lanyard from the side table.

"Going somewhere?" Quincy asked.

"To Truth," she said, tightening the laces on her Converse. "I think Belle wants to talk."

He smirked with crossed arms. "To fight?"

"Maybe," Avi said, smirking back. "I'm ready this time."

"Hey," Zazie whispered as Avi zipped her windbreaker. "I thought we were gonna finish bio *Jeopardy!* when the movie goes off?"

"We are. I'll be back in like thirty minutes."

46

AVI STOOD IN TRUTH'S LOBBY waiting for someone to swipe her onto the elevator. She was about to call Belle when Nevaeh walked in, carrying loads of bags from an arts and crafts store.

"Hey, Baby LeBeau," she smiled. "Going up?"

Avi nodded and grabbed two bags from Nevaeh.

"I feel like I haven't had the chance to talk to you in forever," Avi said as they waited.

Nevaeh shook her head with a deep inhale. She knew what Avi was hinting toward.

"Yeah . . . I've been trying to give Belle space, and since you're her sister, I didn't want to . . ." Her voice drifted off.

"No, it's fine. I get it."

They stood side by side, shifting uncomfortably in the silence before Avi felt like she would burst if she didn't ask.

"You know," she started carefully. "Belle never flat-out told me why you two stopped hanging out."

"Really?" Nevaeh's bottom lip twisted, her eyebrows raised. "I told her that getting back together with the big dummy was a bad idea, and she freaked."

"So did I! Wait a minute. I thought you were okay with him."

"At best, I only ever tolerated Logan."

The elevator dinged, and they waited for two girls with glum expressions to exit first.

"Belle stopped talking to you because you said that?" Avi had said far worse things about Logan to his face.

Nevaeh leaned on the opposite end of the elevator as it began its slow ascent. "There was that, and then I called him an arrogant, controlling idiot who didn't deserve her. And I may have called him ashy, but I can't remember if I said that part out loud. Anyways, she called me jealous and accused me of wanting him. I knew right then we needed a break." She stared at the elevator's buttons with crossed arms. "I love your sister like she's blood; I couldn't just stay quiet while she stayed with a guy who spoke to her the way he used to."

Avi's eyes bulged. "You heard it, too?"

"Yeah! One day I caught him yelling in her face like he ain't had no home training. I. Went. Off. Then he tried to act like *I* was the one overreacting. But I don't play that. It was like the beginning of the end for us."

Finally, the sixth-floor number lit, and the metal doors slid open. They headed left down the hall toward suite 604.

"Do you think you guys will make up?" Avi asked.

"We will," Nevaeh said confidently. "We needed a break, but Belle's my best friend. We're gonna start college in the fall without that clown."

Avi gave a weak smile but decided not to say anything. The college thing was up in the air, but if Belle stuck to her plan, then maybe Avi was about to hear good news.

When they entered, Avi set the craft bags on the table and headed for Belle's room. She could see from the crack under the closed door that the light was off. She knocked twice but heard only silence on the other side. Avi checked her phone. There were no messages asking her to meet elsewhere. She pushed off the door and turned to leave when she remembered the palazzo pants she wanted to borrow. Avi knew Belle would say no if she asked, especially after their latest fight, so she pushed the door open and flicked on the lights.

She jumped back with a gasp. Belle's desk chair was upturned next to her cracked ring light. The lamp that usually stood by her bed was on its side, covered partially by the white comforter. Broken glass was strewn across the floor, the picture frames mangled near Belle's beloved white violin—smashed to pieces.

And then, scariest of all, there she was—Belle, lying motionless on the floor, her white carpet stained with blood.

Avi inched toward her, heart hammering louder with each step as she fought the urge to run. Or cry. Or breathe. On her knees, Avi reached out a trembling hand for signs of breath.

Before she could, Belle shrieked in a panic. She paused her feeble attempts to scratch her attacker's face when Avi's cracked voice rang, "It's me!"

Belle looked up at the sound of her voice, frantic tears spilling over the darkening bruise under her left eye. The tears mingled with blood flowing from her nose down to her swollen lip.

"What took you so long?" Belle moaned.

She tried to sit up, but Avi pushed her shoulder back down, seeing the pain etched across her face. Not to mention the intense wincing every time she moved the hand cradled to her chest.

"You have to get me out of here before anyone sees."

Avi's mind raced. "Where would we go? I can't drive, and you need help."

"We can—"

"Nevaeh!"

Belle closed her eyes tight in defeat, and a moment later, Nevaeh was in the doorway. Her horror crystallized as she met them on the floor, examining Belle's face, hands, and the purpling bruise on her upper rib cage.

"Should we go to the nurse?" Avi wheezed.

Belle whimpered, "No."

"She's right," Nevaeh said calmly. "Your finger's broken, and that bruise on your side looks bad. We're going to the ER."

Belle attempted to sit up again to retort, but she couldn't bear it.

With an exhale of relief, Avi looked from her sister's bloody face to Nevaeh. "It was—"

"Logan, I know," Nevaeh finished. "Get some clothes on her. I'm gonna bring my car around."

47

AVI STOOD IN FRONT of a vending machine in Brady Hospital, staring at her phone. Her mother's contact information taunted her.

Ten minutes ago, Avi had left Belle and Nevaeh in the gloomy examination room. She told them she needed a drink, but what she really needed was a chance to clear her head.

Now was the time, wasn't it? There couldn't be a better time than now to involve the people who could help.

Under Avi's care, Logan had gone from slapping Belle around to fracturing her pinkie, spraining her wrist, blackening one eye, and bruising two ribs all in one night.

Avi bit her nails and rocked on her toes, attempting to calm the shakes that continuously took over her body. The image of Belle balled up on the floor, motionless, played on an endless loop. She would eventually see that Avi was doing the right thing and come around. She had to.

Call me back.

MOMMY

This had to be a sign. God-sent. Avi raised her thumb to press the call button.

"What's up, Baby LeBeau?" Nevaeh said.

Avi jumped, bumping into the vending machine as she stuffed her phone in her back pocket.

"Oh—hey. I was about to—"

"Call your mom? I saw you looking at her name."

Avi collapsed into the closest seat in the waiting room. She pulled her legs to her chest, face buried in her knees. "I don't know what to do anymore," she said.

"Yeah, it's tough." Nevaeh nodded. She took a seat, wiping her face in her hands. "When we talked earlier, I left out the real reason why me and Belle stopped talking."

Her words forced Avi's eyes up.

"The day after the pageant, I went to your room to bring Belle her stuff. That's when I caught him yelling in her face—I don't even know how he found his way into Hollingsworth, but that's when I cursed him out. She was mad at first that I didn't let her handle it, but a few days later, she admitted that I said a lot of what she wished she could have. It was almost like she was afraid to. I guess I should've known then," Nevaeh said, shaking her head. "Anyways, she ended up breaking up with him, and I was happy about it, but fast-forward to the day after we got back, and I walked in her room while she was putting makeup on her neck.

"Over the break, she'd called me, upset about him showing up at your house, but she didn't . . ." Nevaeh took a second to clear her throat. "The bruises from whatever he did were fading, but they were still bruises. A couple weeks later, I finally said it out loud. I accused him of putting his hands on her, and she blew up. Made me feel like I was losing my mind for even suggesting it. I mean, I *know* her!

"So, when they got back together, I decided I would mind my business. You know—stay in my place for once. She wasn't speaking to me anyway. I, um—I didn't realize how dumb that was until you called me." Her inhale was ragged as she roughly smeared tears across her face.

"Sometimes," Nevaeh continued, "it's hard to know if helping someone you love means making yourself available when they're ready to reach out, or going beyond that and making the move they're too afraid to make."

Nevaeh glanced nervously toward the examination rooms. When she turned back, her eyes were intent. Her voice urgent.

"She's already in there making up a lie about getting in a fight with some girl at the Walmart on MLK. Avi, she's eighteen. They can't call your parents. You have to."

48

AVI SAT WIDE-AWAKE in the queen-size bed, a somber spell cast over Sugah's bright green house. Paisli and Antonio slept on either side of her, snoring in sync.

Not even an hour after she'd called their mom, Sugah was ripping open the privacy curtain in the examination room. If Belle had the power, Avi would've burst into flames from the rage in her eyes alone. That was around 10:00 p.m.

When they got to the house, sometime after 2:00 a.m., Belle hid away in Aunt Naima's old room with Sugah. Another two hours passed as Avi waited in the living room before headlights lit up the front of the house.

Toni burst in through the door like a one-man SWAT team and flew up the steps. Ellis held Avi's face in his hands with promises to talk later.

After making plates for Antonio and Paisli, Sugah coaxed some tea into Avi and sent her upstairs to change. She hadn't noticed the blood on her T-shirt.

On her way, Avi peeked into the room where Belle lay curled in their father's lap, cradled to his chest like a newborn.

"She's going to be fine," her mom whispered, laying her soft palm on Avi's cheek. "Go lay down, cher, you look exhausted."

At exactly 4:13 a.m., their dad met Jovahn, Moe, EJ, and Kai at the front door. Over the snores, Avi listened as he explained what happened. The twins' outrage. Kai's silence. And a refusal to let any of them speak to either Belle or Avi until the morning.

Now, at 6:30 a.m., their dad closed Paisli, Antonio, and Avi's door behind him. They were headed to the police precinct so Belle could give an official statement, file a report, and hopefully be granted a temporary protection order.

It was hard to believe that just yesterday, she and Belle were scrubbing toilets in Zody.

Avi sat by the window, gazing through Sugah's handmade floral curtains until the SUV pulled back into the driveway. But only Belle exited the car. Avi heard her feet creak on each step, then Naima's door shut. As Avi's phone buzzed, Antonio slipped out of the room.

Otw to a meeting with the Headmistress and Headmaster.

MOMMY

Willing her heart to slow, Avi gathered her clothes to shower. She turned the handle, peeking into the hallway before scurrying out. Avi wasn't ready to face Belle—she wanted to plan what she would say, but she was out of her wheelhouse. In almost fifteen years, nothing she'd done had ever made Belle look at her the way she did yesterday. Betrayal, contempt, indignation, and disgust were somehow all center stage on her face at once.

As she dried off, Avi considered apologizing for not letting

Belle know before calling their parents. Not having any warning when something drastic was about to happen was the worst; Avi knew that firsthand.

Perhaps she would try starting with confidence.

I called them because I had to. It was the right thing to do!

Or maybe begging was the way to go. But what was she begging for? Forgiveness? Even if she wasn't sorry? No. It was understanding that she wanted.

Avi's fist hovered by the door as she mustered the courage to knock. But every time she psyched herself up to do it, her tail tucked back between her legs.

"Get yourself up off that floor," Sugah ordered half an hour later. She pulled Avi to her feet and forced a tray of tea, two boiled eggs, and buttered toast into her hands. "I've been walkin' past these steps, seein' you sit outside this door waiting for a perfect moment that's never gonna come. You're gonna go in there and talk to her."

"I don't think she's ready yet," Avi rushed out.

"You're right, and it's not gonna go well either, but you two have to get past this hard part."

Sugah knocked on the door twice. "Belle, baby," she said gently. "I have your breakfast here and some hot tea."

She fished a long silver key out of her vest. "I have to run to the store and check on the restaurant, but I'll be back soon."

Avi's mouth dropped open. "Wait, you're not coming in?"

"Oh, no. This is between you two. Chin up."

Before Avi could ask for a second to gather her thoughts, Sugah nudged her in.

Belle lay over the purple duvet with earphones in and her back to the door. Antonio sat next to her, watching reruns of

Avatar: The Last Airbender. With Sugah's wave in their direction, he scampered off the bed and followed her out.

Avi wanted so badly to be on the opposite side of that wooden door with them. Instead, her feet stood glued to the floor as the teacup rattled on the tray.

"I don't have an appetite," Belle croaked.

Avi placed the tray on the nightstand and took the hot mug in her hands before walking to Belle's end of the bed. She lay with her head propped on a decorative pillow. The swelling in her lip was down, but the bruise under her eye was purpling. She wore a finger splint on her pinkie and pointer fingers, a black wrist brace on the other hand. An ice pack the size of a bonnet rested over her left side.

Avi inhaled deeply before taking two steps into Belle's line of sight.

The moment she saw her, a growl emitted from the very pit of Belle's stomach. "Why are *you* here?"

"I—um—well, Sugah wanted me to bring you breakfast. It's on the nightstand when you get hungry."

"Get out."

Avi looked down at the paneled floor, then up at Belle again. "I also wanted to check on you," she croaked. "Ask how you're doing." Avi took a cautious step forward. The scalding tea spilled over the sides as her hands shook, but she was too concerned about any sudden movements from Belle to care about burns.

When she didn't say anything, Avi took another step, this time holding the mug out.

"Maybe this will help you feel better."

In a clumsy move, Belle rose out of the bed, smacking the

tea from Avi's hands. The mug and spoon clattered on the hardwood floor, the tea splashing her bright pink socks.

"Does it look like I want tea?" she hissed, getting in Avi's face. "Do you even get what you did? Everyone already knows!"

Fury radiated from Belle's skin as she snatched her phone from the bed. "See for yourself what they're calling me."

The screen showed the PresCliff anonymous gossip page. Avi scrolled through tweets from the last few hours. Each was about Belle and Logan. There were speculations about their relationship, countless memes, concerns about Belle's well-being, as well as those about Logan's reputation. Then came a poll asking, "Who's the liar?" with Belle's and Logan's names as options. It already had seventy-four votes.

One tweet from a nameless account claiming to belong to a Preston sophomore read:

> I heard that he tried to break up with her again, so she made a plan to ruin his life by having her bestie N.W. beat her up.

Worst of all was an anonymously submitted version of Belle's senior photo, poorly edited to give her two black eyes, a broken nose, and missing teeth. The caption read, "The perfect doll lies again."

Avi was at a loss for words. Sure, Belle had been worried about people judging her, but Avi hadn't thought that people would take sides quite like this. Wasn't it obvious that Logan was at fault? Who were they to ask for picture proof? And take polls? How could they be that cruel? Avi searched for names, but of course, every PresCliff post was anonymous.

But the retweets weren't. She scanned the twenty-seven

retweets of the doctored photo. These were people they knew. Not friends, but kids she sat in classes with. Students they all ate lunch with and passed by every day on campus.

"I can't believe this," Avi said, her voice barely above a whisper.

"Really? Because I can," Belle snapped.

Avi took a closer look at the picture, hoping for a clue. "Who would do this?"

"It doesn't matter! This is exactly what I told you would happen. Now, I'm a liar, and according to @JustLyfe1, 'a hoe trynna ruin another black boys chance at success.' Oh, and to top it all off, I had to go to the police station this morning so that stupid officer could look at me sideways while I tried to report his good friend Walsh's son about an 'argument that got a little out of hand.' "

"They— He said that to you?"

"Yes!" Belle shrieked, and her eyes bulged. "What the hell aren't you getting, Avi? They almost arrested Mommy because of how she reacted. One thing! I asked you to do one thing. Keep your mouth shut," she said shakily. "Let *me* deal with my problems."

Avi shook her head defiantly. "No. No! You were hurt. You still are. How was I supposed to not say anything?"

"Because you promised."

"And he promised not to hit you anymore!"

They were face-to-face. Eye-to-eye. Both huffing audibly for minutes, it felt. Belle looked away first, shooting Avi a dangerous glare and facing the white wall opposite the bed.

"I'm recanting my statement."

"Belle, that's not funny."

"And I'm not playing with you—or anybody else. I'm eighteen. I can do what I want." She bit on her nail nervously and sat on the edge of the bed. But she must have landed too roughly, because her hands flew to her side.

With a ragged exhale, she said, "Going to the police was a bad idea, and I never should've agreed to it."

Avi lowered onto the bed, gazing imploringly at her sister with a soft hand to her cheek. "Belley, he seriously hurt you this time. He broke your ring light and smashed your violin. He put you in the hospital."

"No, *you* put me in the hospital," Belle said, jabbing a finger in her face. And they both stood. "You called Nevaeh after I asked you to get me out."

Avi took a step back, reeling from the menacing look in her sister's eyes.

"This Twitter page, everyone calling me out my name, Logan being arrested. None of it would've happened if you'd just kept your promise!"

Avi flinched at her words but held her hands up in surrender between them. "Look, I know everything seems bad right now, but—"

"But what? These aren't things people forget. *This* is how I'll be remembered. Being cofounder of Cheetah Plans won't matter. Being dance captain, my three-point-nine GPA, the excess community service hours. Nobody will remember any of it. From now on, I'll either be the lying hoe or the sad victim who was too weak to leave."

"But you know none of that's true. Belle, I'm sorry for going behind your back, but I couldn't watch you do it alone anymore."

"Then you should've been there for me!"

Avi jumped when Belle's hand shot out, but she reached past her to wrench the door open.

"From now on, we don't speak. I don't see you, and I don't want anything to do with you."

Avi was desperate to say something—anything—to try and make them better, but before she could utter a word, Belle shrieked for her to leave and slammed the door behind her. The sound of the lock clicking into place seemed to seal their fate.

AVI STOOD OUTSIDE for only a moment before turning away. She walked across the hall to her room, where Paisli still slept, and removed her tea-soaked socks.

The sound of the door slamming in her face echoed in her ears. Pounding, now. It was like her brain was rolling, unprotected, in her head.

She walked past the messy living room where the boys slept last night and saw Antonio lying on the couch. Hot grits, pancakes, and sausages sat on the crowded stove as Avi entered the kitchen, grumbling, "Morning," to her brothers.

Kai and EJ grunted, looking sullen at the table in front of empty plates. Moe sat at the island, shifting food in his bowl with his fork.

She was pouring orange juice to wash down her Tylenol when Kai asked, "Did you talk to her?" through a wide yawn.

Avi nodded.

"Did she seem okay?" EJ asked.

She swallowed the pills before responding. "One of you would probably do a better job comforting her. I don't think she'll be speaking to me again anytime soon."

"I don't blame her," Moe said without looking up from his phone.

Avi set the glass down. "Excuse me?"

"I said, 'I don't blame her.'" He enunciated every word, staring Avi dead in the eyes.

"M, c'mon. Don't start," EJ sighed.

"No, I wanna know how you let this happen?"

"I didn't *let* it happen," Avi scoffed. "I wasn't even there."

"Yeah, exactly," Moe said, rising slowly from his chair. "You weren't there, but you knew this was happening. I think it's funny how you run your mouth about everything else, but Belle has to be hospitalized before you decide to pipe up and say something about this guy putting his hands on our sister."

Avi looked down at her bracelet, twisting the charms to avoid their eyes.

"This is why you were running behind her earlier this year?" EJ asked.

She nodded. "I thought if I kept a close eye on her, then . . ."

"Then what?" Kai asked.

"I thought I might be able to help her and protect her."

Moe's glare was callous. "But now you see how dumb that was, right? How long have you known?" he demanded.

Avi didn't want to say it out loud. The answer was too shameful.

"I asked *how long*?"

"January second," she said, barely above a whisper.

"Avi," Kai said incredulously.

"Seriously?" EJ asked in disbelief.

"What the hell," Moe said, walking around the island. "We're supposed to be there for each other, Avi. Why didn't you say something?"

"They'd broken up by the time I found out, and then she made me promise not to say anything," Avi said breathily. They were all looking at her. Expecting her to make sense when nothing did anymore. "It was supposed to be over. She wasn't supposed to be in danger anymore. But then they got back together. I begged her not to, but she didn't listen."

Avi felt the familiar burn behind her eyes, the tightening in her chest. She couldn't control the quake in her voice. Every word sounded small and unconvincing.

"All of a sudden, she was happy again. I told her he was bad for her, but she wouldn't listen to me. Only to Logan. I didn't know what to do."

"All that's cap!" Moe was yelling now, his eyes ablaze. "You know exactly what you should've done. If it was you, Belle never would've let that go on. If it was you, she would've told somebody that could help. Belle would've protected you, Avi. She always has. Why couldn't you do the same for her when it counted?"

"Morris," boomed their father's voice from the doorway. No one had heard them come in.

Avi couldn't take another word. She flew past her parents and up the stairs, with Kai on her tail.

49

THE TOP OF SUGAH'S MAHOGANY chest held dozens of family photos. Graduations, birthday parties, wedding receptions, Christmas portraits—so many happy moments gazing at Avi as she lay in the bed, alone. And front and center on the chest sat a decade-old picture of Avi and Belle in matching pink Resurrection Sunday dresses. Belle's front teeth were missing as she smiled so widely her cheeks met her eyes. Avi hugged Belle's waist as she gazed up at her.

Now Avi was sure she couldn't look Belle's way without repercussion. She flipped over only to come face-to-face with Moe's stony-faced eighth-grade picture. There was no escape in this house.

There were three knocks on the door. She shot up, attempting to smooth down the unruly flyaways in her uncombed puff before the silver knob turned.

Her dad crossed the doorway, and Avi sighed in relief. Any more hostility from her siblings today, and she would undoubtedly crack.

He unbuttoned the cuffs on his blue shirt and rolled up

his sleeves. Anger, concern, and something else Avi couldn't quite place played across his face, but exhaustion won out.

"Your brother is gonna come in here and apologize to you later," Ellis said, taking a seat by her feet.

"For what?"

"He was out of line. You already know that."

"But was he?" Avi asked. "I thought so, too, at first. But he made a lot of points. Valid points." She cradled her knees to her chest, feeling the mattress give as her dad settled farther onto the bed.

"Talk to me."

The burn in the back of her eyes returned. Avi hadn't allowed a single tear to fall. Not since she'd decided to grant her sister the right to hate her—when she'd decided to tell. To reveal all the secrets they'd kept for months. The very decision that made Kai and the twins look at her like she was a stranger.

"Belle made some bad choices over the last few months, but she was scared, even if she didn't know it. I knew it, and I still didn't say a word. Daddy, nothing Moe said was a lie. I waited until she had to go to the ER before I said something, and even then, it was a hard call to make. It's like, I don't get where my head's been, and if Nevaeh hadn't been around, we probably would've made things worse." She swallowed hard, pressing her nails into her palms.

"When I found her like that. On the floor, with blood on her face. It didn't look like she was breathing. I actually thought she might be dead," Avi whispered. "What kind of person knows their sister's in trouble and does nothing?"

She took in a ragged breath and traced a finger along the paisley design on Sugah's comforter. "Now, hate's coming from every direction, and if I were them, I'd feel the same way." She bit her lip. "I do."

"You said Belle was scared even if she didn't know it," her dad said, leaning in, his stare intense. "What about you?"

"What about me?"

"You weren't scared?"

"Not of Logan," she said plainly.

Her dad squinted slightly and touched his thumb to her cheek. "But the situation. It terrified you, right?"

Avi's nod forced her tears to roll.

"Belle told us everything she asked you to do," he said. The shake in his tone forced Avi's cedar-brown eyes onto his. Somehow Avi saw her own guilt mirrored in her father's eyes.

"That much weight on your shoulders—it's unfair," he said, nodding. "And I know that the pressure you were getting from Belle to stay quiet was strong. But with everything in me, I know that your intuition was stronger. Avi, the devil's in the details, and you knew something was up all along."

This truth was the hardest yet. Something had always been off with Logan, and Avi knew it. She saw it in his eyes that day at the mall. She saw the texts. She heard him yell. She knew the day he showed up uninvited at their front door.

"You didn't trust your gut, and that's why you're experiencing this particular type of guilt. But," he said, cupping her chin, "in no way is all this on you."

Her dad exhaled, tilting his head back toward the ceiling. When he looked down again, he took Avi's hand in his.

"There's a reason Belle felt she had to hide this from your

mama and me, and I honestly believe that's on us. But there's an even greater reason that Logan felt he could put his hands on my daughter and keep goin' about his business like he wouldn't pay for it. And for the rest of his life, that's gonna be on him. I'll make sure of it. Do you believe me?"

He searched Avi's eyes, and the ferocity roaring in his own gave Avi the reassurance she needed. She nodded, knowing that Logan would get what he deserved. If her father said it would happen, there was no question.

"Give it some time. Hate isn't what you're receiving from Morris or Belle. I get what it may feel like"—he said, cutting off Avi's retort—"but I can guarantee you, that's not it. We're all angry and consumed with guilt right now. Regardless, you gotta be careful how you treat yourself. If you're not, I can almost guarantee you'll bring innocent people down with you," he said, jabbing a finger at the comforter. "You'll get so caught up in your head, so caught up in your hurt, that you won't even consider the collateral casualties stewing in your pain right alongside you. *That's* what happened with your sister. Promise me you'll be gentle with yourself." Avi nodded. "I want to hear your voice," he commanded.

"I promise."

With that, he kissed her forehead and stood, wrenching the door open. There was Paisli—eyes wide, a hand raised and poised to knock.

"You okay, Pai?" their dad asked after a moment.

Paisli's mouth fell open, then closed and opened again. Avi straightened, watching her little sister's eyes dart back and forth between her and their father.

"Paisli, what's wrong?" Avi asked, starting to get concerned.

She inhaled sharply, seeming to snap back to her senses as Ellis laid a hand on her shoulder. "Nothing. . . . Uh, Sugah says lunch is ready."

"Okay." He draped an arm over her shoulders. "You still look a little tired. Maybe you wanna lie down again after we eat." Before they left the room, her dad paused, looking back. "If Morris didn't get the position you were put in before, he gets it now. He'll be up here to apologize in a second. It's your choice what you do with it."

50

BEING BACK ON CAMPUS after a week was bittersweet. On one hand, it was liberating to be out of Sugah's house. For so long, the green house had meant summer vacations, hearty Southern meals, and preapproved laziness. But seven days of Belle's glares and angry outbursts made Avi's haven feel more like her own personal hell.

Avi was surrounded by people, but she still felt intense loneliness—all from missing one person, who was there. It felt strange. No one could convince Belle to speak to her again, although their parents and even Sugah had tried.

Plus, being back on campus meant Avi had to walk around, pretending not to hear people talk about her family behind her back. And, occasionally, to her face. Moe still wasn't necessarily speaking to Avi, but before they went on their separate campuses, he roughly bumped her shoulder with a reminder—"Don't let anybody punk you." It was good advice; Avi hoped she wouldn't need to use it.

But on Avi's first day back, Jamal, a junior she'd never spoken to before, walked up to her at the Cliff and asked, "Is this whole thing a stunt to raise Belle's YouTube viewers?"

The question caught Avi off guard. She froze with a hand hovering near the napkin dispenser, a blank look on her face. Her immediate response was shock, but to her surprise, indignation or rage didn't follow. She was filled with dismay and confusion instead.

For hours, Avi had stared at the purple walls in Sugah's room, imagining scenarios and questions she might receive from classmates. But when they got back to campus, she discovered she hadn't managed to prepare herself for the nasty, anonymous Internet rumors to materialize as walking, talking faces who believed everything they read.

Kai, who felt guilty for idolizing Logan and dismissing Avi's warnings, happened to be sitting at a nearby table with Jah and Thalia when he overheard Jamal's question. He immediately stood and advanced on Jamal with a string of harsh swears—earning himself a write-up and a detention in the process.

From then on, Avi made sure not to find herself alone on campus. She went with Rhyon and Zazie to their extracurriculars, trying to avoid solo run-ins with other students and keep her mind busy. Before she found her sister that night, Avi had been in the process of developing an action-adventure idea about two spy siblings (in the spirit of *Mr. & Mrs. Smith*) to upload to Wattpad. But since then, she found that every creative bone in her body was useless, so much so that she yearned to be back on the *Cliff News* for the first time since she quit. If she couldn't create, then she might as well carry Zazie's photography equipment or act as an assistant for the modeling team.

After the one incident in the Cliff, the week passed fairly

uneventfully. Avi sat in Algebra II, listening to Professor Blue speak about their upcoming final, then pairing up with Rhyon to complete a worksheet. As they finished problem three, Quincy walked in. His book bag hung on one shoulder as his midnight eyes scanned the room.

The smile they exchanged was hesitant and half-hearted, just like all Avi's responses to Quincy had been the past few days. Things between them were off, and it was her fault. Quincy had called and messaged numerous times while she was away, but she hadn't known what to say to him. It was difficult to let anyone in unless they were family . . . at least at first. Eventually, Avi responded to Zazie's and Rhyon's calls. And when she did, it was the first time she found herself smiling in Sugah's house that week. But letting Quincy back in was challenging in a different way.

It wasn't until the night before they returned to campus that Avi finally called Quincy. Their conversation was short, meaningless—and the urgency in his voice unsettled something in the pit of her stomach. Before he could even get in a proper goodbye, she rushed him off the phone with promises that they would talk on campus. She couldn't figure it out herself. Nothing about him had changed, so why was this so hard all of a sudden?

Avi hoped that seeing Quincy in person would make things feel like they had before. Warm. Sweet. Whole. Like the moon settling in its rightful place. But now, as Quincy pulled a chair to Avi's desk, his intent eyes set on her, the feeling was inexplicably off.

Rhyon scooted her desk away to give them some privacy.

"Hey," Quincy breathed. He was so close that his familiar

scent of mint and laundry detergent washed over her. "You're okay?" Each time they'd spoken, this was always the first thing to tumble out of his mouth.

She nodded uncomfortably, crossing her arms on the desk.

"And how's Belle?" Always the second question.

She squinted her eyes at him. "You didn't ask my brothers already?"

"Yeah. But I figure you'd know best. You guys are the closest." Quincy couldn't have known that Belle had practically disowned her, but hearing him say that still set her off.

"We're not," Avi spit. "You're better off talking to the twins."

"I want to talk to you," he said softly. "A lot's been going on, and we haven't had a chance to."

Avi bit her lip and relaxed her tone. "I'm sorry. Things have been . . . dramatic, lately."

"EJ said the same thing." He shrugged. "But I thought I should check on you. In person."

"I'm pretty much the same as I've been on the phone."

"But you seem a little off to me."

Avi scoffed. "Since you sat down here?"

"Since everything happened," Quincy said seriously. "I kinda got used to being the first person you told everything to—or at least I thought you were telling me everything—and then you didn't respond for a week. Then when we did talk, it was awkward, and you didn't want to see me for the past few days. I mean, it's fine. Family stuff is hard. But . . . I guess I'm worried."

Avi didn't get why Quincy being so understanding was so off-putting. She usually loved being able to read his every thought and cherished the expressions on his face. But that wasn't the case today. She didn't like what she was reading.

"I wasn't the one who had to go to the hospital. You don't have to worry about me." Avi tugged at the collar on her shirt. Was it suddenly boiling in here?

"That doesn't mean this shit's not affecting you, too. Look," he said, scooting his chair even closer. *Too close.* "Maybe I don't exactly get why you've been moving funny lately—"

The hairs on her arm stood on end. "I haven't been 'moving funny,' I'm—"

"—but Moe told me how rocky things have been with you and your sister, and—"

"Quincy, stop!" Avi's voice came sharp and panicky.

Classmates cast her curious glances, and Quincy looked stunned. She muttered an apology before her eyes fell to the papers on the desk.

Why did he have to go there? She wasn't ready to talk about that with anyone. Especially not in the middle of class.

"Mr. McClain," Professor Blue said from his desk. "I'm sure Miss LeBeau isn't the only student who would benefit from your assistance. Make your rounds."

Quincy nodded and slid the chair back to its empty desk.

In her ear, he said, "I'll call you tonight," before moving away.

Tears threatened to spill from Avi's eyes. She was sick of the constant overwhelming waves of emotion she no longer had control over. She was exhausted by her inability to be kind to her very sympathetic, undeniably sweet boyfriend. She watched Quincy sit down with another pair at the front of the room as Rhyon scooted her chair back in place.

51

We should meet up today so we can talk

QUINCY

About what?

AVI

How you're really doing

And us

QUINCY

I told you I'm fine

AVI

That's a lie

QUINCY

And we're fine

AVI

That's a lie too

QUINCY

I gotta get to class

AVI

MADAME DELCOUR'S CLASS listened attentively as Avi and Fallon presented their joint paper on "La Revue Nègre: Josephine Baker." The two managed to write their entire six-page research paper without having to see each other. It was beautiful. And fairly easy with the help of joint Google Docs. They both picked parts. Avi did the final edits to make it flow. Fallon made the poster board. And boom. A painful group project made painless.

As they headed to their seats, Madame Delcour said, "Class, the study guide and past quiz answers have been posted on BriarWeb for the upcoming final. Chapter reviews begin Monday."

Avi handed Madame Delcour their research paper before scooping up her bag and walking out the door.

The past few days had been full of April showers—fitting for the mood she was stuck in. But today, it was sunny and bright, with only a slight breeze. Avi walked out of the building and tied her lavender cardigan tightly around her waist before heading for Hollingsworth.

She needed to pack a bag for their weekend trip to Sugah's. It had been nearly two weeks since they'd returned to school, and Avi was more than ready to be with her sister again—even if the feeling wasn't reciprocated. According to the doctors, Belle was physically well enough to return to school next Monday. If it was anything like the past two weeks, she and Belle would need each other. Hopefully, this weekend would be one of reconciliation.

Fallon leaned against the railing outside Johnson, smiling down at the phone in her hand. Avi quickened her step, wanting desperately to continue their silent streak. Since Avi returned to school two weeks ago, Fallon had wholly ignored her existence. She didn't acknowledge her in classes, wouldn't look Avi's way in the halls of Hollingsworth, and failed to make even one snarky remark.

Avi preferred it this way. She could've gone her entire life without having to speak to Fallon ever again. Maybe it was something in the air or the sinister smile on her face, but the moment Fallon glanced up, Avi could feel her need to disrupt their peace.

"Avielle, one sec," Fallon purred as she blocked the sidewalk.

"What's up?"

"Nothing. We just haven't had the chance to catch up in a minute."

"We have," Avi said with raised brows. "Neither of us took it. I thought that was working for us."

"I know things have been . . ." Fallon considered her words for a moment with pursed lips. ". . . *tough* for your family for the last few weeks. It's been the same for mine. I wanted to be considerate. You know, give you some space. Unlike all these hound dogs, harassing you."

"And what changed?"

"Time's passed." She shrugged. "How's Belle?"

"Fine."

Avi tried stepping around Fallon, but she moved in front of her.

"That's it? 'Fine' is all I get?"

"If you cared, you would have come to my grandma's house with the rest of your dance team."

"Excuse me for not knowing if she wanted to see me, considering what she accused my cousin of. I assume the stuff people were writing about her on Twitter couldn't have helped."

Avi pressed her lips together, waiting for Fallon to be honest. She could tell it was coming—it was in the fold of her arms. The way she lowered her voice and smiled to disguise the poison that always leaked from her lips.

Leaning in, she said, "Belle probably thought everyone would believe her story, huh?"

Avi's nose flared.

"Believe me, there are a lot of people who think she's telling the truth. But the rest of us know just how much the Perfect Doll loves attention."

Avi's hands tightened on the straps of her shoulder bag. "The Perfect Doll," she repeated.

She knew immediately why that phrase sounded familiar. The doctored picture of Belle that someone had submitted anonymously to the PresCliff page was captioned "The perfect doll lies again." Avi had spent hours staring at the picture, allowing herself to be enraged over and over again. How many times had she read that caption treating her sister's trauma as a joke? Even though Belle said it didn't matter who'd posted the photo, the caption had always tugged at something in Avi. It felt different from the other posts. It felt personal.

Fallon would've been one of the first people to find out—not to mention eager to spread a rumor to cover for her family. This fit Fallon's specific brand of cruelty.

"You made that picture, didn't you?"

Her smile faltered for the tiniest fraction of a second. "Please! Everyone saw the same post I did, and the consensus is that your lying sister set my cousin up."

"Fallon," Avi huffed with as much warning as she could muster, "you belong in a room with padded walls. Get out my face."

This time, when Fallon tried to step in front of her, Avi nudged her to the side. All week long, students had made small, ignorant comments hinting toward the same. Avi was determined to walk away like she had every other time.

"Fine, you can go," Fallon called. "But I thought you'd want to hear about Logan's reduced punishment."

Feet away, Avi spun around, her book-laden backpack landing hard on her hip. Passing students slowed their steps.

"Oh, that got your attention? Word is, your sister recanted her statement to the police," Fallon announced to loud murmurs. "Even admitted to causing the damage herself. I guess she felt bad about trying to ruin his life. Or maybe she finally got sick of lying; I don't know. But there is a plus side to all of this, Avielle. At least she won't be seen as the poor damsel who let a boy hit her. Just the pathetic girl who lied about it."

Avi's bag hit the sidewalk with a thud as she rushed at Fallon. Before her hands could close around her neck, a solid figure obstructed her path. With tears of rage as she was half carried, thrashing, away, Avi saw Fallon check her hands, bloodied from tipping backward on the pavement.

It wasn't until Avi was back inside the glass doors of Eckford that she realized it was Quincy pinning her hands to her sides.

With all the strength she could muster, Avi shoved him away. "Why would you do that?" she cried.

"Hitting her isn't gonna help anything, Avi." *How can he sound so calm?*

Outside, people were being dispersed from the walkway by a teacher as some guy helped Fallon to her feet. Avi tried to go around him, but he held her back.

"Get off of me," Avi yelled. "Why do you think you get to decide what I do?!"

"I'm trying to help."

"I don't need your help," she said gruffly. "I need you to stay away from me."

"Avi," Quincy said evenly. "You gotta be able to see when you're making a bad choice. You already made a big one; don't make another."

Avi leaned away, finally seeing his supposed care and patience over the last few weeks for what it was. Judgment. Condescension. Who did he think he was, throwing the biggest mistake of her life back in her face? As if she could feel any worse. As if those weren't the same thoughts keeping her up every night.

"You know what?" Avi said quietly. "You don't get to say that. You're the first bad choice I made and I don't need you, okay?"

A look of sheer betrayal warped his face, and almost

instantly, Avi regretted her words. With wounded eyes, Quincy released her wrist, letting go as if she'd burned him.

"Say less," he said, taking a step back. "If I'm such a bad choice, then we should end this. Right?"

Avi shook her head, swallowing the lump in her throat as she edged backward. It was too much. *Everything* was too much.

"I don't have time for this." She pushed open the glass door and ran down the steps to grab her bag and cracked phone from the sidewalk. Fallon and the crowd were long gone, and Belle's recantation was the most pressing matter. Not possible videos of Avi trying to attack Fallon. Or the end of her first relationship.

As Avi stomped toward Preston, she looked back. Quincy was gone.

52

Belle recanted her statement???

AVI

AVI ASKED HER GROUP chat with Moe, EJ, and Kai, pressing send as she stomped onto Preston's campus.

She was shaking with fury by the time she rammed open the doors of Preston's admin office. Her parents weren't answering their phones to say whether Fallon's claims were true. So, she was going to the one other person who might have that information.

Avi flew past the woman at the front desk, ignoring her futile greeting. With one look at the empty secretary's desk, she decided to let herself into Headmaster Walsh's office.

"You're ending Logan's suspension," she fumed.

Headmaster Walsh sighed deeply at Avi's sudden intrusion but motioned to the chairs in front of his grand cherrywood desk. "Please, have a seat."

"I don't want to sit. I want to know why Logan's suspension is over when he should've been expelled weeks ago!"

Walsh cleared his throat. "Miss LeBeau, you have to

understand that your sister recanting her statement and making it clear that she will not testify in court is basically admitting that she was upset and most likely fabricated parts of the story."

"That is not—"

"Furthermore," he said, raising his voice, "I have full faith that the lack of evidence and Belle's refusal to lie on the stand will result in a dismissal of all charges. Now, I do admit that there was an altercation, and for that, Logan is remorseful. For that reason, I will not be suspending his punishment, but reducing it to in-school suspension. Graduation is next month. He needs to be here."

Avi couldn't believe the crap gushing from Walsh's mouth. Their whole family was full of it.

"There was 'some kind of altercation'?" she sputtered. "My sister is walking around with a black eye, a broken finger, and bruised ribs. Not to mention the destruction of her property. *Your son* did that!" Avi jabbed at the framed picture of Logan on the headmaster's desk, and it fell to the floor with a satisfying shatter. "When it's Preston's property being destroyed, you seem to care a lot more. Remind me again what punishment you wanted to give Zazie over those stupid posters?"

Headmaster Walsh stood, buttoning the jacket to his navy-blue three-piece suit. He strolled around the desk and leaned where the frame sat seconds before. The pungent scent of his expensive cologne assaulted Avi's nose as his snakelike eyes pierced hers.

Calmly, he said, "That is all a lie."

His nonchalance was like a slap in the face.

"No, *you're* the liar, and you're gonna fix this."

Walsh chuckled. "You know what, Miss LeBeau? I have a real problem with you and your entire family thinking it's okay to waltz into my office and tell me how to do my job."

Avi crossed her arms over her chest. "Well, I have a problem with someone raising a child who doesn't know how to keep his hands to himself."

Walsh's eyes flicked up with warning. "That is strike number two. You don't want to get to three, Miss LeBeau."

Avi stepped back and took a deep breath.

With a veneer of politeness, she said, "Headmaster Walsh, refusing to testify is not admitting that nothing happened. Your officer friends bullied Belle. Your niece humiliated her, and your son abused her. Logan should be in jail. Now you're telling me that he won't even serve his full suspension."

"That is exactly what I'm telling you," Walsh said, straightening up. He walked back to his chair. "I will not continue to punish my son because of the lies told by a silly teenage girl who wasted his time."

"You know what?" Avi's tone was sharp, her hands curled into fists. "You're a fraud just like your stupid son. I see where he gets it from."

Walsh slammed his hands on his desk, making Avi jump as he waved a finger in her face.

"That is strike three. Young lady, get out of my office now, or I will personally have security escort you out in the same handcuffs they put on my son."

He opened the heavy office door, and Avi turned to leave.

As she walked past him, Walsh spat, "Your parents will be receiving a call."

53

We're dealing with it. Be there at 5:00

MOMMY

What? That doesn't make sense

EJ

Are you sure?

KAI

I just got kicked out of Walsh's office.

AVI

What happened?

KAI

Stay there. I'm omw

EJ

Me too

KAI

AVI SAT ON A BENCH in front of the admin building, rubbing her face in her hands. The day hadn't started so badly. Breezy classes. Great lunch. Beautiful weather. But it was taking a nasty turn.

She leaned back, anxiously bouncing her foot on the brick sidewalk—when she saw Logan heading toward her. He wore a polo shirt and ridiculous Tony Stark–like sunglasses, and there was an actual pep in his step.

"I thought you weren't supposed to be on campus during your suspension," Avi called when he passed her.

Logan stopped and smiled like they were old friends as he removed his sunglasses.

"Avi. Hey, I'm glad I ran into you."

"Oh?"

"Yeah." His arms swung at his sides. "I haven't been able to get in contact with Belle in a minute. Will you give her a message for me?"

"You're kidding."

"No. She loved that violin, and I realized I never apologized for breaking it. I was upset, and—"

"Wait. So, you'll admit to breaking the violin, but you won't admit to hitting Belle."

"I didn't," he said in a low voice. His eyes cast at his red shoes. "The whole thing was a huge misunderstanding. She should've waited for me. I was coming back to—"

"To what?" Avi asked, standing. "Finish her off? Good thing I showed up then, huh?"

Logan kept his head down, jingling the keys in his pocket as a student jogged up the steps into the admin offices.

"No answer?" she asked, emboldened by his uneasiness.

"Did you know there's a camera outside our house? Right on the front porch."

Logan's head snapped up, and Avi smiled at the instant fear covering every inch of his face. It was nice to see him sweat for once.

"I saw everything that happened that day," she said, crossing her arms over her chest. "Logan, how are you only sorry about breaking the violin?"

His shoulders straightened as he slipped the sunglasses back on his face and took a step toward her. "You still don't get me and Belle." He shrugged. "We're good together. Partners."

"But you didn't want a partner. You wanted an obedient trophy to stand quietly at your side and look pretty. That's not Belle. You should've asked. She would've told you."

Logan leaned in so closely, she felt the heat of his breath on her face. "And I'm telling you. You don't know her like I do."

"I don't believe you," Avi said, shaking her head. "I don't believe you're this calm. Whoever that scared boy was who showed himself when I mentioned a camera, that's the real you. You lie and pretend. And when you thought no one would see, you treated Belle like she was worthless. Even if I don't know my sister like I thought I did, I know exactly who you are."

Logan ran a hand over his mouth. "You got a mouth just like her. You know that?" He pointed a finger in her face. "Watch it, little girl."

Avi brushed his hand away. Students passed by. Faculty walked the grounds, and security patrolled this area. What was he going to do? "Or what?"

"Wait a second," Logan chuckled, and his eyes brightened with delight. "I know what this is. Yeah, I do. It kills you that Belle chose me over you. Over *everybody.* Doesn't it? That's why she's at the police station now, you know. Because I said 'please.' Because I told her, 'I love you.' And don't get me wrong, I do. But I know for a fact that you begged her to break up with me, and . . . nothing. You hate to see it. You do," he chuckled. "But we're gonna be together again in a matter of weeks. She's going to NYU for me, and there's nothing you can do about that.

"Hey, I wanna hear it," he said boastfully. "Tell me it kills you, Ellie."

"Don't call me that," Avi spat. "What kills me is stupidity. I mean, what kind of *idiot* talks that much BS to someone who just told them she has proof he did something he told the police he didn't?"

She held a finger to her ear, inviting Logan to scream, *It's me. I'm the dummy!* But he didn't. He glared, and the hatred burning in his eyes could start a wildfire.

"It would be smart for you to remember that I'm not my sister, and I'm not scared of you—or of destroying your future. So run to your daddy, so he can—"

Avi's head hit the ground before she even saw Logan's meteoric arm swing back. Too quickly, she snapped up, and the stars lining her vision swirled.

Remembering the threat she was facing, Avi whipped around expecting to see Logan standing above her. Instead, she saw a raging ball of limbs rolling in the grass.

"EJ," Avi muttered.

She watched, unmoving, as EJ straddled Logan. Fists flew one moment. In the next, the boys rolled in the grass, each trying to overpower the other.

Noemie yanked Avi up, pushing her glasses in her hands before she was ready as a crowd of eager students stampeded past to see the cause of the commotion. Shouts of excitement and goading littered the air for far too long before Kai and Professor Blue were able to pry Logan out of EJ's chokehold.

When campus security arrived a minute later, Logan still lay coughing in the grass while Blue pinned EJ's arms behind his back. Dozens of phones recorded, and cameras flashed as campus security tried to disperse the crowd. Logan's right eye was swelling alarmingly; EJ's lip bled down his chin.

Avi only came to her senses when security began leading EJ, Kai, and Logan into the admin building. Her heart drummed thunderously against her chest as she moved her legs to follow, but Noemie held her back.

"Take her to Briarcliff's nurse," Blue commanded. "Now!"

Hearing the urgency in Blue's voice, Avi finally felt the searing sting in her cheek.

54

AVI RECOUNTED EXACTLY what led to the fight for Briarcliff and Preston security, Rhyon, Zazie, and finally Headmistress Malone.

She sat on a hospital bed in the nurse's office, covered in white sheets and propped up against a stiff pillow. She held an ice pack to her cheek as everyone fussed unnecessarily. Because of the rings Logan was wearing, there would be bruises, but nothing long-lasting. The stinging had subsided, though her cheek remained sensitive to touch. Nurse Moody gave Avi medicine for her migraine and strict instructions to take it easy for the rest of the day. Even though they said she'd be fine, they wouldn't let her leave.

"Your mother was hysterical on the phone," Headmistress Malone said. "She asked that you stay put until she gets here."

For Malone, Avi had included her encounter with Headmaster Walsh—his indifference, his accusations against Belle, and his threats to have Avi removed in handcuffs. Though she did omit breaking Logan's picture. It wasn't one of those need-to-know things.

Given the headmaster's reaction to Avi—who had merely

shot off at the mouth—she was worried about how EJ would be punished. He'd actually injured the headmaster's precious son. Was he sitting in handcuffs as they spoke? Walsh clearly despised her entire bloodline even before she entered his office and berated him. How was he going to feel now that her brother had blackened Logan's eye and almost successfully choked him out in front of God only knew how many cameras?

"He was defending you," Zazie said consolingly from the edge of the bed.

"Right. They'd be dead wrong to even try it." Rhyon's eyes were glued to her phone as videos from the fight flooded her feed. "Whew. E didn't hold back!"

Zazie leaned over to see. "Logan's lucky Moe was in baseball practice."

Rhyon turned the phone toward Avi, but she waved it away. She didn't need to relive it.

She leaned back on the pillow with her eyes closed, inhaling the overwhelming smell of bleach as the bed squeaked beneath her.

"I didn't have to do all that," Avi sighed, more to herself than to the room.

"Do what?" Malone asked as she walked back through the doors, sliding her phone in her blazer.

"Lash out! Belle's gonna be so pissed. I could see Logan getting angry and still couldn't make myself shut up."

She dropped the bag of ice from her face and ran a hand over her ponytail. If their relationship had been fractured before, this would break it. Repeatedly, Belle asked her to let her fight her own battles. And what did Avi do? Quite literally approached the angry bear, poked it with a stick, and threw its wrongdoings in its face.

"And you shouldn't have to," Malone said. She picked up the ice pack and placed it gently against Avi's cheek. "You should be able to speak your piece without fearing some boy will smack you." She searched Avi's eyes for understanding. "When your mother gets here, I'll head over to Preston to check on your brother. There were witnesses. There's nothing Walsh can do to cover this one up."

A door banged open in the hall.

"Where is she?" her mother's voice demanded shakily.

"In here," Malone called.

She rushed in with Paisli and began to inspect Avi's body.

"Where's Daddy?" Avi asked as her mom held her face, tilting it side to side. She winced.

"With EJ and Kai."

Toni moved to her arms, then ran her hands up and down her legs. When she tried to pull down her calf socks, Avi shrieked, "It's just my face!"

She allowed her mother to examine her left cheek until movement at the door caught her eye. Belle stood there, in sweats, hugging herself. The bruising on her face was almost healed, but her eyes were bloodshot and heavy.

"We'll give you all some privacy," Professor Malone said as she steered Rhyon and Zazie unwillingly toward the door.

"Thank you for staying with her, Alexandria," Toni said as they embraced.

After they filed out, Avi held her breath as Belle neared

the bed. The silence was suffocating as they stared at one another. Their mom looked on, unsure. The bed creaked as Paisli sat down, and Avi finally remembered her voice.

"You came," she squeaked.

Belle lifted a hand and then lowered it, eventually resolving to cross her arms awkwardly over her stomach. "Are you okay?"

"I'm fine. Really. All I needed was this ice pack and some Tylenol."

Without warning, Belle's hand flew to her mouth to stifle a sob.

"They wouldn't tell us what happened over the phone," she cried. Their mom moved to rub a hand on Belle's back, her other still resting on Avi's uninjured cheek. "We knew there was an argument and a fight. Not if you and EJ were okay."

"What happened?" Paisli asked quietly.

Avi told the story in its entirety. Paisli's eyes grew wide at the discovery of Fallon's betrayal, especially since Fallon was one of Belle's Cheetahnaire sisters. Their mom wore a look of disgust hearing of Walsh's nonchalance. Belle flinched when she learned it was Logan's fist that had put Avi in this room.

Paisli's troubled eyes, their mother's rage, Belle's silent tears, and a pregnant pause filled the air as Avi scanned the faces around her. They were all speechless.

Avi wiped at her face, ignoring the pressure in her cheek as she thought out an apology. The things she shouted at Logan. The way she'd provoked and threatened him. How she'd ignored her sister's request to mind her business. What could she say? What words made her actions—and the thundering avalanche of reactions—justifiable? She was lying on a hospital bed. EJ could be arrested.

She opened her mouth to begin, just as Belle stopped pinching the bridge of her nose. For the first time in a long time, she met Avi's eyes. And the look she wore wasn't enraged. It wasn't sad or resentful or brimming with distrust. It was remorseful.

"He wouldn't have thought he could come back on campus if I hadn't been so dumb today," she said with a shake of her head. "I don't know what I was thinking."

"It's okay," Avi began, but Belle interrupted her.

"It's not. You don't get it. I was there! I was back at the precinct," she said, jabbing at the bed. "I got my keys and snuck out when Mommy, Daddy, and Sugah weren't looking. I took my car, walked in that precinct, and was waiting for Detective Jones so I could officially recant my statement. The only reason I turned my phone back on was to call Logan and tell him it was almost done. And then the messages flooded in. That you were in the nurse's office, and EJ was in Preston security's custody." She smiled, but the regret in her eyes spoke volumes. "That's what it took. Logan had to attack you and EJ for me to realize . . ." Her voice trailed off.

Belle sat on the bed, staring at her fidgeting fingers.

"You know," she exhaled raggedly. "For the past few months, I've been trying to make everything look perfect when it wasn't. Fallon was right about that. Because . . . I've lied about a lot. I was so caught up trying to impress people who don't even matter. And too consumed with helping Logan 'make it' that I didn't realize I was drowning. It's sad," she said, meeting Avi's eyes, "how far you can sink before you realize you can't breathe anymore. You tried to force me up, and I steadily pulled you down. Didn't I? Just like Daddy said."

Belle placed her hands gently on either side of Avi's face, wiping her tears as she whispered, "I'm sorry. I didn't realize I couldn't breathe. I didn't see how I was forcing you to hurt with me. I promise I didn't mean to."

Avi nodded, not yet able to clear enough air in her throat. She felt the thread that had been so raggedly cut re-form seamlessly between them.

"I want everything for all of you," their mom said, "but you have to know you deserve it without suffering. Especially when it comes to love. You all *have* to understand that."

When their mom opened her arms, they didn't hesitate to lean in.

Paisli peeled away first, clearing her throat. "As long as we're sharing, and everyone's already calm . . ." She blew out her cheeks, shifting on her feet. "I've known about Logan for as long as Avi. Maybe even a few hours before."

"What?!" Mommy thundered.

"No, I know," Paisli said, shaking her head. "That day we made the sister tag video, when he showed up, Avi told me to stop being nosy, but I couldn't help myself! As soon as I went to my room, I watched the clips on the surveillance app. I wanted to say something, but I knew Belle would be mad that I'd invaded her privacy, so I didn't. And then I couldn't sleep that night."

Avi watched, baffled, as Paisli paced back and forth along

the edge of the bed. Belle's mouth hung open, frozen with shock.

"I heard you two in the kitchen fighting over the videos and agreeing not to say anything, so I didn't, either." She made an about-face, and her hands flew to her chest with relief. "Belle, I was so mad at you for making Avi not say anything. It didn't make sense! And then I blamed you for letting him do that." Her voice cracked with shame.

"That's why you wouldn't answer my calls?" Belle asked.

Paisli bit her lip, nodding. "When we went to Sugah's, I tried to tell Daddy that I'd known, too. But I knew how sad you were, Belley, and then you were so angry." She turned to Avi. "I wasn't really asleep when you came in the room after Belle yelled that day. I heard her. And then when I heard Moe yelling . . . Avi, I tried to speak up. I did. But I got scared, and I didn't want everyone to be mad at me, too. I'm sorry I let you be sad alone."

Avi took Paisli's hand in hers.

"Wait a minute," Toni said, raising a finger. "What are these clips you're talking about?"

Belle spoke up before Paisli could. "The day you and Daddy went on your date during winter break, Logan showed up at the house."

"I saw that when I checked the footage the next day. You said he was in town to visit his cousin and stopped by."

"But the camera picked up more," Avi said.

"He choked me that day," Belle said quietly. "And when Avi confronted me with the videos, I deleted them."

"Belle, no," their mom gasped.

"I know! I wasn't thinking straight."

"That's the type of hard evidence we could use."

Paisli's shoulders straightened. "They'd really help that much?"

"Yeah, but I deleted them from the panel months ago."

"Why, Pai?" their mom asked. "Do you know how to recover them?"

"I swear, this is the last secret I kept," Paisli said, standing on the balls of her feet. "After I saw the videos, I saved them because I was planning on telling at first. Then you guys agreed not to say anything, so I sent them to my email because Mommy checks my phone."

"I check your email, too."

"That's why I created a new one. But that's all that I've ever used it for. I swear."

"I could kiss you," Avi said, smirking.

Belle took her face and did just that.

"When we get back to Sugah's, we'll talk the details over with Daddy," their mom said.

"Oh yeah! What's happening with E?" Belle asked.

Toni slipped her phone out of her jean pocket. "Looks like EJ's in the clear for now. I'm gonna talk to the nurse, and then we can head out."

55

PRESTON'S MAIN PARKING LOT sat full despite the evening sun. As Avi lugged her small suitcase on the pavement, she weaved through cars far ahead of Toni, Belle, and Paisli. She pressed the lock button to hear the beep three times before she saw their empty SUV only a few yards away.

Avi looked down to press the unlock button when she heard jangling keys across the lot. A heavy duffel bag hung from Logan's shoulder, and his black eye shone against a raised red welt on his cheek. Avi stopped midstep, hoping he wouldn't see her, but the suitcase handle slipped from her hand and slammed to the ground.

Logan's head snapped up, and he moved away from his red truck toward her.

"Avi, I'm so sorry," he started, desperation in his eyes.

But Belle was in front of her before he could get out the words. Just a whisper of her name escaped his lips.

"Not another step," their mom said, moving in front of her daughters.

Avi could hear her mother's ragged breath as she dug

through her huge purse, muttering, "Little boy, you must think I'm playin' games. That's okay. I got something for you."

Belle placed a hand over her mother's, urging her to stop.

"Belle," Logan said, forcing their attention back on him. "You have to do something." His tone was shaky. Scared.

She tried to move toward him, but Toni's arm shot out.

Belle looked at her intently. "Trust me."

Avi's blood ran cold as their mother slowly lowered her arm. She watched her sister move toward Logan. It was torture, the few seconds it took for her to near him. To look up at his tall, broad frame. Belle wouldn't go back to him. Not after everything they'd been through. She couldn't.

Avi tried to move forward, but her mother held her shoulders.

"Thank you for talking to me," Logan exhaled. "I know I don't deserve it. I know I hurt you. But if you don't help me, I'll lose everything. For good this time. My scholarships, my acceptances. They won't even let me walk at graduation. Belle, babe, I need you."

With another step, Belle closed the space between them, nodding. She reached her arms up, moving to hug him, and Logan's shoulders slumped in relief.

Their mom's protest cut short as Belle jerked her left leg up, nailing him between the legs. Without hesitation, she grabbed the back of his head and kneed him in the face.

Blood spurted from Logan's nose as he met the ground.

Belle tucked an escaped coil behind her ear, gazing down with newfound disgust as her ex rocked in the fetal position, seemingly unsure if his nose or balls needed more attention.

She squatted beside him. "You're on your own this time," she said, low and even.

The words hung in the air, along with Logan's whimpers and Paisli's raucous laughs. Their mom wrapped an arm around Belle's shoulders.

"We'll drive to the admin office to pick up the boys, okay?"

Belle nodded as they turned and packed into the SUV.

As they drove off the lot, Avi turned to see Logan finding his footing, but Belle called her name.

"Let's be done looking at the bad parts."

Avi leaned in as Belle draped an arm over her shoulder. She ran a hand over Paisli's head in her lap, remembering her favorite quote on Professor Lovette's wall: *"Is solace anywhere more comforting than in the arms of a sister?"—Alice Walker*

EPILOGUE

ZAZIE FLOATED THROUGH G-12, smudging their hollow room one final time before they headed home. As Avi carved their initials into the doorframe—keeping up with tradition, of course—she couldn't help but be reminded of how Zazie had done the same for Belle before she walked back into her dorm.

The transition back for the last month of school was tough for them all, but now that the truth was out, there was little that gossiping classmates could say. Avi and Zazie offered Belle their room to sleep in, but she refused. Something Dr. Cashmere was teaching her about reclaiming her space. She slept, studied for finals, dressed for prom (in an elegant two-piece sky-blue number), and prepped for graduation—all in that room. It helped that Nevaeh was by her side every step of the way. Belle framed the picture they'd taken together on Senior Decision Day in their Spelman tees.

"Y'all ready?" Rhyon asked, slamming her door shut with the broadest smile on her face. "Libertad" was the word she used when Kieley left for North Carolina yesterday. She took the knife from Avi and carved "+ R.B." next to "Z.L. + A.L."

Avi was halfway down the hall, hugging her floormates and dodging their moving boxes when she remembered the floral decorative box in her closet. She ran back to the room and scooped the pink-and-blue box into her arms.

Inside was the finished outline for her new Wattpad short story. Also a "New Student Org Proposal" sheet Avi picked up on her way out of Briarcliff's admin offices. She was ready to leave the *Cliff News* behind her, and new ideas for how to do just that had begun to sprout. Wattpad was fun, and she looked forward to posting this summer—but maybe the *Cliff News* didn't have to be the only way to reach readers on campus. On top of the org sheet lay the English tutoring work-study form Professor Lovette had given her for next year. And an apology letter from Egypt, who felt awful upon discovering Belle's misfortune and wrote to both sisters—turns out Cori was right about her, to an extent. Maybe they'd never be friends, but there was a line of disrespect she promised never to cross again.

The last thing in the box was a half-written poem inspired by Quincy:

The Stillness of You

It's the sound, the feel,
The stillness of you
That let me know before we were Us,
You'd be the one I could trust.
Trust in the words you say
Your eyes, smile, walk,
but you walked away.
Stay?
Know I was lost in my mind,
in tears, my fear and

Your light, life
Our peace and need
To feel, worth it.
You're worth every bit.
I can be too.
Did you know I still think about you?

It was unfinished, just like their relationship.

Besides his text to make sure she was okay the night Logan hit her, they hadn't spoken. She wanted to talk, but she could only guess that he wasn't ready, since he'd declined all her requests. The text she sent this morning to let him know she was leaving at noon was left on read.

In the lobby, Avi, Rhyon, and Zazie handed in their keys, and Housemother Lisa hugged the three tightly, kissing them each on the cheek before holding the doors of Hollingsworth open for them one last time.

Next month was their study abroad trip to Amsterdam, so tearful goodbyes weren't necessary. That didn't stop Zazie from pulling them both in for a last suffocating group hug.

As they walked toward the cars out front, Rhyon nudged Avi's hand.

Sitting stony-faced on the rails outside of Rashad Hall was Quincy, in a white tee, Nike shorts, and the diamond earrings he'd worn the day they met.

Avi promised to call Zazie and Rhyon tonight before heading his way.

"Hey," she said, tightly gripping the box resting on her hip. "I didn't think you'd come."

Quincy scratched his chin. "Me neither. My cousin's gonna be here in a few, but I ran into Kai, and he thought I should hear you out."

"I'm glad you're here," Avi said, taking a step closer. "I don't know what came over me that day. Or what I was thinking. I was confused, and Fallon made me so upset that I—"

"That's not an apology, Avi."

She swallowed hard, nodding. "I'm sorry, Quincy. From the bottom of my heart, I apologize. I swear, I didn't mean anything I said to you that day." She rubbed a hand up and down her arm. "Belle's therapist thinks I may have been projecting some bad feelings about Logan—and relationships in general—onto you, but I . . ." She bit her top lip, exhaling deeply. ". . . I don't really understand it, either. I wish I could go back in time. I wish we could just forget it ever happened."

"But we can't," he said, shrugging. Quincy stepped off the railing, standing at his full height with crossed arms. "You can't get mad and say whatever wild shit you want to people you're supposed to care about. I can't forget that. Didn't you tell me Maya Angelou said, 'When someone shows you who they are—' "

"—believe them," she finished, flapping her hands in the air. "Yes, I did. But you *know* me. Quincy, you just kept pushing me that week, and I—I said something I didn't mean . . . but you know that's not me!"

"Really? Because I didn't know you could say that to me. That I was the first bad choice you made." He shook his head, inhaling deeply. "Imma be real with you. You know my history. You know I have a thing with my dad and . . . rejection,

I guess. I'm not saying I don't understand why you were lashing out, but I think the truth comes out when people are mad. Like that's how you really feel."

"It's not."

"Avi, I accept your apology, but we can't just pick up where we left off after that."

She bit the inside of her cheek. "What would help?"

Quincy stuffed his hands in his pocket. "Time. *Maybe* . . ." His voice faded as the sun glinted off the bracelet on her wrist. "You're still wearing the charm."

Avi raised her hand to her chest. "I told you I wouldn't take it off," she sniffed. "But if you want it back . . ."

He shook his head. "I don't. It was a gift. And I'd be lying if I said I didn't still like it on you."

She took a step closer to him, grasping tightly at the crumb of hope in his words. "You're right. We can't pick up where we left off, but maybe . . . one day, we could start something new. And when you're ready to talk—"

"I'll call you," Quincy said, nodding. And then he smiled, and Avi felt the familiar trembles in her heart.

His phone chimed then. "I gotta head out, but maybe we'll see each other this summer."

She stilled as he bent to kiss her lightly on the cheek.

Avi turned toward the sidewalk, where her classmates and their families bustled about. There was Paisli in the passenger seat of Belle's Nissan. And Belle, leaning on the hood of the car, waiting. The lavender blazer Avi had received for completing her first year at Briarcliff lay folded over her sister's outstretched arms.

AUTHOR'S NOTE

DAYS AFTER I GRADUATED from Spelman in 2017, I sat on the floor of my childhood bedroom reflecting on my achievements, the lifelong relationships I'd formed, and the woman I was because of my collegiate matriculation. While I was sad that my time at Spelman was over, I couldn't help but be outrageously proud that I was becoming the woman I've always dreamed I could be. And then I thought: Who would I be if I'd began this transformation at fourteen, instead of eighteen? What if instead of just four, I'd spent eight years creating these bonds, learning life-changing lessons and receiving an education that one can only get at an HBCU?

And the first threads that would become *Briarcliff Prep* began to form.

While Briarcliff Preparatory and Preston Academy are completely fictional, Historically Black Boarding Schools were born out of necessity in the late 1800s and existed in great numbers in the 1900s. Though only a handful of these schools are still up and running, their history, culture, and existence were/are rich, important, and critical. Not having attended an HBBS myself, I did extensive research, took creative liberties, and weaved in some of my own experiences, growing up in a majority African American school in PG County, Maryland, and going on to attend the number one HBCU in the country, into this story. And while I'd love for everyone to enjoy these schools and this story as a whole, I feel it's important to note that I wrote this story with young Black women in the forefront of my mind.

Womanhood, especially Black womanhood, is something I hold near and dear to my heart, which is why I named several of the buildings on Briarcliff's campus after women I admire or included their names, quotes, or works in this book. My hope is that readers may take the opportunity to appreciate and learn about these trailblazers for themselves. Some of these notable women that I carry with myself day-to-day are Maya Angelou (a poet, dancer, actress, memoirist, and civil rights activist) of the Angelou Auditorium, Zora Neale Hurston (a writer, anthropologist, and folklorist) of the Hurston Bookstore, Toni Morrison (a novelist, editor, professor, and Nobel Prize winner) of the Morrison Center. And, of course, my Spelman sister, Alice Walker (writer, poet, and social activist) whose works, notably *The Color Purple,* convinced me to unabashedly write this story combining the highs, lows, joys, and sadness that come with womanhood and almost certainly accompany Black womanhood, whether young or old.

With love,

BRIANNA PEPPINS

ACKNOWLEDGMENTS

I'D LIKE TO first shout a special thanks to my Lord and Savior, Jesus Christ, for guiding, redirecting, and loving me every step of the way.

To my Mommy, I get my love of reading from you and I know for a fact I wouldn't be the woman I am, or even a writer, without you. Thank you for teaching me to be bold, introducing me to the greats, and for going the extra mile to ensure I was prepared for every obstacle thrown my way. To my Daddy, thank you for always being a listening ear, my Marvel partner, and for accepting my neediness with open arms. Your love and support has been invaluable, and I know what it means to be resilient because of you.

A huge thanks to everyone at KT Literary, especially Jas Perry. Jas, you did everything you promised you would as my literary agent and more. I still count signing with you as my best career move to date. A million times thank you for believing in me.

Thank you to Emily Meehan, who first acquired Briarcliff and to Britt Rubiano for taking over and seeing value in this story. To Christine, I'm always so blown away by your sharp eye. Thank you for treating BP with so much respect and for championing my first book baby.

Thank you to everyone at Disney Hyperion, who has rooted for BP and worked behind the scenes, especially Kieran Viola, Crystal McCoy, Christine Saunders, Ann Day, Matt Schweitzer, Holly Nagel, Dina Sherman, Danielle DiMartino, LaToya Maitland, Maddie Hughes, Sara Liebling, Guy Cunningham, Mark Amundsen, Jenny Langsam, Sharon Krinsky, Marybeth Tregarthen, Monique Diman, Michael Freeman, Jess Brigman, Kim Knueppel, Marci Senders, Mili Nguyen, Kori Neal, Lia Murphy, Vicki Korlishin, and Loren Godfrey. To Zareen Johnson, you amazed me with BP's cover design, and Kingsley Nebechi, seeing your cover art for the first time made me burst into tears. You're a true talent.

To my big sister, Carmell, you set the ultimate example for what sisterhood should mean, and I count myself as blessed to love and be loved by you. Antoine, you're the overprotective, big brother I've always needed, and I'm reminded of what confidence really means every time you enter a room. Alyssa, I chose you to be the very first person to read *Briarcliff Prep* because your opinion meant the most to me. I strive to be and do better because I know you're paying attention. Trinity, God handed me my first friend when He gave me you, and I hope you know that I'm forever grateful.

Neila, Kennedi, KJ, Aubrey, and Legend, it's been a dream watching each of you grow, and I hope you all know you can always depend on me. To Kaylee, I gave Avi your middle name, I wrote the first draft of BP with you by my side, and now I write with your picture on my desk. I've always been so inspired by you, and there's nothing you can't do in my eyes.